ST PIRAN'S:
THE WEDDING!

BY
ALISON ROBERTS

SYDNEY HARBOUR
HOSPITAL:
EVIE'S BOMBSHELL

BY
AMY ANDREWS

ST PIRAN'S: THE WEDDING!

BY
ALISON ROBERTS

MILLS & BOON

First published in Great Britain 2013
by Mills & Boon, an imprint of Harlequin (UK) Limited.
Harlequin (UK) Limited, Eton House, 18-24 Paradise Road,
Richmond, Surrey TW9 1SR

© Harlequin Books S.A. 2013

Special thanks and acknowledgement are given to Alison Roberts for her contribution to the *St Piran's Hospital* series

ISBN: 978 0 263 89882 8

Harlequin (UK) policy is to use papers that are natural, renewable and recyclable products and made from wood grown in sustainable forests. The logging and manufacturing process conform to the legal environmental regulations of the country of origin.

Printed and bound in Spain
by Blackprint CPI, Barcelona

Dear Reader

Two years ago I had the pleasure of being part of the *St Piran's Hospital* series.

I loved my story about Luke and Anna, and adding to the conflict of the characters Josh and Megan, whose tense relationship ran throughout each of the stories in the *St Piran's* series.

When the series finished, it certainly looked as if these two star-crossed lovers could never get a happy ending of their own. Not only was there a wife still in the picture but, shockingly, she was now pregnant! I was honoured to be asked to revisit *St Piran's* and find a happy ending for Josh and Megan, but I also thought: Hmm…this will be quite a challenge. Challenge is a good thing, I reminded myself. It takes us out of our comfort zone and makes us stretch our wings and achieve more than we might have thought we could. And isn't it true that the more you put into something, the more you get out of it?

I really hope you love this story as much as I did in the end.

Happy reading!

With love

Alison

PROLOGUE

'CODE ONE, DR Phillips.' The registrar slammed down the phone as he swung his head. 'Theatre Three.'

Megan's pager began sounding at precisely the same moment, with the particular sound reserved for an absolute emergency.

The surge of adrenaline made everything else irrelevant. Even signing her resignation. Her ticket to finally escape.

She dropped her pen on top of the paperwork and leapt to her feet.

'Let's go.'

A code one was a life-threatening emergency. A life was at stake. More than one life, potentially, if Megan was being summoned. For a paediatrician to be called in with the same paging system used for something like a cardiac arrest meant that a newborn baby could be in need of specialist resuscitation. For it to be happening in Theatre meant the baby was arriving by emergency Caesarean. There were no scheduled Caesareans for the St Piran's maternity department today so this one must have come in via the emergency department.

The registrar, Matt, was keeping pace with Megan as she ran for the elevator.

'Suspected uterine rupture,' he said.

Megan nodded, holding her finger on the button as if that would speed up the arrival of the lift. Then she turned away.

'Stairs,' she snapped. 'It'll be quicker.'

'She'll be bleeding out, won't she?' Matt was right behind her. 'The baby won't stand much of a chance.'

'Depends.' Megan was taking the stairs two at a time. 'Internal blood loss can sometimes slow down or even stop simply because it's filled the available space and that puts pressure on ruptured vessels. The real danger comes when you open that space and release the pressure.' She blew out a hard breath as she pushed open the fire stop door on the theatre suite level. 'But you're right. It's critical for both of them.'

The main corridor in St Piran's theatre suite was deceptively quiet. The flashing orange light above the door of Theatre Three was a beacon. But so was something else that Megan hadn't expected to see.

A lone figure, at the end of the corridor, in front of the tall windows. A figure that stopped pacing and was now poised, reminding her of a wild animal sensing danger.

There was no mistaking the intensity of the stare Megan knew was directed at her.

'Get some scrubs on,' she ordered Matt as they reached the door to the change rooms. 'Then go in and make sure we've got everything we might need on the resus trolley. Check the incubator. I'll be right there.'

The figure was moving towards her. It might only be a silhouette because of the background light of the fading day beyond the windows but Megan knew exactly who it was.

Josh O'Hara.

Oh…*God*…

Why now? When she'd successfully avoided being alone with him for months.

Ever since that final, devastating kiss.

She could have avoided it now, too. Why hadn't she gone straight into Theatre with her registrar?

Because there was only one reason why Josh would be pacing the corridor like this. Why he wouldn't be in the Theatre with a case that would have been in his emergency department only minutes ago.

Megan was holding her breath. She'd never seen Josh look this tense. Distraught, even. Not even when he'd come to tell her that he loved her but they had no future.

Or…maybe she had. Once. So long ago now that the memory of his face was only a faint chord in the symphony that nightmare had been.

They'd had more than one turning point in their star-crossed history, she and Josh.

Clearly, this was another one. The third.

Bad things came in threes, didn't they?

That meant that this had to be the last. Of course it was, because escape was only days away for Megan now. She'd be on the other side of the world very soon. Just not quite soon enough.

Megan sucked in enough air to be able to speak. 'It's Rebecca, isn't it?'

His wife. They might not be living together as man and wife at the moment but they were still married.

A single nod from Josh. God, he looked terrible. He always looked like he could use a shave but right now his face was so pale it looked like he hadn't been near a razor for a week. And he must have been virtually scrubbing at his hair with his fingers for it to look so dishevelled. The expression in his eyes was worst of all, however. Blue fire that was born of desperation. Guilt. Despair.

And shame, perhaps, for what he had to beg for?

'The babies…' The words came out strangled. 'Please, Megan. Do your best for them. They…they won't let me in.'

Of course they wouldn't. He was far too emotionally involved. This was his family in Theatre Three. The whole family. As if it hadn't been hard enough for Megan that Rebecca was going to give him a child, she had to go one step further and present him with a complete family. Two babies.

And it might be up to her to save the lives of Josh's children.

The irony would be unbearable if she gave herself even a moment to think of it. Fortunately, she didn't have a moment to spare. As if any reminder of the urgency was needed, her registrar burst out of the changing room and went into the theatre.

Even then, something made Megan hesitate for just a heartbeat and, without any conscious thought, she reached out to touch Josh's arm in a gesture of reassurance. Not that she needed to touch him to ramp up the tension. Megan opened her mouth to say something but there were no words available.

With a curt nod, she turned away and went to throw on some scrubs.

Of course she would do everything she could to save his family. She would do it for any of her patients but if heroics were called for in this case, she wouldn't hesitate.

After all, it was Josh who had saved *her* life all those years ago.

* * *

That touch on his arm was almost enough to utterly unravel Josh.

His breathing ragged, tiny sounds escaping that could have been the precursors of gut-wrenching sobs if he couldn't pull himself together, Josh went back to his pacing.

Back to the window end of the corridor where he was far enough away to keep his agony private but close enough to see who came and went from Theatre Three.

He got his breathing back under control and silent again but guilt was still threatening to crush him.

This was his fault. If Rebecca died, he would know where the blame could be laid. Why had he allowed himself to be pushed so far away? In recent weeks she had refused to see him. Or talk to him even. The only information he had been given had been that Rebecca was 'fine'. That her GP was looking after her, with the implication that he was doing a better job than Josh ever had.

God…if it hadn't been so hard, he would have been able to ask the questions that might have told him something wasn't right. He might have given in to the urge to turn up on her doorstep and make sure she was 'fine' for himself.

As recently as this morning, he'd thought of doing exactly that on his way to work but it had been all too easy to talk himself out of it. He hadn't really wanted to start his day by stopping by his old house, had he? If he was really honest, he wanted to avoid laying hands on the woman he'd once loved but should never have married.

But the way he felt about Megan had been the reason he'd married Rebecca at all, wasn't it?

Oh…*God*…the threads of his life were so tangled. So confused… The pain of his childhood, knowing how much his mother had loved his father and seeing how she'd been destroyed bit by bit as she had been cheated on time and again. The conviction that, if this was what love was all about, he wanted nothing to do with it.

Knowing that he was falling deeper in love with Megan with every passing minute of that night they'd spent together.

Turning his back on her and everything that that kind of love could lead to.

Marrying Rebecca because he had been lonely. And because it had been safe. He had liked her. Respected her. Loved her the way you could love a good friend. A *safe* kind of love.

Had he allowed himself to be pushed so far out of Rebecca's life because it had been so hard to face the irrefutable evidence that he'd cheated on Megan by having sex with Rebecca that one, last time? When he'd known the marriage was over and it was only a matter of time before he and Megan could finally be together.

But Megan believed he had cheated on his wife when he'd gone to *her* bed.

He couldn't blame her for hating him for it.

At least he'd had the chance to save Megan's life that time, ironically in not dissimilar circumstances, but right now he'd been rendered useless. He couldn't even try to save Rebecca.

Did people think he wouldn't *want* to?

She was the mother of his children, for God's sake. Still his wife, even if it was in name only.

He had loved her once.

Just…not the way he'd loved Megan.

A part of him, so ruthlessly and successfully

squashed months ago, was still capable of reminding him that he still loved Megan in that way. And always would. Not that Josh was going to acknowledge the whisper from his soul. It was a love he had chosen to forsake.

For his career and his sanity, that first time.

The second time it had been for his unborn children.

What would he have left if things weren't going well in Theatre Three?

He'd lose his wife.

His children.

And he knew what that pain was like. It was years ago now but the memory of holding that tiny scrap of humanity in his hands would never leave him. He'd known, on some level, that it had been his own son that Megan had lost that day. That he had been holding. It was too neat a fit, not only with the dates but with the power of that night. The connection that had felt like it would last for ever. The kind of connection that made it feel right to create a baby. Make a family.

He'd lose Megan again, too, if things weren't going well in Theatre Three.

No. A fresh wave of pain ramped up the confused agony Josh was grappling with.

He'd already lost Megan. Months ago.

Something made him stop the caged-in prowl back and forth across the corridor end. Made him freeze and whip his head sideways.

Of course it was Megan. In green theatre scrubs now, with her hair covered by a cap. Moving decisively from the door of the changing room to the one beneath the flashing orange light. She didn't look in his direction.

Despite, or perhaps because of, the overwhelming

emotions he was having to deal with, Josh allowed himself to be distracted from the agonising, lonely wait for just a heartbeat.

Baggy, shapeless clothes like theatre scrubs did nothing to stop Megan being the most beautiful woman Josh had ever known. It didn't matter what she wore. Scrubs. Tattered old jeans. The gorgeous gown she had worn as a bridesmaid in a royal wedding party.

Oh…no…Tasha. Josh reached for the mobile phone clipped to his belt. He needed to let his sister know what was happening. She could be the one to break the news to their mother.

What time would it be in San Saverre?

As if it mattered. Tasha would want to know the trouble that both her brother and her best friend were in right now.

Her loyalty would be tested. She knew the empty space he was in now, having sacrificed a relationship with the woman he truly loved for the sake of his children. To keep a marriage, even in name only, so that he wouldn't repeat history by being the kind of man their father had been. She would know how devastating it would be, being faced with the prospect of losing those children.

But she would also know how hard this had to be for Megan. To be expected to save his babies that were being carried by another woman. The babies she could never have given him because losing *their* son, all those years ago, meant she could never have another child.

Josh had to stifle an audible groan.

He was a reasonably intelligent man. He was damned good at the job he did, running the emergency department of St Piran's.

How was it that he always messed things up so badly when it came to his relationships with women?

He could save lives.

But he was just as good at breaking hearts.

It was his fault Rebecca hadn't had medical help in time to prevent this catastrophe.

His fault that Megan had become pregnant with his first child.

His fault that she'd lost the baby. That she'd never have another.

No wonder Megan had blanked him at Tasha's wedding. He'd done it to her, hadn't he?

Twice.

Every time he'd come to a point in his life where he was losing control...faced with the absolute vulnerability of loving someone—*Megan*—enough to give them the power to make or break him...he had frozen. Backed away and stayed with what he knew. What seemed to work.

He was an emotional coward.

Or a control freak?

As a modus operandi it was fine as far as his career went. Kept him on top. Moving forward. He could deal with a thousand people professionally and win acclaim. But he didn't seem to be able to deal with even one person on an intimate level and not cause serious harm.

What made anybody think he would be a good father?

Maybe he'd end up just like his own father had been. Worse than useless.

Maybe he would fail *all* his children before they even had a chance of life.

No.

The word was wrenched from deep inside Josh.

These babies couldn't die.

Megan wouldn't let them.

The baby looked dead.

Delivered to Megan's area of the theatre seemingly within seconds of the emergency surgery starting, the nurse laid her limp burden down under the lights, gave the paediatric team a grim glance and moved swiftly back towards the main table. Another baby would be delivered almost as quickly.

The resuscitation protocol was automatic for Megan. Airway, breathing, circulation, drugs.

She couldn't allow the fact that this was Josh's baby anywhere near the conscious part of her brain. Even a hint of distraction, let alone panic, could be disastrous.

'Suction,' she ordered.

Making sure the newborn's head was at the correct angle to keep the airway open and holding the end of the soft tubing at a length that couldn't go too far and trigger a laryngeal spasm, Megan cleared away any possible obstruction. Against the soft chugging of the suction machine, Matt was gently stimulating the baby's body by rubbing the skin with a warmed towel.

To one side of them, the tension was escalating.

'Pressure's dropping again.' The anaesthetist's tone was a sharp warning. 'Ectopic activity increasing.'

'We've got to get this second baby out. Where the hell's the suction? I can't see a damned thing…'

On Megan's side of the theatre the baby was showing no signs of starting to breathe.

'Bag mask.' Megan's order was clipped.

With the tiny mask covering both the mouth and nose of the infant, she gently depressed the soft bag to deliver the tiny amount of air needed to inflate the lungs. Again. And again.

'Not pinking up,' Matt noted.

'He's in shock.' Megan signalled for a technician to take over the bag mask. 'Start chest compressions, Matt.'

'You going to intubate?' Matt was already slipping his hands around the tiny chest, keeping his thumbs in front ready to start compressions.

'In a minute.' Megan could see over her registrar's shoulder. The second baby was lying on a towel a nurse was holding flat on both hands as the cord was cut. She was close enough to be able to see if there were any signs of life.

There weren't.

They needed a second paediatric team in here but there hadn't been one available. It was up to Megan and Matt here. At least they had a second resuscitation trolley set up.

'Keep up the CPR,' she instructed Matt. 'One hundred and twenty beats per minute. He may need some adrenaline. We'll need to cannulate the umbilical vein as well as soon as we can. Let's see where we are with baby two.'

Baby two was a girl. Just as flat as her brother was.

Or maybe she wasn't. After the first puff or two of air from the bag mask, the tiny girl gave a gasp and began trying to breathe on her own. It wasn't enough, though. The heart rate was still falling.

At ten minutes the Apgar score for both babies was still unacceptably low. They needed intubation, stabilisation and transfer to PICU—the neonatal intensive care unit.

They were both alive, however, and Megan was fighting to keep them that way.

The battle on the other side of Theatre Three was not going so well.

Part of Megan's brain was registering the increasing tension as she slid a small tube down the first baby's airway to secure ventilation. The obstetric surgeon had found the torn abdominal artery but too much blood had been lost. The fluid replacement and the drugs being used were not enough. Rebecca's heart had stopped.

CPR continued on the mother as Megan checked the settings on both incubators and watched the recordings being taken on both babies reach a level that meant it was safe to transfer them to PICU.

As the second incubator was wheeled from the theatre, she heard the defeated note in the surgeon's voice.

'Time of death...sixteen forty-three.'

November in Cornwall could provide a bone-chillingly grey day with an ominous cloud cover that threatened a torrential downpour at any moment.

The rain held off for the duration of Rebecca O'Hara's funeral but the background was suitably grim for the final farewell of a young mother who had never had the chance to see her babies.

'I hope nobody gets too sick today,' somebody muttered as the congregation filed into the chapel. 'Looks like practically the entire staff of St Piran's is here.'

There were whispered conversations in every pew.

'Who's that sitting beside Josh?'

'Tasha. His sister. The one that married the prince. I didn't know she was pregnant.'

'No. On the other side. The older woman. Is that his mother?'

'Yes. Her name's Claire. I heard that she's planning to move to Penhally to help him look after the babies.'

Further up the aisle, St Piran's CEO, Albert White, was sitting with a member of the board of directors, Luke Davenport.

'Thank goodness the babies are doing so well,' he muttered. 'Josh looks wrecked enough as it is.'

'It's all so sad.' Luke's wife, Anna, tightened her grip on her husband's hand. 'All of it. Rebecca was so unhappy for so long. I think she really believed that the babies would make everything all right.'

She exchanged a glance with her husband. One that suggested that—given enough time—maybe things would be all right eventually.

For Josh, anyway.

At the very back of the church, a woman noted for her tendency to gossip wasn't about to rely on meaningful glances.

'You'll see,' she muttered to the colleague sitting beside her. 'Now that the wife's out of the way, he'll be married to his fancy piece in no time flat. You just wait and see.'

'Shut up, Rita,' her companion hissed.

For once, Rita did shut up. She spent the next few minutes watching as the final people squeezed in to take up the last of the standing room at the back of the church. She'd been watching the congregation ever since she'd arrived. Early.

'Where *is* Megan?' Rita finally had to ask. The organ music was fading and the funeral director was taking his place to start the service.

'Haven't you heard?' The person on the other side seemed amused that Rita was out of the grapevine loop for once. 'She left St Piran's yesterday.'

'Where's she gone?'

'Africa.'

'She's coming back, though…isn't she?'

'Doubt it. Her resignation was permanent. She's joined *Medécins San Frontières*.'

'But—'

'*Shhh.* Leave it, Rita. It's over.'

CHAPTER ONE

Almost two years later

WHY ON EARTH had she come back here?

Penhally, Cornwall, on this November day seemed grim. Grey and bleak.

And so *cold*. Megan was quite sure the temperature was a single digit and having come from an African summer where a cool day could still be thirty degrees Centigrade, this was like being inside a fridge.

It didn't help that she'd lost so much weight in recent weeks, of course. Dengue fever took a huge toll, especially the second time around. Her old coat hung so loosely on her that Megan could wrap it around her body like a blanket. Which was exactly what she did as she stood there, shivering, a suitcase by her feet, looking out over Penhally Bay as the taxi disappeared down the hill.

The sky was a deep, ominous grey and looked ready to unleash a torrent of rain at any minute. The sea looked equally menacing with whitecaps on the steel-grey water, moored yachts rocking on the swells and huge breakers crashing onto dark, wet sand. Seagulls circled overhead and the sharp, plaintiff notes of their cries echoed perfectly how Megan was feeling.

It was too cold to stand here in the street, that was for sure, but the view as she turned towards the cottage was just as dispiriting. The gate was barely visible in the wild growth of what had been a neatly trimmed hedge. The small garden was a wilderness but not high enough to disguise the coils of long-dead plants in the hanging baskets on either side of the front door or the broken panes in the lattice windows, some of which had curled pieces of cardboard trying to fill the small squares.

How long had it been since the last tenants had gone? Since she'd fired the rental agency who had failed to fix the issues like the broken pipes that had driven the tenants away? At least six months, but Megan had been too far away and too busy to cope with the hassle of putting new arrangements in place. Angered too by the flood of queries coming in from developers who were always waiting in the wings like vultures to get their hands on such a desirable piece of real estate.

And then she'd been too sick.

It was a ridiculously hard effort to push the gate open and drag her suitcase along the flagged path now choked with weeds and the branches of perennials like lavender that looked like they hadn't been cut back since she'd left two years ago. Megan felt the prickle of tears at the back of her eyes. This had all been so pretty once. Not that she'd ever managed to keep it as picture-perfect as her grandmother had but she'd tried her best to keep it the same.

To preserve the memories of how it had been in her childhood, when this cottage and her beloved gran had been the most precious things in her life.

And that, of course, was what had brought her back now.

This was where her roots were.

Not that she'd actually been brought up here. No…
After her parents were tragically killed in a car accident, Megan had gone to live with her grandmother in
London. But Gran had been brought up in Penhally and
that was where she'd taken Megan for a seaside holiday, every summer. They'd rented this very cottage,
year after year, and the memories of those weeks had
always been tinged with the rosy perfection of being
the best time in the best place in the world. The cottage had been the home of her heart for as long as she
could remember.

When she'd been so dreadfully ill, nearly losing her
life after losing the baby, Megan had been forced to
finally tell her grandmother the truth. Despite being
already frail, Gran had gathered up all her strength,
wrapped it all with the unconditional love she had for
her granddaughter and declared that they needed a new
beginning, starting with a seaside holiday. When she'd
found that their beloved rental cottage was on the mar-
ket, Gran had simply moved their lives back to her home
town and, by doing so, had allowed Megan to put the
pieces of her shattered life back together.

So this cottage and its memories, the sea and the
village all added up to *home*. And home was the place
that drew you back when you needed comfort. A safe
place to recover and reassess your life.

Besides, the cottage badly needed sorting out. It
would have been unforgiveable to let it crumble into
some sort of ruin. Megan could hear the kind of 'tsk-
ing' sound her grandmother would have been making
as she pushed open a front door stiff with disuse and
stepped into a space that felt just as cold as it was outside. A space that reeked of damp and mould and mice.

Oh…*hell*…

This was far worse than she'd expected.

It wasn't just the evidence of appalling neglect. The horrible smell of the rubbish left by the tenants littering the hallway or the ominous sound of trickling water coming from the kitchen. Or was it the bathroom upstairs? Probably both.

It wasn't the knowledge that there would be no electricity on yet and it mightn't even be safe to have it turned back on until she found someone to check the wiring. It wasn't even the wave of incredible weariness as Megan contemplated the energy it would take to sort any of this out.

No. It was the feeling of being so alone.

The result of the emotional punch of the memories of *not* being alone in this house.

Not that Josh had ever stayed here. But this was where it had ended, wasn't it? Her feet seemed to be literally treading memory lane. Taking her down the hallway and into her kitchen while her head and her heart conjured up the figure of Josh following her.

Her feet crunched through pieces of broken glass on the kitchen floor.

Her heart had been broken long ago. How on earth could it still hurt this much?

Because it was here that Josh had prised that jug of water out of her hands? Just before he'd kissed her as if it was the end of the world and she was the only thing that mattered to him.

Here that Josh had told her how much he loved her?

When he'd told her that he couldn't be in love with her any more because his *wife* was pregnant.

She could actually hear echoes of his voice.

I love you so much, which is why this is the hardest thing I've ever had to do...

It was just one night, weeks before you and I...

I love you, Megan...but no child of mine will grow up as I did, without a father. I won't do that. I have to make this work...

Yes. That had been when her heart had really broken. With the realisation that Josh had been lying to her when he'd told her the marriage was over. When she realised he'd still been sleeping with his wife at the time as he'd shared *her* bed.

That was when she'd known that it was truly all over. When any hope had died. She had known that, despite the love they had for each other, they could never, ever be together. Nothing could change that. If Rebecca's death hadn't even made a dent, then being back in Penhally certainly wasn't going to. That sense of betrayal was clearly still there. She'd thought she'd got over it all but the pain she was feeling right now was proof that she'd only managed to hide from it.

The chirrup of her mobile phone announced a text message. It was from Tasha—the only friend she'd really kept in touch with over the last couple of years. Maybe because Tash had also left Penhally. Or because she'd understood. How ironic was it that Tasha was Josh's sister?

U there yet? The message read. *How's it going?*

Megan's breath came out in a snort of wry amusement as she pulled off a woolly glove and tapped a response.

Just got here. Bit messy.

Would Tasha wonder what she was referring to? The house? Her emotional state? Her life?

Maybe she knew. *Hugs*, came back. *U OK?*

I will be. Thnx. Call u soon.

Tasha would be worried about her. Her friend had

been dubious about the return. Why not come somewhere sunny to recuperate? she'd suggested. Like San
Savarre? Or London, which would be close enough to
make sorting things out a little easier and she wouldn't
be so alone because Charles would be there, wouldn't
he? Being with such a good friend who knew the whole
story would be the best protection from being vulnerable to ghosts from the past.

She could cope, Megan had assured Tasha. It
wouldn't be for long. Yes, she knew that Josh had moved
from the smart St Piran town house he'd shared with Rebecca and was living closer to Penhally now. Of course
he had moved. He'd needed a bigger house and a garden for the children and for his mother, who'd gone
to live with them. By tacit agreement, she and Tash
rarely talked about her brother but in those early days
Megan had needed to know that the babies had survived
their dramatic entrance to the world and had gone on to
thrive. She hadn't really needed the later snippets that
had told her Josh was a perfect father to little Max and
Brenna. Or that his emergency department at St Piran's
hospital was considered to be the best in the county.

Or that there were no women of any significance in
his life. That he'd taken some sort of vow not to mess
up anybody else's life.

His children and his career were all that mattered
to Josh now. He probably wouldn't even be interested
that she was visiting the area. There was no reason for
their paths to cross other than the fact that this was a
small village.

Megan closed her eyes to the view of Penhally Bay
she still had in front of her through the kitchen window.

Maybe it was time to really let go of the past.

All of it.

Sell her grandmother's cottage and move on for ever.

If the memories were this hard to handle, how on earth did she think she would cope if she actually met Josh again?

The sooner she got out of here the better.

Maybe she didn't even need to think about fixing up the cottage. It wasn't as if it would make much difference to the kind of money a developer would be happy to offer.

She did need to find a place to stay for the night, however, and she really didn't want to contact any old friends from St Piran's even though she knew they would be happy to help.

The information centre in the village should be able to direct her to somewhere that would have a room available. Too weary in both body and spirit to face carrying her suitcase, Megan locked it into the cottage, taking only her shoulder bag as she set off to walk down the hill.

When she went back through the gate, however, the small path down to the beach caught her eye.

Just a look, she told herself. A glimpse into part of her past that wasn't associated with Josh. If she could feel the sand beneath her feet and close her eyes and breathe in the salty air, maybe she could remember something happier.

A summer's day, even. Building sandcastles and collecting shells and pieces of seaweed. Sitting on the damp sand with her bare legs stretched out in front of her, waiting for the thrill of the last wash of a wave to foam around her. Running back to the cottage to show Gran her new treasures.

* * *

Maybe it should have been running into Josh unexpectedly that she should have prepared herself for.

The dog on the beach was large enough to be quite frightening as he came loping towards Megan with a piece of driftwood clamped between his jaws. In the periphery of her vision, however, Megan could see a woman and children who had to be the dog's family because the beach was otherwise deserted. Nobody with children would have a vicious dog, would they? Besides, his teeth were occupied with the large piece of driftwood. And his tail was wagging in a very friendly manner.

'Crash!' The woman called firmly. 'Come back here.'

Crash? The name was unusual enough to ring a bell. He'd only been a gangly, half-grown puppy then, of course, but Megan could remember him wearing a big, white ribbon around his neck at a summer beach wedding. Luke and Anna Davenport's wedding.

It wasn't Anna coming towards her now, though.

'I'm so sorry.' The woman, bundled up warmly in a coat, hat and huge scarf, was very apologetic. 'He's a bit too friendly, so he is. But he wouldn't hurt a fly.'

She had a strong Irish accent and the lilt took Megan immediately into a space she really didn't want to be. Was everything and everybody here going to make her think instantly of Josh? She took a deep breath and focused on the dog.

'It's fine,' Megan said. 'I don't mind.' To prove it, she scratched the dog behind one of his ears, which was easy to do because Crash was leaning on her leg. 'Isn't this the Davenports' dog?'

'Indeed it is. We mind him during the day when

they're both working. The children love him to bits, so they do.'

The children were half hidden behind folds of the woman's coat as she held their mittened hands. Megan could see cute hats with ears on them and bright plastic boots. A pink pair with red flowers and a green pair with eyes that made them look like frogs. The owner of the frog boots peered out from the folds of coat.

'Cash naughty,' a small voice pronounced.

Crash wagged his tail harder.

The woman looked down to smile at her charges. 'Say hello, children.'

But the children said nothing. Neither did Megan. Her gaze had also dropped and she could see that the children were no bigger than toddlers. That they seemed to be close enough the same size as each other to be twins.

And…oh, God…the cheeky smile on the little boy's face had a charm out of all proportion to his age. His eyes were too dark to determine their colour but they were so…alive. His face danced with mischief and Megan could feel the pull of a personality that went past being cute or attractive.

It was the kind of pull that made it impossible not to get sucked in.

To fall in love.

The kind of connection that could be overwhelming. That had the capability of derailing, if not destroying, a life.

Megan sucked in a deep breath. How ridiculous to be…what, *afraid* of a child?

But it was more than that, wasn't it? Much, much more.

Her gaze jerked up again and now she could see past

the folds of the scarf and a woollen hat pulled low over
her forehead. She could see a woman who looked to be
well into her sixties but could be younger because those
lines suggested a life that had not been easy. Behind the
spectacles she wore, Megan could now see the colour
of her eyes and her heart skipped a beat. She knew who
had inherited that shade of indigo blue.

'Oh, my goodness. You're Josh's mother…Claire
O'Hara?'

'Indeed I am.' Claire blinked in surprise. 'Have we
met?'

'Just once. At the hospital. When the twins were still
in the intensive care unit. The day before…'

The gaze Claire O'Hara directed at Megan was intense. And then it turned distinctly wary. 'Oh…You're
Megan Phillips. The doctor. I'm so sorry. I didn't recognise you. It was such a terrible time…the day before
poor Rebecca's funeral and…'

'There's no need to apologise.' Megan was still
caught by the undertone she couldn't fail to have missed
in the older woman's gaze. Recognition of more than
her identity.

Had Josh filled her in on his star-crossed lover history?

Unlikely. But this was a small village and St Piran's hospital grapevine was robust thanks to people
who loved to gossip, like that dreadful woman—the
ward clerk in the NICU…what was her name? Ruth?
No…Rita.

Oh…Lord. Had Josh's mother heard about the way
they'd met, way back when Megan had been a final-
year medical student? That she'd become pregnant after
a one-night stand with Josh, who hadn't been remotely

interested in seeing her again? That he'd saved her life but that their son had been too premature to survive?

That baby—Stephen—had been Claire's grandson.

Even if she hadn't caught up on ancient history, she couldn't have missed the scandal of the way she and Josh had been drawn back to each other when he'd moved to St Piran's.

"Poor Rebecca", she'd said. Because her daughter-in-law had been badly treated by her husband, who had given up on their marriage and had been more interested in another woman? That Megan was the "other woman"? And that, in the end, they hadn't been able to keep their hands off each other?

Or maybe she felt sorry for Rebecca because she'd died knowing that Josh was only staying in the marriage for the sake of the children.

Megan was acutely embarrassed. Ashamed, even. The way she might have felt if Claire was her own grandmother and she'd disappointed her beyond measure. It had been a mistake to come back here. A dreadful mistake.

Except that Claire wasn't eyeing her as if she was the cause of all her son's troubles. 'And you look…different,' she continued. That wary expression had completely gone now. Claire's face actually creased with a kindly concern. 'You're so pale, dear. Are you all right?'

'I'm…um…fine.' Megan nodded for emphasis and then tried to cover her embarrassment at the undeserved sympathy by looking down and smiling at the children. They stared back, wide-eyed and still shy.

'This is Max.' Claire smiled. She turned her head. 'And this is Brenna.'

They were so impossibly *cute*. Small faces with perfect features and she could see now that their eyes were as blue as their grandmother's and their father's. She wondered if the hair beneath the animal hats would be glossy and black and so soft to run your fingers through it, just like Josh's. Or had they inherited their mother's blondeness?

Josh's children. Josh and Rebecca's children. Living proof that he'd gone back to his wife's bed after his marriage was supposedly over, leaving him morally available to Megan.

Maybe something of how hard this was showed in her face.

'Up,' Brenna demanded, dropping her grandmother's hand to hold both arms in the air. 'Up, Nan. Pick me *up*.'

Claire had to let go of Max's hand to pick Brenna up. Max immediately toddled off, at some speed, towards the waves. Crash loped after him.

'*Max*. Come back. We have to go home now. It's starting to rain.'

It *was* starting to rain. Big, fat, icy drops of water began pelting the small group on the beach.

Claire tried to put Brenna down to run after Max but the little girl shrieked a protest. Crash had dropped his lump of wood and was circling Max, who looked determined to get closer to the wild surf.

'I'll get him.' Megan dropped her shoulder bag and took off.

It took only seconds to reach the toddler but the burst of energy it took was enough to make Megan feel faint. She really wasn't fine at all, was she?

It was just as well that Max's little legs had also exhausted their energy reserves. He grinned at Megan. 'Puddle?' he asked hopefully.

Oh, help…he was totally irresistible with that crooked little smile and the hopeful expression on his face.

'Not today, sweetheart.' She scooped up the toddler and held him in her arms. 'It's not sunny enough, is it?'

Her steps almost faltered as she carried the child back to Claire. She was holding Josh's son. The closest she had ever come to holding the child she could have had herself. The shape of the soft little body cuddling into her was delicious. When Max wrapped his arms around her neck to hang on tighter, Megan felt a flash of pain in her chest, as if her heart was cracking. An old scar, perhaps, being torn open?

Thank goodness it was raining. If any tears escaped, at least nobody would know except her. All she wanted was to grab her bag and escape the moment she got back to Claire, but how could she leave her now? The rain was coming down harder and she had to get two small children and a very large dog off the beach and—presumably—into a car. Or was Josh now living this close to Penhally beach? To her cottage?

'The car's not far,' Claire said. 'Just down the road a bit.' She put Brenna down and took a leash from her coat pocket, which she clipped to Crash's collar. Holding the lead with one hand, she held out her other hand to Brenna. 'Can you walk now, pet?'

'No-o-o. Up.'

Relief that Josh wasn't going to turn out to be a close neighbour made Megan take a deep breath.

'Let me help,' she said. 'You're getting wet and you've got a bit of a handful here.'

'Don't I know it?' Claire picked Brenna up, managing to keep hold of the leash. 'And there I was thinking that it would make my day easy if I gave them all a quick run on the beach before we did our messages in the village. I don't know where these tots get their energy from.'

Megan had to hide a smile as she found herself struggling to keep up with Claire on the way back to the car. Limitless energy was clearly an O'Hara trait.

Not that she could leave Josh's mother to cope alone once they reached the car either. The wind had picked up and was threatening to blow the heavy doors closed and it was a mission to strap two wriggling toddlers into their car seats and then shove a folder double stroller out of the way to make room for a big dog to jump into the back hatch of the station wagon.

Finally, everything seemed to be sorted but as Claire reached up to pull the hatch down, she suddenly stopped. She closed her eyes and bent her head, her breath escaping in almost a groan.

'Are you all right?'

'Oh, I'm fine, I am. Just need to catch my wind.'

But Megan could feel a prickle of awareness. One that she'd learned never to ignore.

'Sit down for a minute,' she said. 'Here…' She pushed the stroller further back and guided Claire to sit on the edge of the car floor. Crash shuffled sideways to make room. The car was pointed into the wind and with the hatch cover still up they were fairly well protected from the weather. 'You are a bit short of puff, aren't you?'

'It's the cold, that's all.'

But Claire was virtually gasping for air. She started loosening the woollen scarf around her neck but abandoned the action to start rubbing the top of her left arm through her coat sleeve.

'Have you got any pain in your chest?' Megan asked.

Claire shook her head. 'It just gets…tight…that's all. In the cold…and…if I hurry.'

'But your arm hurts?'

'Only an ache… It's nothing… Goes away…'

Except it didn't seem to be going away this time. And Claire's face looked grey. Even as Megan watched with mounting alarm, beads of perspiration appeared beneath the edge of the woollen hat.

'Go.' A small voice came over the top of the back seat. 'Go, Nan. Go-o-o…' The plea trailed to a miserable sound. Beside Max, Brenna began to cry.

Claire tried to stand up but had barely begun moving before she collapsed backwards.

'I don't…I don't feel very well…' She tugged harder at her scarf and it came away and rippled to the ground.

'Do you have any history of heart problems?' Megan asked. 'Do you carry spray for angina or anything?'

'No…I'm fine…' Claire's face was crumpling. She looked terribly afraid. 'I *have* to be,' she whispered.

Megan had stripped off her gloves and was feeling for Claire's pulse. The rapid, uneven beat made it very clear what had to be done. She reached for her shoulder bag to find her mobile phone.

'I'm calling an ambulance,' she told Claire calmly. 'You need medical attention.'

'No…I'll be fine… Just give me…a minute…'

But the emergency services had answered Megan's call with commendable swiftness and she was already describing their location.

'Cardiac chest pain,' she told the dispatcher. 'Radiating to the left arm. Arrhythmia.'

'You're a doctor?' the dispatcher queried.

'Yes.'

'An ambulance is on its way. Are you able to stay with the patient?'

In case of a cardiac arrest?

'Of course.'

Megan made Claire as comfortable as she could while they waited for the ambulance. She took off her own coat to provide the older woman with some extra warmth. Picking up the scarf, she saw why it had been difficult for Clair to loosen. It had become caught on a necklace chain, which had broken.

Not that she pointed that out to Claire but, to prevent a possible treasure being lost, she put the chain into her own coat pocket, leaving the scarf in the back of the car. Her actions were brisk and organised but automatic because she was busy providing as much reassurance as she could, knowing that any stress could make this much worse. If Claire was, as she suspected, having a heart attack, then anxiety could tip the balance and stop her heart completely.

Would she have the strength herself to keep up CPR until an ambulance arrived?

Thank goodness she didn't need to find out. The ambulance arrived only minutes later and the crew had Claire on a stretcher and attached to a monitor within a very short time. She had an oxygen mask on by the time the rhythm settled on the screen of the life pack and a paramedic was preparing to insert an IV line.

'Marked ST elevation,' her crew partner noted. 'Looks like an infarct all right.'

'Are you on any medication?' the paramedic asked Claire. 'Are you allergic to anything that you know of? Have you had any aspirin today?'

Claire was shaking her head in response to all the questions. Things were happening too fast for her to find any words. The children in the car were both crying loudly now but Megan was still holding Claire's hand.

'It's going to be fine,' she reassured Claire yet again. 'These people are going to look after you and make sure you get checked out properly at hospital.' She turned to one of the crew members. 'Claire's son is Josh O'Hara at St Piran's. He may well be on duty at the moment so you might like to let him know in advance who you're bringing in.'

'Will do.'

Megan tried to let go of Claire's hand but the grip tightened. She leaned closer to hear the words that were being muffled by the oxygen mask.

'But who's going to…look after the children?'

Megan felt a cold chill run down her spine. No. She couldn't offer to do that. It would be too hard. The scars were still too fresh. Best not to go near anything that might pick at them. Her life was taking a new direction now. Having it derailed would be a disaster.

The paramedic was busy with her other hand. 'Sharp scratch coming, Mrs O'Hara.' She slid a cannula into a vein. 'There. All done.'

Claire lifted the hand that Megan was still holding, trying to pull the oxygen mask away from her face. 'I can't do this…the children…'

Her partner was leaning over Megan. 'Chew up this aspirin for me,' he instructed Claire. 'I'll give you a sip of water to wash it down.'

Megan was in the way. She tried to pull her hand free but Claire's grip tightened.

'Please…' Claire's face looked alarmingly grey. Getting stressed was making her condition rapidly worse. 'Can't you help?'

'Yeah…' The paramedic gave Claire a very direct glance. 'Can you drive?'

'Yes, but—'

'You could follow behind the ambulance, then. I'm

sure there'd be someone else to look after Doc O'Hara's kids once you got there.'

Claire was nodding. 'Please, Megan…'

'Otherwise we'll have to bring them in the ambulance. Or wait for back-up.' The paramedic was sounding impatient now. 'And we really need to get going.' The look he gave Megan was a direct warning. Hold this process up any further and if anything goes wrong between here and the emergency department of St Piran's, she would have contributed.

Megan was caught. She couldn't walk away. There were two crew members in the ambulance and one of them had to drive. If the other had to care for two toddlers, there would be nobody left to care for Claire. And she could get worse. Go into a cardiac arrest, even.

Her nod was jerky. 'I'll do it,' she said tightly. 'Are the keys in the car?'

'Yes…oh…*thank* you, lovie.' Claire finally let go of her hand but her eyes filled and tears rolled down her cheeks.

Megan closed her eyes for a heartbeat. There was no help for this, so all she could was do her best to cope with it. At least she had a kind of advantage here. She knew there was a high likelihood that she would have to see Josh and she would have a few minutes to at least try and prepare herself emotionally for that.

No doubt Josh would prefer to avoid this encounter as much as she would. And he probably wouldn't have the luxury of any warning.

Megan opened her eyes and smiled at Claire. 'Try not to worry,' she told her. 'I'll be right behind the ambulance. I won't let anything happen to the children. You'll see them again very soon, I promise.'

The back door of the ambulance slammed behind her after Megan had climbed out.

The vehicle was pulling out onto the road as Megan checked the fastenings on the car seats, fastened her own safety belt and started the car, surprised to see how shaky her hands were.

The beacons on the ambulance were flashing and the siren began to wail as the vehicle picked up speed. Megan wasn't going to try and keep up with it. Not on a wet road when she was feeling shaky. Certainly not with two precious children in the car.

She didn't need to follow that closely anyway.

The route to St Piran's was written on her heart, like everything else about this place.

CHAPTER TWO

'INCOMING, DR O'HARA.' The nurse's voice came from just behind Josh's shoulder as he scrolled through the images on the computer screen.

He grunted an acknowledgement, still focused on the screen. Surely something had shown up on the MRI of his earlier patient to explain her acute neurological symptoms?

'Status two.' The nurse sounded oddly nervous but, then, she was new and had only just learned that flirting with him was likely to earn disfavour. 'Sixty-year-old woman who looks like she's having an infarct.'

'Put her straight into Resus, then. Is Ben around?'

'Yes…but…'

The back of Josh's neck prickled as he turned his head. 'But what?'

'The patient is your mother, Dr O'Hara.'

The prickle ran down the entire length of his spine now, turning icy cold. Josh was on his feet and moving before he gave the action any conscious thought.

'How far away?'

'ETA five minutes. They're coming from Penhally.'

They? Were the children in the ambulance as well? This couldn't be happening. Not now, when his life was exactly the way it was supposed to be. The children, the house, his job—none of it would have been possible without his mother's help.

An infarct? Claire O'Hara had never had a day's illness in her life. She'd never smoked. She was as slim now as she'd been in her twenties. Her blood pressure was fine. She had energy to burn.

Or did she? Had she been pushed too far by him taking up the amazing offer of her helping him to raise the twins?

If this was yet another disaster in his life, could the blame be laid, yet again, at *his* feet?

Ben Carter, another emergency medicine consultant at St Piran's, was already in the resuscitation area. The defibrillator was being tested. A twelve-lead ECG machine was standing by. He glanced up and saw Josh.

'Don't panic,' he said quietly. 'We don't know exactly what we're dealing with yet.'

'Status two infarct,' Josh snapped. 'Unstable. What the hell happened? Have you had any details? Where was she? Did she…*arrest* somewhere?'

'No. That much I do know. She's status two because she's throwing off a few ectopics. She's on oxygen and she's had aspirin, GTN and morphine. Her breathing's improving.'

'Improving? My God, how bad *was* it?'

'Josh…' Ben stepped closer to put a hand on his colleague's arm. 'I've got this, OK? It'll be good for Claire if you're here but you need to stay calm.'

'What about the children? Were they with her?'

'I don't know.' Ben was looking past Josh now. Towards the double doors sliding open to admit a stretcher and ambulance crew. A nurse was pointing them towards the resus room. He turned to a nurse. 'Has the cardiology registrar been paged?'

'Forget the registrar,' Josh said. 'Get Anna Davenport down here. This is my *mother*, for God's sake.'

Claire looked terrified as she was wheeled into the resus room.

'Josh...' she gasped, reaching out a hand. 'Thank heavens you're here.'

'Of course I'm here.' Josh took hold of the hand. He knew he was getting in the way as the ambulance crew transferred Claire to the bed and gave Ben a handover but, for the first time in years, his mother needed *him* instead of the other way round. He kept his eyes on her face as the staff stripped away the clothing from her upper body and started adding extra dots so they could take a more comprehensive recording of the electrical activity in her heart. Ben was drawing off bloods for urgent analysis.

'Let's sit you up a little bit, Mrs O'Hara,' a nurse said, slipping another pillow behind Claire. 'And I'm just switching the oxygen over to this plug on the ceiling so we can get rid of the portable tank. No, don't take your mask off.'

Claire ignored the nurse, pushing the mask clear of her mouth. 'The twins, Josh...they're...'

'Please keep your mask on.' The nurse gently moved Claire's hand. 'It's important that you get some oxygen at the moment.'

'I can hear you.' Josh leaned closer. 'What about the twins?'

'They're fine.' The paramedic was loading the portable oxygen cylinder back onto the stretcher. 'The doctor who called the ambulance for Mrs O'Hara said she'd be bringing them straight here. She can't be far behind us.'

'A doctor?' Josh was confused. 'Was she at the medical centre?' Getting treatment, even, for some condition she'd never let him know she had?

'No. She was at the beach. With the children and a big dog.'

'Crash. Oh, no…' The woman coming swiftly into the resus room sounded as though she was starting a conversation with an old friend. 'What's he been up to now, Claire?' She was smiling down at her patient. 'More importantly, what on earth have you been up to?'

The smile was reassuring but Josh could see the concern in the face of the head of the cardiology department. Concern that increased as a technician handed her the sheet of paper from the twelve-lead ECG machine. Ben was also reading the ECG over her shoulder.

'What is it?' Josh forgot his confusion about a doctor being on scene when Claire had become ill. He hadn't missed the significant glance passing between Anna and Ben.

'Left anterior,' Anna said calmly. 'ST elevation of up to three millimetres. Have we got anything back on the bloods yet? Cardiac enzymes? TNT?'

Josh had to take a deep breath as he heard Ben relay the earliest results. He didn't want to let Claire know how serious this could be. An infarct that knocked out part of the left ventricle was more likely to have serious consequences. Every minute counted now so that they could save as much cardiac function as possible.

Anna had turned to Claire. 'You're having a heart attack, Claire,' she said gently. 'But there are things we can do to minimise the damage it might be doing to your heart. I'm going to take you up to the catheter laboratory and we can see exactly where the blockage is in your coronary arteries. We'll clear it if we can and might put something called a stent in to keep the artery open.'

'You're going to…operate on me?' Claire's face was as white as the pillow behind her.

'Not exactly. You'll be awake. We put a tiny tube inside an artery and that goes into your heart. It's very clever.'

'And Anna's very good at it,' Ben put in. 'You'll be in the best hands, Claire.'

'We'll give you a sedative,' Anna added. 'You'll be awake but it won't hurt and we won't let you get too anxious.'

'No.' Claire shook her head. She tried to peer past the medical team crowded around her bed. 'I can't go. Not yet. She said I'd see the children again. Very soon.'

'*Who* said?' Josh could feel the tension of this whole situation spiralling upwards. They couldn't let Claire get any more upset because there was still a definite risk of her rhythm degenerating into a fatal arrhythmia. Who had his children? Where were they?

'She does.' Claire's lips were trembling. 'The doctor.'

'*What* doctor?'

'The one who…looked after them…when they were born.'

'Megan Phillips? But that's impossible. She's in Africa.'

'Not any more.'

Josh froze as he heard the voice coming from behind Ben and Anna on the other side of the bed. Everybody turned to see who was at the entrance to the room. Holding the handles of the double stroller that contained the twins.

'*Daddy*.' Both Max and Brenna's faces lit up with smiles as they spotted their father. They held up four little arms.

But Josh didn't even see the plea. His gaze was locked on the woman behind the stroller.

Oh, my God...

Megan.

For just a heartbeat, the world stood absolutely still.

Nothing else mattered.

That his mother was dangerously unwell. That he had two tiny, defenceless children calling for him. That he was the head of a department of St Piran's Hospital that was gaining widespread recognition as a centre of excellence in emergency medicine.

None of those things could even exist in the space Josh was sucked into for just a second.

A space of such intensity, it pulled the oxygen from the air around him and made it feel impossible for him to breathe.

The space he'd been in on that New Year's Eve party when he'd met Megan properly for the first time. When he'd sensed the power of truly falling in love. The power that had held his mother captive and broken her life.

He'd been there again in the trauma of that emergency when it had looked as though Megan might die. When he'd sensed the power of what a parent's love for a child could be as well, and had vowed never to let that power control him either.

During the course of that one, incredible night when he'd shared her bed for only the second time—just before he'd found out he was going to become a father.

On the day he'd had to do the hardest thing in his life, and tell her it was all over.

In that moment when he'd had to beg her to do her best to save the lives of Rebecca's and his children.

Daddy.

The echo of the word penetrated the space. Grounded Josh instantly. He was where he needed to be. Living his life the way it had to be lived.

The way he *wanted* to live it.

Nothing could be allowed to change that. Somehow, he had to resist the incredible pull that that space could exert. It felt like his life was depending on it. It was almost ironic to have his mother in the same room. The example he'd grown up with of the damage that that kind of love could inflict.

Stepping towards the newcomers, Josh was aware of the tension around him. The kind that came from a collective holding of breath, waiting to see what was going to happen.

Their story was hardly a secret, was it? Not that Anna or Ben knew that he'd slept with Megan while he'd still been married. While his wife had been in the early stages of pregnancy with the twins. But everybody knew their early history by now. And if anybody had missed the way they'd been drawn back to each other when he'd first come to St Piran's, the hospital grapevine would have filled them in. Maybe everybody *did* know about that night in the on-call room.

Oh…Lord…Tash knew everything. How much did his mother know?

Josh pulled the barriers of his professional image around him like a force field.

'Megan… What a stroke of luck you were there for my mother when she got sick. And thank you so much for taking care of my children.'

He stooped to release the safety straps around the twins. Not that he squatted down fast enough to miss the change of expression on Megan's face. Had she been holding her breath like everyone else in here? Hurt by his deliberate focus on his own family? Himself?

He hadn't even asked her how she was despite some alarm bell ringing faintly in the back of his head. As he stood up, with a twin under each arm, he couldn't help taking another look at her. That warning bell hadn't been a false alarm. She looked...terrible.

So thin. So pale. Something was wrong. Her emerald-green eyes looked dull enough to be frightening.

Except that Josh had no right to have an emotional stake in Megan's wellbeing any more.

And even if he did, this wasn't the time. Or place.

He held her gaze for the briefest moment, however. He couldn't help it. He knew his concern would be transparent but that didn't matter either. He tried to send a silent message.

We'll talk. Soon.

'The babies...' Claire's voice wobbled. 'Let me give them a kiss before I have to go.'

Megan's heart was hammering in her chest.

How ironic would it be if she provided another cardiac emergency for Josh to deal with?

What had she expected to happen here? A moment of pure fantasy where the existence of anyone else—including his mother and children and colleagues—simply evaporated? And Josh's face changing as though he was witnessing a miracle? That he would come towards her in slow motion and sweep her into his arms? Kiss her again just like he had that last time...?

Maybe some tiny, secret part of her had hoped exactly that.

It didn't mean that she'd wanted it to happen, though. Or that she could have coped with going down that

track. It was the last thing she wanted when she'd fought
so hard to find her new direction. A completely different track.

Josh had done exactly the right thing. Been professional. Cold, almost. But then, when she'd been trying to
process that, feeling dizzy and bewildered, he'd looked
at her again. *Really* looked at her. And she'd known that
this wasn't it. This moment couldn't count as their first
meeting after a long absence.

That had been postponed due to unforeseen circumstances.

Circumstances that were slightly chaotic right now, as
staff bustled around, taking care of Claire and preparing
to move her to the catheter laboratory even as Josh gave
her the chance to kiss and cuddle each of the children.
Max grabbed one of the wires attaching an electrode
to the cardiac monitor and pulled it free, which set off
an alarm. The sound frightened Brenna, who clung to
her father and had to be persuaded to give her grandmother a quick kiss.

Meanwhile, Megan simply stood there, clutching the
handles of the stroller. She could hardly walk out, could
she? Not when these people were old friends. How rude
would it seem to Ben and Anna if she just left?

Besides, she felt frozen. Watching Josh. Seeing the
easy way he held his small children and talked to them.
Knowing that his light tone and smile was an act. That
the way those lines had deepened around his eyes advertised how much stress he was under right now.

And…he looked as gorgeous as he ever had. His pal-
pable charm hadn't changed either and it was being directed towards the twins right now and they looked as
if they were being won over by that lazy smile as eas-

ily as she always had. He must have raked his fingers through his hair a fair few times to get it looking so rumpled, and to her horror Megan could feel the urge to smooth it with her own hands. To push that wayward lock back from his forehead and cup his face with both her hands so that she could really look and discover every tiny change that time had wrought.

She gripped the moulded plastic handles of the stroller more tightly. Forced herself to smile in response to Ben's greeting.

'We'll have to catch up. I'd love to hear about Africa. You here for a while?'

No. She needed to escape as fast as she could.

'I…I'm not sure yet.'

Ben's pager sounded and he excused himself hurriedly. Megan wished she had one clipped to her own belt. A reason to disappear.

But she couldn't leave quite yet. Anna needed to know that her dog was locked in the back of Claire's car out in the car park and the cardiac surgeon had been busy on the phone for the last few minutes, juggling her responsibilities so that she could join the cardiologists and be involved in this emergency angioplasty case.

Anna finished her call and nodded at someone. A loud clicking noise announced that they had disengaged the brake on Claire's bed. It was time to move.

'You coming up with us, Josh?' Anna queried. 'Not that you can stay in the cath lab, of course, but you're welcome to come in while we set up.'

Ben stuck his head back into the room.

'You're covered here, mate. Give me a call later and we'll sort out what happens tomorrow.' He smiled at Claire. 'I'll come up and see you in the ward later. You'll be feeling a lot better by then.'

Josh stood there, holding a twin on each hip.

Megan stood there, holding the handles of the empty stroller.

As Ben vanished, Josh's gaze shifted to settle on Megan.

So did Anna's.

The whole room seemed to pause and the atmosphere was electric. Josh couldn't take the twins with him to go with his mother. Everybody was clearly waiting for her to make an offer to help out.

It was too much to ask. Way too much. Josh had plenty of staff here, didn't he? Any number of nurses who would probably fight for the chance to earn his appreciation by babysitting.

But Josh was looking at her and it was like that graze of a glance he'd given her when he'd picked the twins up. The one that recognised *her*.

Not as a separate person.

As part of what they had once been. Together.

With a huge effort Megan broke the eye contact as she tried to marshal the wild tumble of thoughts and emotions in her head. She looked at Anna.

'I've got Crash outside in Claire's car,' she said. 'What would you like me to do with him?'

'Oh…help…' Anna caught her bottom lip with her teeth.

'Sorry, love.' The beeping of the monitor recording Claire's heart rate increased its tempo noticeably. 'It's my fault. I took him to the big beach for a run with the twins and—'

'It's OK.' Anna's gaze flicked to the monitor. 'Don't you worry about anything, Claire. I can sort this. Oh, help…if only Luke hadn't left already. I could have called him to take Crash *and* the twins home.'

'Did Luke decide to go, then?'

Josh had moved towards Megan. He put Max down and began fitting Brenna back into the stroller. Max turned around and headed back towards Claire's bed.

'Not so fast, cowboy.' Anna scooped the toddler up and came towards the stroller as well. She was close to Megan again, but her gaze was on Josh. 'Yes,' she told him. 'He'll be halfway to New Zealand by now.'

Megan blinked. New Zealand? This whole situation was starting to feel surreal. Anna noticed her expression.

'Luke's father has had a stroke. It doesn't sound too bad but his mother is freaking out completely. When he checked flights late last night, he found he could get a ticket for a dawn flight leaving Heathrow. He drove to London at one a.m.'

'Of course he wants to support his mother. I'll think of something else.' But the desperate note in Josh's voice was so uncharacteristic it told Megan just how tightly he was hanging on here. Did he feel like his world was collapsing around him?

His mother was seriously ill.

His ex-lover had appeared in his life again.

He had a child-care issue on his hands.

Who could he turn to?

Another silence. Megan couldn't ignore the trouble Josh was in here.

Just because he'd broken her heart…because they could never be together…it didn't mean that she had to stop caring, did it?

Even if it did, it didn't mean that she was capable of stopping.

'I can look after them,' she said quietly. 'All of them.'

Both Josh and Anna's faces lightened instantly.

'I couldn't ask you—'

'Would you really?' Anna spoke over Josh's exclamation.

'I can't take them home, though,' Megan added. 'My cottage is a bit...uninhabitable at the moment.'

'Take them to my place,' Anna suggested. 'The key's just upstairs in my office. You know where our cottage is, don't you?'

'Yes. You had your wedding on the beach just down the hill.'

Josh was shaking his head. 'It would be better to take the twins home. My keys are right here. And they might be happier if they have their own stuff around.'

Meaning that they might not want to be with her? A complete stranger?

The look Josh gave her was apologetic. As if he was reading her mind.

'I mean, there's all their toys. And the food they like. And their PJs and beds if things don't...'

The unspoken warning that things might not go as well as expected was enough to make them all suddenly anxious to get going.

'Fine.' Megan nodded. 'I'll take them home to your place, Josh. Only...'

He turned his head, already moving to go and find his house keys.

'Only I don't know where you live.'

'Anna can fill you in.' Josh kept going.

Anna smiled. 'That's easy. Josh bought the Gallaghers' farm, next door to my place. On the St Piran side. Crash has a basket on the veranda. He won't wander— it's always been his second home.'

Josh was back, thrusting a set of keys into Megan's hand.

'Thank you *so* much.' Stooping swiftly, he touched the twins' heads. 'Be good for Megan,' he told them. 'I'll be home soon.'

Claire's bed was moving past them now, with most of the staff disappearing as well. Any moment now and Megan would find herself alone with Josh's children and the keys to his house in her hand.

How surreal this all was had just gone off the Richter scale. Was she the only person who found this unbelievably bizarre?

No. Claire was watching Megan as her bed was manoeuvred through the door of the resus room. There was concern in her face. And sympathy? Something else as well.

Maybe a message. One that said: *You can do this. We all know how strong you are.*

It wasn't true. Nobody around here knew how strong she had become over the last two years. Maybe if she'd had that kind of strength way back, none of this would have happened, but at least she had it now.

She *could* do this.

And if she succeeded, it would prove to everyone just how far she had moved on with her life.

She could prove it to Josh.

She could prove it to herself?

CHAPTER THREE

How WEIRD WAS this?

To be going home to his children, knowing that Megan Phillips was there. Looking after Max and Brenna, like a stand-in mother.

In his house.

Like a stand-in wife?

No.

Josh wasn't going into that space. The idea of he and Megan being together had died a long, long time ago.

The moment he'd told her that Rebecca was pregnant.

Parking his car next to where the family wagon was, Josh walked towards the rambling, old farmhouse that looked out over the ocean. It was far too dark and drizzly to see anything, especially in the welcoming glow of the house lights, but could hear the sea and the wash of waves was a familiar, comforting pulse of sound.

Crash was on the veranda. Watching. Ready to protect his second home from any intruder. His tail began waving as soon as Josh climbed the steps, however, and a damp nose nudged his hand in welcome.

He let the big dog into the house with him as he entered.

Josh knew he needed some moral support. He just didn't realise how much until he walked inside and

ALISON ROBERTS   55

could smell hot food and hear the sound of voices and
could feel...

Could feel Megan's presence in his house. Even before he entered the big, open-plan living area where the
children were snuggled up on the couch on either side
of Megan, listening to a story.

Josh had to pause for a moment. To listen to the soft
lilt of Megan's voice. To soak in the tilt of her head and
the way his children were tucked into the crooks of her
arms as if it was the most familiar, and loved, place in
the world for them.

Dear Lord...if things had been different...it could
have been *their* son listening to Megan reading that
story. Getting sleepy and needing to be tucked up in
bed. Leaving his parents to have a quiet evening together bathed in that flickering firelight.

That soul-deep yearning had been successfully buried for years now.

But it hadn't gone away, had it?

Perhaps it was fortunate that Crash didn't get stopped
in his tracks and mesmerised the way Josh had been.
The dog padded far enough into the room to interrupt
the story.

'*Cash*.' Max wriggled free of Megan's arm and slid
down from the couch, running to throw his arms around
the big animal.

'*Daddy*.' Brenna also wriggled free and made straight
for Josh, who was glad of the need to move and pick his
daughter up. He had to give her a good cuddle and kiss
as well and that covered a few more awkward seconds.
And when he looked up, Megan's gaze was on Crash.

'Sorry,' she said. 'I didn't realise he was allowed inside. I shouldn't have left him out in the cold like that.'

'That's his spot,' Josh assured her. 'It means Anna

can drop him off or collect him without worrying about disturbing us.'

Us.

God...it sounded as if he was including Megan.

'She'll be here to pick him up soon,' he added hurriedly. 'She had a few things to catch up on and wanted to check on Mum again.'

'How is she? Did James get to see her in the end?'

Josh nodded. 'Yes. He agrees that bypass surgery isn't necessary. Anna put in four stents and everything's looking great. The damage should be minimal and Mum will be able to come home in a day or two.'

'That's wonderful.'

'Yes. I'm sorry it all took so long, though.'

'No worries. You said it might.'

He hadn't thought it would take this long, though. That phone call to update Megan on progress and fill her in on what the children might need had been hours ago.

'Thank you so much,' he said now. 'I don't know how we would have managed it you hadn't been there.'

Megan turned her head away. 'I'm sure you would have managed just fine.'

Of course they would have.

Just like Josh had managed when Megan had finally walked out of his life, physically, months after her emotional departure.

Just when he'd needed her most.

'When did you get back from Africa?'

'Today.' Megan turned back, a wry smile shaping her mouth.

Welcome home.

The words hung there, unspoken.

Josh cleared his throat. 'Max, don't let Crash lick

your face, mate. Come on…it's high time you two were in bed.'

Megan closed the story book and put it on the table beside the couch. 'I'll leave you to it.'

Josh had scooped up Max as well. He had to peer over two small heads to catch Megan's gaze.

'Couldn't you stay for a few more minutes…?' He had barely had the chance to thank her properly, let alone talk about anything other than today's drama. He should let her leave but… His mouth seemed to be moving of its own accord. Producing words that weren't getting filtered through any of the usual channels.

'For a coffee or something?' he was saying. 'To… I don't know… I don't feel like we've even said hello yet.'

A long pause this time, during which Megan got slowly to her feet.

Was it his imagination or did she close her eyes and dip her head a fraction, almost as if she was praying for strength?

Whatever it was, it lasted only a heartbeat and then she spoke very quietly.

'I'll put the kettle on, then.'

Megan was sitting at the kitchen table with a half-empty mug by the time Josh returned.

'Sorry. That took a bit longer than usual. I think they're missing their gran.'

Megan smiled. 'I'm sure she's missing them as well. They're…gorgeous kids, Josh.'

'They are, aren't they?' He tried not to sound too full of pride as he went to the mug on the bench beside the kettle.

'I didn't finish making your coffee.' Megan was

watching him. 'I didn't know whether you still took it black or…or if you'd started having sugar or something.'

'Same old,' Josh said lightly. 'Some things never change, do they?'

Their eye contact was fleeting but significant. Things *did* change over time. Little things, like how you had your coffee. Big things, like how you lived your life.

Megan was looking around as if she was trying to find a way of changing the subject.

'This place is wonderful. I'd never have thought of you living on a farm, though.'

Did she think of him, then? Josh found it unexpectedly hard to take his next breath. His chest felt tight with some nameless emotion. Relief? *Hope*? He fought to shake it off.

'It's not a farm any more. Doug Gallagher died suddenly eighteen months ago and June decided to sell up.' He poured boiling water into his mug. 'The neighbours on the other side wanted the land but not the house so she subdivided. We've only got about three acres or so around the house. More like a big garden than a farm.'

'Must be perfect for the kids with all this space and the beach just across the road.'

'Seems to work well.' Josh sat down at the end of the table, at a right angle to Megan.

It felt too close.

It didn't feel close enough.

He had to close his eyes for a moment. To focus and get through the wave of confusion.

'It is perfect,' he heard himself saying aloud. 'I'm lucky enough to have the perfect life.' Who was he trying to convince here? Megan or himself? 'It's a bit further away from work than the apartment,' he added, 'but that was no place to try and raise children.'

'No.' The mention of the St Piran's townhouse he had shared with Rebecca had chilled the atmosphere, and Megan's tone, noticeably. Or had it been his declaration that he had the perfect life? One that didn't contain her? Maybe he'd gone too far in erecting protective boundaries.

'I needed to get away, anyway,' Josh added quietly. 'To make a fresh start.'

Megan seemed to be finding the colour of her remaining coffee fascinating. 'As you do,' she murmured.

The tiny silence couldn't be allowed to continue because anything could have taken root and flourished enough to get spoken aloud. Things like…

I've missed you. So, so much.

It would be much safer to stick to less personal topics but there was something personal that Josh couldn't ignore any longer.

'Are you OK, Megan?' Oh, help…the query sounded far too intimate. Dangerous territory. He had to back off fast. 'Physically, I mean?'

He couldn't read the glance he received in response. Women were so good at that. Making you feel like you couldn't have stuffed your foot any further into your mouth if you'd tried.

'I'm getting over a rather nasty bout of dengue fever. Second one in a six-month period.'

'Sounds horrible.'

'It's certainly not pleasant. I'm having a bit more trouble getting my energy level back this time. And I'm still getting a bit of joint pain.'

Josh didn't like that. It made him feel like he did when one of the twins got sick. Or fell over and skinned a knee. The feeling of needing to make it better.

'Do you need anything? Anti-inflammatories or…
multivitamins or something?'

Megan shook her head. 'I'm fine, Josh. I just need
a bit of time, that's all.' She glanced up and her face
was amused. 'I'm a doctor, remember? I can look after
myself.'

The amusement made her face more alive. Brought
a hint to her eyes of the kind of sparkle they used to
have. Josh wanted to keep it there.

'Doctors make the world's worst patients,' he reminded her with mock severity. 'Sometimes they have
to be told exactly what they should be doing.'

To his disappointment, the amusement faded from
Megan's eyes and she sighed. 'I *have* been told,' she said
sadly. 'That's the only reason I left Africa.'

'The *only* reason?' The question popped out before
Josh could stop it and it earned him another one of those
inscrutable looks.

'I need to sort my cottage out. It's turned into a bit
of a mess.'

How ridiculous was it to feel disappointed? What
had he expected? That Megan would say she'd come
back because she'd wanted to see *him*? He wouldn't
have wanted that, anyway.

Would he?

A wave of something like confusion made Josh's next
query tentative. 'Are you planning to live in it again?'

'No.' The head shake was decisive. 'But renting it
out hasn't worked out so well. I might have to sell up.'

And then she'd have no ties to Penhally left at all.
That was a good thing.

Wasn't it?

'Where will you go?' Josh could feel himself frowning. 'Back to Africa?'

'I can't. Not if I stay with MSF, at least.'

'Why not?'

'I've got immunity to two types of dengue fever now. I'm also female and Caucasian. It puts me in a high-risk bracket to get the haemorrhagic form of dengue and that can be fatal. It's not a risk that MSF is prepared to let their medical staff take.'

Josh felt his gut tighten. 'Surely it's not a risk *you'd* be prepared to take either?'

Megan's silence spoke volumes. She wanted to go back, that much was crystal clear.

Why? What would make anyone want to risk their lives like that? Something was nagging at the back of Josh's mind. A cryptic conversation he'd had with Tash a while back. Not that they ever talked about Megan these days—he'd made sure it had been a no-go subject ever since the wedding—but she'd said something about how happy Megan was finally. And she'd had a smile that suggested…

'Is there someone in Africa?' Josh heard himself ask. 'Someone…special?'

'You could say that.' Megan nodded and she had the same sort of smile on her face he remembered Tash having. A…loving kind of smile.

Josh had to look away. He gulped down a mouthful of coffee and tried to think of something…*anything*… to change the subject.

He didn't want to hear about the new love of Megan's life.

It was good that she was happy.

It wasn't as if either of them would ever consider being together. Not now.

Josh had to regain control of what was happening

here. Of his life. He'd almost lost it today, what with his mother's health scare.

With seeing Megan again.

But the shock was wearing off. Those odd frissons of confusion were fading. Knowing that Megan had moved on to someone else should be all he needed to put things back into perspective.

To help him remember what it had been like two years ago.

There was anger in the mix, deep down, wasn't there? Anger that Megan had not believed him when he'd said that his marriage was truly over before he'd gone to her bed. That sleeping with Rebecca that one, last time had been nothing more than a moment of weakness. Of feeling guilty and sorry for the woman who'd made the mistake of marrying him.

That anger had helped a lot in those months of Rebecca's pregnancy when he had been struggling with having had to end things with Megan before they could even get started properly.

And then his world had collapsed around him. Rebecca had died and he'd been left with two tiny, fragile babies and he'd been facing the impossible.

And what had Megan done?

Walked out and gone to the other side of the world. She hadn't even gone to the funeral.

No. Josh couldn't think of a way to change the subject. All he could do was sit there and stare at Megan.

She had found someone *else*?

Thank God Anna chose that moment to arrive at Josh's house to collect Crash.

They could both hear the front door opening and closing again. And Anna's cheerful call.

'It's only me. Anyone downstairs?'

Even though she was avoiding eye contact, Megan could feel the way Josh had been staring at her. As though he was shocked that she could have moved on with her life?

What the hell had he expected her to do? Sit and watch him raise Rebecca's children and pine for what might have been?

'In the kitchen, Anna.' Megan grabbed her coffee mug and pushed her chair back. She should have left Josh's house long ago. She shouldn't have come in the first place. Right now, she couldn't remember what it was she'd thought she was going to prove by doing so.

Whatever it had been, it felt like she had failed.

When she'd seen him gather Brenna into his arms and hold her like that. Pressing a kiss onto her soft, dark curls... The shaft of pain had felt like the knife that was permanently lodged in her heart had been twisted violently.

Their son had never known his father. Never had a cuddle or been kissed so lovingly. Stephen had never had a chance.

She and Josh had never had a chance.

And it was so...*unfair.*

'Gosh...' Anna breezed into the kitchen. 'It's raining cats and dogs out there now. Thanks for letting Crash inside.' She was grinning. 'Not that it's going to be easy dragging him away from your nice fire to go back to our cold cottage.'

'Want some coffee?' Josh sounded brusque. 'The kettle's still pretty hot.'

'No... My slow cooker is calling. I threw the makings of a beef stew in there this morning and it should be extremely well cooked by now.'

'It's been a long day,' Josh agreed. 'Did you get the chance to check on Mum again?'

'Of course.' Anna's smile was relaxed. 'She's fine, Josh. No pain and her rhythm's back to normal. I told her she's going to end up being in far better health from now on. Give her a week or two and she won't know herself. Oh, and I saw Ben in the car park. He said to tell you that ED's covered for the next couple of days. He's not expecting to see you anywhere near St Piran's unless you're coming in to visit your mum.'

'Thanks. I'll certainly need to be at home tomorrow. I'll have to sort out some extra child-care arrangements to take the pressure off Mum for a while.'

Megan had already rinsed out her mug but she did it again to avoid turning around and becoming a part of this conversation. Just because she'd stepped into the breach today it didn't mean she wanted to continue spending time with Josh's children.

In fact, she really *didn't* want to spend any more time with them. Or with him.

'I'd better be going,' she said brightly. 'And let you both get on with having your dinners.'

'I can drop you home,' Anna offered.

'No… I'll call a taxi.'

'Don't be daft. It's only a few minutes down the road to your cottage. You'll be waiting ages for a taxi in this weather.'

'I'm not staying at my cottage.'

'Why not?' Josh was frowning. 'Oh…you said it was uninhabitable, didn't you? How bad is it?'

'Pretty bad. Some pipes burst and the place got flooded months ago. The tenants moved out and left all their rubbish behind. There's no power. Probably no water either, except for what's still leaking out of the pipes.'

'Good grief…' Anna looked horrified. 'No wonder you can't stay there. Have you found somewhere in the village? I can drop you there.'

'I…um…haven't found anywhere yet. I was on my way to do that when I met Claire at the beach.'

'So it's my fault you haven't found somewhere to stay.' Josh was pushing his fingers through his hair in a gesture that Megan remembered all too well. 'You can stay here. We've got plenty of room.'

Megan could feel her jaw dropping. Stay under the same roof as Josh for a whole night for the first time in her life? Wake up and have breakfast with him? And his children? Why was fate throwing this stuff at her? Just how far did she have to go to prove she had moved on from Josh?

'Don't be silly.' It was Anna who spoke. Not that she could have read any of Megan's thoughts from her expression because she had moved to the door to summon Crash. She turned back to Megan with a smile. 'It's perfect timing. I'll be lonely while Luke's away and our spare room is all set up.' Her smile widened. 'Do you like beef stew?'

'I…ah…' Megan was shaking her head. Anna's cottage was just down the road. Next door to Josh. It was still too close for comfort.

'Just for tonight,' Anna said persuasively. 'You can sort out something else if you want to tomorrow, when it's not dark and raining. You look exhausted, Megan.'

She was. Emotionally as well as physically.

Just for one night? That's all it would need to be, wasn't it? She might even decide to sell up and be leaving all of this behind her by tomorrow.

'And it'll give us a chance to catch up.' Anna was looking wistful now. 'I've missed having you around, Megan.'

The persuasion was working. Megan felt far too weary to make any further protest. And she would enjoy Anna's company. The company of female friends was something she had missed badly after leaving here.

'OK,' she agreed. 'Just for tonight. Thanks, Anna.'

'Hooray…' Anna threw her arms around Megan and hugged her. 'It's so good to see you again.' She stepped back, still beaming. 'Isn't it, Josh?'

Megan didn't turn her head to see what reaction Anna's assumption that Josh was happy to see her had provoked but she got an inkling by the curiously raw note in his voice.

'Yes… It is.'

What else could he have said?

No, it was excruciatingly painful to see Megan again.

He'd thought he had it all finally sorted and now he was feeling like his perfectly ordered world had big cracks in it.

He would have preferred to never have laid eyes on her again.

But he couldn't have said any of those things in front of Megan. And they weren't even true. Not the one about preferring to never see her again, anyway. It might have been easier, certainly, but he would have always wondered where she was. How she was. Who she was with.

In the wake of both women and Crash leaving the house, Josh ransacked the fridge for enough leftovers to make himself a meal. He thought enviously of the hot beef stew Anna and Megan would be eating by now. Or was he more envious of Anna having the opportunity to find out more about Megan than she would ever be prepared to tell him? What would they be talking about?

That new *special* person in Megan's life? The one she was prepared to risk her life for by going back to Africa?

It should be *him*.

The thought came from nowhere and hit Josh like a sledgehammer. It wasn't framed as a regret. Or any kind of desire.

It was just there. A statement of fact. *He* was the person Megan should be with if she was going to be with anyone. Always had been. Always would be.

How could she get past that so easily?

Because it wasn't true for her? Maybe it never had been. She'd found it easy enough to condemn him for sleeping with Rebecca, hadn't she? She'd never shown the slightest sign of forgiving him. Not even when he'd found himself at the most harrowing point of his life as a single father with premature twins.

At least his mother had been there for him. She had provided the glue that had let him stick his shattered life back together. It might present a very different picture from what he had imagined would be his future but… dammit…it was a good life.

Good enough, that was for sure. Better than most people had. He had a brilliant job. A wonderful home. His mother reminded him regularly how lucky they all were. How different it was from the cramped flat in London where she'd tried to raise him and his siblings after his father had finally walked out on them all for good. He was so lucky to have his mum here to help, too. Family. And he had two amazing children who were more important than anything else could ever be.

Including Megan?

Yes. Josh shoved his plateful of food into the microwave and set it to heat.

He'd made that decision long ago. The moment he'd known he was going to become a father. When he'd vowed not to be like his own father. He was well on the way to honouring that vow now. He couldn't—*wouldn't*—let anything undermine that.

Maybe he needed to take a new vow now. Not to be like his own mother. To try again and again in the name of love, only to be hurt beyond anything remotely acceptable. Because it wouldn't only be him who got hurt now, would it? It could be his children. His mother even. And that would turn him into his father again. God…life could be a complicated business sometimes.

A new vow wasn't really needed, was it? He could stick to the original one and he'd been successful so far.

Josh turned away from watching the plate go round and round inside the microwave. He had time to ring the coronary care unit at St Piran's and check on how his mother was doing. The sooner life got back to normal for them all, the better.

As if to underline the resolution, a faint cry came from upstairs. One of the twins had woken and needed comfort.

Josh left the kitchen.

'I'm coming,' he called. 'It's OK, darling. Daddy's here.'

Where he needed to be. Where he *wanted* to be. You could only live in the present, couldn't you?

You had to trust that the future would turn out all right.

And you had to let go of the past.

CHAPTER FOUR

PALE SUNLIGHT WAS filtering through the curtains in Megan's room when she woke up the next morning from one of the best sleeps she'd had for a very long time.

Perhaps the red wine she had shared with Anna over the meal of beef stew and crusty bread could take the credit. Or maybe it was the cathartic effect of having a heart-to-heart conversation with another woman, including more than a few tears being shed. The lullaby of the sound of surf had probably had a calming influence as well.

Whatever the reason, Megan was astonished by how good she felt as she luxuriated in that boneless relaxation of waking slowly from a very deep sleep, stretching cautiously and revelling in the fact that her joints were not giving even the slightest twinge. And then it occurred to her that it was November in Cornwall and for the sun to be high enough to be coming in her window meant that it had to be—

Good grief…ten a.m.?

Discarding the borrowed nightwear, Megan dressed in yesterday's clothes and hurried out of the room, although she knew Anna must have left for work long ago. Sure enough, there was a note propped up on the kitchen table with a set of keys beside it.

Wanted to let you sleep as long as possible.

Help yourself to breakfast. There's cereal, toast and eggs around.

I got a ride to work so here are my car keys. You can drop them in to me later which will give everybody else a chance to say hi ☺

Love, Anna.

PS—you're more than welcome to stay again to-night. Your turn to cook?

PPS—enjoy the sun while it lasts!

Crash was nowhere to be seen. Back at day care at the O'Haras'? Thank goodness Anna hadn't asked her to drop him off. Megan didn't think she was ready to see Josh again yet. Maybe she never would be.

He had the perfect life. A job he loved. A fabulous home. Family around him. His mother and…and his *children.*

Megan had none of those things right now.

But…she did have plans, didn't she? She needed to hang onto that and decide what the next step should be.

Mulling over her options while she had a cup of coffee and toast didn't make things any clearer. Washing up her dishes, Megan looked out towards the little bay over the road from the Davenports' cottage. The surf still looked pretty wild but the clouds were white and billowing today, moving fast enough for the sun to make frequent appearances.

Getting a little bit of exercise and a blast of fresh, sea air was irresistible. Megan put her warm coat and gloves on and borrowed one of Anna's woolly hats to keep her hair from driving her crazy.

Gusts of wind strong enough to douse her with salt spray and almost knock her off her feet made it a strug-

gle to walk in one direction on the beach but when
Megan reached the end of the bay and turned around,
it suddenly felt like she was flying. She held her arms
out wide and laughed aloud from the childlike joy of it.

Seagulls were swirling overhead, riding the strong
air currents, and they sounded as if they were shrieking from the excitement of it all. Megan didn't shriek
but she was still laughing by the time she got back to
her starting point and she'd never felt more alive. As if
her blood was actually fizzing in her veins. She had to
stop for a minute then to catch her breath and she looked
up and down the bay, hugging herself with both arms.

She loved it here. So much.

The buffeting in the cold air and the fresh, sticky
feel of salt spray she could taste on her lips had done
more than restore her zest for life. It seemed to have had
a cleansing effect as well. Not that Megan could have
said exactly what had been blown away.

Maybe the disappointment of finding the home of
her heart virtually derelict.

The backwash of the emotional disturbance that seeing Josh again had caused.

Or maybe doubts about the big decisions she needed
to make about her future.

Whatever it was, right now it had gone and Megan
was left feeling at peace.

At home.

She couldn't deny the sense of belonging to this little
corner of the world. Could she really turn her back and
walk away for ever?

It would be an easy way out, that was certain. But
would she always miss it? Be haunted, as Charles
warned her might happen, by thinking she had left unfinished business behind?

Worse than that, now that she'd seen the cottage, would she be left thinking she had dishonoured the memory of her grandmother—the woman who'd always been there for her? Who'd taken a frightened four-year-old and guided her towards adulthood with infinite wisdom and warmth?

'What should I do, Gran?'

The only sound in the wake of her plea for advice was the crash of the surf. Even the seagulls were silent for a moment. Megan took a last, deep gulp of salty air before turning to leave the beach.

She couldn't leave. Not yet, anyway. The sustaining memories held in this place were bigger than the heartbreaking ones. It was a sanctuary she couldn't afford to throw away if there was another answer. And she owed it to Gran to fix up the cottage as much as she could before she made any final decision.

Resolutely, Megan began walking back to Anna's cottage, wrapping her coat around her body to keep warm and sticking her hands in her pockets to keep the wind from sneaking into any gaps.

Even through the woollen gloves, she could feel something in her pocket. A small, hard object. She remembered what it was as she pulled it out. Claire's chain, which had caught on her scarf and broken yesterday. It was only now that Megan registered what was hanging on the thin silver chain. A tiny, silver shamrock.

Very Irish, she thought with a smile. And probably treasured. Was Claire fretting about losing it? She could take it in when she returned Anna's car keys. On the way, she could sort out a rental car for herself and find some tradesmen to come and start urgent work on her cottage.

* * *

By mid-afternoon, with the sun already taking a bow for the day, Megan pulled into the doctors' car parking area at St Piran's feeling weary but satisfied with her day.

She sat in Anna's car for a minute after turning off the engine. Just because she could. Because today was so different from yesterday and she could take her time. Because that awful stress of being afraid of what she would find here was gone.

Megan knew that Claire was going to be fine. She would probably have a new lease on life now and be healthier than she'd been in a long while.

She knew that she didn't have to imagine what it would be like to see Josh again. To wonder if her feelings would be strong enough to turn her carefully reconstructed world upside down. To be afraid that he might actually hate her for walking out of his life when he'd badly needed his friends.

And, as it was with the cottage, she could accept that this hospital was an important part of her personal history. That it held a lot of memories worth treasuring and that avoiding it was not only immature but it could lead to regrets.

Locking the car, Megan walked towards the sprawling, modern structure that housed a renowned medical facility. A helicopter was approaching, hovering just before coming down on the heli-pad. Such a familiar sound here because the A and E department had the reputation of being able to handle anything and it was the first choice in the area for any major trauma.

Thanks to Josh.

Children were also brought here rather than to other hospitals within easy flight distance because the paediatric department was equally first rate. They had the facilities, equipment and dedicated staff to cope with any traumatic or medical emergencies.

It was so familiar.

And so different from what Megan had been forced to get used to in a developing country that had far too little available in the way of facilities, even basic equipment and supplies, and far too few staff. It had been so easy to feel that she was making an important contribution there but was saving a little life in Africa any less satisfying than saving one here?

No. Parents were parents the world over and they all loved their children. It was just…different. The challenges were different and often unbearably frustrating because it could be purely luck that made something available there that would be taken totally for granted here, like an incubator or even antibiotics.

There were familiar faces to be seen on her way to the cardiology ward, including one of the midwives Megan had known well.

'Brianna…hi.'

'Megan…I heard you were back in town. How are you?'

'I'm fine. And you? Obviously back at work?'

'Only part time. The twins are setting new heights in being "terrible twos".' But Brianna was smiling, clearly loving motherhood.

Twins. There was something in the air around here. Reminders of Josh around every corner? Megan could feel herself trying to pull a protective layer around her heart. Putting up some 'road closed' signs.

Brianna was still smiling. 'I've got to run. Home call to make to a new mother. But I'd love to catch up. Are you back for good?'

Megan shook her head with more emphasis than necessary.

'Oh, shame. We could sure use you. Did you know there's a consultant paediatric position being advertised as we speak?'

Again Megan shook her head. She hadn't known. Didn't really *want* to know, in fact.

'I'm just visiting,' she said, forcing a smile. 'But we should definitely have a coffee or something.'

Just visiting. The words echoed in her head after she'd said goodbye to Brianna. They felt wrong, somehow.

Did she still belong here, in the same way that part of her would always belong to Penhally? Did she belong in Africa now, where part of her heart would always be? Or maybe she needed to be somewhere that she had belonged to long ago. London.

Megan didn't know and it was a disturbing feeling. As if she was drifting.

Lost.

At least the map to the cardiology ward was well remembered and easy to follow. Megan found Claire sitting up in bed, reading a magazine.

'Oh, my dear…' Claire's smile lit up her face. 'I'm so pleased to see you. I don't know how I'm going to thank you. Josh tells me you probably saved my life.'

The heartfelt gratitude was embarrassing but it was impossible not to return such a warm smile.

'I've got something else you might be pleased to see.' Megan fished in her pocket. 'The chain was broken but I had it fixed for you today when I was in Penhally.'

'My chain…' Claire took it from Megan almost reverently. 'Oh…'

'It looked like it might be special.'

Claire nodded, her face misty. 'My Joshie gave it to me for Mother's Day. He bought it with the first money he earned from his paper round. I think he was about six or seven.' Claire pressed the hand holding the chain to her heart. Her smile was rather wobbly now. 'Sorry,' she sniffed. 'It's all a bit...'

'Emotional. I know.' Megan's smile was sympathetic. 'You've been through rather a lot in the last twenty-four hours. I understand completely.'

More than Claire would know, in fact. Megan had been on a bit of a roller-coaster herself. She watched as the older woman's fingers trembled, trying to open the catch on the chain.

'Can I help?' She took the chain and Claire bent her head forward so that she could fasten it behind her neck. When she leaned back on her pillow her face was disconcertingly close. Those blue eyes so familiar.

'Thank you, lovie. Please...sit down for a minute. Have you got the time?'

'Of course.' Megan took off her coat and perched on the edge of the chair beside Claire's bed. She couldn't help casting her eye over the monitor still recording an ECG and up at the IV pole, where the bag of fluids was empty. Did she still need a line in and fluids running to keep a vein open in case of emergency?

'You're looking good,' she told Claire. 'Are the doctors happy with you?'

Claire nodded. 'I'm allowed to go home tomorrow as long as I behave myself today. They're going to do a... an echo-something-or-other in the morning.'

'An echocardiogram?'

'That's it. They did tell me what it would show but it all sounded very technical.'

'It gives them a way of looking at your heart and seeing how well it's pumping. They can measure the blood that comes out with every beat and give it a number. It's a percentage of the blood that was in that part of the heart. They call it an ejection fraction.'

Good grief...Megan knew she was hiding behind professionalism here. Avoiding talking about anything too personal because this was Josh's mother. The grandmother of Rebecca's children.

Claire seemed to see straight through her. She leaned forward and patted Megan's arm.

'I'm so glad you've come back,' she said softly. 'Josh will be too.'

But she hadn't come back. Megan opened her mouth to reiterate her visitor status but Claire was nodding.

'You're a star,' she told Megan. 'I saw your picture. In that refugee camp. You were holding a dear little baby and there were so many children all around you.'

Megan's eyes widened. 'Where on earth did you see that?'

'In that newsletter thing that comes from the organisation you work for. What's it called again?'

'Medécins Sans Frontières,' Megan said faintly. 'The MSF. Doctors without borders.'

'So it is.' Claire's gaze was oddly direct. 'Josh gets it delivered every month.'

'I...ah...' Megan had no words. Josh had been following where she was and what she'd been doing for the last two years? That was...unexpected. Flattering? Confusing, that was for sure.

'He needs things to keep him interested.' Claire's tone was almost offhand. 'Poor man, all he's got in his life are the children and his work. It's not enough, is it?'

Megan could only stare at Claire, her jaw still slack. What was Claire trying to say?

She didn't have to wonder for more than a heartbeat.

'He'd never admit it for the world.' Claire's voice was no more than a whisper. 'But he's lonely, so he is.'

Megan took in a slow breath and tightened her jaw. Lonely? With two gorgeous children and his mum living with him? With his job and all his colleagues? His *perfect* life?

He was *lonely*?

And she was supposed to care about that?

For heaven's sake, Josh O'Hara didn't have to be lonely if he didn't want to be. He could have any woman he wanted. Back when she'd first met him, when he'd been no more than a talented but very junior doctor, he'd had the reputation of being a notorious womaniser. He'd been a legend. To have him even noticing the naïve bookworm of a final-year med student that Megan had been at the time, let alone focusing his well-deserved legendary skills in the bedroom on her for a whole night, had been unbelievable. When he'd been back with his ultra-cool friends days later and had ignored her, she'd known exactly how easily replaceable she'd been.

So what had changed? He was still impossibly good looking. In that unfair way men were capable of, he was only getting more attractive as he got older. He was still supremely confident, with good reason, given the accolades the emergency department of St Piran's Hospital regularly garnered. He was a prime example of pure alpha male and Megan could be absolutely sure that no woman in her right mind could be immune to the lethal Irish charm with which he could capture anybody he fancied.

So, if he *was* lonely for feminine company, why wasn't he doing something about it?

And why did the mere thought of him being lonely echo in her own heart like this?

Because, despite the new directions in which she had taken her life, she was lonely too?

Did she really think she could move on and find a way to ignore the person-shaped hole in her life that would never be filled?

There was no point in allowing that train of thought. If Josh was lonely, it had nothing to do with her. She couldn't allow it to. With a huge effort Megan focused on what was right in front of her.

An IV line that had blood backing up its length because the bag of fluids was completely empty and exerting a vacuum effect. She reached out and pushed the call bell.

'You need your IV sorted,' she told Claire. 'And I should really be getting going.'

It wasn't a nurse who answered the call bell. It was Anna.

'Hey...' She grinned at Megan. 'You called?'

'Hardly needs a consultant cardiac surgeon to remove a cannula or hang some more fluids but this is good. Saves me having to page you to give you your car keys.'

'How did you get on? Was it useful?' Anna glanced at the IV tubing taped to Claire's arm.

'Enormously. Thank you so much. I zipped all round Penhally and sorted out some contractors to start work on the cottage. They're charging like wounded bulls but the plumber and electrician both said they could start tomorrow.'

'Fantastic.' Anna was eyeing the monitor beside Claire's bed. 'It's all looking great,' she told her patient, 'but I'd rather keep your IV in for a bit longer.

Think of it as an insurance policy against any complications. If it's there, we won't need it. Now…where's the trolley? Ah, there it is…' She moved to the corner of the room but turned to look at Megan as she pulled open a drawer. 'If they're not starting till tomorrow, that means you won't be able to stay there yet.'

'Probably not for a few days, no.'

'So you'll stay and keep me company?'

'If you're sure…' Being so close to the beach was as much of a draw card as Anna's company. 'And, yes, I'd be delighted to cook tonight. I'm going to go and pick up my rental car now and will do some shopping.'

'Oh…' Claire had been following the conversation, looking from one younger woman to another and back as though following a tennis match. Now she was beaming. 'You'll be just down the road, then, lovie. You'll have to come and have a cuppa, so you will.'

Anna excused Megan having to respond. She'd come back with a new bag of saline from the trolley drawer but exclaimed in frustration when she went to hang it on the hook.

'It's past its expiry date. It shouldn't even be in the trolley. That really isn't good enough.' Discarding the bag, she went back for another one.

Megan's jaw dropped. 'You're not going to throw it out, are you?'

'Have to. It expired a month ago.'

'But that's such an arbitrary date. You can see it's all right.' Megan held the bag up to the light. 'No goldfish swimming around. This stuff lasts for ever. It's only salty water. We wouldn't hesitate to use it in Africa.'

'Plenty more where that came from.' Happy with the new bag, Anna was changing over the giving set, pushing the spike into the port on the bottom of the bag. 'And not only fluids. I'll bet there are hundreds of things like cannulas and syringes that have to be discarded at every stocktake because they've gone over the date. Hospital policy. Hey…maybe we should gather them all up and post them to Africa.'

'That's not a bad idea. In fact…' Megan felt a fizz of real excitement '…it's a *brilliant* idea. My clinic would be over the moon to get a crate of supplies like that.'

'We could do some fundraising, too.' Claire didn't want to be left out of the discussion. 'There's plenty of grannies like me in the district and we'd love a good cause to have a bake sale or something for.'

'Oh, I couldn't ask you to—'

Claire held up her hand in a stop sign. 'Don't you say another word, lovie. I've been lying here wondering how I was ever going to be able to thank you for saving my life and this is it. I can not only say thank you to you but we can do something for all those poor children in Africa at the same time. It's perfect.'

Perfect. There was that word again. Funny how it was starting to grate.

'Go and talk to Albert White,' Anna advised. 'You'll need the CEO's permission before you start gathering up the old stuff. I'll ask Luke who else you could talk too as well. You could fill dozens of crates if you got some other hospitals on board with the idea.'

If nothing else, the excuse of going to talk to Albert White took Megan away from Claire and her disturbing confidences about her son's state of happiness. It also stopped Megan worrying about the downside of staying longer at Anna's place with it being next door to the O'Haras. It was a godsend to have something other than herself or Josh to think about as she walked through the hospital corridors, and the more she thought about it, the better the idea seemed.

By the time she knocked on the CEO's office door, she was more excited about it than she could remember being about anything for a very long time.

The last thing Josh O'Hara expected to see when he emerged from the lift on his way to visit his mother was Megan Phillips shaking hands with Albert White.

'Josh…' Albert was positively beaming. 'I heard about your mother. I'm delighted to hear today that she's doing very well.'

'You and me, both.' But Josh was looking at Megan, who seemed to be avoiding his gaze. She looked oddly… nervous? What was going on?

'You're not working today, are you, Josh?' Albert continued. 'Didn't Ben tell me he had things covered in Emergency?'

'I'm just here for a visit.'

'All by yourself? Where are those little ankle-biters?'

'Being babysat by one of Mum's friends from her grandmothers' group. Only she's a great-grandmother. You remember Rita—the ward clerk in NICU who re-tired a while back?'

Albert's eyebrows rose. 'Who could forget?'

Josh snorted softly. 'I know. She's a much nicer person these days now that her feet don't hurt from too much standing. Her great-grandson, Colin, goes to the same playgroup mine do. They call it "afternoons with the oldies" or something similar. Anyway…'

'Yes, yes. Must get on. I'll leave Megan to tell you the good news.'

Josh stared after the CEO as he bustled away.

'Was he actually rubbing his hands together?' he murmured.

'Probably.' Megan was biting her bottom lip.

'And didn't I see you two shaking hands? It looked like you'd made some kind of a deal.'

'Mmm.' Megan was still avoiding direct eye contact.

Josh sighed inwardly. He had a feeling that whatever it was, it was going to make life a little more complicated for him.

Megan was eyeing the button to summon the lift. Josh leaned against the wall. She'd have to reach around him to get to the button.

'So...is it a big secret?'

Megan sighed audibly. 'No. And you'll find out soon enough, I suppose. Anna had this idea...'

He listened to the plan of collecting out-of-date supplies like IV gear and drugs and old equipment that was being replaced and donating them to Megan's clinic in Africa. He had to agree it was a brilliant idea but he was only half listening to the words coming out of Megan's mouth. What was even more riveting was the way her mouth was moving. The flicker of real passion he could hear in her voice and see in her eyes.

It had the effect, he thought, that holding a shot of whisky under the nose of a recovering alcoholic might have.

So tempting.

He actually had to fight the urge to put his finger against Megan's lips and stop the words. And then to cover her lips with his own and silence them for a very, very long time...

And then Josh realised that Megan had stopped talking. He tried to pull back her last words from the ether before they evaporated completely.

'I'm not quite sure what this has to do with my department.'

'Albert made me an offer I couldn't refuse.'

'Which was?'

'He'll donate everything suitable that St Piran's can spare. He'll contact his fellow CEOs from other hospitals in the district and get them to pitch in. He'll endorse a hospital fundraiser to cover the shipping costs.' Megan was biting her lip again. 'He'll even throw in a ticket so that I can travel with the load and make sure it gets to the right place.'

Josh shook his head in amazement. 'That's an amazing offer all right.' But he couldn't shake the image of Albert walking away rubbing his hands together as though he'd got the better end of the deal. 'What does Albert get out of it?'

'Me,' Megan said simply. 'I've agreed to work here for the next few weeks to get a big project off the ground. He needed a paediatric specialist to oversee it.'

Josh was grateful for the wall he was leaning on. Now he could understand exactly why Megan had looked nervous. She knew that he wouldn't like this.

'The project's the paediatric triage and observation suite to go into A and E, isn't it?'

It had been a pipe dream for such a long time. The busy emergency department with all the sights and sounds and smells that went with major trauma and life-threatening medical problems was a terrifying place to bring young children, especially when they were sick and even more vulnerable. And often, admitting them to a ward was not necessary but they did need observation for a period of time because, if you had the slightest doubt, you couldn't afford to send them home. A dedicated, child-friendly space that still had the capability to deal with life or death situations would put his department even more securely amongst the best in the country.

'Mmm.' Megan finally looked up. 'I couldn't say no, Josh. I did try, I can assure you.'

Really?

Maybe she was doing this to punish him.

Seeing her again had disturbed his equilibrium markedly. Feeling her presence in his house and seeing her close to his children had made visible cracks in the foundations of his new life. Even when she wasn't there, he could feel the way it *had* been last night. It had haunted him all day. So much so that he'd accepted with alacrity Rita's offer to babysit. So that he could escape. Not only to visit his mother but to find refuge in the other half of his life.

His work.

How could he handle knowing that he would see her here every day? For weeks?

Megan had found her new life. In Africa. She'd found someone *special*.

Did she want to rub his nose in that? To remind him, on a daily basis, just how much he'd messed up his own life?

It was then that Josh realised he'd been holding eye contact with Megan just a shade too long. That he'd been searching her face for confirmation. But what he saw was something quite different.

Anxiety.

Fear, almost.

Why was *she* afraid?

'I could try and talk to Albert again,' Megan said quietly. 'If it's a problem.'

Josh could feel his head moving. Not in assent. He

was slowly shaking it from side to side in a negative response.

Because he knew why Megan was afraid. She didn't want to be working near him any more than he wanted her to be. Because she was unsure about whether she could handle it.

And she could only be that unsure if she still felt the same way about him as she had before she'd walked away two years ago. Before he'd ended things to stay in his marriage and be the father he'd had to try and be for his children.

But he wasn't married any more, was he?

Was that going to make a difference? Could he afford to even think about letting it make a difference?

Josh had no answer to that internal query.

And maybe that was what he needed to find out. It might be the only way he could avoid being haunted for the rest of his life by what might have been with Megan Phillips.

He could talk to Albert himself but if the incentive that had been offered had been massive enough to swing the deal when Megan was clearly feeling vulnerable, how could he do anything that might wipe out the reward she wanted so badly? If she didn't have something like this to keep her here, she might leave again, and Josh knew that if she left on such a disappointing note he would never see her again.

Besides, the CEO knew what he was doing.

Megan was perfect for the task.

Josh was still shaking his head. He added the hint of a smile as he eased himself away from the wall and allowed Megan free access to the lift button and escape.

'It's not a problem,' he said decisively. 'We're lucky to have you on board. When are you going to start?'

'In a day or two. As soon as I've got the renovations on my cottage underway properly. Maybe Thursday?'

'Excellent.' Josh tried, not very successfully, to widen his smile. 'See you then, Megan.'

He walked away. He knew Megan would have pushed the button for the lift but he also knew that she wasn't watching for it to arrive.

She was watching him.

He could feel it as clearly as if it were her hands and not her gaze touching him.

CHAPTER FIVE

WHAT *HAD* SHE been thinking?

Megan was shredding salad vegetables with far more force than required as she groaned inwardly yet again.

'I must be crazy,' she said aloud.

'Hardly.' The voice came from her mobile phone, which she had on speaker mode, propped on the kitchen windowsill. 'It's not every day that you get such a generous donation. It'll make a huge difference to the clinic, you know that.'

'But it's not a donation, is it? I'm going to have to earn it. By working…with Josh. He'll be looking over my shoulder the whole time. This is *his* baby. He was talking about it years ago. Before I left.'

'What's really worrying you, Megan?' The male voice was kindly. 'Not being able to do the job justice, or having to work that closely with Josh?'

'I—I'm not sure. It's complicated.'

'Relationships always are. You've got some serious history with Josh, we both know that.'

'It's not just him, Charles. It's the cottage and the hospital and…and Gran. When I think of family, I think of this place. These people. It's…confusing.' She twisted the iceberg lettuce in her hands, dividing it into smaller and smaller pieces.

'Which is precisely why you need to take time to get your head around it all.'

'But maybe that's the wrong thing to do.' Megan was separating lettuce leaves now and pulling at them to break them up even further. 'Maybe I should just pack it all in and come to London. What's the weather like?'

'Cold and grey.' She could hear the smile in his voice. 'I'm sitting beside the fire. I think Mrs Benson's got some roast beef and Yorkshire pudding in the oven for my dinner.'

'Mmm…nice. We're having fish and salad.' Megan eyed the lettuce she'd shredded into minuscule pieces, the tomatoes that had been diced to within an inch of their lives. Cucumber that should be discs but was now tiny triangles. 'I'm not sure it was such a good idea after all.'

'It's healthy. I'm pleased that you're looking after yourself. Oh, there's the bell. I'd better go and present myself in the dining room. Talk to you soon, love. When are you going to start the job?'

'On Thursday. I'm meeting all the contractors at the cottage tomorrow to make a list of everything that needs doing.'

'Don't overdo things.'

'I won't.'

Having said goodbye, Megan scooped the sorry salad into a bowl and turned her attention to crumbing the fresh fish fillets she'd bought in St Piran.

It was all Claire O'Hara's fault, she decided.

Telling her that Josh was lonely.

No. It was her own fault, for remembering what Claire had said in that moment when she could have said no to Albert. When, having come up with his brilliant idea, he'd given her a very significant glance and asked if—given her…ahem…history with Josh—she thought they would be able to work together again.

She could have said no. She probably could have said no and still received permission to collect at least something to contribute to the clinic, but the lure of being able to make a really significant difference had been huge.

And when she thought about working with Josh, all that came into her head was Claire's voice.

But he's lonely, so he is.

Why had he told her that his life was so perfect? Was he trying to protect her in some way?

And why did it bother her so much if he *was* lonely?

Because she understood? Because the words resonated at such a very deep level in her own heart?

Because the kind of love that she and Josh shared would never, ever go away completely—on either side—and because they could never be together, there would always be that empty…lonely space inside.

The fact that they couldn't make it work was sad but it didn't mean that she didn't want Josh to be happy. To close off that lonely space and move on.

Did it?

Charles had been wise, Megan concluded, slipping the fish into the oven to bake. She had to face this head on and find out exactly what was going on in both her head and her heart. She'd promised Charles that she would do that before making those final, irrevocable decisions about her future.

When she was really sure of herself, she could make sure that Josh knew that she was stronger now. That she didn't need protection. That she'd moved on successfully and was on the way to making her life as perfect as possible, too.

Did they both need to believe that in order to finally let go?

'Did you order this, Megan?'

'What is it?'

The nurse, Gina, started unrolling a large, laminated poster. A line of text became visible. 'It's a paediatric resuscitation chart.'

'Oh…good. That's to go on the wall behind where the IV and airway supplies are going in the main resus area. There should be a paediatric Glasgow coma scale and a classification of shock chart coming as well.'

'OK.' But Gina looked curious as she unrolled the chart a little further. 'Aren't doctors supposed to know all this stuff about weights and drug dosages and things off by heart?'

Megan nodded, looking up from where she was sorting packets of supplies. 'Think of it as an insurance policy,' she said. 'In an emergency situation, the more time you can save and the more accurate you can be, the better.'

Behind Gina, she could see Josh approaching. This new area of the emergency department, taken from part of the plaster room and a couple of offices, was still a mess a week after the transformation had begun. There were workmen installing ceiling tracks for X-ray equipment, putting pipes in for an oxygen supply, sorting lighting and electrical fittings for monitors and computers, and installing phone lines and the fixed furniture like the central nurses' station.

When this exciting project was finished, St Piran's would have a six-bed observation unit where babies and children could stay for up to twenty-four hours without needing admittance to the main ward. They would also have two resuscitation areas. A main one that would have everything needed for a life or death emergency and a second one so that they could cope with more than one serious case at a time. The division between the two areas could be folded back, if necessary, to allow access to the state-of-the-art gear that would be going into the main part.

The whole concept would be something that many hospitals would envy. Josh O'Hara would get the credit for its inception and execution. No doubt it would generate huge publicity and kudos and his already stellar career would skyrocket even further. If he was at all concerned about how the result would affect his own reputation, he wasn't showing it right now. Josh looked relaxed and confident. His shirtsleeves were rolled up and a stethoscope was dangled carelessly around his neck.

It was by no means the first time Josh had wandered out of the main department to see what was happening with the set-up of the new paediatric wing and, of course, Megan had been rattled by the close professional scrutiny that had so many deeply personal undertones but she was finally starting to relax.

The tone of their interaction had been put into place on the first day. This was Josh's territory. The career half of his perfect life. He clearly had no idea that his mother had suggested it wasn't so perfect to Megan and he seemed determined to demonstrate how happy he was in his work.

He talked easily and passionately about the new project, happy to discuss any queries or ideas Megan put forward. He interacted with his colleagues in a totally relaxed manner but she was left in no doubt about the respect he was given as head of department. And she'd seen him, in passing, treating patients. On one occasion holding someone's hand to reassure them, on another leading a full resuscitation on a badly injured trauma victim.

Megan had taken her cue from Josh. She was here as a colleague in a professional capacity, nothing more. To her relief, it wasn't proving as hard as she'd expected. Nobody could know how aware she was of Josh's proximity. How she could hear his voice across the whole department, even when he was speaking quietly. How she could sense his approach when she wasn't expecting him or looking in the direction from which he was coming. Like she had when Gina had been showing her the poster.

Megan acknowledged his approach with a tiny tilt of her head but continued talking to Gina.

'There are so many variables with paediatric patients,' she said, pleased to hear her voice sounding so steady despite the awareness of Josh infiltrating every cell of her body. 'And size and weight can make a critical difference to what size ET tube you might want to grab or, say, how much diazepam you want to give to treat a seizure.'

Josh was smiling as he stepped closer to Gina. He took the chart and unfurled it completely, holding it up against a wall to admire it. The movement made the muscles of his shoulders move under his shirt and the light caught the dusting of dark hair on his arms but Megan's attention was caught by his hands. Watching those long, clever fingers as they traced the different text boxes on the colourful chart.

'You can't weigh a sick baby or toddler easily,' he

was telling Gina, 'but you can measure their length. Look…' He pointed to one side of a graph. 'I've got a two-year-old who's come in in status epilepticus and I want to give him an initial dose of IV diazepam. Here's his age. A quick measure shows me he's quite big for his age at just over a hundred centimetres so he's close to twenty kilograms, and I can double-check the dose I want to give him here…' Josh's hand made a rapid swoop towards a new box containing drug dosage information. Something in Megan's stomach mirrored the swoop.

'Cool.' But Gina was looking at Josh, not the chart, and the hero-worship was all too obvious.

She was young, Megan noted. And very pretty. It was also quite obvious that Josh had no need to be lonely if he didn't want to be. Not physically, anyway. Something much less pleasant than the previous sensation settled in her stomach. Deliberately, she dragged her gaze downwards and stared at the package in her hand. An ET tube. Cuffed. Smallest size.

'Want me to stick the poster up now?' Gina asked.

'No.' Megan's tone was a lot crisper than she'd intended. She smiled at Gina to disguise her inward turbulence. 'Put it on one of the trolleys in the corner of the observation room. I've got the mural painter in Resus at the moment, checking out how she can work around the fittings that are going in.'

'Mural?' Josh was finally looking at Megan directly as Gina moved away. She could feel it. 'In the resus room?'

She wanted to look up but resisted. Too hard to meet his gaze and still sound completely professional. So she reached for another handful of packages from the carton as though sorting ET tubes was too important a task to interrupt.

She risked a very quick glance upward, so as not to appear rude. 'Not as bright or complicated as the walls and ceiling in the observation area. I'm going for some leafy beanstalk plants with caterpillars on them and butterflies scattered over pale blue walls. A few on the ceiling too, where there's any space.'

'Sounds time consuming. I hope it won't put us behind on the target to have all the radiology gear installed by tomorrow.' She could hear the frown in Josh's voice. She could also feel the intensity of the look he was giving her go up a notch or two. But when she looked up, she found that he was watching her hands, not her face.

What was it about hands? She only had to let her gaze rest on his, even if they were perfectly relaxed and just curled on the table in the staffroom or on his thigh when he was sitting down on the couch in there for once, and it always gave her that odd curl of sensation. The way it had when she'd been caught watching him trace the information on that resuscitation chart. Was it the memory of touch?

Did Josh get that by looking at *her* hands?

Megan sucked in a quick breath. 'It fits in with the overall philosophy of making this whole area as child friendly as possible,' she said evenly. 'You get conscious patients in Resus too, you know. Trauma victims, for example. If you can distract them from their pain and fear at all, it's going to help not only the assessment but it can potentially improve their status.'

It was quite true. Megan could almost hear Josh talking to the media about it when he was proudly showing off the new facility. Shock, from internal blood loss, he might say, is made worse by how fast the heart is beating. If you can calm a child down, you can slow the heart rate and potentially slow the rate of bleeding. People would lap it up. Everybody who contributed to the fundraising efforts would know that money hadn't been wasted in decoration for its own sake. Parents would feel happier knowing they could take their child into a place that went the extra mile.

Megan managed to smile as she looked up at Josh. 'I'll bet you could distract Brenna from something scary or sore by getting her interested in the big blue butterfly in the corner, or trying to find the yellow caterpillar with green spots on a leaf somewhere.'

The mention of his daughter did the trick. The intensity with which he'd been watching Megan faded rapidly and Josh relaxed. He even smiled back. A real smile that made the corners of his eyes crinkle.

Something crinkled inside Megan yet again.

Rebecca's daughter, she reminded herself, not only Josh's. The child that had been conceived when his marriage was supposed to be over.

'I take your point,' Josh conceded. 'A pretty resus room is commendable. What are you doing there?'

'Sorting airway supplies and deciding how we want to arrange them for ease of access. I'm thinking sets of the most commonly used sizes of ET tubes, cuffed and uncuffed, with guide wires but having appropriate LMAs and needle cricothyroidotomy kits with them as well to cover any complications.'

'Mmm.' Josh seemed to be listening intently and approving of what Megan was telling him.

Except that there was just a hint of a far-away gaze in his eyes. As though he was listening to her voice and thinking of something quite different. Had he remembered that it was her birthday today? Did he even know? And if he did, was that too far into personal territory to be allowable in this new phase of their relationship? Or should that be 'non-relationship'? Megan's train of thought became scrambled enough for her to sigh inwardly and grasp at something to ground her in reality again.

'How's Claire this week?'

'Doing really well, thanks.' Yes, she could see the way Josh blinked and refocused. 'Still getting tired easily but she's managing fine, thanks to her granny group friends. Oh...I had a message for you, in fact.'

'Oh?' Good grief... She was definitely losing the ability to concentrate right now. Was that what Josh had been doing a moment ago? Being so aware of the sound of a voice that the words became almost meaningless?

Funny how you could feel a voice as much as hear it.

'They want to get involved in the Africa project. They're thinking of starting a toy drive. Mum asked if I could ask you to come and talk to her as soon as possible and tell her the kind of things they should be collecting.'

'Oh...' Megan bit her lip. 'That's very kind of them but, in general, toys wouldn't be the first priority. The really useful things might be exercise books and pencils and paper and crayons and picture books and...' Megan stopped, embarrassed. It was so easy to get carried away and start sounding over excited.

But Josh was smiling. 'That's what you need to tell mum and her cronies. I'm sure they'd be delighted to collect whatever would be most useful.'

'I'll do that. Thanks for passing on the message.' It might be an effort to turn away from that smile but Megan managed. She could even focus on the task at hand again. Out of the corner of her eye she saw Josh stare at her a moment longer but then he, too, turned away, rolling up the resuscitation chart as he let his gaze roam around what was happening away from this corner of the project.

The memories were all there, of course. And that powerful, indefinable pull between them, but it was all manageable. Under control.

It was, Megan mused, like looking at something magical. A tropical pool, maybe, on the hottest of days. Still and deep and so cool looking, surrounded by lush greenery. You knew that if you slipped into the water the sensation would be such bliss you might die from the sheer pleasure of it but you also knew that there were vicious piranhas circling beneath that smooth surface and the pain would be unbearable. The will to survive was enough to keep your feet on dry ground, no matter how uncomfortable or hard that might be.

Gina reappeared from the direction of the main department.

'Dr O'Hara? You're wanted. The condition of that little girl with asthma has deteriorated.'

'Coming.' Josh discarded the poster and began moving but his head turned. 'You've been given practising privileges here again, haven't you, Megan?'

Megan nodded. Albert White had made sure that it was legally covered. What's the use in having expertise like yours in the department, he'd said, if it couldn't be used if needed?

'Would you mind?' Josh was still moving but his head tilted in an invitation for her to follow him. 'She's on maximum therapy already and I thought we had it sorted. A second opinion would be welcome.'

'Sure.' Megan was on her feet and catching up. The thrill of anticipation was due to it having been so long since she'd faced a potential emergency with everything she might need at hand, she told herself.

It had nothing to do with the prospect of working side by side with Josh.

Six-year-old Bonnie was being given a continuous infusion of salbutamol but she was struggling to breathe. She could only manage sentences of one or two words in response to Josh's questions and the outline of her ribs was visible even through the hospital gown due to the effort she was making to shift air.

'What's the oxygen saturation?' Megan queried, her hand on Bonnie's wrist, trying to count an extremely rapid heart rate.

'Down to eighty-six percent,' Josh told her. 'It's dropped. Respiration rate is up from forty to fifty-six.' He was frowning. 'Let's start a loading dose of aminophylline and get a chest X-ray to exclude a pneumothorax.' He raised his eyebrows at Megan, who nodded her agreement.

'We could start her on some positive pressure assisted ventilation, too.' She squeezed Bonnie's hand. 'We're going to change your face mask, sweetheart and give you one that's going to make it a bit easier for you to breathe. It's nothing to be scared about, OK?'

But Bonnie looked terrified. So did her mother, who was sitting close to the head of the bed, holding Bonnie's other hand. Megan moved closer to Josh and lowered her voice.

'We need an arterial blood gas. And we need to get her up to PICU as soon as she's stable.'

Josh murmured his agreement. He was still frowning. Somewhere behind them someone was shouting and a staff member was threatening to call Security if they didn't calm down. An X-ray technician bustled into the resus area and began moving equipment that clanked loudly against something else. An alarm was sounding on some monitoring equipment nearby.

Josh caught Megan's gaze. A gesture with his hand encompassed the undecorated walls with the array of potentially frightening supplies and machinery. 'The sooner we have our unit up and running, the better,' he muttered, 'don't you think?'

'Mmm.' Except it wasn't going to be *their* unit, was it? Megan was never going to work here again on a permanent basis. The realisation gave her a curiously sharp pang of regret.

She was working here right now, though, and over the next fifteen minutes her energies were directed solely to trying to help Josh stabilise Bonnie. Despite all their efforts, however, her condition was getting worse. Single-word responses became no responses at all and the child's level of consciousness was dropping noticeably. The level of oxygen in her blood, having gone up for a brief period, dropped with an alarming plunge. Her fingernails took on a bluish tinge.

'I'm going to intubate,' Josh decided. 'Rapid sequence. Megan, can you pre-oxygenate and then give me some cricoid pressure, please?'

Megan took her position and held the mask over Bonnie's face, turning up the flow of oxygen to try and get as much into her bloodstream as possible before any attempts to breathe were interrupted by the anaesthesia and intubation procedure.

She was ready to push on the front of the now unconscious Bonnie's throat to help Josh visualise the vocal cords and slip the tube into the correct position but his first attempt was unsuccessful. Megan could see the beads of sweat forming on his forehead. She reached above his head to silence an alarm on the monitor that was insistently beeping.

Josh looked up. He didn't have to say a word—the communication was simply there telepathically. If the next attempt was unsuccessful they would have to do something more invasive, like puncturing Bonnie's airway from the front of her neck. They couldn't afford to have her paralysed and not ventilated adequately for more than a few minutes. Megan had more experience with the smaller and sometimes difficult airways of children. She also had smaller hands that were capable of defter movement.

It wasn't anything like an admission of defeat on Josh's part to swap positions. He was simply taking the best advantage of the resources available.

The pressure of needing to perform to the best of her ability was countered by the knowledge that Josh had enough confidence in her to give her the chance. Megan didn't realise she was holding her own breath until she felt herself release it in a sigh of relief when the tube slipped into place and she could hear the air entry into Bonnie's lungs with her stethoscope as Josh squeezed the bag attached to her face mask.

The tension was still there for the next few minutes as they hooked Bonnie up to the ventilator and adjusted settings until they were happy with the way she was breathing and the amount of oxygen that was circulating in her bloodstream. And then Megan went with Bonnie to the paediatric intensive care unit to see her settled in and her care passed to the medical team on duty.

Finally, Megan returned to the main part of the emergency department because she wanted to tell Josh that the little girl appeared to be stable and she was already showing some signs of improving.

Josh was standing beside the triage desk, along with several nurses. He was holding a huge bunch of red roses wrapped in Cellophane. He didn't see Megan approaching because he was reading the small card stapled to the Cellophane.

Red roses. The most romantic of flowers. Who was the lucky recipient? Megan wondered. Or had someone sent them to Josh? Either way, she was experiencing a rush of emotion that was a long way from being pleasant.

Until Josh looked up and smiled at her.

'These are for you,' he said.

The unpleasant heaviness in her belly twisted and tried to break up and form something entirely different. Except that Josh's smile wasn't reaching his eyes.

'Apparently, it's your birthday,' he added.

'Oh… Happy birthday, Megan.' The chorus came from several staff members but Megan barely heard them. If Josh was surprised to learn that it was her birthday today, it meant that the flowers couldn't possibly have come from him.

And that meant…

Josh had her pinned with his gaze. 'So, who's this Charles?' he asked, his tone deceptively casual.

This was it. A defining moment. There was a choice to be made. Did Megan stick to her new plans for her future or was she going to allow the past to hold her back?

Could she finally accept that what she had once wanted more than life itself was never going to happen and take the final step that would set Josh—and herself—free?

There really wasn't a choice to make, was there?

Megan took a deep breath and spoke into the waiting silence, ignoring all the expectant faces around her, except one. She was speaking to Josh here.

'Charles is my fiancé,' she said quietly.

CHAPTER SIX

FIANCÉ?

Megan had a fiancé?

He shouldn't feel this shocked, Josh realised. What had he expected—that Megan would stay single for the rest of her life because she couldn't marry *him*?

The chorus of 'happy birthdays' had turned into a round of congratulations. And questions. Who was Charles? Where had she met him? How long had they been engaged?

'He's a tropical diseases specialist,' he heard Megan telling them. 'I met him when he came out to Africa. He lives in London and…and we only got engaged very recently.'

'Is that why you're not wearing a ring?'

'Ah…yes…'

The hesitation was tiny. It might not have even been significant except for the way Megan's gaze finally moved to meet Josh's intent stare. The contact was brief but he registered two things. That there was more to this engagement than Megan was saying and that she was shocked by the way he was staring at her.

Fair enough. Josh pasted a smile on his face. Fortunately he had long since let go of that bunch of flowers.

'Congratulations, Megan,' he heard himself saying in

a perfectly normal voice. 'I hope you'll be very happy. Now, you'll have to excuse me. I want to go and see how Bonnie's getting on.'

It was a good enough reason to walk out of the department, wasn't it? Josh hadn't banked on being followed, however. He increased his pace.

'Josh...wait...' Megan was closing the gap. 'That's what I came to tell you.'

'What?' He didn't turn his head. 'That you're *engaged*?'

'No...' The word was a sigh. 'That Bonnie's doing well. Tidal volume's increasing and her blood chemistry's improving. She's quite stable.'

'Good. I'd still like to see for myself.' Josh kept walking.

'Josh...' This time the word was a plea. 'Don't be like this...please...'

Her voice was quiet enough to carry no further than his own ears but two nurses coming towards him along the corridor were giving him frankly curious stares. And then they gave each other a significant glance. He could almost hear the newsflash that would hit the hospital grapevine in the very near future.

It's happening again. They can't even work together for five minutes without the sparks flying. What is it with the chemistry between those two?

No. It wasn't happening again. Or it wouldn't be if he could get a grip and stop behaving like a petulant teenager. He forced himself to slow down. To turn and give Megan a direct look.

'I need coffee,' he was saying as the nurses passed them. 'How 'bout you?'

He hadn't banked on the cafeteria being so deserted for once, any more than he had on Megan following him. They ended up sitting at one of the prized tables by the windows and there was nobody to overhear their conversation.

Megan had been very quiet during the walk to the cafeteria and while they fixed their drinks. Now she wasn't even tasting her coffee. She'd sat down at the end of the table, at a right angle to him, the way they'd been in his own kitchen. As though she didn't want the barrier of the table between them. Did she feel like he had? So close but not close enough?

'I'm sorry,' she said. 'I...should have told you about Charles the other night.'

Josh made a noncommittal sound. She had, hadn't she? When she'd talked about that 'someone special' still in Africa?

'It's...complicated,' Megan continued. 'I'd like to explain.'

Josh wasn't at all sure he wanted to hear anything more about Megan's engagement. He averted his gaze. 'Why? What's the point?'

The silence made him look back and the expression on Megan's face made him catch his breath. His question had made much more of a direct hit than he'd intended. She looked...stricken?

Why? Was she embarrassed at letting him know she'd found someone she loved more than him?

Ashamed that this was evidence that she'd found it easy to move on?

Or did she wish that things could have been different?

Megan's lips were moving. They trembled, which made the words sound shaky.

'I don't want you to hate me,' she whispered.

Josh could actually feel something melting inside him.

That anger at the way Megan had refused to believe him when he'd tried to explain how he'd ended up in Rebecca's bed that night. At the way she had walked out of his life at such a dark time when Rebecca had died. He could feel all the resentment he'd clung to just melting. Evaporating.

How could he ever hate the only person he had and ever would truly love?

He had chosen to end things between them. He'd pushed her out of his life so that he only had to think about being a good father and he'd had good reason to do that. The best reason because he'd known how dangerous it was to rely on having a love like that in your life. Having his mother alone and looking older than she should for her years was a reminder he could tap into every day, with the added bonus of remembering what that relationship had been like for himself and his siblings. How it was the children who could be hurt most.

He'd done the right thing. The only thing he could have done, anyway. He'd honoured his vow. But it didn't mean that he didn't want Megan to be happy, did it?

Of course it didn't.

'I don't hate you,' he said aloud. The smile he could feel tugging at his lips came from somewhere very deep. Very tender. It was just there. Kind of like the way his hand moved to cover one of Megan's. 'I could never hate you, Megan.'

He had to let go of her hand. But not quite yet. The warmth and silky feel of her skin was irresistible. His thumb moved over it. The memories of this hadn't done reality justice. He needed to capture it properly.

'Charles is…' Megan's voice sounded curiously thick, as though clogged by tears she was holding back.

'It's not perfect, you know…but…but what we had—it's gone, Josh—and I…I had to try and move on…'

'Of course you did.' The movement of his thumb had become something to comfort Megan now. 'I'm happy for you. Really, I am.'

'You'll move on, too.' He could actually hear Megan swallow.

'No.' Josh pulled his hand away.

It wasn't going to happen because the choice was unacceptable. He couldn't be with Megan because, even if he could somehow exorcise the ghosts of his own childhood, it was too late. She had found someone else. And to be with anyone else would be a shell of a marriage. The way it had been with Rebecca. He'd only end up messing with someone else's life and he'd vowed never to do that again.

'You still blame yourself, don't you? For everything.'

Josh said nothing.

This time it was Megan who, after a long and increasingly tense silence, reached out and caught his hand.

'It wasn't your fault,' she said softly but fiercely. 'I'm just as much to blame for getting pregnant that first time. And I didn't tell you. That was wrong. You thought it might be your son you were trying to save that night in Emergency but even then I didn't tell you. I let you wonder about that and be haunted for years and years. I…I'm sorry, Josh. I know it was a terrible thing and neither of us will ever forget but it's far in the past now. We need to let it go.'

'I married Rebecca,' Josh muttered. 'I can blame myself for making her life miserable.'

'She chose to marry you,' Megan said quietly. 'And, from what I heard, you'd made it very clear that you didn't want children. But you gave up what you *did* want, didn't you? For the children. For her.'

Josh had a lump that felt like it had sharp edges stuck in his throat. Oh, yes…he'd given up what he'd really wanted and it had felt like something was trying to die a slow and painful death inside him during those months when he'd pushed Megan away.

He couldn't tell her that, though, could he? Not when she had moved on and found someone else.

Except…she was still holding his hand. Really holding it now. Somehow their hands had moved and now their fingers were intertwined. Josh could feel himself being drawn closer. His head was moving. Something in Megan's eyes was pulling him closer and closer.

Any moment now and he would be close enough to touch her lips with his own. In his peripheral vision Josh could see a group of staff coming into the cafeteria. If he kissed Megan right now, it would be all over St Piran's in a matter of minutes. And the worst thing was, he didn't give a damn.

Right up until the realisation hit him that this newsflash would come right on the heels of the news that Dr Phillips was engaged to some eminent specialist from London. Another relationship would be under threat. And it would be his fault.

History would be repeating itself.

Somehow, Josh found the strength to break that magnetic pull. To untangle their fingers and move himself away.

The group of nurses on early dinner break were heading for a table near theirs now.

'So…it's going well, isn't it?' Josh said, a little more loudly than he needed to. 'Our paediatric wing is going to be something for St Piran's to be proud of, don't you think?'

Megan knew instantly that Josh was trying to put them back onto a professional footing that wouldn't attract any more than mild curiosity from other staff.

It was a million miles away from the space they'd been in only seconds ago.

What exactly had happened there? She could have sworn that Josh had been thinking about *kissing* her.

And, dear Lord…all she had been able to think about was how much she wanted him to.

'Hey, Megan…' The midwife, Brianna, was amongst the group of nurses. She veered closer, a packet of sandwiches in one hand and a bottle of water in the other. 'I've been hearing great things about what's happening in A and E.'

'Yes, it's going really well, thanks.' Megan's smile included Josh. They could do this, it was intended to imply. They could put both their conversation and their interaction with each other back onto a purely professional footing.

Brianna was smiling at Josh. 'Is it true that a member of the royal family is going to come and cut the ribbon for the opening?'

'I believe so.' Josh's smile was as lazy and gorgeous as any Megan had ever seen. She could still see the lines of tension creasing the corners of his eyes, though. Could Brianna sense the undercurrents happening here?

Apparently not. 'How exciting,' she was saying to Josh. 'You'll be all over the news on telly. You're going to be *so* famous after this'

Josh's smile faded. 'I'm not interested in being famous,' he said. 'It's St Piran's I want to put on the map. And not because it has the flashest emergency department but because of the standard of care people get when they come through our doors.'

'Mmm…' But Brianna was grinning. 'Maybe we'll all be famous.' She turned back to Megan. 'You'll still be here, won't you? For the grand ceremony?'

'I expect so.' It was only a couple of weeks away, wasn't it? Megan hadn't made any plans to leave before then. In fact, she still hadn't made any definitive plans for what was coming next in her life. Decisions had to be made. Was she using this new project as a means of procrastinating? 'I've still got a lot of work to do on the cottage to get it back into shape.'

'I saw all the vans parked outside when I drove past yesterday,' Brianna nodded. 'Looks like you've got every tradesman in Penhally on the job.' She glanced down at the packet of sandwiches in her hand. 'Oh, help. I'd better eat or my break will be over. Nice seeing you again, Megan. You're looking a lot better than when you arrived. I think being home must be agreeing with you.'

Being home? Was that how everybody was seeing this visit?

If she was honest with herself, it was how it felt. Breathing in the sea air every morning. Working in a hospital that was as familiar to her as her own home. Being with people she knew so well. People she respected and liked.

Being close to Josh…

She couldn't really call it a comfort zone with the kind of undercurrents she'd been so aware of just a few minutes ago but she couldn't deny the attraction of the familiarity. The feeling of home. A huge part of who she was belonged here and it was going to be a terrible wrench when she left again.

Megan could feel Josh watching her.

'You're not living back in the cottage again, are you? With all that work still going on?'

She nodded. 'I felt a bit in the way after Luke got back from New Zealand. It's not so bad. I can navigate through all the ladders and paint pots. I have hot water and electricity again. I'm going to start on the garden this weekend.'

Oh…help. Should she tell Josh that Charles was planning a visit to come and help? But then she might feel obliged to tell him more about why they'd become engaged and that might lead to a conversation that would take her in the opposite direction from that she needed to go. Bridges might well get burned behind her if that happened and right now those bridges were an insurance policy.

This was the easiest way through it all, wasn't it? She was getting married to someone else and moving away and that would be an end to it all. For good.

But Josh was making a face that suggested even working in her garden was a bad idea.

'I was supposed to tell you,' he groaned. 'And Mum will have my guts for garters if you don't say yes.'

'About talking to her? The toy drive thing? I'll pop in after work.'

Josh shook his head. 'About Saturday. It's the twins' second birthday party. She's decided that you have to be the guest of honour.'

'Oh…I don't think that's…' A good idea? Of course it wasn't. It was a family occasion. A celebration of exactly why she and Josh could never be together.

It was a horrific idea, in fact. No way could she put herself through that.

Except that she made the mistake of meeting Josh's gaze and it was clear that he knew precisely how hard it would be. And not only for her.

'There's going to be lots of people there,' Josh told her quietly. 'And as far as Mum and everybody else is concerned, you saved the lives of Max and Brenna when they were born. Just before…before you left Penhally. And you saved the life of their grandmother virtually the minute you got back. They want to thank you and they've decided that the birthday party is the perfect venue. They'd be very disappointed if you couldn't come.'

Megan swallowed. Hard.

'You don't need to stay long. It's a lunchtime party. You could just come for a cup of tea or something. Please?'

He cared so much, Megan realised. He didn't want his mother to be disappointed. He was quite prepared to do something that was probably going to be as difficult and uncomfortable for him as it would be for her, for the sake of someone else he cared about. How could she not be caught by that plea when that ability to care about others was one of the things she loved so much about this man?

'OK.' The word was a whisper. 'I'll come. I'll talk to Claire about what time and things when I see her later.'

The warmth of the smile Josh gave her stayed with Megan for some time. Well after they'd left the cafeteria and gone back to finish their day's work. The evidence of how Josh could put the needs of others over his own needs stayed alongside the memory of that smile and they were both on her mind as she drove home.

And then it happened. Not in a blinding flash but bit by bit. Random thoughts that came out of nowhere like pieces of a jigsaw puzzle and floated until she began slotting them into place. When the final picture came into view, it was enough of a revelation to make her pull off the road. Not that there was a patch of beach to walk on here but it was a parking area designed to let people appreciate the wilder parts of the Cornish coastline. Even in the dark, the white foam of the surf as it boiled over the rocks at the bottom of the cliff was spectacular and the sound of the sea loud enough to make coherent thought too hard.

The picture was still there, though.

Josh…unable to prevent himself from doing what someone else wanted him to do so badly.

A marriage that had been in tatters. A marriage that Josh had felt guilty about having embarked on in the first place simply because he'd been lonely.

A woman who had been bitterly disappointed in how it had turned out. Who had been obsessed by her need to have a baby.

Josh had said that she'd done it on purpose. Because she'd wanted a baby. It had been her way of trying to keep them together.

Had it been a desperate, last-ditch attempt to save her marriage or to try and at least get pregnant?

Had Rebecca planned some kind of seduction and empowered it by playing on her husband's guilt? Megan remembered what Tasha had tried to tell her but she had been too desperately unhappy to listen. The marriage had been over for a long time, she'd said. Rebecca had probably been lying in wait on the bed in a skimpy set of underwear or something.

She'd been playing games.

Just this one more time…

How could Josh have been cruel enough to refuse? If he had, it wouldn't have been the action of a man who cared as much as she knew he was capable of caring.

It had only been that one time. Josh had told her that, too. A *mistake*, he'd said, and his voice had been agonised enough that she knew he'd been telling the truth.

And it had been weeks before he'd come to *her* bed that night. Had it been the final point of his marriage? One that had been definitive enough for Josh to know he had to leave it behind and move to where he really wanted to be?

How could *she* have been so judgmental?

She'd made it all about herself, hadn't she? She'd been so hurt by the idea that he'd slept with Rebecca even on a single occasion when they'd both been caught by the pull of the irresistible tide that had drawn them back together.

Megan had thrown up an impenetrable barrier right there, on the spot. A barrier that had made it unthinkable that she could ever be with this man she'd loved so much because he'd slept with his wife.

Once.

She'd seen the twins as evidence of his infidelity, for heaven's sake. Those gorgeous children who were the only children of his own Josh would ever have. Children he could never have had if he had been with her. They had his genes. His looks. His personality, probably, judging from the little she'd seen of them.

They were half-Josh. How could she not love them, if she let herself?

But she'd run away. Put thousands and thousands of miles between herself and those tiny babies. Between herself and Josh when he must have needed all the support he could get.

And right now, with tears coursing down her face, Megan could see it for what it had been.

A *mistake*.

They'd both made them. The difference was that Josh had known instantly about the mistake he'd made. It had taken two years and being forced to come home for her to recognise hers.

And the saddest thing of all was that there was nothing she could do about it. It was far too late. She'd run and she'd been away long enough for Josh to put his new life together. A life that he was determined to protect for the sake of the people he loved most.

His children.

A life that didn't—*couldn't*—include her.

CHAPTER SEVEN

A BIRTHDAY PARTY for two-year-olds was bound to be an emotional roller-coaster. Shrieks of delight and peals of laughter were punctuated by the odd bout of tears and even a tantrum or two.

Beneath a sea of balloons and streamers, the furniture in the O'Hara house had been pushed back to give more space both for the children to play and for the small crowd of accompanying adults to supervise as well as enjoy a social gathering of their own.

Claire's fellow grannies from the play group were there, including Rita who had brought her granddaughter Nicola Hallet and her great-grandson Colin. Brianna was there with her twin daughters Aisling and Rhianna. Anna and Luke had brought Crash.

'On request.' Anna laughed. 'But he's our fur child and he fits the age group.'

The look that passed between Anna and Luke at that point had more than just Megan wondering if a less furry child was a not-so-distant prospect but there was no chance to ask her friend whether she was keeping a secret.

The party was full on. Timed for the middle of the day so that the young participants could go home for a sleep when it all got a bit much, there were gifts to open and games to play before the food was served.

Megan had offered to help in the kitchen where Claire and her friends were setting out tiny sandwiches cut into the shapes of animals and heating small pizza squares and chicken nuggets, but Claire shooed her back into the living area to have fun. On her way out of the kitchen Megan saw the dessert platters of bite-sized pieces of fresh fruit and two cakes. One a pink pony-shaped creation and the other an impressively green dinosaur with lurid, candy-covered chocolate buttons for spots. She was smiling as she joined the main gathering. Saving the bright food colouring for just before the toddlers were taken home was smart thinking.

Fun was the last thing Megan had expected to have when she'd steeled herself to follow up her promise to attend this party. She had spent the last few days in a state of confusion that had bordered on unbearable. Charles was driving down from London today and he had every right to expect that she would have achieved her purpose for staying on here by now. That she would have come to terms with her past and would be able to face her new future with confidence.

But, if anything, after the startling insight of how much she could blame herself for this whole, sad, star-crossed-lovers' story that she and Josh had created, it had only become harder to untangle the web of memories and emotions. It was much, much easier to let herself become distracted. To be drawn into the moment by concentrating on her work or the new project of collecting donations for the clinic or…amazingly…having *fun*.

Her trepidation had vanished only seconds after she'd walked in, carrying her gifts. It had evaporated the moment the twins had spotted her and come running.

'*Meggy.*'

That they'd been more interested in receiving cuddles than the brightly wrapped gifts was testament to how they were being brought up, Megan decided. She was the one to use the gifts as an excuse to call time from the tangle of warm little limbs wrapping themselves around her body.

Around her heart.

Josh was right there, a proud smile on his face, when his children remembered to say thank you for their gifts.

And then the children had wriggled back into the festivities and it was just Josh so close. Before Megan had had a chance to centre herself. She could still feel the overwhelming pull of those cuddles. The unconditional love...

'Great choice.' Josh was still smiling but there was a question in his eyes. 'Well done.'

Megan ducked her head. It was almost too much, receiving praise from Josh on top of the emotions his children had just stirred in her. And she didn't want to answer that question. The one about how she felt about these children. Maybe she didn't even want to think about it.

'The assistant in the toy shop has to get the credit,' she said. 'She told me that dress-ups were always a winner at this age.'

So now Max had a bright yellow Bob the Builder hard hat on, a tiny tool belt clipped around his waist and a miniature high-vis vest over his own clothes. And Brenna had pulled on the tutu skirt with the elasticised waist and put the sparkly tiara on her dark curls and was refusing to let go of her wand with the star on the top. She was waving it like a stern conductor as she danced to each burst of music for the game of musical cushions.

All the children followed her lead and were dancing with varying degrees of competence and balance.
Josh's smile was as misty as those of any of the watching adults. He was actually forgetting to stop the music
so that the children could make a dash for available
cushions.

Megan found herself watching Josh instead of the
game, knowing that her own smile was also coming
from a very tender place in her heart.

Something had changed in the last few days.

Something very fundamental.

The anger had gone, hadn't it? That sense that Josh
had betrayed her by sleeping with Rebecca.

And with it had gone the entire foundation on which
she'd built her conviction that they could never be together. It seemed to have simply crumbled away.

Where did that leave her now?

Emotionally available?

Not really. There was Charles to consider now. And
the pull of what she'd left behind in Africa.

Megan certainly couldn't forget about Africa. It
seemed like it was the only thing people here wanted
to talk to her about.

Wendy, the grandmother of three-year-old Shannon,
couldn't wait to tell her about the bake sale planned for
the next week.

'We're hoping to raise over a hundred pounds,' she
told Megan. 'We're going to spend it at the bookshop.'

Margaret, who was at the party with two grandchildren, four-year-old Liam and his younger brother
Jackson, overheard Wendy and rushed to join the conversation.

'Mr Prachett at the bookshop is giving us a great dis-
count and he's found a line of picture books that have

no text but still tell stories. And he's going to donate lots of pencils and paper, too.'

'The school's on board,' Wendy added. 'Every child has been given an exercise book and they're decorating the covers in art class.'

Another granny, Miriam, offered Megan a cup of tea and a proud smile. 'I'm in charge of clothing donations,' she said. 'I've got two huge crates in my sewing room and I'm washing and mending and ironing everything before it gets packed. We're only accepting lightweight items like cotton dresses and shorts and T-shirts. Will that be all right, do you think?'

'I'm sure it'll be wonderful,' Megan responded. It was impossible not to be touched by the enthusiasm and generosity of these women. 'You're all wonderful. I can't believe how this project keeps growing and growing.'

'It's you who's wonderful,' Miriam said. 'We're having fun collecting things but we're still in our own comfort zones, aren't we? With our families safe and healthy around us. You're the one who was prepared to go to the end of the earth to really help.'

Josh was supervising a bubble-blowing contest but was standing close enough to overhear Miriam's words. When he looked towards them, his glance had none of the admiration of the women around her.

'Megan's an angel,' he said crisply. 'Just ask my mother.'

The tone was light enough to make the people around her smile. Maybe it was only Megan who could hear that the words covered something painful. They both knew the real reasons for her heading to Africa two years ago and it hadn't been entirely altruistic, had it?

Would she do it again, knowing what she knew now?

Fortunately, Josh had turned back to the bubble blowing and there were much easier questions to answer.

'What's it like?' Wendy asked. 'In the camp?'

Megan deliberately censored the first impressions that always came to mind. The unbearable heat and filth. The suffering of so many people. 'Huge. Like a fair-sized city, really, with a hundred and thirty thousand people in the camp and another thirty thousand or so around the edges.'

'It can't be an easy place to live.'

Megan shook her head. 'No. It's hot and dirty and there are pockets of violence but it's the disease that's the worst of it. There are probably eight thousand children suffering from malnutrition and so many orphans who lose their parents to things like AIDS. And then there are other diseases like dysentery and malaria and dengue fever to cope with.' She deliberately stopped herself going any further. A birthday celebration was no place to be telling things like they really were. She could do that somewhere else. At one of the fundraising events, maybe.

But the older women were hanging on every word. They tutted in sympathy.

'And the clinic? Is it like a medical centre or a proper hospital? Do you have operating theatres and maternity wards and things?'

'Oh, yes…it's a proper hospital but very different from St Piran's, of course. And we struggle to cope with what we have to work with.'

Megan's attention was caught by what was happening behind Margaret. Brenna was having trouble with her bubbles because she wasn't holding the loop anywhere near her mouth when she was blowing. Josh was crouched beside her. He closed her little fist over the handle of the loop and dipped it into the soapy water and then held it up in front of her mouth. She could see him miming what she needed to do with her lips and breath.

Brenna sucked in a big breath and whooshed it out and a stream of small bubbles exploded into the air. Her face lit up with a grin that went from ear to ear and Megan could see the way Josh's eyes crinkled as he grinned back. Even if she hadn't been able to read the love he had for his daughter on his face like that, she would have been able to feel the glow of it.

'Sorry, what was that?' She'd completely missed something Wendy had been saying.

'I read in the paper that other hospitals are joining St Piran's to donate old equipment and drugs and things. Isn't that marvellous?'

'It certainly is.'

'Dengue fever.' Miriam was frowning thoughtfully. 'That's what you got sick with, wasn't it?'

'I'm much better now.'

'You look it. Must be the lovely sea air around here that's done the trick.'

'Mmm…' But Megan was having trouble focusing on her health or anything else right now. She was still watching Josh and remembering another time when she had read that kind of infinite love on his face. Way before Brenna had been born. Before he'd even known she was a possibility.

That love, seen in the half-light of that on-call room, had been purely for *her*.

And Josh would have seen the mirror image of it on her own face.

She could feel the glow of it all over again. So much so she needed to take off the cherry-red cardigan she had on over the soft white shirt she had teamed with her jeans. Had Josh sensed something of what she was thinking? Was that why he was suddenly there, his hand extended?

'Let me take that for you. I can hang it up with the coats.'

'Yes…' Wendy was nodding with satisfaction. 'You've got a nice bit of colour in your cheeks now, dear.'

Megan could certainly feel that colour, which must have heightened as Josh's hand brushed hers in relieving her of the cardigan. Feeling flustered, she avoided meeting his gaze, but that didn't help because she found herself looking at his hand. Holding an item of her clothing.

Oh, help… She had to excuse herself.

'I might see if your mum needs some help in the kitchen,' she muttered.

'See?' Josh had raised an eyebrow. His lazy grin was charming every female within range. 'I told you she was an angel. You could just enjoy yourself, Megan. You don't have to work, you know.'

Megan shook her head with a smile. It must be time to serve the party food and it was just too disturbing, being this close to Josh and remembering things like that moment in the on-call room. *Feeling* things like the way that had made her feel.

Something huge had certainly changed but was it only on her side?

She was only half the equation here.

Josh had built his own foundation to anchor the barrier of them ever being together. The concrete had been poured the day he'd come to tell her that Rebecca was pregnant. Megan had probably added some steel reinforcing rods herself when she'd walked out without even having the courtesy of attending Rebecca's funeral.

He must have been so hurt by that. The subtle edge to that "angel" comment he'd made suggested that it hadn't been buried far below the surface. And maybe it had just added to the anger simmering in the wake of her accusation that he'd been lying about his marriage being over. That he'd treated her like a bit on the side.

Could he ever forgive her for that?

He'd said he didn't hate her.

That he could *never* hate her.

And, when he'd said that, he'd looked…as if he'd wanted nothing more than to close the gap between them and kiss her senseless.

There was still something there between them, that much was obvious.

A big something.

But was it big enough? Could it be trusted? Did she even want to find out? Or would she end up back at square one, the way she already had when it came to Josh O'Hara?

Twice, in fact.

There had to be a limit on how many times you could go through that kind of emotional trauma and still survive.

The sensible thing to do would be to run. As fast and as far away as she possibly could.

Josh watched Megan making her way into the kitchen. The room instantly felt emptier without her which was ridiculous given the number of people milling about.

Not to mention a very large dog. Crash was being extraordinarily patient with all the small people who wanted to stroke his nose or try to climb onto his back but Luke was hovering nearby.

'Might be time we took off,' he said to Josh. 'I sus-

pect all the Davenports are ready for a blast of fresh
air on the beach. If we stay much longer, all these kids
are going to start feeding treats to Crash and the consequences won't be pretty.'

Josh grinned. 'Fair enough. Thanks for bringing
him.'

The noise level was rising steadily around them, with
Shannon staging quite a spectacular tantrum, lying on
her back and drumming her heels on the floor. Josh
and Luke shared a grimace. 'No wonder you want to
escape,' Josh muttered. 'It's enough to put you right off
having kids, huh?'

But Luke just smiled. 'Bit late for that,' he murmured.

Josh opened his mouth but was too stunned for any
word to emerge. And then it was too late. Small hands
were tugging on his trouser leg.

'Daddy...*up*.'

Claire appeared in the doorway as Josh scooped
Brenna into his arms.

'Who's hungry?' she called above the noise. 'And
who needs some juice?'

Shannon stopped shrieking but the noise level didn't
diminish as the tribe of excited, hungry children flowed
past Josh towards the kitchen. Luke and Anna used the
exodus as a means to slip away with Crash, and Josh
watched them go, still somewhat dazed by their apparent news.

It seemed like whichever way he turned, things were
changing around him on an almost daily basis. And
they had been, ever since the disruption of his mother
getting sick.

Ever since Megan's unexpected return?

That she was here in Penhally at all was surprising

but the fact that she was still here at this party was startling enough to signify an even bigger change.

'Here…' Claire put a glass of sparkling wine in his hands as soon as he walked into the kitchen. 'Give that to Megan.'

'I'm not sure she'll want to stay long enough for a drink.'

His mother made a sound that Josh recognised from his childhood. He needed to do what he was told. With a wry smile he headed for Megan, fully expecting her to reject the offer. She hadn't wanted to come to this party at all and he couldn't blame her for that. Josh had expected her to drop in only long enough to be polite. To have a cup of tea and say happy birthday to the twins and then find an excuse to slip away from the chaos, like Luke and Anna had done.

But Megan looked more than happy to accept. Her smile was instant. Brief, but happy enough to light up her face.

'What a lovely idea. Thanks, Josh.'

'You're welcome.' The words were polite. They should have come accompanied by a smile to answer hers but Josh's lips felt oddly stiff. His fingers were tingling, too. Had Megan been as aware as he was of that tiny touch of skin to skin as the glass had been transferred?

There was certainly something very different about the way Megan was looking at him today.

About the way she was smiling at him.

Maybe the biggest change of all had happened a few days ago and was only now filtering through. He'd hardly seen her since that conversation they'd had in the cafeteria. Maybe because he didn't trust himself around her? If Brianna and her friends hadn't come in when they had, would he really have kissed Megan?

Did he still want to?

She was smiling again right now. At Claire this time, nodding as she raised her glass to her lips. His mother's expression was anxious. Did she like the wine? Was she enjoying herself? Megan's smile said that she did. And she was. The tip of her tongue appeared as if chasing an errant drop of wine from her bottom lip and Josh was aware of a sudden heat, deep down in his belly. He almost groaned aloud.

Yes. The answer was most definitely yes. For a long, long moment he couldn't take his eyes off Megan's mouth. God help him, but he'd never wanted to kiss anybody as much as he wanted to kiss Megan Phillips at this moment.

Megan's gaze suddenly shifted, jerking up to meet his as if she'd felt the force of that shaft of desire.

It was impossible to look away. To deny what he was feeling.

To one side of him, Brenna was climbing onto a chair, a mangled chicken nugget in her small fist.

'For you, Daddy,' she announced imperiously.

'Mmm…' But Josh couldn't move. Couldn't even look down. Not yet

Not when he could see that Megan knew exactly what he'd been thinking about. How he was feeling.

And she wasn't looking away…

A faint flush of colour had painted her cheeks again and her lips parted slightly. Never mind that the room was packed with people and there had to be at least a dozen conversations going on, adults helping little ones to eat or pouring juice or drinking their wine and chatting to each other.

Far too many people for such a small space and yet, for that instant, it felt like it had in the cafeteria days ago. As if nothing else mattered and he was alone in the world apart from Megan.

'*Dad*-dy...'

Josh lowered his head and obediently opened his mouth. The chicken nugget was posted home accompanied by a squeal of glee from his daughter and the moment was well and truly broken.

That flush of colour seemed to stay on Megan's cheeks after that. Was it the wine? Maybe it was due to the compliments that Claire kept heaping on Megan to anyone who was listening.

'She saved my life, you know. If she hadn't been there on the beach that day, I probably wouldn't be here, celebrating my grandchildren's birthday. She's my angel, so she is. Where's my camera? I need a photo.'

Rita was only too pleased to arm herself with the camera and take a picture of Claire and Megan side by side and smiling.

And then she wanted one of Megan with the twins.

'She was the doctor who saved them when they were born, you know.' Claire had to wipe a tear away. 'My angel, so she is...'

Josh stood back and watched as Claire engineered the picture she wanted. Brenna was happy enough to sit on Megan's knee but Max took a bit more persuasion. He was busy flattening chicken nuggets with his plastic Bob the Builder hammer. His grandmother bribed him by saying that he would be able to blow out the candles on his cake as soon as the picture was taken and in short order there was Megan with both his children on her lap.

Josh suddenly found it hard to take his next breath. Brenna was reaching up, unable to resist the urge to play with the tumble of Megan's hair. She seemed to change her mind at the last moment, however, and touched Megan's face instead. Unusually gentle for such a small child, Brenna traced the outline of Megan's smile.

Claire was dabbing her eyes with her handkerchief as Rita snapped some photos.

She was right, wasn't she? If it wasn't for Megan, this party might not be happening. She had been the person who had been there to hold them and care for them when they had taken their first breaths.

What a different picture that would have been from the happy, family chaos they were in the midst of here. Josh could paint that different picture in his mind all too easily. The bright lights and tense atmosphere. The hiss of oxygen and the beeping of monitors giving alarming readings.

How hard had that been on Megan?

Harder than it had been for him, banished to pace the end of the corridor and agonise over what might be happening?

Of course it must have been.

He'd begged her to save his babies, knowing that he couldn't face the agony of losing another child. But the child he *had* lost had also been Megan's and, although he'd done his absolute utmost to save the baby she'd named Stephen, he'd failed. And yet he'd expected Megan to do whatever she could to save the twins and he'd had absolute faith that she would. She'd made sure that he'd been left with the gift of life that he'd failed to give her all those years ago.

She must have been devastated at having to be a central player in such an ironic twist of fate. No wonder she hadn't hung around for Rebecca's funeral. She'd already done far more than it had been reasonable to expect and it was thanks to her that he had these precious children in his life.

And that he still had his mother.

His chest still felt tight and now Josh had a lump in his throat as well. How selfish had it been to harbour resentment at Megan for taking off the way she had? To have hung onto the anger that she hadn't believed him when he'd tried to explain the anomaly of sleeping with Rebecca that one last time? How arrogant had it been to assume she would trust him when he'd let her down so badly in the past? Turning his back on her after that first night together.

Failing to save *their* child.

And she had been afraid to tell him she'd moved on and become engaged to another man because she didn't want him to hate her?

As if the kind of love he had for Megan could ever, *ever* flip over to the dark side of that coin.

If anything, in this moment, seeing her here in his house, holding his children, he loved her more than ever. The power of that first night they'd had together was trickling back faster and faster.

Threatening to drown him.

A power that was becoming intense because this scene felt so *right*. Megan as the mother of his children. It felt as right as it had to create a new life together on the night they had been discovering each other for the first time.

But what could he do about it?

Too much damage had been done. Megan had finally taken definitive steps to move on from it all. What was it he'd overheard someone saying? Oh…yeah…she'd gone to the end of the earth in order to do that. And she'd found someone else there. This Charles that she was now engaged to.

Megan wasn't available so it didn't matter a damn how right any of this felt. He had no right to mess up whatever it was Megan had decided she wanted for the rest of her life. He had to let go.

Be happy for her?

But…what about the change he was so aware of today? The way Megan was looking at him?

Her smile…

The utter confusion Josh could feel seemed to be contagious. Max was suddenly overcome by the emotional overload of the exciting birthday party. He hit his sister with his plastic hammer and Brenna shrieked with outrage and then burst into heartbroken sobs.

Claire tried to rescue Megan but Brenna wasn't having any of it. She wound her arms around Megan's neck and howled more loudly. A kick from her small legs sent Max tumbling off Megan's lap and his face crumpled ominously. Josh moved in to collect his son. He picked Max up and held him tightly, making soothing noises to circumvent an additional meltdown. It would be time enough when things had calmed down to have a talk to him about what it was acceptable to use his new hammer on. It was certainly pointless right now.

'Maybe we'd better postpone the cakes,' Claire suggested, and there was a murmur of agreement from other adults. The twins weren't the only toddlers who were reaching the end of their tethers. The guests began to sort themselves out to go home.

Megan was on her feet. She had her arms wrapped around Brenna and she was rocking the small girl and making the same kind of soothing noises Josh had been making to Max. His son had now recovered his good humour.

'Juice?' he begged. 'Thirsty, Daddy.'

'I'll fix that,' Claire said. 'Can you give out the goody bags for everybody before they go?'

'Sure.' A glance over his shoulder before he moved to the front door to give out the farewell gifts showed him that Brenna was now almost asleep in Megan's arms. Her eyes were shut and a thumb was in her mouth. Her other arm was still wound around Megan's neck, though. There was even a small fistful of that tumble of brown curls, anchoring Megan's head in place.

When he got back to the kitchen, there were only a couple of guests remaining and Max was sitting at the table, eating pizza and staring hopefully at his cake.

'Later,' his grandmother was saying. 'It'll be our teatime treat.'

Megan was nowhere to be seen.

'She's gone upstairs to put Brenna to bed,' Claire told him. 'Maybe you could check on them?'

'Sure.' But Josh didn't return his mother's smile. Poor Megan. She'd not only attended a party she hadn't wanted to go to, she'd been firmly cast in the role of stand-in mother.

How on earth was she coping with that?

It had been a huge relief when Brenna's sobs had receded and the stiff little body she'd been holding had begun to relax. That boneless sensation of a child falling asleep in her arms had been so sweet Megan hadn't dared risk waking her by accepting Claire's offer to take her. Instead, she'd said she would put Brenna down for a nap herself.

To find Brenna's tiny fingers still clutching a handful of her hair when she eased her onto her small bed was enough to bring tears to Megan's eyes. She really hadn't wanted anyone else to comfort her, had she?

Kneeling beside the bed and leaning in close enough not to have her hair pulled painfully or disturb the toddler's slumber, she gently disentangled the connection, although she needn't have worried about waking Brenna who was deeply asleep now, her head sinking into her pillow. Dark eyelashes made fans above plump, flushed cheeks and a cupid's bow of her mouth made tiny movements as if sucking on something, even though the favoured thumb had been discarded.

For a long moment Megan stayed where she was, kneeling beside the bed. She smoothed some errant curls back from Brenna's face and then simply watched her sleep, marvelling at such perfect skin and the expression of such innocence that made sleeping children look like angels.

So precious.

So vulnerable.

The vice that squeezed her heart was all too easy to recognise and Megan had to close her eyes for a moment and try to take in a deep, steadying breath.

How had this happened?

How, in God's name, hadn't she seen it coming and put a better protective barrier in place?

It was too late now. She'd fallen in love with Brenna.

With Josh's daughter.

Megan heard the soft sound of movement behind her. Or maybe she sensed Josh easing himself silently into the room. Still on her knees, Megan turned her head, knowing that her eyes were bright with tears. That her distress must be written all over her face. She loved a child who could never be hers. And now she was facing the man she loved and *he* could never be hers either.

She could see pain that mirrored her own on Josh's face. He murmured something that was inaudible but the tone was one of pure empathy. He held out his hand to help Megan to her feet and it felt only right that he didn't let it go. That he drew her into his arms and held her.

They were both suffering here. The swirl of their entire history, mixed with feelings that were too powerful to fight. And Megan didn't want to fight any more. She needed this moment. It felt right. As though there'd been something worthwhile in all the pain over so many years.

Because even a moment as perfect as this made it all worthwhile.

And then Megan moved from where her face was buried against Josh's shoulder. She turned her head and looked up to find Josh looking down at her. Neither of them could look away. There was something far too powerful for either of them to fight happening now.

Slowly…so slowly that she could have easily stopped it happening if she'd thought about it for even a nanosecond, Josh's head dipped and his lips came close enough to touch hers.

So softly. The love she could feel in that gentle touch was so pure that Megan knew she would remember it until she drew her last breath.

And then, faster than thought itself, the touch ignited and the flame of passion licked every cell of her body. Megan could feel her lips parting beneath Josh's, her body arching into his, a tiny cry of unbearable desire escaping her throat. A whimper of need that was so deep it felt like it was tearing her apart.

A tiny part of her brain remained in control, however. Or maybe it was Josh who was still aware that they were standing beside a bed that contained his sleeping child. It was impossible to unleash the passion but equally impossible to drag themselves away from each other. Every time they tried and the contact became light enough to break, they both pressed closer. Went a little deeper each time.

It was a familiar sound that broke the spiral.

Not the whimper of a child waking or the sound of someone coming up the stairs.

It was an electronic chirp. The sound of a text message arriving on the tiny mobile phone Megan had in the back pocket of her jeans.

A second chirp sounded as she and Josh finally stepped back from each other and the noise was just enough of a prompt to break the stunned immobility of the way they were staring at each other.

Megan read her message. She could feel the curiosity emanating from Josh. She couldn't meet his gaze.

A warning bell was sounding in the back of her head. Taking the shape of the thought she'd had what seemed like only minutes ago.

That things were changing and it was dangerous because she could get badly hurt all over again.

That the safe thing to do would be to run. As fast and as far away as she could.

'It's Charles,' she said, her voice totally without expression. 'He's waiting for me at the cottage.'

There was a moment's charged silence.

'You'd better go, then.' The words from Josh were as toneless as her own had been.

Megan still couldn't look at Josh. Nothing was being said and yet everything was being said.

'Mmm.' A strangled sound. 'I'd better.'

He wasn't watching her as she fled. Megan knew that without even turning back. He hadn't moved an inch. He was standing there, his head bowed, his gaze fixed on his daughter.

CHAPTER EIGHT

THAT KISS HAD changed everything.

Maybe that wasn't a good enough excuse for Josh to be where he was now, too late in the evening for it not to seem significant, standing in front of the door to Megan's cottage. But he'd been agonising over it ever since Megan had virtually run out of his house, according to Claire, stopping only long enough to snatch up her bag and jacket.

She'd left her cardigan behind, draped over one of the chairs that had been pushed to one side in the living room, and it had only been found when the children had finally been been put down for the night and Josh and his mother had been clearing away the remnants of the birthday party.

Returning an item of clothing wasn't much of an excuse, but Josh needed to meet this Charles.

To find out what his competition was like?

No. His motivation wasn't that juvenile.

Taking a deep breath, Josh raised his hand and lifted the brass door knocker. He rapped it briskly, three times.

He hadn't been able to think of anything other than Megan since that kiss. The kaleidoscope of memories, emotions and a determination to be honest with himself had swirled around and around in his head, sliding and colliding until *finally* they seemed to have fallen into place.

He had treated Megan abominably, he could freely admit that. He'd convinced himself he was being strong and doing the right thing but he'd been covering the fact that he was an emotional coward. And, yes, maybe he wasn't doing the *right* thing now but it was the honest thing to do.

He understood why Megan had left him when he'd been at the lowest point of his life, consumed by guilt at the death of a wife he'd never loved enough. Terrified by the prospect of being a solo father to two fragile, ultimately vulnerable, babies.

He had forgiven Megan for that. He had forgiven her for not believing him when he'd told her that his marriage was over. For thinking that he was sleeping with his wife at the same time he'd gone to Megan's bed.

His knock went unanswered. He could hear some classical music coming from inside the cottage but there was no sound of any voices. The thought that he might be disturbing something intimate prompted Josh to lick suddenly dry lips. To take another deep breath. He would try just once more. He rapped three times again, and then added another couple of raps, slightly louder.

The bottom line was that he could forgive Megan anything at all because…he loved her. It was as simple as that. And as complicated. He could even forgive her for marrying someone else and moving on with her life without him if he could believe that she would be happy doing that.

But Josh also understood why Megan had fled from his house earlier today, in the wake of that kiss.

It was still there.

Whatever they'd discovered on that first night together and rediscovered when they'd found themselves working together in St Piran's all those years later was still there.

Stronger than ever, maybe, because it had been denied and locked away.

Because of his stupid, misguided tunnel vision.

How had he ever convinced himself that he could only be the father he was determined to be for his children by denying love or commitment to anything other than them or his career?

He could never be the best father—the best anything, for that matter—without Megan in his life because he could never be the person he could be if he had her by his side.

He could never feel *whole* without her.

And, thanks to that kiss, Josh was convinced that it was the same for Megan, whether she was prepared to admit it or not.

So why the hell was she planning to marry someone else?

Just what did this Charles have that *he* didn't?

Maybe he was about to find out. The door was opening in front of him. Expecting it to be Megan, Josh felt his lips curling into a smile but the smile drained away when he found himself facing the man who had to be Charles. It was an effort not to let his face freeze into lines of…shock?

Whatever he'd expected Megan's fiancé to look like, it wasn't this. Charles was much, much older than he was. Pushing sixty? He had completely grey hair, wire-rimmed spectacles and…and he was wearing a *waistcoat*. He looked like he could be Megan's father. Or a favourite uncle. There was a kindliness about his face and his smile looked genuine but his eyes were sharp. This man missed nothing.

'You *must* be Josh,' he said into the awkward silence. 'Please, come in. Megan's having a bath but she'll be down in a minute, I expect.'

'I...ah...' This was so unexpected that Josh was completely thrown. Just what had he thought he would do when he got here anyway? 'I just came to return this,' he said, holding out the garment in his hand. 'Megan left it behind at the party. Perhaps you could give it to her?'

A hand was extended but not to accept the item of clothing. It was asking for a handshake.

'I'm Charles Cartwright,' the older man said. 'Megan's friend. Please do come in. I've heard so much about you, I'd like to meet you properly.'

Megan's *friend*?

He couldn't walk away now without appearing rude. Besides, Josh's level of confusion was rising. What kind of a fiancé described himself as a friend? Maybe Megan wasn't engaged at all and that was why she wasn't wearing a ring. Had she told everybody she was engaged to protect herself?

Perhaps all he needed to do was convince Megan that she didn't need that kind of protection. That he'd finally grown up and got over himself. That he could be everything that she needed him to be.

That it might not be as easy as it sounded became more apparent with every step Josh took into the cottage.

It was impossible not to remember the last time— the *only* time—he'd ever been here before. There was an air of redecoration chaos and a strong smell of paint that made it feel different now but nothing could erase those memories.

Steeling himself to do the hardest thing in his life.

Putting it off, just for another minute, resisting the urge to pull Megan into his arms from the moment she'd answered the door. Following her into the kitchen after accepting the offer of a drink.

And then he'd snapped when Megan had betrayed her nervousness by spilling the water when she'd tried to pour it. That kiss was seared into his memory just as deeply as today's now was but…they were so different.

The kiss in the kitchen that day, more than two years ago, had been one of desperation. A last kiss, before he had to tell her what he knew would kill the hope and love he could see in her eyes. When he had to say that he couldn't be in love with her any more.

And today's kiss? The only desperation there had been the need to get far closer than they could through a kiss. Far closer than their surroundings and circumstances would allow.

But they'd both wanted that, hadn't they?

The real difference was that today's kiss had been tinged with *hope*.

Or was he imagining that?

Josh's confused whirl of thoughts circled back and tried to start again. Why had he come here? What did he hope to achieve? The only thing Josh was certain about was that he was nervous. More nervous than the last time he'd entered this cottage because then he'd known what the outcome would be.

Now it felt like the rest of his life was hanging by a thread that was so tangled up he had no idea how to start unravelling it.

Charles was leading the way into the living area of Megan's cottage. It was cosy. The curtains had been drawn to shut out the rest of the world and the fire was a soft glow of embers waiting to be tickled back into life with some new fuel. A couple of wine glasses, one with a few mouthfuls of ruby liquid remaining, had been pushed to one side of the coffee table. The rest of the table was completely covered with photographs.

Josh had to step closer. To see what had been going on in this intimate atmosphere?

'Snapshots of Africa,' Charles said from behind him. 'Can I get you a glass of wine, Josh?'

'No... Thanks,' Josh added belatedly, knowing his refusal had sounded terse enough to be rude.

He couldn't look away from the photographs because Megan was in every one of them. Never alone, but often the only white face amongst a crowd of smiling colleagues. Or standing with family groups against the background of a tent city. Working in what looked like an overcrowded and pressured clinic setting. Mostly, with children. Treating them. Surrounded by them. Holding them.

'I brought copies of all the ones I thought Megan would like to have,' Charles said quietly. 'I'm a bit of an amateur photographer.'

'They're very good,' Josh heard himself saying politely.

But they were more than very good. The images were amazingly evocative. They captured the barren landscape, the poverty and suffering, the harsh climate so clearly Josh could feel himself stepping into that foreign world.

There was a profile shot of Megan, wearing her stethoscope, her head bent as she listened to the chest of a tiny child who lay in its mother's arms. One of those heartbreaking children who were all ribs and stick-like limbs and huge, huge eyes.

Megan's hair was piled up and clipped to the top of her head but some of that luxuriant tumble of curls had escaped, as it always did. The stray lock looked black—soaked with perspiration and glued to the damp skin of her neck and cheek. Josh could actually feel the urge to touch the photograph. To try and smooth that lock of hair back from Megan's face. To say something to ease the lines of distress he could see in her fierce concentration. In the lines of the way she was holding her mouth and the creases around her eyes.

He couldn't resist picking up another image. One that made him suck in his breath sharply the moment he saw it. He couldn't stop staring at it, even though he knew he was glimpsing something private. A picture Megan hadn't known was being taken because she was sound asleep, slumped in an old wicker chair, her head uncomfortably tilted so far to the side it was virtually resting on her shoulder, but still there was a hint of a smile curving her lips.

She wasn't alone, of course. Tucked under each arm was a tiny baby, their faces so black against Megan's white coat and the blankets they were cocooned in. The babies were also deeply asleep and all three of them looked utterly at peace.

So *happy*.

'Lovely shot, isn't it?'

'Mmm.' Josh could barely produce an audible sound. He was seeing a part of Megan's life he could never share. A part of the woman he loved that was completely unknown.

'They're twins,' Charles told him. 'The girl is called Asha, which means Life. And the boy is Dumi—the Inspirer.'

'Special names,' Josh murmured.

'Megan chose them. She saved their lives when they were born and she fought for them every step of the way after that. Day and night for weeks, it was Megan who fed them and changed them and cuddled them when they cried.'

'What happened to their mother?'

'She came into the camp in the late stages of her pregnancy and it was too late to start any treatment for her advanced AIDS. She died within hours of giving birth.'

'And the babies?' Josh felt his heart sink like a stone. 'Are they...? Did they...?' He couldn't bring himself to say the words. Megan would have been devastated if—

'They were lucky.' He could hear the smile in Charles's voice even though he didn't look up from the photo. 'We at least had the time to give the drugs that can help prevent transmission of the disease from mother to child. Neither of them were infected with HIV during the pregnancy and they were delivered via Caesarean and then bottle-fed, of course. They're both thriving.'

Thank goodness for that. Josh's relief was tinged with a sense of unreality, however. How weird was it knowing that Megan had been living a life that paralleled his own to such a degree? A lone parent figure for fragile twin babies.

'When was this picture taken?' he asked.

'Six months ago, when they were about eight weeks old, I think.' Charles sounded oddly hesitant. 'The twins were the main reason it was so hard to persuade Megan to come home and recover properly from the dengue fever. It would have been impossible if I hadn't suggested—' He broke off suddenly, his head turning. 'Megan...we have a visitor.'

'So I see. Hello, Josh. What are you doing here?'

Megan was dressed again after her bath, in jeans and a warm pullover, but her feet were bare and her hair hung down in damp tendrils that she was still squeezing dry with a towel.

She looked…good grief…*frightened*?

Vulnerable, anyway. Heartbreakingly vulnerable. Because of him. Because he was here and threatening to break…something.

Slowly, Josh put the photograph down. He held out what he was still holding in his other hand. The cherry-red cardigan.

'You left this behind at the party. I thought you might need it.'

'Oh…' Megan came forward to claim the article of clothing. 'Sorry…'

What for? The inconvenience of it needing to be returned? Or for what had happened that had made her flee his house in such a hurry that she'd left it behind?

The moment was astonishingly awkward. It was Charles who cleared his throat and tried to break it.

'Megan's been telling me about all the fundraising efforts going on for the clinic. It's a wonderful thing you're all doing.'

'It's Megan who can take the credit,' Josh said. He had to clear his own throat because his voice came out sounding oddly raw.

'She's also told me about the new paediatric wing for your emergency department. That's going to put St Piran's on the map in a big way. You've got a brilliant career ahead of you, Josh, by all accounts.'

Josh made a vaguely dismissive sound. Yes, he already had, and would no doubt continue to have, a brilliant career.

But it wasn't enough, was it?

Charles was clearly struggling to find a topic of conversation to break the loaded silences.

'And your twins turned two today? Megan tells me they're beautiful children.'

Josh managed to make another affirmative noise. Yes, his children were beautiful. They were everything to him and he would lay down his life in a heartbeat for them, if it was necessary.

But…right now…it still didn't feel *enough*.

He needed something more in his life.

He needed Megan.

At least part of what he was feeling had to be showing on his face. In his inability to even make polite conversation. No wonder Megan was starting to look embarrassed. Stricken, even?

'I'd better go.' Josh started moving but it felt like he was walking away too soon. That he hadn't touched on whatever it was he'd wanted to achieve by coming here.

'I forgot.' The words came out in a kind of a growl as he swung back to face Megan. 'We're doing a test run of the technology in Paediatric Resus tomorrow. X-ray and monitoring and so forth. You might want to be there to see how it comes together.' He tried, and failed, to smile. 'It doesn't matter, of course. If you're busy.'

The look that passed between Megan and Charles was palpably significant but Josh couldn't read the message. His gut was forming an unpleasantly rock-like mass inside him.

'I'll be there,' Megan said quietly. 'What time?'

'Three p.m. We're hoping that a Sunday afternoon might be a quieter spell. There are a lot of people who want to see if it's going to fly.' Josh forced himself to acknowledge Charles with a smile. 'You'd be most welcome to come too, Charles. You might want to see what Megan's been up to while she's been here.'

'Thank you, but I'm due back in London early to-morrow afternoon.' Charles was smiling back at him. 'And I've got a pretty good idea of what Megan's been up to. She knows I approve.'

Had there been some kind of hidden meaning there? Josh had arrived at Megan's cottage feeling agitated because he'd known something had changed. Or hadn't changed, more to the point, in the wake of that kiss. He was driving away feeling like he'd found more questions than answers.

There was a part of Megan he didn't know. The part that was bound up with Africa. That was *friends* with Charles Cartwright. A very important part. But he was missing something here, and he had no idea what it was.

Josh was still feeling agitated. And confused.

Totally at a loss as to what he could do about any of it, in fact.

The new paediatric wing of St Piran's emergency department was not quite finished but it was still crowded on this Sunday afternoon. The scenario being run of dealing with a child with multiple trauma after being knocked off his bicycle might be a pretence but to the medical staff involved this was no game.

From where she was standing in the second resuscitation area, Megan was close to the junior star of the show who was getting ready to play his part. Thirteen year old Jem, the son of Nick Tremayne, who was a Penhally Bay GP, had volunteered for the role.

'I'm going to be a doctor when I grow up,' he told Megan. 'Just like my dad. I'm already learning first aid. And I've done this for real, too, when I had my accident.'

'I remember.' Megan nodded. How could she forget? That had been when her path had crossed that of Josh's again so unexpectedly. A route that had only led, again, to an emotional disaster.

'I don't remember this bit of it, though,' Jem said sadly. 'I was unconscious.'

'That's what you have to pretend to be now.' His father was helping one of the volunteer ambulance crew to fasten a collar around his neck. 'And no giggling. This is serious stuff.'

'OK.' Jem lay flat on the stretcher, closed his eyes and groaned. He tried it again, obviously hoping for a more dramatic effect.

Josh appeared though the doors leading to the main resus area. 'The paediatric trauma team have been summoned by pager,' he announced. 'On my count these doors will open and we'll take it from there in real time.'

He looked extremely tense, Megan thought. Not surprising, given that there were so many observers here. Word had spread fast. Albert White was here as CEO. There were quite a few of St Piran's consultant staff present, including Luke and Anna Davenport, and Nick had brought some of the other local GPs with him. There was also a reporter from a local newspaper accompanied by a photographer.

The tension was instantly contagious. Never mind any personal issues between them, if a major glitch showed up in this scenario, it could be due to a poor choice she had made about the design and predicted flow patterns.

It wasn't like Josh to be grim, though, even if he was stressed. He didn't smile at Megan when he spotted her.

He practically scowled at her, for heaven's sake. So she'd arrived a little later than she'd intended. Did it matter that much? He was also looking less than amused by Jem's acting.

'Cut the sound effects, Jem,' he said briskly enough to sound like a reprimand. 'We can do without the groaning, OK?'

A minute or two later and they could hear Josh's count. 'Three, two, one…'

The doors swung open. Megan followed the stretcher that was supposedly arriving from the ambulance bay and pressed herself into a corner, out of the way. The paramedic who was helping started his handover, describing a serious incident in which a child had been struck by a car at speed.

'GCS on arrival was fifteen. Blood pressure was one-three-five on ninety. Resp rate thirty-six. Oxygen saturation ninety-nine per cent on air.'

As airway doctor, Ben Carter was leading the paediatric trauma team, consisting of other consultants, registrars, nurses and technicians. He requested another primary survey as soon as their patient was transferred to the bed.

The angle of the lights was checked, monitors switched on and trolleys moved closer. Megan could see the way Josh was following the movement of every person involved. He stood there, completely focused, looking tense enough to snap.

Findings were relayed via Josh, who was directing the scenario.

Strong peripheral pulses.

Pupils equal and reactive.

Tender abdomen.

Obvious midshaft, femoral fracture.

'IV line in and secured.' A registrar had taped a tube to Jem's arm. 'Hanging normal saline. Oh…where's the hook?'

An impatient sound came from Josh's direction as the minor missing detail was noted and fixed.

Ben was ordering blood tests and then X-rays. 'Neck, chest, abdomen and pelvis. We'll need CT on standby given the mechanism of injury.'

A nurse moved to test the phone lines. The X-ray technician manoeuvred overhead equipment. The staff were already wearing lead aprons, although no real X-rays were going to be taken. This was about testing the ceiling tracks and making sure that they could get the images that were needed quickly.

Josh stepped closer as soon as the process looked like it was not going to present any problems.

'The pelvic X-rays have shown fractures,' he announced. 'Your patient's now becoming restless and confused. He's vomited twice and his GCS has dropped below nine. Heart rate is rising and blood pressure is dropping.'

Ben nodded. 'We'll intubate prior to moving him to CT, then.'

Now they would all be able to see how well Megan's choice of positioning for equipment would work. The team had to pull in a ventilator and suction equipment, find ET tubes and laryngoscopes and draw up the drugs.

Megan didn't realise she was holding her breath until it became clear that everything was going like clockwork and then she released it in a long sigh. This was *great*.

The reporter thought so, too. He was scribbling madly on his notepad. The photographer was actually grinning as he took shot after shot.

Why wasn't Josh looking happier?

He almost seemed to be brushing off the congratula-tions that came in the wake of the successful test run.

'There's still a bit of fine tuning to be done,' Megan heard him tell someone. 'It has to be perfect before we officially open for business.'

'When's that going to be, Dr O'Hara?' The reporter pressed forward as people began to disperse.

'As soon as possible. You'll have to ask Dr Phillips. She's the one in charge of the project.'

The reporter nodded. 'And is it true that we've got a member of the Royal family coming to cut the ribbon? The Queen, even, or William and Kate?'

Josh managed a smile. 'You'll have to ask Dr White that one.'

But the reporter was distracted now. Behind Josh, Jem was sitting up on the bed, peeling off his neck brace.

'That was *so* cool!' he exclaimed. 'I could open my eyes just a crack and see through my eyelashes. I still looked unconscious, didn't I, Dad?'

'You sure did,' Nick told him. 'Good job. It wasn't scary, was it?'

'Nah.'

'What's your name, son?' The reporter asked. 'And how old are you? Can we get a photo?'

'Cool. I'll put this back on.' Jem lifted the neck brace.

'No, just hold it. Let's get your dad in the photo, too. You're Dr Tremayne, aren't you? What do *you* think of this new development at St Piran's?'

Megan decided to escape while she could. Why had Josh tried to deflect credit onto her? This whole project was his baby, everyone knew that. He'd been dreaming of it coming together for years now. Was he not happy with how things had gone today?

Where was he, anyway?

Ben Carter had gone back to his duties in the main department with most of the registrars and nurses who'd been involved in the practice run.

'Josh?' He shrugged in response to Megan's query. 'Hasn't come in here. He's probably lapping up a bit of the publicity. Hey…it went well, didn't it? Good job, Megan.'

She'd write a note, Megan decided, and leave it on Josh's desk. If he had a problem, he could come and talk to her about it.

The last thing she expected to find was Josh himself in his office.

No. Maybe the last thing was that fierce glare she was being subjected to.

'Sorry to disturb you.' She knew her tone was cool. 'I didn't think you'd be in here. I was going to leave you a note.'

'Why? Because you couldn't bring yourself to talk to me face to face?'

Megan gave her head a small, sharp shake. 'Don't be daft. I thought you'd be busy talking to that reporter or something.' The glare was getting on her nerves. She hadn't done anything wrong that she knew about. 'What's up with you today, Josh?'

'What's that supposed to mean?'

'You got out of bed on the wrong side or something. You're…angry about something.'

'Damned right I am.' Josh stalked across the office and pushed the door shut behind Megan. He turned to face her.

'You can't do it.' The words burst out of him.

Megan already knew what the answer would be. Her mouth went dry but she had to ask anyway. 'Can't do what?'

'Marry Charles.'

She sucked in a breath. She'd known that herself last night, the moment she'd seen the two men standing side by side in her living room.

Her lover and her friend.

Her past and her future.

Safety…and danger.

Charles had known it all along, of course, bless him, but he'd been waiting for her to wake up.

Should she tell Josh why the engagement had been mooted in the first place? That it was no longer a realistic option?

No. Dammit. What right did Josh have to glare at her like this? To be telling her what she could or couldn't do?

So she didn't say anything. She just held Josh's angry glare. Her heart was thumping so hard it was probably visible. She couldn't move. Couldn't even breathe right now. The sheer *power* of this man over her was unbelievably stunning.

The moment stretched until it was unbearable. Josh snapped first.

'Why him?' Josh took in an audible gulp of air. He was rubbing the back of his neck with his hand—a sure sign that he was deeply agitated. The expression on his face was…desperate? He opened his mouth again.

'Why not *me*?'

CHAPTER NINE

MEGAN'S BREATH CAME out in an incredulous huff of sound.

'You're not available, Josh,' she shot back. 'And even if you were, you couldn't give me what Charles could.'

The words might be cruel but they were true. It was the reason her plans had gone in the direction they had.

Josh had flinched. 'Which is?'

'Security,' Megan said decisively. But then her voice wobbled and went quiet. 'Love…' she added.

Josh was gaping at her now. 'How can you *say* that? You know how much I love you. *I'm* not the one who's moved on.'

'I…haven't. I…'

But Josh didn't appear to be listening to her. He'd stepped closer. Megan bowed her head as he took hold of both her shoulders. She could feel the strength in that grip. The tension. And yet the touch was still gentle.

'Can you honestly say you don't still love me, Megan?'

She had to lift her chin. To meet a gaze so intense it burned.

No. Of course she couldn't say that.

She didn't need to say anything. Josh had always been able to read her like an open book. She couldn't

look away. Neither could Josh. Not a word was spoken
but it felt like a whole conversation was taking place.
And the tension was leaving Josh's hands. His fingers
moved, skimming her neck to touch and then cradle
her face.

'Oh…Megan…' The words were a groan. Josh tipped
his head until their foreheads were touching and they
stood like that for a long, long moment. And then Josh
pulled her into his arms. So close she could feel his
heart thudding against her own. She could feel his lips
moving against her ear.

'I *can* love you,' he whispered. 'If only you'll give
me another chance. I've been blind. Stupid. I need you,
darling. I want you. I…I love you. *So* much.'

Oh…*God*…

The words echoed in her own heart. They stirred
up memories of similar words spoken in the past. And
more… So much more. They stirred up memories of
those intimate moments. The touch of those hands on
parts of her body that had lain dormant ever since. The
feel of his lips…and his tongue…on her mouth and her
breasts and…*ohh*…the feel of him inside her. The absolute perfection of that connection that she'd never
found—never *would* find—with anyone else.

How could she fight that, if there was even a small
chance that, this time, they could make it work?

She couldn't. She couldn't fight. Couldn't protect
herself any longer. She had to take this risk because if
she didn't, she would always wonder if it *could* have
worked. If cowardice had made her miss her chance
of true love and as happy-ever-after as this life could
offer anyone.

'I love you, too,' she heard herself whispering back
to Josh. 'I always have. Always will.'

'Oh, thank God for that.'

They loosened their hold on each other just enough to be able to see each other's faces. Josh still had a worried crease on his forehead.

'What about Charles? Your...engagement?'

'Charles has known all along how I feel about you, Josh. The engagement was only ever a...a means to an end, I guess. He's a friend, that's all. We weren't sleeping together.'

Megan's heart skipped a beat as the words left her mouth. She could see the effect of them on Josh. The knowledge that there was no barrier there any more. Josh wasn't married any longer. He was prepared to make a commitment. The children were being safely cared for by their grandmother.

He could take her hand and go home with her and they could go to bed together and make love. A fresh start.

The beginning of the rest of their lives?

'But... Oh, hell...' Josh groaned. 'Everybody around here thinks it was a real engagement. They'll blame me for breaking it up. There he goes again, they'll say, messing with people's lives.'

'It's got nothing to do with anybody else,' Megan said. 'Except for the children, of course. And your mum. And Tasha.'

'They'll all be thrilled that I've finally come to my senses. They all adore you. Especially Max and Brenna.'

'And I love them, too, but...' It was all too easy to get carried away by the heat of passion, wasn't it? There *were* other people to consider here. 'Maybe we can wait until the dust settles,' Megan suggested slowly. 'We don't have to rush out and tell anyone.'

We need to be sure about this was the silent message she was trying to send. *So that nobody gets hurt.*

Especially her? There was no doubt that Josh was genuine in *wanting* to make this commitment but was he actually *capable* of it? Maybe there was no way to protect herself any longer but, by keeping it a secret, she could keep a shred of dignity if it went wrong. Again.

Yes…the fear was still there. Easily dismissed right now but would it ever go away completely?

I am sure came back in that intense gaze, but then Josh seemed to take a deep breath. Did he want some kind of insurance policy too? Did he have that same tiny flicker of fear? Whatever he was thinking, he was clearly happy to follow Megan's lead.

'Things *are* crazy right now. We've got the official opening of the paediatric ED wing coming up and there's still a lot to do.'

The fact that Josh was happy to agree to her suggestion made that fear flicker a little brighter but Megan doused it. She took a deep breath herself. 'And there are all the donations to pull together and get shipped off. I'm supposed to go and talk to Albert about that tomorrow. He's getting worried about storing all the stuff that's coming in from other hospitals.'

'And Mum's going to be tearing her hair out in the next few days if she keeps tripping over all the cartons piling up at our place.'

Yes. There was a lot to do for the next little while. It would be best for all concerned to postpone that fresh start to their lives. Maybe they both just needed a little time. To trust completely.

Josh was smiling down at Megan. '*We'll* know,' he murmured. 'And that's what matters, isn't it?'

'Mmm.' This *was* all they needed. A little time. And

then the fear would burn itself out and things would be perfect. Megan's breath came out in a sigh as Josh lowered his head to kiss her tenderly. 'I...I can't believe how happy I am right now.'

'Mmm.' Josh broke the contact of their lips for just a heartbeat. 'Me, too.'

He hadn't been exaggerating to say that life was crazy right now.

And it was all so damn exciting!

Josh's life as a single father and full-time clinician had always been quite hectic enough, especially at this time of year with Christmas approaching. This year Christmas was barely registering yet, despite the decorations beginning to go up around the hospital.

Everywhere he turned at the moment, people were telling him how brilliant he was and how proud they were to be associated with St Piran's. They also wanted more of him. His secretary was complaining that it was becoming a full-time job trying to schedule all the requests for interviews and television appearances that were being lined up to follow the official opening of their emergency department extension. Not only that, the media had got wind of the hospital's involvement in Megan's project for Africa and somehow he was getting way too much of the credit. He seemed to be becoming the face of St Piran's and people were liking what they saw.

Over the last couple of days Josh had been hounded by a television company that was trying to persuade him to agree to base a reality TV show around the new paediatric emergency unit.

'We'll do a re-enactment of the story leading up to the emergency,' the producer had enthused. 'We'll have all the drama of the medical crisis and then we'll follow up. Interviews with the family and the staff. Real emotional stories, Doc, and we won't shy away from the gritty stuff. We'd have no trouble selling this worldwide. You'd be a superstar.'

Heady stuff, but Josh wasn't interested. What he wanted was to have an emergency department that was renowned for its excellence. One that would be the first choice for any case that was within range of an ambulance or helicopter.

The local air rescue service was making noises about needing another chopper and more staff to cope with the expected increase in workload the hype over the new facilities was generating. He needed to slot in a response to their request for an urgent meeting.

On top of all that, there had been more than one fundraising event to try and attend. With space on a cargo plane already booked and the deadline rapidly approaching, it seemed like the whole of Penhally Bay and St Piran were at a fever pitch to get their projects completed and packed up.

Josh had a new anxiety as he drove home each day, that the stress of all these unusual activities would be too much for his mother so soon after her heart attack, but, if anything, she seemed to be thriving on it all.

'Dinner's going to be a bit late,' she apologised on this occasion. 'Rita's on her way over to help me with the last of the book bags. She was going to come after dinner but Colin's come down with the horrible cold the whole family's had and she's promised to help out tonight.'

'I can fix dinner, if that would help,' Josh offered. He could see that Rita wasn't going to be the only visitor to the house today. Megan came out of the kitchen in the wake of Brenna, who had heard her father come home and was rushing to greet him. Megan had a wash-cloth in her hands.

'Warning,' she called. 'Major stickiness coming.'

Josh couldn't have cared less about the sticky hands that were already in his hair as he picked Brenna up for a cuddle. Finding Megan in his house was becoming a regular event due to Claire's pleas for advice on co-ordinating all the community donations for the clinic. If his mother was aware of any change in his relation-ship with Megan, she certainly wasn't showing any sign of disapproval. Not only was Megan being invited into the house more often, she was being invited to step fur-ther into the lives of his children. Helping to feed them. Reading them stories. And more.

'Would you mind getting the children into their bath, love?' Claire asked Megan now. 'I'm getting worried that we won't get this last crate finished and the truck's coming tomorrow.'

Josh surveyed the train wreck of his living area. Max was sitting amongst a pile of beautifully decorated ex-ercise books, trying to tear open a box of crayons.

'No, Max.' Claire rushed to rescue the crayons.

'Mine,' Max declared.

Josh saw Megan trying not to smile. She held out her hand. 'Hey, Max. How 'bout you come and show me your favourite toy for the bath? Is it a duck?'

'No.' Max scrambled upright. 'My *boat*.'

Josh looked at Brenna. 'Do you want Daddy to come and help with the bath too?'

'Yes. Daddy *and* Meggy,' Brenna shouted.

Max sneezed loudly and his grandmother sighed. 'I hope you're not getting Colin's cold,' she told him. 'Let me find you a tissue.'

The doorbell rang as she finished speaking and Claire flapped a hand in consternation, at a loss to know what to attend to first. Megan was really smiling now.

'Don't worry. I can sort the tissue.' She scooped Max into her arms before anyone could protest. Josh followed her up the stairs. He could hear his mother greeting her friend at the door, his daughter telling him something that made absolutely no sense, and even the strains of a Christmas carol coming from the radio that was on in the kitchen.

It sounded like home. Family. And Megan was here in the midst of it all.

A taste of the future?

Megan looked up from turning on the taps as he entered the bathroom. She caught his gaze and her own face lit up.

She understood perfectly.

In no time at all the bath contained two very happy toddlers, who were splashing and crowing with delight as Megan soaped their plump little bodies and then tipped buckets of warm water over them to rinse off the suds. The splashing was getting vigorous enough to make the adults kneeling beside the tub distinctly damp. Stray curls of Megan's hair were sticking to her face and Josh could feel damp strands of his own hair flopping into his eyes. He pushed them back.

'I need a haircut,' he muttered. 'Goodness only knows how I'm going to fit in an appointment before the opening.' His fingers rubbed his jaw as he dropped his hand. 'And I'm going to have to find time to shave more often.'

'You look great.' Megan slanted him a look that ignited a slow burn somewhere deep inside. 'When they see you on telly, women all over the country will be whimpering.'

Josh smiled back. 'Whimpering, huh?' He only had to tilt his body slightly for his shoulder to come into contact with Megan's body.

The eye contact had caught and was holding. Sending some very clear messages.

Oh…help… How long could they keep this up? This knowing that they had made a commitment to each other? That they wanted each other so much that it hurt? The anticipation that was building might be delicious but it was becoming unbearable.

It was just as well Max sneezed again at that point.

'Time to get you out, captain.' Josh caught the plastic tugboat in Max's hands just before it got smacked onto the water to create another satisfying splash. 'Small boys who are coming down with colds need to be tucked up in bed in their PJs.'

'Good thinking.' Megan had a towel ready to wrap around the slippery little body.

Brenna had her arms up, ready for her turn to come out of the bath. Josh wrapped her in a towel and started to dry her.

'Did Mum tell you that Tasha rang?'

'No.' Megan's teeth caught her bottom lip. 'I've been so slack…I've barely been in touch with her since I got back here.'

'You'll get plenty of time to catch up. She's coming over for the opening.'

'Is she?' Megan was guiding Max's feet into the holes of his pyjama legs. 'That's fantastic news.'

'It is. Alessandro can't make it but he's put their private jet at her disposal. Nice for some, huh?' Josh grinned. 'She said she was really coming because she wants to see you. The opening is just a bonus.'

'That's not true. She's just teasing.'

'I know. But she was really thrilled to know that you're still here. And I think she might have guessed about…you know…'

'Did you say something?'

'Not exactly.' Josh focused on doing up the buttons on Brenna's pyjama jacket. 'But she thought I was sounding unusually happy and demanded to know why. I said that things were looking up—that the changes at work were pretty exciting and that Mum had a new lease on life what with the African project. I…um… apparently wasn't very convincing.'

Megan smiled. 'She'll know soon enough. Everybody will.'

'Can't be soon enough for me.'

They had both finished dressing the children in their nightclothes. It was time to move but the pause button seemed to have been pushed again as they shared a long, significant glance.

'I'll get them into bed if you want to head downstairs and see how Mum is getting on. Don't want her overdoing things.'

'She's loving it.' Megan raised an eyebrow. 'I'm starting to wonder where she's going to direct all her newfound energy once this project is finished.'

'Don't worry.' Josh shook his head. 'Wait till you see what Christmas is like around here. She'll have more than enough to keep her busy and happy.'

Brenna had been listening, wide-eyed, to her father. 'Kiss miss,' she said clearly.

Josh caught Megan's laughing gaze. 'Oh, yeah…' he murmured. 'I'm planning to, don't you worry.'

* * *

Two days later, the contributions from hospitals all over Cornwall and from the communities of Penhally Bay and St Piran were packed onto a cargo plane and started the long journey to Africa.

Megan watched the plane take off.

She was alone at the airport. Claire would have loved to have come but Max was really miserable with his cold and Tasha was arriving tomorrow and all sorts of preparations needed to be made. There had been no way Josh could take the time to come with her either. The opening ceremony for the emergency paediatric unit was only a few days away now.

That was OK. Megan knew how important Josh's career was to him and making this long drive simply to see a plane take off had been purely sentimental, really, but the project had been hugely significant to Megan.

Life-changing, in fact.

If Anna hadn't come up with the idea in the first place and Megan hadn't run with it, she probably wouldn't have stayed long enough to not only deal with the past but to move past it into a future that was bright enough to blind her.

Was that why she had tears in her eyes that she had to blink away more than once on the long drive home?

Maybe it was partly due to this being the culmination of such astonishing generosity by so many people. It had all been a bit overwhelming, in fact. Especially when she'd seen Albert White early that morning. The CEO had handed her a large white envelope.

'Open tickets,' he'd told her. 'I know the consignment will get held up in customs and so forth for a while, but we know how much you'd like to make sure it gets to its destination and the board of trustees wanted to show their appreciation for the work you've put in over the last few weeks. It's a return airfare,' he'd added, 'because we're hoping very much that you'll want to come back. There's a consultant position in Paediatrics that's still available, you know.'

The envelope was still in her handbag but Megan had no idea when, or even if, she'd be able to make the long trip back to Africa herself.

Did she even want to now?

And what about that job offer?

Did she want to work full time again? Or work at all when she could be a full-time mother to the twins?

That they were Rebecca's children had become insignificant now that she'd opened her heart to Max and Brenna. She already loved them as much as a birth mother could have. You didn't have to give birth to feel like a real mother. Asha and Dumi had taught Megan that.

Another set of twins. A whole world away.

Would she ever see them again?

Why was it that making a choice had to involve some kind of loss? To be with Josh for the rest of her life was more than she could have dreamed of for her future but the joy was tinged with sadness as well.

Life was a funny business.

That sense of loss and sadness was still with Megan when she finally arrived home to a dark, chilly cottage. She flicked on some lights, contemplated lighting the fire but went to her kitchen to make a hot drink first. She dropped her handbag onto the table, ignoring the way it fell open and tried to spill its contents, and busied herself filling the kettle and switching it on.

The knock at her door came just as the kettle came to the boil and Megan knew instantly who it would be.

Any regret over losses made by her choices evaporated under the glow of joy as she went to answer the door.

Josh was leaning against the doorframe, his grin lazy and utterly gorgeous.

'I missed you today,' he said softly. 'Thought I'd pop in and say hello.'

'Oh…that's nice.'

More than nice. Megan was being backed up against the wall of her hallway. Josh kicked the door shut behind him with his foot an instant before his lips covered hers. She reached up to touch his face but found her hands grasped and held on either side of her head, also against the wall.

She was glad of the support because there was no mistaking where this kiss was going and she was melting inside at the onslaught to her senses. No way could her legs have held her up without some assistance.

Josh finally raised his head. 'I couldn't wait any longer.' His voice was hoarse with need. 'I haven't even been home yet.'

'You're with me.' Megan smiled. 'You *are* home.'

She could see the effect of her words as Josh's eyes glazed from the force of his desire. His hands were busy, undoing the buttons of her shirt. A second later and they were sliding inside her bra to cup her breasts. The shaft of sensation as his thumbs brushed her nipples was exquisitely painful and Megan couldn't see straight any more either.

'Not here,' she managed to gasp. 'Upstairs. Bed.'

'Oh, yeah…' Josh groaned. *'Bed.'* He scooped Megan into his arms as easily as if she'd been one of the twins and headed for the stairs. He didn't put her down until he was standing beside her bed and he didn't put her down on her feet. He dropped her, flat on her back, onto the bed and leaned over her, loosening his tie.

'Oh, Megan. You've got no idea how hard it's been, waiting for this.'

'I think I do.' Megan watched Josh hauling off his clothes but she didn't touch her own. Josh could do that, too. When he unbuckled his belt and let his trousers drop to the floor, her breath caught and Megan had the passing impression that it might be possible to die from desire that was *this* strong but even if it was possible, she didn't give a damn.

As the trousers hit the polished boards of her bedroom floor they made a noise that rapidly became recognisable as the ringtone of Josh's phone.

He made a very impatient sound. 'I'll turn it off.'

Naked, except for his underwear, he shook the trousers to extract the phone from the pocket. He glanced at it.

Megan could swear she felt the world stop spinning right then.

'It's Mum,' Josh muttered. 'She wouldn't ring unless it was important.'

Megan tried, and failed, to ward off a chill of premonition. 'You'd better answer it.'

He did. Megan knew that it was something serious as soon as he began speaking because Josh's voice took on the crisp focus that she'd only ever heard in the emergency department. When something important needed sorting out. The questions he was asking only confirmed her fear.

'When did it happen?

'How long did it last?

'Where are you now?

'Take his clothes off. Sponge him down with some tepid water. I'm on my way.'

Ending the call, Josh didn't pause for a moment. He was doing up the button on his trousers before he even turned back to Megan.

'Max has had a febrile convulsion,' he told her. 'Mum's called the ambulance but she's scared stiff. I have to go.'

'Of course. Oh, poor Max…'

She should be able to see this from a clinician's point of view. To be involved and caring but not panic the way a parent would. But she couldn't. The fear that gripped Megan was that of a mother, desperately afraid for her precious child.

'I'll come too.' Megan pushed herself to a sitting position. She tried to start doing up her buttons but her hands were shaking too much.

And Josh was shaking his head as he pulled on his shirt. 'No need. It's probably nothing. He's had a cold. This is most likely just an ear infection or something.'

But it could be something much worse. Meningitis? Encephalitis?

'Where the hell is my other shoe?' Josh was swinging his head, searching.

'Over there,' Megan told him. 'By the window.'

How could Josh be sounding like this? Like a doctor instead of a parent? This was weird…

Unless he could sense how Megan was feeling? Was he trying to push her back? To remind her that Max wasn't really *her* child?

That Rebecca was—and always would be—the twins' mother?

She had intended to get off the bed and help Josh find what he needed but Megan couldn't move now.

She was frozen with something like horror. And there was no need for her to move anyway. Josh was moving fast. Totally focused on what he needed to do.

What he'd needed when he'd arrived here was the last thing on either of their minds.

It'll be all right, Megan told herself. As long as he kisses me before he leaves.

But Josh didn't stop long enough to kiss her goodbye. He didn't even *look* at her as he rushed out of the door.

He said something but Megan would never know what those words had been because she'd been sucked back in time. To when she'd seen him again, an alarming number of days after they'd spent that passionate first night together. When he'd blanked her, as though that night had never happened.

It felt exactly the same right now.

He'd been about to make love to her and then, in the blink of an eye, it had been as though it had never been about to happen.

As though she hadn't even existed any more.

She didn't *matter*.

She couldn't stay here, on the bed, with her shirt still unbuttoned and her hair a tousled mess. Megan did up her shirt, forcing stiff fingers into action, but didn't bother touching her hair as she went downstairs.

It was ridiculous to feel like this.

Like what? *Betrayed*?

His child was sick. Maybe seriously sick. Of course Max had to be the priority.

But she was supposed to be sharing his life. Why had he shut her out? He hadn't even *looked* at her before he'd rushed off.

She couldn't do anything to prevent that old button

being pushed. The one that fired the emotions she'd been devastated by so many years ago. She'd felt so… used that first time. Used and cheap and stupid. Incredibly naïve and so very, very hurt.

What had Josh told her that day he'd come to pass on the news that Rebecca was pregnant? That his children had to be the most important thing in his life. The only thing that really mattered.

Apart from his career, of course.

He'd been far too busy to come with her today. Far too focused on the upcoming public acknowledgement of his brilliant bloody career.

Something far too close to panic was clutching at Megan now as she paced back and forth across her kitchen floor, her arms wrapped tightly around her body. There was no comfort to be found in the hug or the movement, however. Megan shivered. Her home felt cold and empty with the absence of Josh.

So did her heart.

This was exactly what she'd been afraid of. That she would put herself back into this space. Every step she had taken had made her feel closer to Josh. More a part of his family. That the future was safe from the kind of emotional trauma she *knew*, all too well, that he was capable of causing, whether or not it was intentional.

The panic caught and held. Spiralled.

What the hell was she going to do?

With a sob Megan collapsed into a chair beside the table. Her arms flopping onto its surface. Coming into contact with her handbag. Half-blinded by tears, Megan started automatically shoving the spilled contents of the bag back into place.

The last item her fingers closed over was a large white envelope.

With tears still streaming down her face, Megan stared at it blankly. And then she remembered what it contained.

Her fingers trembling, she opened the envelope.

CHAPTER TEN

'SHE'S GONE.'

Josh O'Hara scowled at his sister. 'What do you mean, she's *gone*?'

After a sleepless night, during which Max had been thoroughly checked and declared to be suffering from no more than an ear infection, Josh had taken the day off work so that he could collect his sister from the airport and look after the rest of his family.

Tasha had been desperately keen to see Megan so she'd taken Josh's car and gone to Megan's cottage as soon as she could without offending her family. She'd been gone a couple of hours and had now stormed back into the farmhouse, looking bewildered as she'd made her startling announcement.

Claire came down the stairs, having settled the twins for a nap. 'That paracetamol has worked a treat,' she said. 'Max doesn't even feel like he's running a temperature any more and he went out like a light. He's exhausted, poor lamb, after such a disrupted night. I'm feeling the same myself, so I am. I'm going to make a big pot of coffee.'

She stopped speaking and looked from her son to her daughter and back again.

'What on earth's the matter with you two?'

'Megan's gone,' Tasha said. 'The cottage is all locked up. I went to the most likely car rental agency and was told she handed in the vehicle and her keys very early this morning. She ordered a taxi. To take her to the airport.'

Déjà vu.

Josh could feel the blood draining from his brain, leaving a confused maelstrom of questions.

Why?

How could she do something like this?

Where had she gone?

What the hell has just happened here?

Snatches of answers were trying to compete.

You blanked her again, didn't you?

When you got the news about Max, she ceased to matter, when only minutes before she'd been the only thing that mattered.

He'd shut her out. Hurt her unbearably and she'd reacted the way she always had. By running away.

Surely by now she felt she could trust him? Running away was… It was verging on cowardly, wasn't it?

The blood was returning now. Boiling back as something like fury began to nibble its way through all the other devastating emotions swirling around.

Both Claire and Tasha were staring at him.

'Kitchen,' Claire commanded. 'We all need some coffee.'

Moving in a vaguely zombie-like fashion, Josh did as he was told. He needed to sit down, that was for sure. To try and get his head around this. Half of him was furious. The other half was numb. Stunned by a blow he hadn't expected.

Didn't deserve?

Maybe he did. For his past stupidity if not for how badly he'd handled this latest crisis.

He barely heard the chatter going on between Claire and Tasha as they made coffee.

'I'll do it, Mum. You sit down. You look exhausted and you've had a heart attack recently, for heaven's sake.'

'I'm fine. Or I will be when I know what on earth is going on around here to make Josh look like the world has ended. Out of the way, Natasha. Or make yourself useful and find some mugs.'

A chuckle from Tasha. 'You certainly sound like your old self. I'm sorry I couldn't come over when you were in hospital. I was feeling a bit sick myself for a few days there and we didn't know what it was.'

'You didn't say.'

'I didn't want to worry you. And I'm fine now, except for first thing in the morning.'

'Oh…' Claire dropped the lid of the biscuit tin. 'Are you…?'

'Yes.' The joy in Tasha's voice made Josh turn his head and tune in properly. 'I'm pregnant. Three months along now.'

'Why didn't you tell us?'

Tasha sat down at the table and sighed. 'I felt bad, you know? About telling Megan. Knowing that she can never have her own babies. It wasn't something I could tell her in a phone call or a text and…and I thought I could tell her face-to-face. Today. She texted me this morning but now her phone's turned off.'

'What did she text you about?' Josh demanded.

'Max.' Tasha closed her eyes. 'She wanted to know if he was OK. I told her everything was fine and I'd see her soon.'

'And?'

'And nothing. That was it.' Tasha shook her head. 'I could have walked past her at the airport without even knowing. Why has she gone? I would have thought the opening of the emergency paediatric unit was just as important for her as it is to you.' She opened her eyes and glared at Josh. 'This has got something to do with you, hasn't it? I know how much Megan loves you. Did you give her a reason to think it was all on again and then do something to show her that nothing had changed?'

It was Josh's turn to close his eyes. 'Something like that, I suppose,' he muttered.

There was a long silence. The groan from Josh broke it. 'I knew it was like this,' he said. 'I was right to want nothing to do with love. It only wrecks your life. Some-one always gets badly hurt.'

'Oh, *rot*,' Tasha said. 'Alessandro and I are as happy as any two people could be, thank you very much.'

Claire had totally forgotten about the coffee she was preparing. She sank into another chair at the table, her fingers at her neck, playing with her silver shamrock. She looked troubled.

'Do you love Megan, Josh?'

'Yes. Totally. As much as it's possible to love any-one.' He could feel his face settling into grim lines. 'But what's the point? She's gone. Again.'

'Wasn't she engaged? To that man from London?'

'Charles?' Tasha sounded astonished. 'No *way*...he was just a friend.'

'Not any more,' he told his mother.

Claire nodded. 'It was a second-best thing, then. Like you and Rebecca.'

'What's made her run away?' Tasha asked gently.
'Do you know?'

Josh didn't answer. If he did, he'd have to take the
blame, wouldn't he? And he wasn't the only one at fault
here. Megan had run away. Blanked him back in the
most blatant way possible. He had every right to be
furious with her, didn't he? Not that he expected his
mother or sister to buy into that. He was outnumbered
here, he could feel it.

'If you don't know, you need to find out,' Claire
said. 'For a bright boy, Josh, you can be a bit simple
sometimes.'

'I would have thought you'd understand better than
anyone,' Josh told her.

'What?'

'You loved Dad, didn't you?'

'Yes, of course I did. I wouldn't have married him
otherwise.'

'You loved him enough to take him back, time after
time, after his affairs. You believed it could work and
he just hurt you again and again. Hurt all of us.'

'Oh…' Claire looked devastated. 'You were just a
child. I thought I was doing the right thing, trying to
keep the family together.' She looked ready to cry. 'How
could I not see the damage that was happening?'

'Hey…I turned out just fine,' Tasha put in.

'Joshie was the oldest,' Claire said sadly. 'I leaned
on him. I let him see more than he should have seen
about how tough things were.' She reached out to touch
her son's arm. 'But you can't compare my marriage
to what you and Megan have. Have always had, from
what I've heard.'

'Why not?' It didn't bother Josh that his mother knew

far more than he'd realised. Nothing mattered right now except that he'd lost Megan.

Again. Maybe for good this time.

'The love in my marriage was one-sided,' Claire said sadly. 'Rory was fond of me, certainly, but he didn't *love* me. The balance was too wrong and *that* was why it never worked.'

Tasha was nodding. 'If you have real love on both sides, it's like a see-saw. Sure, it tips up and down a bit but you can always find the balance and when it's there, it's like a bridge into another world. Not a perfect world but...' Her smile was misty. 'It's as good as it gets.'

Josh knew that world. It was the space he could be in with Megan and no one else.

'You know how much you love your children,' Claire added. 'What that's like.'

Josh's smile felt rusty. 'It's the best feeling in the world.'

'Well, love between parents and children is pretty much a given,' Claire said sagely. 'When you get that kind of love between people who choose to be together, it's different but just as powerful.'

'Yes,' Tasha agreed. She had her hand on her belly. 'And when you combine all the different sorts of love in your life, that's when the real magic happens.'

'Like the sun that can shine through the worst of any weather,' Claire said softly.

'Or at least dry the puddles afterwards.' Tasha laughed. Then she sobered and patted Josh's hand. 'You and Megan have that. Put the past behind you once and for all and start again.'

The numbness was finally wearing off. The fury was still there but part of it was being directed internally now. Josh knew exactly what he needed to do. What he *had* to do. But was it too late?

'I have no idea where she's gone.'

'I think you do,' Tasha suggested.

'And if you don't, you can find out, for heaven's sake.' Claire sounded impatient. 'Ring that friend of hers that she isn't engaged to any more. Find out what plane she got on.' She clicked her tongue irritably. 'What on earth are you waiting for?'

Bleached, bone-thin cattle stirred the parched ground and made the dust swirl. Fortunately, there was no breeze to shift it any closer to where Megan was sitting beneath a skeleton tree that offered only a hint of shade.

Back at the camp for less than twenty-four hours, she was finding it a struggle to cope with the heat and the smell and how appallingly tired she was. The flight had been incredibly long. Plenty of time to catch her breath and reflect on her knee-jerk reaction of escaping Josh.

Why couldn't she get past the automatic response? Maybe it had been justified way back after their first night together because she'd had nothing to hang any kind of faith on. Now she *knew* how much Josh loved her.

But she'd known that last time, hadn't she? And then he'd come to her home and told her it was over—that they could never be together. Because the welfare of his children had to come first.

And it had been the welfare of those children that had sparked this reaction. Did she really think he would have come back from seeing Max at the hospital to tell her that he'd made a mistake and he couldn't include her in his life?

At that moment, yes... Her panic had been caused

by the fear of exactly that happening and the only way Megan had thought she could protect herself had been to somehow make it *not* happen.

And now here she was, having ensured that the worst-case scenario was firmly in place. The way she had when she'd made the mistake of not believing Josh when he'd tried to explain about sleeping with Rebecca again?

He wasn't even going to attempt to explain himself this time, though, was he? Megan had turned her phone on first thing that morning only to find her battery was flat. It was charging again now but unless there were texts or calls she'd missed in her travels, she wouldn't be hearing anything today.

It was opening day. The pinnacle, so far, of Josh's career. He'd already proved he could push her away for the sake of his children and Megan knew his career came a close second in his life priorities. It would be almost dawn in Cornwall right now. Was he awake already? Had he had a haircut? Would he shave for a second time, maybe, before heading off to face all the cameras and lights?

Megan shifted slightly, to ease the pins and needles in her arms.

'You're getting to be big lumps,' she told the two babies she held. She kissed one grizzled scalp and then the other, earning a toothless grin from Asha and a wave of two chubby fists from Dumi. 'Big, fat, healthy lumps. How good is that?'

One of the group of Somalian women Megan was surrounded by, Fatuma, was crouched beside her in the shade of the bare tree, holding a child of her own. She looked up and smiled. 'Fat.' She nodded. 'Is good.'

Megan kissed the babies again. 'It is,' she said softly.

Speaking in Somalian, she continued, 'Thank you so much for helping to care for them, Fatuma.'

'It is my honour,' was the reply. 'You saved my baby. I help yours.'

Megan nodded gravely. The exchange of gifts was respected.

For a minute both women watched the older children playing in the bare field near the cattle. They all held long sticks and there was a stone that was being scooted across the ground by being hit. Shrieks of laughter could be heard and it was a sound that could, temporarily at least, reduce the grim reality of these surroundings.

Still, Megan sighed.

'I wish they *were* really mine,' she said.

'They are the babies of your heart. They *are* yours.'

Megan nodded again. It was true. She had missed them so much. If she wasn't able to adopt them as a single woman and take them home, she would stay here despite the risk of dengue fever.

'Lots of insect repellent, I think,' she murmured.

Fatuma looked puzzled but then shaded her eyes to look towards where the sun was glinting off the corrugated-iron roof of the clinic buildings.

'Truck coming,' she sighed. 'More and more people.'

Idly, Megan followed her gaze. The truck was one of those ancient ones with a big wooden crate on its flat deck. A crowd of people stood in the crate, filling the space to uncomfortable levels. Not an unusual sight. What was unusual was a face amongst them that simply didn't fit.

A white face.

The truck stopped near one of the camp registration tents and the people spilled out over the back.

The heat suddenly seemed unbearable to Megan.

She could feel a trickle of sweat gluing the folds of her shawl to her back. Exhaustion and jet lag seemed to be combining to make her feel very odd. Unwell, even.

Or maybe it was just because missing Josh was so painful it was like having part of herself ripped away. The pain came in waves and this one was strong enough to have her hallucinating.

Imagining that the tall, lean figure leaping from the back of that truck was actually Josh. That he had come to the end of the earth to find her. That he was striding towards her, flanked by an entourage of curious children, through the shimmer of heat and clouds of dust like some kind of mirage.

Blinking didn't make things any clearer. Lack of oxygen wasn't helping but Megan couldn't take a new breath because...

Because it *was* Josh.

Unbelievably, Josh was here. In Africa. Clearly hell-bent on finding her. And as he got even closer, she could see the grim lines on his face.

'Megan Phillips,' he growled as soon as he got within range of being heard. 'Don't you *ever* run out on me like that again.'

This was the part of Megan that Josh had never met before.

Having released the pent-up combination of anger at the way she'd run out on him, fear that he might have lost her completely and sheer exhaustion from the hideously long journey, Josh took a deep breath and soaked in the relief of seeing her again.

Crouched on the arid African dirt, with a shawl covering her head and wrapped around her body, Megan was clearly a welcome companion for the other women who were so well shrouded only their faces were visible. Expressionless faces that were regarding him with barely restrained hostility in the silence that had fallen after his heated reprimand by way of a greeting for Megan. Even the children playing nearby were standing still, as frozen as everybody else by this startling turn of events.

'Y-you…you *c-can't* be here,' Megan stammered.

'Why not?' Oh…*God*…she didn't want him to be here?

The woman closest to Megan touched her arm and said something in her own language. Megan answered in the same language. The words were incomprehensible but the tone was clearly reassuring. Her companion got to her feet with graceful ease and, by some unseen signal, all the others followed her lead. The children still clustered around Josh were shooed away. Someone offered to take the babies from Megan but she shook her head, smiling.

When the crowd had virtually melted away, Megan looked directly at him.

'Isn't it the opening today?' she asked quietly. 'The new wing of *your* department?'

Josh merely shrugged. 'Ben Carter's looking after that. He was happy to cope with all the publicity and I was more than happy to let him have the glory.'

'But…' Megan looked completely bewildered. 'It's been so important to you. You've dreamed about this happening for years.'

Josh stepped forward and crouched down in front of Megan. He wanted to take her in his arms but she still had her arms full of babies. And he still didn't know whether he was welcome here or not.

'It's not as important to me as you are,' he said

slowly. 'I've dreamed of being with you a hell of lot longer than having a paediatric wing in my emergency department.'

A spark of what looked like hope flashed in the emerald-green depths of Megan's eyes but then they clouded again. She seemed to be having trouble processing his words.

'The children,' she whispered. 'Oh…*Max*.' She looked incredulous now. He'd left a sick child to come here?

'Max is fine.' Josh was unconsciously using the gentlest tone he had. The one that was so useful to soothe a frightened patient or its parent. 'He's on antibiotics for his ear infection and he'd bounced back, the way children so often do. Mum's looking after them. And Tasha's helping. Getting some quality "auntie" time. And some practice.'

The hint wasn't picked up. He could see Megan swallow hard.

'You're really here,' she murmured. 'You came all this way. For me?'

'For you,' Josh confirmed. 'I needed to apologise for the way I shut you out the other night. I just wasn't thinking and I'm so sorry I scared you.' His smile was crooked. Self-effacing. 'I know it's not much of an excuse but I am a man. I'm not good at multi-tasking.'

A snort of something like laughter escaped Megan. Unable to resist touching her, Josh reached towards her face, wanting to stroke her cheek. His hand became hijacked halfway there, however, caught by a tiny, dark hand. The grip was remarkably tight.

'Hello, there.' Josh smiled at the baby. 'Are you Asha?'

'No. That's Dumi.'

'May I?' Josh moved to pick up the baby. 'I know what it's like, juggling twins.'

Megan said nothing. She was watching Dumi, who gurgled with pleasure and held up both arms when he felt Josh's hands around his body. Josh gazed down at the small face and felt an odd tightness in his chest when Dumi's face suddenly split into a wide, toothless grin.

'He likes you.' Megan smiled for the first time since he'd arrived.

'He's gorgeous,' Josh said. 'They both are. Beautiful babies.'

'My babies,' Megan said softly. 'I'm going to adopt them. That's why I asked Charles to marry me in the first place because I thought the process would be a lot easier if there were two parents available, but…I could still do it, I think. I'm going to try, anyway.'

Josh nodded solemnly. She'd been a mother to these babies since the moment they'd entered the world. This was the unknown part of the woman he'd always loved and understanding this bond she had with these babies only made him love her even more.

'It would be good for them to have a father, though, wouldn't it?'

Megan's eyes were wide. Watching him intently.

'My babies would love to have a mother,' Josh continued. Oh…help…could he put what he wanted to say into the right words? 'You love Max and Brenna, don't you? Enough to be their mum?'

Did she love the twins she'd left behind in Cornwall?

Did it compare with the love she had for this man, who'd traversed the globe to find her? A love that was threatening to overwhelm her?

'Of course I do,' Megan whispered. 'They're part of you. How could I not love them?'

'Snap.' Josh smiled slowly. 'And I've just found the part of you that I knew was missing.' He took a deep breath. 'Come home with me, my love. Marry me. We'll both adopt Asha and Dumi and bring them up with a big brother and sister.'

'Oh…' The words painted a picture of a perfect future. One that Megan hadn't even dared to dream of when she'd put her trust in Josh's new commitment. She gave her head a tiny shake. 'Whatever would your mother say if she found herself a grandma to African babies?'

'She'd be thrilled to bits,' Josh said. 'You know what she said when she was driving me to the airport?'

'What?' Josh was leaning closer. So close the babies they were holding were able to reach out and grasp the hand of the other. They both gurgled happily.

'She said I would be a better father if I was a truly happy man, and a blind person could see that I was never going to be happy without you. That I needed you. That we all needed you. *Make sure you bring her back*, she said, *for all our sakes*.'

He leaned even closer and Megan felt herself sway towards him. Over the heads of the two babies their lips met in a gentle kiss.

'I love you,' Josh whispered. 'More than I'll ever be able to tell you.'

'Snap.' Megan's voice wobbled. Tears of joy were very, very close.

'Give me the chance to show you. Every day. For the rest of our lives. Could you do that?'

Megan could only nod. She could do more than that. She could use every day of the rest of their lives to show Josh that she loved him every bit as much. Starting right now. She closed the gap between them and kissed him again.

How tender could a kiss be? How much love could it convey? How sure a promise of the future could it seal?

A lot, apparently.

Much more than enough, anyway.

On both sides.

EPILOGUE

A BIRTHDAY PARTY for twelve-year-olds was bound to be a noisy affair.

Especially in the O'Hara household, with so many blessings in the way of family and friends.

Claire O'Hara's knees were a little stiff these days, so she moved from where she was standing on the edge of the veranda watching the game of football happening on the lawn to sink down into one of the comfortable wicker chairs.

'You all right, Claire?' Megan came bustling out of the house, a bunch of carrots dangling from her hand but paused, concern furrowing her brow. 'Is your knee bothering you again?'

'I'm just fine, lovie.' She eyed the carrots. 'Are you heading for the ponies?'

Megan grinned. 'We'll never get the girls back inside for food if I don't drag them out of the paddock. Want to come with me?'

'I went up before. You'd better take your camera. The ponies are looking very pretty with all their plaits and ribbons.'

'Good thinking.' But Megan didn't move to rush back into the house.

She wasn't looking at her mother-in-law any more,

either. A tall figure had broken away from the game of football and was coming towards the house. Even from this distance Claire could see that her son only had eyes for one person right now. She could feel the connection between the two of them, getting steadily stronger with every step Josh took. The strength of that connection never failed to take her breath away.

Was it really ten years since Josh had come back from Africa and brought Megan back into their lives for good?

Such incredibly happy years.

Oh, there'd been the anxious wait about the adoption of Dumi and Asha and it had taken a while but what a honeymoon, to have gone back over there and brought the new babies home to complete their family! Claire had stayed in the farmhouse only long enough to re-alise what a superb twin-wrangler and mother Megan was and then, with one of those lovely twists that life could suddenly produce, she took over Megan's little cottage for her home and it was perfect. An easy walk to the lovely beach that made it so perfect for all her grandchildren to visit.

Josh had reached the veranda now and he and Megan were just standing there, smiling at each other—as though it had been only yesterday that they'd fallen in love.

'Need any help?' Josh queried.

'You're doing great,' Megan said softly. 'You and Alessandro really know how to keep a bunch of small boys happy.'

'We've had plenty of practice,' Josh laughed.

Yes. The O'Hara children's royal cousins were here for this celebration. Three little boys in the last decade and Marco, Alessio and Rocco were out there having a wonderful time kicking the football with Max and Dumi. Even better, Tasha was in the house behind them, feeding the brand new and much longed for princess, Alandra, named for her father.

'I'm going to round up the girls,' Megan said. 'Anna and the others have got the table all set. How's Luke going firing up the barbecue?'

'I'm just going to check.' Josh turned away but not before he'd given Megan one of those lingering kisses that always made Claire's eyes go all misty. He turned back once more. 'You all right, Mum? You're not sitting out here all by yourself, are you?'

'No. I've got company.' Claire dropped her hand to where she knew it would encounter the roughened fur of an elderly companion. Crash was nearly thirteen now and getting stiffer in the joints than she was but he was a part of this family. So were Anna and Luke and their two children. Six year old Chloe loved to tag along in the wake of the older girls and nine year old Ben was a keen surfer and a best friend for Max and Dumi. As close as anyone could get given the bond between the brothers, that is.

Claire had to blink more mistiness away as Josh and Megan left to attend to party business. Who would have thought that two sets of such very different twins could blend to become such a perfect family? Eleven year old Dumi stood a head taller than twelve year old Max already but he had a gentle soul and the whitest, happiest smile that brightened the lives of anyone fortunate enough to be within range. The boys adored each other.

Brenna and Asha were completely different, too. Brenna was a total tomboy and Asha as feminine as they came but the two girls had also bonded as babies and now shared the passion of ponies. How Megan found the energy to ferry them to pony club and events was astounding given that she had been working part time at St Piran's ever since all the children had started school. Josh was just as amazing. His career still seemed to be on an upward trajectory, with his skills as a consultant in such demand and a new book due to be published on setting up and running an emergency department. He still loved to work on the front line, however and somehow he found the time to be involved with the boys' football practices and matches. Somehow, Josh and Megan had found a balance. Professional, personal and parental and they could work as a team and keep everybody happy.

The noise level increased. Claire stayed in her chair with Crash at her feet as the party attendees streamed past her on their way to the food. She smiled and Crash thumped his tail as children and adults greeted him and 'Nanny Claire' on their way past.

'Are you having a good birthday, Max?' she asked her grandson.

'The best,' he said, pushing his mop of black curls back and grinning at her. Heavens, but he was the spitting image of his dad at that age.

And so much happier…

'To be sure,' Dumi added with a cheeky grin and the Irish accent he'd perfected to make his grandmother laugh.

It never failed.

Claire was still smiling as the excited troop of girls began to appear from where they'd been dressing up the ponies.

Behind them, she could see Megan. And Josh.

Walking hand-in-hand.

She lost sight of them for a moment, as the girls

swept past but then she saw them again. All by themselves for a precious moment, in the garden of their home, with the beautiful backdrop of Penhally Bay sparkling blue in the sunshine.

They didn't see Claire watching them.

How could they, when they both so intent on kissing each other?

With an effort, accompanied by the happiest of sighs, Claire got out of her chair to make her way inside and join the happy gathering of her family and friends.

Life was good, so it was.

* * * * *

SYDNEY HARBOUR HOSPITAL: EVIE'S BOMBSHELL

BY
AMY ANDREWS

*This book is dedicated to all the loyal Medical Romance™ fans
who always look for our books and love a good series!*

First published in Great Britain 2013
by Mills & Boon, an imprint of Harlequin (UK) Limited.
Harlequin (UK) Limited, Eton House, 18-24 Paradise Road,
Richmond, Surrey TW9 1SR

© Harlequin Books S.A. 2013

Special thanks and acknowledgement are given to Alison Ahearn
for her contribution to the *Sydney Harbour Hospital* series

ISBN: 978 0 263 89882 8

Harlequin (UK) policy is to use papers that are natural, renewable
and recyclable products and made from wood grown in sustainable
forests. The logging and manufacturing process conform to the
legal environmental regulations of the country of origin.

Printed and bound in Spain
by Blackprint CPI, Barcelona

Dear Reader

Ever since the *Sydney Harbour Hospital* series hit the shelves readers have been asking for Finn and Evie's story. And I can't blame them, because I have to admit to more than a passing fascination myself as I wrote their sub-plot in Mia and Luca's story. But I just kept thinking: There's no way Finn can be redeemed—it'll never be done. I pity the one they ask to do that.

And then they asked me to do it…gulp!

But in all honesty I was ecstatic to be chosen, because I'd already written a prequel for Finn and Evie quite a few months prior—their very first meeting—so I've been invested in their HEA for a while and I do so like a challenge…

But how do you redeem a man who's as emotionally shut down as Finn? Evie's been trying for years to reach him with no success. Well, it wasn't easy. I had to strip him right back and throw a huge curve ball at him, and then have the one person he's always counted on subconsciously to be there, despite his perennial bad mood, walk away.

Yep, Finn was a tough one—but Evie was tougher. She refused to take his scraps, demanding all of Finn. Demanding the fairytale. Refusing anything less.

And she got it too.

I hope you enjoy their journey to Happy-Ever-After-land.

Amy

**Praise for
Amy Andrews:**

'A spectacular set of stories by Ms Andrews,
the ITALIAN SURGEON TO DAD! duet book
features tales of Italian men who know how to
leave a lasting impression in the imaginations of readers
who love the romance genre.'
—*Cataromance.com* on
ITALIAN SURGEON TO DAD! duet

'Whether Amy Andrews is an auto-buy for you,
or a new-to-you author,
this book is definitely worth reading.'
—*Pink Heart Society Book Reviews* on
A MOTHER FOR MATILDA

Amy also won a RB*Y
(Romantic Book of the Year) Award in 2010 for
A DOCTOR, A NURSE, A CHRISTMAS BABY!

PROLOGUE

EVIE LOCKHEART BELTED hard on the door, uncaring if the whole building heard her. Loud rock music bled out from around the frame so she knew he wasn't asleep. 'Open up now, Finn Kennedy,' she yelled, 'or so help me I'm going to kick this fancy penthouse door right in!'

She glared at the stubbornly closed object. It had been two weeks since he'd been discharged from hospital after the less than stellar success of his second operation. Two weeks since he'd said, *Get out. I don't want you in my life.* Two weeks of phoning and texting and having one-sided conversations through his door.

And it was enough.

She was sick of Finn shutting her out—shutting the world out.

And if she didn't love him so much she'd just walk away and leave him to rot in the cloud of misery and denial he liked to call home.

But memories of the infection he'd picked up after his first operation and the state he'd got himself into as he'd tried to self-treat were never far from her mind and she was determined to check on him whether the stubborn fool wanted her to or not.

She was about to bash on the door again when the lift

behind her dinged and Gladys stepped out. She'd never been happier to see Finn's cleaner in her life.

'Gladys, I need Finn's key.'

The older woman's brow crinkled in concern as she searched through her bag. 'Is he all right? Is he sick again?'

'No,' Evie dismissed. Gladys had found Finn collapsed on the floor overwhelmed by his infection and still hadn't quite got over the shock. 'He's probably fine but I'd like to see it with my own two eyes.' *Then I'm going to wring his neck.*

Gladys stopped her frantic search. 'He was fine yesterday,' she hedged.

Evie had to stop herself from knocking the dear sweet little old lady, who also happened to clean her apartment along with many others at *Kirribilli Views,* to the ground and forcibly searching her bag.

'He told you not to give me the key, didn't he?'

Gladys looked embarrassed. 'I'm sorry, Evie. But he was very firm about it.'

Evie suppressed a scream but she stood her ground and held out her hand. 'Gladys, I'm begging you, one woman to another, I need to see him. I need the key.'

Gladys pursed her lips. 'You love him?'

Evie wasn't surprised that Gladys was in the gossip loop, given how long rumours about she and Finn had been floating around Sydney Harbour Hospital and how many of its staff lived at Kirribilli Views. She nodded, depending on the incurably romantic streak she knew beat inside the old cleaner's chest.

'Yes.' Although God knew why. *The man was impossible to love!*

Gladys put her hand in her bag and pulled out a set

of keys. 'He needs someone to love him,' she said, holding them out.

'He needs a damn good spanking,' Evie muttered, taking the keys.

Gladys grinned. 'That too.'

'Thanks,' Evie said.

'I'll leave his apartment till last today,' the elderly woman said, and turned back towards the lift.

Finn glared at her as the door opened and Evie felt the glacial chill from his ice-blue eyes all the way across the room, despite the darkened interior from the pulled-down blinds. 'Remind me to sack Gladys,' he said as he threw back the amber contents of a glass tumbler.

Evie moved towards where he was sitting on the couch, noticing how haggard he was looking. His usual leanness looked almost gaunt in the shadows. His regular stubbly appearance bordering on scruffy. His dark brown hair messy as if he'd been constantly worrying at it with agitated fingers. The light was too low to see the streaks of grey that gave him that distinguished arrogant air he wore so bloody well.

How could a man look like hell and still cause a pull low and deep inside her? And how, *damn it all*, could he stare at her with that morose belligerence he'd perfected and still not kill off her feelings for him?

Finn Kennedy was going to be the death of her. God knew, he'd already ground her pride into the dust.

The coffee table halted her progress and she was pleased for the barrier as the urge to shake him took hold. 'You're drunk.'

'Nope.' He poured himself another finger of Scotch from the bottle on the coffee table. 'Not yet.'

'It's three o'clock in the afternoon.'

He raised his glass to her. 'I appreciate this booty call, but if you don't mind I have a date with my whisky glass.'

Evie watched him throw it back, despairing how she could get through to him. 'Don't do this to yourself, Finn. It's early days yet.' She looked down at his right arm, his lifeless hand placed awkwardly on his thigh. 'You need to give it time. Wait for the swelling to subside. Rupert's confident it'll only be temporary. You'll be back operating again before you know it'

Finn slammed his glass down on the table. 'Go away, Evie,' he snapped.

Evie jumped but refused to be cowed. He'd been practically yelling at her and telling her to go away for their entire relationship—such as it was. But there'd been other times—tender moments, passionate moments—and that was the real Finn she knew was hidden beneath all his grouchy, arrogant bluster.

She understood why he was pushing her away. Knew that he didn't want to burden her with a man who would be forever less in his eyes because he might not ever again be the one thing that defined him—a surgeon.

But surely that was her choice?

'No. I love you and I'm not going anywhere.'

'I don't want you to love me!' he roared.

Evie came around to his side of the table until she was standing right in front of him. 'Well, you don't always get what you want in life Finn—*not even you.*' She shoved her hands on her hips. 'If you want me to leave then you're going to have to get your butt off that lounge and make me.'

'Oh, I see,' he said, his lip curling. 'This *is* a booty call.'

She endured a deliberately insulting look that raked over her body as if she was sitting in a window in Amsterdam.

'What's the matter, Princess Evie, feeling all horny and frisky with nowhere to put it? *Been a while, has it*? You really needn't have dressed for the occasion. Us one-armed guys can't afford to be choosy, or hadn't you heard?'

Evie had just come from lunch with her sisters and as such was dressed in a pencil skirt that came to just above her knee and a satiny blouse that buttoned up the front and fell gently against her breasts. Her hair was loose and fell around her shoulders.

She ignored him. She would not let his deliberate insults deter her from her goal. 'Let me help you, Finn. Please.'

His good hand snaked out and snagged her wrist. He yanked and she toppled forward, her skirt pulling tight around her thighs as she landed straddling his lap, grabbing at his shoulders for stability.

'Is this what you wanted?' he demanded. 'You want to see how I do this with one hand?' He groped a breast. 'Or this?' he persisted, letting his hand slide down to where her skirt had ridden up, pushing his hand up beneath the fabric, gliding it up her thigh, taking the fabric with him until it was rucked up around her hips and her legs were totally exposed, his hand coming to rest on the curve of one cheek.

Evie felt the drag of desire leaden in her belly as she fought against the seductive allure of her erect nipples and the quivering flesh in his palm. The heat in his gaze burnt into her with all the sear factor of a laser.

'You want to help me feel like a man again?' he sneered, his breath fanning her face. 'You want to take a ride on the one thing I have that *is* fully functional? You want to *screw*, Evie?'

Evie steeled herself against his deliberately crude taunts. He was lashing out. But she wasn't going to respond with the venom his remark deserved.

Because that's what he wanted.

'I just want to love you, Finn,' she said quietly, refusing to break eye contact even though she knew he was trying to goad her into it. Her pulse roared in her ears and her breath sounded all husky and raw. 'Let me love you.'

Evie watched as all the fight went out of him. His hand dropped from her bottom and then he looked away. 'I can't even touch you properly, Evie.'

She grabbed his face and forced him to look at her, his stubble almost soft now it was so long—more spiky than prickly. 'You have this,' she said, her thumb running over the contours of his mouth. 'Which, when it isn't being vicious and cruel, can melt me into a puddle.'

She grabbed his left hand with her right hand and brought it up to her breast. 'And this,' she said, her nipple beading instantly. 'Which knows its way around a woman's body as well as the other.'

Evie saw his pupils dilate as he dropped his gaze to look at his hand on her breast. He stroked his thumb across the aching tip and she shut her eyes briefly.

'And,' she said, dragging herself back from the completely wanton urge to arch her back, 'this.' She tucked her pelvis in snugly against his and rubbed herself against the hard ridge of his arousal.

'And I can do the rest.'

She put her hands between them and her fingers felt for his button and fly and in that instant Finn stopped wrestling his demons. His mouth lunged for hers, latching on and greedily slaking his thirst as his good hand pulled at her blouse then yanked, popping the buttons.

He grunted in satisfaction, his mouth leaving hers, as her hand finally grasped his erection. His grunt became a groan as he blazed a trail down her neck, his whiskers spiky and erotic against the sensitive skin. He yanked her bra cup aside and closed his hot mouth over a nipple that was already peaked to an unbearable tightness.

Evie's eyes practically rolled back into her head and there was no coherent thought as she mindlessly palmed the length of him and cried out at the delicious graze of his teeth against her nipple.

She wasn't aware his hand had dropped, distracted as she was by the combined pleasure of savage suction and long hot swipes as his tongue continually flayed the hardened tip in his mouth. She wasn't aware of him pushing her hand out the way, of him shoving her underwear aside, of him positioning his erection to her entrance, until it nudged against her thick and hard, and then her body recognised it, knew just what to do and took over, accepting the buck and thrust of him, greedily inflaming and agitating, meeting him one for one, adjusting the tilt of her pelvis to hit just the right spot.

It was no gentle coupling. No languid strokes, no soft caresses and murmured endearments, no long, slow build. It was quick and hasty. Just like their first time. Parted clothes. Desperate clawing at fabric, at skin. At backs and thighs and buttocks. Hitting warp speed instantly, feeling the pull and the burn from the first stroke.

Except this time when Finn cried out with his release, his face buried against her chest, he knew it was goodbye. That he had to get away. From Sydney. From the Sydney Harbour Hospital. From Evie.

From this screwed-up dynamic of theirs.

But for now he needed this. So he clutched her body to his and held on, thrusting and thrusting, prolonging the last vestiges of pleasure, finding a physical outlet for the vortex of grief and pain that swirled inside.

Holding on but saying goodbye.

CHAPTER ONE

Five months later

'WHERE IS HE, Evie?' Richard Lockheart demanded of his daughter. 'Prince Khalid bin Aziz wants Finn Kennedy and only Finn Kennedy to do his quadruple by-pass and he's going to donate another million dollars to the hospital to show his appreciation. Sydney Harbour Hospital needs him, Evie. Where is he?'

'I don't know,' Evie said staring out of her father's office window at the boats sailing on the sparkling harbour, wishing she was riding out to sea on one and could leave all her troubles behind her.

'Evie!'

She turned at the imperious command in his voice. 'What makes you think that I know where he is?' she snapped at her father.

'I'm not stupid, Evie. Do you think hospital gossip doesn't reach me all the way over here? I know you and he have a…had a…thing. A fling.' He shrugged. 'Whatever you want to call it. I'm assuming you've kept in touch.'

If Evie needed any other proof of how out of touch her father was with her life, or with life in the trenches generally, she'd just found it. If he knew Finn at all he'd know that Finn wasn't the keeping-in-touch type.

In the aftermath of their frenzied passion five months ago she'd hoped there'd been some kind of breakthrough with him but then he'd disappeared.

Overnight. Literally.

Gladys had told her the next day that he'd gone and handed her a note with seven words.

Goodbye Evie. Don't try and find me.

After all they'd been through—he'd reduced their relationship to seven words.

'Evie!' Richard demanded again, at his daughter's continuing silence.

She glared at her father, who was regarding her as if she was two years old and deliberately defying him, instead of a grown woman. A competent, emergency room physician.

'The state of play between Finn and I is none of your damn business.'

'*Au contraire*,' he said, his brows drawing together. 'What happens at this hospital *is* my business.'

Richard Lockheart took the *business* of Sydney Harbour Hospital very seriously. As its major benefactor he worked tirelessly to ensure it remained the state-of-the-art facility it was, carrying on the legacy of his grandfather, who had founded the hospital. Sometimes she thought he loved the place more than he'd ever loved his wife and his three daughters.

Evie sighed, tired of the fight already. She was just so bloody tired these days. 'Look,' she said, reaching for patience, 'I'm not being deliberately recalcitrant. I really don't know where he is.'

She turned back to the view out the window. His

brief impersonal note had been the final axe blow. She'd fought the good fight but there were only so many times a girl could take rejection. So she'd made a decision to forget him and she'd navigated through life these past five months by doing just that. By putting one foot in front of the other and trying not to think about him.

Or what he'd left behind.

But there'd only ever been a finite amount of time she could exist in her state of denial and the first flutterings this morning had brought an abrupt end to that. She couldn't deny that she was carrying his baby any longer.

Or that he deserved to know.

She turned back to her father. 'I think I know somebody who might.'

Evie had spent the last three afternoons pacing back and forth outside Marco D'Avello's outpatients rooms, waiting for his last expectant mother to leave, summoning up the nerve to go in and see him then chickening out each time as the door opened to discharge a patient.

Today was no different. It was five o'clock, the waiting area was empty and his door opened and she sprang from the seat she'd not long plonked herself in for the hundredth time in half an hour and headed for the lift.

'Evie?'

His rich, beautifully accented voice stopped her in her tracks. Evie had to admit that Emily, his wife and a midwife at the hospital, was an exceptionally lucky woman to wake up to that voice every morning. Not to mention the whole dark, sexy Italian stallion thing he had going on.

Just waking up with the person you loved sounded pretty good to her.

He walked towards her. 'I have been watching you outside my door for three days now.' His voice was soft. 'Would you like to see me?'

Evie dithered. She wasn't sure what she wanted. She didn't know what an obstetrician could tell her that she didn't already know. And yet here she was.

'Come,' he murmured, cupping his hand under her elbow.

Evie let herself be led. Why couldn't she love someone like Marco? Someone who was gentle and supportive?

And capable of love.

She heard the door click behind her and sat in the chair he shepherded her towards. 'You are pregnant. Yes?' he said as he walked around to his side of the desk.

Evie startled gaze flew to his. 'How did you…?' she looked down at her belly, placing her hand over the bump that was obvious on her spare athletic frame if she was naked but not discernible yet in the baggy scrubs she wore at work.

Marco smiled. 'It's okay, you are not showing. I'm just a little more…perceptive to this sort of thing. I think it goes with the job.'

Evie nodded, her brain buzzing. She looked at him for long moments. 'I'm sorry. I don't know why I'm here.'

He didn't seemed perturbed by her strange statement. She was pregnant. He was an obstetrician. It was where she should be. Where she should have been a lot earlier than now.

He just seemed to accept it and waited for her to talk some more.

'I haven't told anyone. No one knows,' she said, trying to clarify.

'How many weeks?'

'Eighteen.'

Marco frowned. 'And you haven't seen anyone yet?'

'I've been…busy.' Evie felt her defences rise, not that Marco seemed to be judging her. 'It's always crazy in the emergency department and…time gets away…'

She looked down at her hands still cradling her bump because what excuse was there really to have neglected herself, to have not sought proper antenatal care?

She was a doctor, for crying out loud.

'You have been well?'

Evie nodded, dragging her gaze back to Marco. 'Disgustingly. A few weeks of vague nausea in the beginning. Tired. I've been really tired. But that's it.'

She'd expected the worse when she'd first discovered she was pregnant. She'd figured any child of Finn's was bound to be as disagreeable as his father and make her life hell. But it had been a dream pregnancy to date as far as all that went.

Which had only made it easier for her to deny what was really happening to her body.

'We should do some bloods,' Marco said. 'Why don't you hop up on the couch for a moment and I'll have a feel?'

Evie nodded. She made her way to the narrow examination table and lay staring at the ceiling as Marco palpated her uterus then measured the fundal height with a tape measure. 'Measurements seem spot on for eighteen weeks,' he murmured as he reached over and flipped on a small ultrasound machine.

'No,' Evie said, half sitting, pulling down her scrub top. 'I don't want to…I don't want an ultrasound.'

She didn't want to look at the baby. Not yet. She'd made a huge leap forward today, finally admitting the pregnancy to someone else. She wasn't ready for a meet and greet.

And she knew that made her all kinds of screwed up.

'I'm sorry,' she apologised. 'That's probably not the reaction you're used to.' She couldn't explain why she didn't want to see the baby—she just knew she didn't. Not yet.

Marco turned off the machine and looked down at her and Evie could tell he was choosing his words carefully. 'Evie…you have left it too late to…*do* something about the pregnancy.'

Evie struggled to sit up, gratefully taking Marco's proffered hand as she sat cross-legged on the narrow couch. She had thought about termination but as with everything else pregnancy related she'd shoved it determinedly to one side.

She'd spent the past eighteen weeks not thinking about the baby—her body aiding and abetting her denial by being virtually symptom-free.

She looked at Marco. 'I know. I don't want to.'

She stopped. *Where had that come from?*

Termination had been an option and one, as a doctor and a woman, she firmly believed should be available, but suddenly she knew deep down in the same place that she'd known she loved Finn that she loved his baby too. And that nothing would come between them.

He may not have let her in, let her love him, but there would be no distance between Finn's child and her.

She gave Marco a half-smile. 'I'm sorry. I don't think

I really accepted until the baby moved a few days ago that I was actually pregnant. I'm still trying to…process things.'

He smiled back. 'It's okay. How about we listen to the heartbeat instead and get some bloods done as a first step?'

Evie nodded and lay back and in seconds she was listening to the steady whop-whop-whop of a tiny beating heart. Her eyes filled with tears. 'There really is a baby in there.'

Marco smiled at her gently and nodded. 'Your baby.'

Evie shut her eyes. *Finn's baby.*

Finn Kennedy eased his lean frame into the low squatter's chair and looked out over the vista from the shaded serenity of the wide wraparound veranda. He liked it here in this rambling old house perched on a cliff top overlooking the mighty Pacific Ocean. He gazed over acres of deep blue sea to the horizon, the constant white noise of the surf pounding against the rocks far below a wild serenade.

He liked the tranquillity. For too long he'd been keeping himself busy to block out the pain, drinking to block out the pain, screwing around and pushing himself to the limit to block out the pain.

Who knew that stopping everything and standing still worked better than any of that?

His muscles ached but in a good way. The hard physical labour he'd been doing the last five months had built up his lean body, giving definition to the long smooth muscles in his arms and legs. He felt fitter and more clear-headed than he had in a very long time.

He clenched and unclenched his right hand, marvel-

ling in the full range of movement. He formed a pincer
with his index finger and thumb and then tapped each
finger in turn onto the pad of his thumb, repeating the
process over and over. To think he'd despaired of ever
getting any use of it back. It was weaker than his left
hand for sure but he'd come a long way.

'As good as a bought one.'

Finn looked up at the approaching form of Ethan
Carter, with whom he'd served in the Middle East a
decade ago. 'I doubt I'll ever be able to open jam jars.'

Ethan shrugged, handing Finn a beer. 'So don't open
jam jars.'

Finn snorted at Ethan's typical Zen-like reasoning as
he lowered himself into the chair beside Finn's. Ethan, a
Black Hawk pilot, had trained as a psychologist after his
discharge from the army and *Beach Haven* had been his
brainchild. An exclusive retreat for injured soldiers five
hundred kilometres north of Sydney where they could
rest, recover, rehabilitate and refocus their lives. Only
partially government funded, Ethan worked tirelessly
to keep up the very generous private funding that had
come Beach Haven's way.

Neither of them said anything for a while, just looked
out over the ocean and drank their beer.

'It's time, Finn.'

Finn didn't look at Ethan. He didn't even answer him
for a long moment. 'I'm not ready,' he said eventually.

Prior to coming to *Beach Haven*, Finn would have
thought being away from Sydney Harbour Hospital,
from operating, was a fate worse than death. Now he
wasn't sure if he ever wanted to return.

Dropping out and becoming a hermit in a beach

shack somewhere was immensely appealing. Maybe he'd even take up surfing.

'Your arm is better. You can't hide here for ever.'

He turned to Ethan and glared at him with a trace of the old Finn. 'Why not?'

'Because this isn't who you are. Because you're using this to avoid your issues.'

'So I should go back to facing them in a high-stress environment where people's lives depend on me?'

'You've healed here, Finn. Physically. And mentally you're much more relaxed. You needed that. But you're not opening up emotionally.'

He shrugged and took a slug of his beer. 'I'm a surgeon, we're not emotional types.'

'No, Finn. Being a surgeon is what you do, not who you are. Beyond all those fancy letters after your name you're just a man who could do nothing but sit and cradle his dying brother while all hell was breaking loose around you. You couldn't help him. You couldn't save him. You couldn't stop him from dying. You're damaged in ways that go far beyond the physical.'

Finn flinched as Ethan didn't even try to pull his punches. In five months they hadn't once spoken about what had happened all those years ago. How Ethan had found a wounded Finn, peppered with shrapnel, holding Isaac.

'But I think you find some kind of emotional release in operating. I think that with every person you save, you bring back a little bit of Isaac. And if you're not going to open up about it, if surgery is your therapy of choice, then I think you should get back to it.'

More silence followed broken only by the pounding of surf.

'So you're kicking me out,' Finn said, staring at the horizon.

Ethan shook his head. 'Nope. I'm recommending a course of treatment. You're welcome to stay as long as you like.'

Finn's thoughts churned like the foam that he knew from his daily foray to the beach swirled and surged against the rocks with the sweep and suck of the tide. He knew Ethan was right, just as he'd known that this reprieve from the world couldn't last.

But his thoughts were interrupted by the crunching of tyres on the gravel drive and the arrival of a little red Mini sweeping into the parking area.

'Are we expecting an arrival today?' Ethan frowned.

'Not as far as I know,' Finn murmured.

They watched as the door opened and a woman climbed out. 'Oh, crap,' Finn said.

Ten minutes later Evie leaned against the veranda railing, looking out over the ocean view, the afternoon breeze blowing her loose hair off her shoulders. It ruffled the frayed edges of her denim cut-offs and blew the cream cotton of her loose, round-necked peasant blouse against her skin. She breathed the salt tang deep into her lungs.

'Wow,' she said, expelling her breath. 'This is a spectacular view.'

'It's all right,' Finn said, irked that he was enjoying the view of her perky denim-clad backside a hell of a lot more than the magnificent one-hundred-and-eighty-degree ocean view.

Since he'd slunk away in the night after their explosive session on his couch he'd thought about Evie a lot. Probably too much. Some of it R-rated. Most of it involving her big hazel eyes looking at him with love and compassion and pleading with him to let her in.

Up here he'd managed to pigeonhole her and the relationship she'd wanted so desperately as a bad idea. Standing a metre away from her, the long, toned lines of her achingly familiar, he had to clench his fists to stop from reaching for her.

Once upon a time he would have dismissed the impulse as a purely sexual urge. Something he would have felt for any woman standing here after five months of abstinence. A male thing. But solitude and time to think had stripped away his old defence mechanisms and as such he was forced to recognise the truth.

Evie was under his skin.

And it scared the hell out of him. Because she wouldn't be happy with half of him. She would want all of him. And as Ethan had not long ago pointed out, he was damaged.

And it went far beyond that awful day ten years ago.

He didn't know how to love a woman. He doubted he'd ever known. Not even Lydia.

'How did you find me?'

Evie turned to face him, amazed at this version of Finn before her, lounging in a chair, casually knocking back a beer.

Had he ever been this chilled?

Okay, there had been a wariness in his gaze since she'd arrived but this Finn was still a stark contrast to Sydney Harbour Hospital Finn. The old Finn was a serious, driven, sombre professional who oozed energy and drive from every pore. His mind was sharp, his tongue even more so, and his pace had always been frenetic.

His drink of choice was seriously good Scotch.

This Finn was so laid back he may as well have been wearing a Hawaiian shirt and a flower behind his ear. His body was more honed, spare, and his skin had been kissed to a golden honey hue. A far cry from the haggard shadow he'd been when last she'd seen him.

Had he been surfing all this time?

The incredible blue of his eyes, so often frigid with disapproval, were like warm tropical waters amidst the golden planes of his stubbly face. And she wanted to dive in.

She'd been nervous that he'd take one look at her and know she was pregnant. Which was ridiculous given that it would be at least another month, maybe more, before it was obvious to anyone. But she really needn't have worried. This Finn didn't look like he'd be bothered if she'd turned up with his triplets.

Something rose in her chest, dark and ugly. It twisted and burned and she realised she was jealous. This was the kind of Finn she'd longed for, had known was there somewhere. The one he'd never shown her.

'Daddy get a private detective?' he goaded.

His voice had an edge that she recognised as the old Finn and she found herself responding accordingly. She was like Pavlov's dog, still salivating over the slightest crumb.

She cleared her throat as emotion lodged like a fist in her trachea. 'Lydia.'

'Lydia?' Finn sat up. '*Lydia* told you I was here?' Isaac's widow, the woman he'd had a seriously screwed-up co-dependent relationship with in the aftermath of his brother's death, had been talking to Evie?

He frowned. '*You know Lydia?*'

Evie nodded calmly. Well, she'd met her anyway—she still had no clue as to their relationship. 'I met her outside your apartment a couple of days after you left. She came to pick up some stuff for you. Told me you were okay. That you needed space. Time… She gave me her card.'

Finn shut his eyes and leaned back into the canvas hammock of the squatter's chair. Trust Lydia to interfere. He opened his eyes to find her looking at him.

'Your arm is better, I see.'

Finn looked down at it. He clenched and unclenched his fingers automatically, still amazed that he could do so. 'Yes.'

Evie pressed her butt hard into the railing. She wanted to launch herself at him, throw herself into his lap, hug him to her, tell him she'd known it would get better, that he'd just needed a little faith and a lot of patience. But he didn't look so laid back now and memories of what had happened last time she had been in his lap overrode everything else.

There was even more between them now than there'd ever been—more than he certainly knew—and she couldn't think about any of it until she had him back in Sydney, until after he'd operated on their celebrity patient, until after she'd told him about the baby…

'You must be very relieved,' Evie murmured.

Finn didn't want to make small talk with her. His mind had been clear ten minutes ago and now it was all clouded up again.

Seeing Evie after five months' break made him realise how much he'd missed her wide hazel eyes and her interesting face. How much he'd taken her presence for granted when they'd worked in the same hospital, when she'd been there for him during his ops. How much he'd come to depend on seeing her, even though he'd pushed her away at every turn.

He'd been able to ignore all of that five hundred kilometres away from her—out of sight out of mind. But it was impossible to ignore now. She made him want things he didn't know how to articulate.

And he wanted her gone.

So he could go back to ignoring her and all the stuff that bubbled to the surface whenever she was around all over again.

'Why are you here?' he demanded.

Evie swallowed at his sullen enquiry. His gaze was becoming chilly again and she shivered. 'Prince Khalid bin Aziz.'

Finn frowned at the name from his past. Several years ago he'd revived a man who had collapsed in front of him on the street a couple of blocks from the hospital. He'd had no way of knowing at the time that the man was a Saudi oil prince. There'd been no robes, no staff, no security. He'd just been another heart to start and Finn's medical training had taken over.

But it had certainly worked out well for the hospital, which had benefited from a huge donation.

'What does he want?'

'He wants you.' *Not as badly as she did, however.* 'He needs a quadruple bypass and he wants you *and only you* to perform it.'

Finn gripped his beer bottle harder as Evie opened a door he'd shut firmly behind him and a surge of adrenaline hit him like a bolt from the blue. He could almost smell the chemical cleanliness of the operating room, hear the dull slap as an instrument hit his gloved

hand, feel the heat of the overhead lights on the back
of his neck.

He shook his head, quashing the powerful surge of
anticipation. 'I'm not ready to come back.'

Evie's looked down at him as he absently clenched
and unclenched his right hand. Her heart banged loudly
in her chest. *What on earth was he talking about?* Finn
was a surgeon. The best cardiothoracic surgeon there
was. He had to come back. And not just for the amir.

For him. For his sanity. For his dignity. The Finn she
knew *needed* to work.

'You look physically capable,' she said, keeping her
voice neutral.

Finn pushed up out of the chair as the decision he'd
been circling around for five months crystallised. He
walked to the railing, keeping a distance between them,
his gaze locking on the horizon. 'I don't know if I'm
going to come back.'

Evie stared at his profile. 'To the Harbour?'

Finn shook his head as he tested the words out loud.
'To surgery.'

Evie blinked, her brain temporarily shutting down
at the enormity of his admission. Quit being a surgeon?
That was sacrilege.

She turned around slowly so she too was facing the
horizon. Her hand gripped the railing as the line between the earth and the sky seemed to tilt. 'My father
will not be pleased,' she joked, attempting to lighten
the moment while her thoughts and emotions jumbled
themselves into an almighty tangle.

'Ah, yes, how is the great Richard Lockheart?'

Evie would have to have been deaf not to hear the

contempt in Finn's voice. It was fair to say that Finn was not on Team Richard. But, then, neither was she.

'Already counting the pennies from the big fat donation Prince Khalid has promised the hospital.'

Evie wondered if Finn remembered that it was through Prince Khalid's misfortune that she'd first met him. At the gala dinner that the prince had thrown in Finn's honour the first time he'd donated one million dollars to the Sydney Harbour Hospital's cardiothoracic department.

Finn had been as unimpressed as she to be there.

He snorted. 'Of course. I should have known there would be money involved.'

Evie had never heard such coldness in Finn's voice before. Not where his work was concerned, and it frightened her. She was used to it regarding her and anything of a remotely personal nature. But not his job.

She'd never thought she'd have to convince him to come back to work. She'd just assumed he'd jump back in as soon as he possibly could.

Just how long had his hand been recovered for?

'So don't do it for him,' she said battling to keep the rise of desperation out of her voice. 'Or for the money. Do it for the prince.'

'There are any number of very good cardiac surgeons in Sydney.'

'He doesn't want very good. He wants the best.'

Finn turned to face her, propping his hip against the railing. 'No.'

Evie turned too, at a complete loss as she faced him. 'Please.'

She seemed to always be asking him for something he wasn't prepared to give. Saying, *please, Finn, please.* And she was heartily sick of it. And sick of being rejected.

And if she wasn't carrying his baby she'd just walk right away. But she was. And he needed to know—whatever the fallout might be.

She opened her mouth to tell him. Not to bribe him into doing what she wanted but because she could see his mind was made up, and before he sent her away for the last time, he had to know.

But Ethan striding out onto the veranda interrupted them. 'Finn—' Finn looked over Evie's shoulder. 'Oh… sorry…I thought I heard the car leave,' Ethan said, smiling apologetically at Evie as he approached.

'It's fine,' Evie murmured.

'What's up?' Finn asked, dragging his gaze away from Evie's suddenly pale face.

'What's the name of that agency you were telling me about?'

Finn frowned. 'The medical staffing one? Why?'

'Hamish's father-in-law had a heart attack and died two hours ago. He's taking two weeks off. I've been ringing around everywhere but no one's available and I can't run this place without a medico on board, it's a government regulation.'

'For God's sake, Ethan,' Finn said, his voice laced with exasperation, having had this conversation too many times before. '*I'm* a doctor.'

Ethan shook his head firmly. 'You're a client.'

Finn shoved his hand on his hip. 'These are extenuating circumstances.'

Ethan chuckled. 'No dice, buddy. Them's the rules.'

'You never used to be such a stickler for the rules.'

Ethan clapped him on the back. 'I wasn't running my own business back then.'

Evie was surprised at the obvious affection between the two men. Surprised even more at the spurt of jealousy. Finn wasn't the touchy-feely kind. He maintained professional relationships with his colleagues and he'd been known to sit at the bar over the road from the hospital and knock back a few whiskies with them from time to time but he was pretty much a solo figure.

He and Ethan, a big bear of a man with a grizzly beard and kind eyes, seemed to go back a long way.

'Problem?' she asked, at Finn's obvious frustration.

Finn shook his head then stopped as an idea took hold. He raked his gaze over her and knew it would probably be something he would come to regret, but choices were limited in the middle of nowhere.

Maybe the current pain in his butt could be Ethan's silver lining. 'Evie can do it.'

'What?' she gaped, her pulse spiking. 'Do what?'

Ethan smiled at Evie apologetically. 'I'm sorry. He's not very good with social nuances, is he?'

'She's a fully qualified, highly trained, *very good* emergency doctor,' Finn continued, ignoring Ethan's remark.

'You can't just go springing jobs on people like that and acting like they have no choice but to take them,' Ethan chided, his smile getting wider and wider. 'Not cool, man. Maybe you should try asking the lady?'

Finn turned to Evie, his palms finding her upper arms, curling around her biceps. 'I'll come back and do Khalid's surgery. But only if you do the two weeks here first.'

Ethan crossed his arms. 'That's not asking.'

Evie felt her belly plummet as if she'd just jumped out of a plane. She wasn't sure if was due to his snap decision, his compliment over her medical skills or his touch but she couldn't think when he looked at her with need in his eyes.

Even if it was purely professional.

'C'mon, Princess Evie,' Finn murmured, trying to cut through the confusion he could see in her hazel eyes. 'Step outside your comfort zone for a while. Live a little.'

'You suck at asking,' Ethan interjected.

Evie swallowed as she became caught up in the heady rush of being needed by Finn. Not even the nickname grated.

Why not?

It would kill two birds with one stone—Khalid got his op and she bought herself some time. And her father had told her to do *anything* to get Finn back.

'Okay,' she said, hoping her voice didn't sound as shaky as it felt leaving her throat.

Finn nodded and looked at Ethan. 'You've got yourself a doctor.'

Ethan looked from one to the other, his bewildered look priceless. Like he couldn't quite believe that in less than a minute his major problem had been settled.

Neither, frankly, could Evie.

CHAPTER TWO

EVIE CLIMBED ONTO the back of the four-wheeler behind Ethan the next morning for the grand tour. *Beach Haven* retreat covered a couple of hundred acres and wasn't something that could be quickly traversed on foot. Finn, who had disappeared shortly after he'd bribed her into staying for two weeks, was still nowhere to be seen. She didn't ask Ethan where he was and he didn't tell her.

Her father hadn't been happy with the two-week delay but as the prince's blocked arteries had been found on a routine physical and hadn't been symptomatic, the surgery wasn't urgent.

Their first port of call was the clinic. It could be seen from the homestead and she'd be able to walk easily to and from along the track, but as it was just the first stop of many today Ethan drove them across.

It looked like an old worker's cottage from the outside but had been renovated entirely on the inside with a waiting area, a couple of rooms with examination tables and a minor ops room. A small dispensary with common medications, a storeroom, a toilet and a kitchenette completed the well-equipped facility. Thought had also been given to disabled access with the addition of ramps, widened doors and handrails.

'Clinic starts at ten every morning. First come first

served. There's rarely a stampede. They usually come to see me.'

Evie cocked an eyebrow. 'For therapy?' He nodded. 'I wouldn't have thought you'd have any takers.'

Ethan shrugged. 'It's a pre-req for a place here. Weekly therapy—whether they like it or not.'

She thought not liking it would be the predominant feeling amongst a bunch of battle-weary soldiers. 'Does that include Finn?'

He nodded. 'No exceptions.'

Evie absorbed the information. Maybe that was why he seemed so chilled? But…surely not. The Finn she knew wasn't capable of talking about his issues. 'I don't imagine those sessions would be very enlightening.'

Ethan laughed. 'He's pretty guarded, that's for sure. But…' he shrugged '…you can lead a horse to water… I can't force him or anyone else to open up. I just hope like hell they do. In my opinion, there's not a man who's seen active duty who couldn't do with some therapy.'

'Is that why you opened this place?' Evie asked. 'A ruse to get soldiers into therapy?'

He laughed again and Evie found herself wondering why it was she couldn't fall for someone like Ethan. He was attractive enough in a shaggy kind of a way with a ready smile and an easy manner.

'Kind of,' he said, his voice big and gruff like the rest of him. 'Returned soldiers have issues. Those who have been physically injured even more so. It's too easy for them to slip through the cracks. Succumb to feelings of uselessness, hopelessness and despair. Here they're able to continue their rehab, contribute to society and find a little perspective.'

'And you're the perspective?' she asked, smiling.

Ethan looked embarrassed but smiled back. 'Any-way…' he said, looking around, 'clinic is done by twelve and then your day is your own as long as you stay on the property and have your pager on you in case an emergency arises.'

'Does that happen very often?'

Ethan shook his head. 'The last one was a couple of months ago when there was an incident with a nail gun.'

She raised an eyebrow. 'Do I want to know?'

He grinned and shook his head. 'Nope.'

Evie nodded slowly, also looking around. 'So, that's it? A two-hour clinic and the odd nail-gun emergency?'

Ethan nodded. 'Think you can cope?' he teased.

Compared to the frenetic pace of a busy city emergency department Evie felt as if Ethan had just handed her the keys to paradise. And there was a beach to boot! 'I think I can hack the pace,' she murmured. 'In fact, I think I may just have died and gone to heaven.'

He grinned. 'C'mon, I'll show you the rest.'

Ten minutes later they pulled up at what appeared to be a massive shed that actually housed an Olympic-sized indoor swimming pool and a large gym area where she caught up with Bob, the physiotherapist she'd met last night. He was in the middle of a session with two below-knee amputees so they didn't chat.

From there it was another ten minutes to a series of three smaller sheds. The side doors were all open and the sounds of electric saws and nail guns pierced the air as Ethan cut the bike engine.

'This is where we build the roof trusses I was telling you about last night,' Ethan said as they dismounted.

With a noticeably absent Finn over dinner last night, Ethan had filled her in on the flood-recovery project the retreat participants contributed to during their stay. Several extreme weather events had led to unprecedented flooding throughout Australia over the previous two years and demand for new housing was at a premium. Roof trusses were part of that. It was a small-scale project perfect for Ethan's ragtag band of clients, which aided both the flood and the soldiers' recovery.

It was win-win.

They entered the nearest workshop, which was a hive of activity. The aroma of cut timber immediately assailed Evie and she pulled it deep into her lungs. One by one the men stopped working.

'I suspect,' Ethan whispered out of the side of his mouth, 'you may well see an increase in visits to the clinic in the next few days. Just to check you out. Not a lot of women around here.'

Evie smiled as all but one lone nail gun pistoned away obliviously. It stopped too after a few moments and the owner turned and looked at her.

It was Finn.

Evie's breath caught in her throat. He was wearing faded jeans and an even more faded T-shirt that clung in all the good places. A tool belt was slung low on his hips. Used to seeing him in baggy scrubs, her brain grappled with the conflicting images.

Her body however, now well into the second trimester and at the mercy of a heightened sex drive, responded on a completely primitive level.

Tool-Man Finn was hot.

A wolf whistle came from somewhere in the back.

'Okay, okay back to work.' Ethan grinned. 'Don't scare our doctor away before her first day.'

One by one they resumed their work. Except Finn,

who downed his nail gun, his arctic gaze firmly fixed on her as he strode in her direction.

'Uh-oh,' Ethan said out of the corner of his mouth. 'He doesn't look too happy.'

Evie couldn't agree more. She should be apprehensive. But he looked pretty damn sexy, coming at her with all that coiled tension. Like he might just slam her against the nearest wall and take her, like he had their first time.

'I don't think happy is in his vocabulary.'

Finn pulled up in front of Ethan—who seriously should know better than to bring a woman into an environment where most of the men hadn't seen one in weeks—and glared at his friend. *Who had clearly gone mad.*

'What is *she* doing here?' he demanded.

Ethan held up his hands. 'Just showing the lady around.'

'She only needs to know where the clinic is,' Finn pointed out.

'Well, apart from common courtesy,' Ethan murmured, his voice firm, '*Evie* really should know the lie of the land in case of an emergency.'

Finn scowled at his friend's logic. 'Now she knows.' He turned and looked at Evie in her clothes from yesterday, her hair loose. 'This is no place for a woman,' he ground out.

Having been in the army for a decade and here for almost five months, Finn knew these men and men just like them. Even hiding away, licking their wounds, sex was always on their mind.

Evie felt her hackles rise. Had she slipped back into the Fifties? She glared at him, her gaze unwavering. 'You ought to talk,' she snapped, pleased the background noise kept their conversation from being overheard. 'What kind of a place is this for a surgeon, Finn? Wielding a nail gun when you should be wielding a scalpel!'

Finn ignored the dig. 'Get her out of here,' he said to Ethan.

Finn scowled again as Ethan grinned but breathed a sigh of relief when Evie followed Ethan out, every pair of eyes in the workshop glued to her butt.

His included.

On their next leg, they passed a helipad and a small hangar with a gleaming blue and white chopper sitting idle.

'Yours?' she asked.

He nodded. 'Handy piece of transport in the middle of nowhere.'

They drove to a large dam area, which had been the source of the silver perch they'd eaten last night. Above it evenly spaced on a grassy hill sat ten pre-fab dongas.

'Each one has four bedrooms, a bathroom, a kitchen and common area,' Ethan explained, as he pulled up under a shady stand of gumtrees near the dam edge and cut the engine. 'They're not luxurious but they're better than anything any of us slept in overseas.'

'So your capacity is forty?'

'Actually, it's forty-five if you count the homestead accommodation,' Ethan said, dismounting and walking over to inspect the water. 'That's over and above you, me, Bob and Finn.'

Evie nodded, also walking over to the water's edge. The sun was warm on her skin and she raised her face to it for long moments. She could hear the low buzz of insects and the distant whine of a saw.

Ethan waited for a while and said, 'So…you and Finn…'

Evie opened her eyes and looked at him. 'What about me and Finn?'

'You're…colleagues? Friends…?'

Evie considered Ethan's question for a while. She didn't know how to define them with just one word. Colleagues, yes. Lovers, yes. Soon to be parents, yes. But friends…?

She shrugged. 'It's…complicated.'

Ethan nodded. 'He's a complicated guy.'

Evie snorted at the understatement of the century. 'You've known him for a while?'

Ethan picked up a stone at his feet and skipped it across the surface. 'We served together overseas.'

'You know his brother died over there?'

'I know.'

'It's really messed with his head,' she murmured.

Ethan picked up another stone and looked at it. 'You love him?' he asked gently.

Evie swallowed as Ethan followed his direct question with a direct look. She thought about denying it, but after five months of denying it it felt good to say it to someone. 'Yes.' She gave a self-deprecating laugh. 'He's not exactly easy to love, though, you know? And God knows I've tried not to…'

Evie paused. She had a feeling that Ethan knew exactly how hard Finn was to love. 'I think what happened with his brother really shut him down emotionally,' she murmured.

She knew she was making another excuse for him

but she couldn't even begin to imagine how awful it would be to hold Bella or Lexi in her arms as they died. The thought of losing her sisters at all was horrifying. But like that?

How did somebody stay normal after that?

How did it not push a person over the edge?

Ethan looked back at the stone in his hand, feeling its weight and its warmth before letting it fly to skim across the surface. 'Yes, it did. But I think Finn had issues that predated the tragedy with Isaac,' he said carefully.

Evie snapped to attention. 'He told you that?'

Ethan snorted. 'No. This *is* Finn, remember. He's always been pretty much a closed book, Evie. At least as long as I've known him. And we go back a couple of years before what happened with Isaac. He's been much, much worse since then but he wasn't exactly the life of the party before that. Part of it is the things he'd seen, the injuries, the total…mayhem that is war. A person shuts themselves down to protect themselves from that kind of carnage. But I think there's even more than that with Finn, stuff from his distant past.'

Evie stilled as the enormity of what she faced hit home. If Ethan was right she was dealing with something bigger than his grief. She looked at Ethan helplessly, her hand seeking the precious life that grew inside her, needing to anchor herself in an uncertain sea. 'I don't know how to reach him through all that.'

Ethan shrugged. 'I don't know how you do it either but I do know that he's crying out for help and after that little performance in the workshop, I think you're the one woman who can do it. I have never seen Finn so… emotionally reactive as just now.'

Evie cocked an eyebrow. 'Is that what you call it?'

He grinned. 'Don't give up on him, Evie. I think you'll make a human being out of him yet.'

Ethan had been right—word had got out. Evie's clinic was bustling that first morning with the most pathetic ailments she'd ever treated. But it felt good to be able to practise medicine where there was no pressure or stress or life-and-death situations and the men were flirty and charming and took the news of her pretend boyfriend waiting back home for her good-naturedly.

She and Bob had lunch together on the magnificent homestead veranda serenaded by the crash of the surf. She yawned as Bob regaled her with the details of the nail-gun incident.

'Sorry,' she apologised with a rueful smile. 'It must be the sea air.'

Bob took it in his stride. 'No worries. You should lie down and have a bit of a kip, love. A siesta. Reckon the Italians have that right.'

Evie was awfully tempted. The pregnancy had made her tired to the bone and by the time she arrived home after manic twelve-hour shifts at Sydney Harbour she was utterly exhausted. She already felt like she was in a major sleep deficit—and the baby wasn't even out yet! She fantasised every day about midday naps and she could barely drag herself out of bed on her days off.

But it didn't seem right to wander off for a nanny nap in broad daylight—was that even allowed?

'Go on,' Bob insisted as she yawned again. 'There's nothing for you to do here and you have your pager.'

Evie hesitated for a moment longer then thought, What the hell?

She pulled the suitcase off her bed—it must have been delivered while she'd been working that morning. She'd tasked Bella with the job of packing two weeks' worth of clothes for her because, as a fashion designer, Evie knew her sister would choose with care. Her youngest sister Lexi, on the other hand, who was thirty-two weeks pregnant and time poor, would have just shoved in the first things that came to hand.

As her head hit the pillow her thoughts turned to Finn, as they always did. Should she tell him, shouldn't she tell him? When to tell him? Here? Back in Sydney? When would be a good time?

But the lack of answers was even more wearying than the questions and within a minute the sound of the ocean and the pull of exhaustion had sucked her into a deep, deep sleep.

Evie woke with a start three hours later. She looked at the clock. She'd slept for three freaking hours?

She must have been more tired than she'd thought!

She certainly hadn't felt this rested in a long time. Maybe after two weeks here she'd have caught up on the sleep she needed.

She stretched and stared at the ceiling for a moment or two, her hand finding her belly without conscious thought.

'Well, baby,' she said out loud. 'Should I track your father down and tell him right now or should I wait till we're back in Sydney and he's done the op?'

Evie realised she should feel silly, talking to a tiny human being in utero who couldn't respond, but she'd spent so much time avoiding anything to do with the life inside her that it suddenly seemed like the most natural thing in the world—talking to her baby.

'Move now if you think I should tell him today.'

Again, quite silly. If she was going to rely on airy-fairy reasoning to inform her critical decisions, it'd probably make more sense to flip a coin.

But then the baby moved. And not some gentle fluttering, is-it-or-isn't it, maybe-it's-just-wind kind of movement. It was a kick. A very definite kick. As if the baby was shaping up to play soccer for Australia.

Crap. The baby had spoken.

Twenty minutes later she'd changed into a loose, flowing sundress that she'd never seen before but which fitted her perfectly. Bella had attached a note to say, 'Designed this especially for you. xxx.'

It was floaty and feminine with shoestring straps—perfect for the beach and the warm September day. And exactly what she needed to face Finn.

Finn couldn't be found around the homestead but Ethan came out as she was standing at the veranda railing, contemplating the horizon.

'Good clinic this morning,' he said.

Evie smiled. 'I've never known a bunch of tough guys see a doctor for such trifling complaints.' Ethan laughed and she joined him. 'I don't suppose you know where Finn might be?' she asked, when their laughter petered out.

'I'd try the beach.' He inclined his head towards the well-worn track that lead to the safety-railed cliff edge and the two hundred and twenty stairs that delivered the intrepid traveller straight onto the beach.

They were not for the faint-hearted…

'He normally swims everyday around this time.'

'Am I allowed to go that far away?' she asked.

Ethan laughed. 'Of course. It's not that far. And even though it isn't a private beach, we kind of consider it as within the property boundaries.'

She smiled. 'Thanks.'

Halfway down she stood aside to let a buff-looking guy in boardies and a backpack run past, his below-knee prosthesis not seeming to hinder him an iota. He nodded at her as he pounded upwards and she turned to watch him as he scaled the stairs as if they were nothing.

Her gaze drifted all the way up the sheer cliff face to the very top. She was dreading *walking* back—running just seemed insane.

Her foot hit the warm sand a few minutes later and her gaze scanned the wide arc of yellow, unpatrolled beach for Finn. She couldn't see him but as she walked closer to the thundering ocean she could see a towel discarded on the sand and she looked out at the water, trying to see a head amongst the continually rolling breakers.

Her heart beat in sync with the ocean as she searched in vain through the wild pounding surf and a hundred disaster scenarios scuttled through her head. She calmed herself with the knowledge that he was a strong swimmer and ignored the ominous power of the surging ocean. Then she spotted his head popping up out of the water. He was quite a distance out but she could see his wet hair was sleek, like a seal's pelt, and his shoulders were broad and bare.

She sat on the sand next to his towel and waited.

* * *

Finn was aware of Evie from the minute she'd set foot on the beach. Some sixth sense had alerted him and he'd watched her advance towards the shoreline, obviously looking for him.

And, of course, she looked utterly gorgeous in a dress that blew across her body, outlining her athletic legs, her hair whipping across her face, the shoestring straps baring lovely collar bones and beautiful shoulders.

Just looking at her made him hard and he was grateful for the cover of ocean.

It had been so long since he'd touched her. He wanted to stride up the beach, push her back into the sand and bury himself in her. But he hated the feelings she roused in him and the loss of control he exhibited when he was with her.

Besides…it would just put them back at square one when he'd tried so hard—and succeeded—at putting distance between them.

He could tell, though, even from this distance, she was here to chat. And, God knew, he didn't want to chat with her. Right now the only thing he wanted to do with her involved being naked and he was going to stay right here until he'd worn the impulse down.

He swam against and with the strong current until he was chilled to the bone and his arm ached. A part of him hoped she'd get sick of waiting and just leave. Or maybe her pager would go off. But she sat stubbornly staring out to sea, watching him until finally the chill was unbearable and, admitting defeat, he strode from the surf.

She handed him his towel as he drew level with her and he took it wordlessly, rubbing vigorously at his body. When he was done he wrapped it around his waist and threw himself down next to her, taking care to leave a gap. She didn't say anything to him as they both sat and watched the ocean for a while, the sun's rays beginning to work their magic on the ice that seemed to penetrate right down to his bones.

Although the ice around his heart was as impenetrable as always.

'I hear you have a boyfriend,' he said after a while.

Evie, her brain still grappling with the perfect words to tell Finn he was going to be a father and her stupid pregnant hormones still all aflutter from his sexy Adonis-rising-from-the-ocean display, didn't register the terseness in his tone.

'A cosmetic surgeon who owns a Porsche and comes from North Shore money,' he continued.

Evie bit back a smile at the ill-disguised contempt in his voice. When choosing her fake boyfriend she'd deliberately chosen all the attributes Finn would despise. 'Well, I figured if I was going to have a make-believe boyfriend I might as well go all out.'

Finn wasn't mollified. 'He sounds like a tosser.'

Evie smiled at the ocean. 'Because he does lips and boobs or because of the Porsche?'

Finn glared at her as she continued to stare at the horizon. 'Is that what you want, Princess Evie? Some blue-blooded prince to keep up your royal lineage?'

She turned to look at him, her nostrils flaring as the scent of sea salt and something her hormones recognised as quintessentially Finn enveloped her. 'I think you know who I want.'

And suddenly the roar of the ocean faded as the pounding of her pulse took over. The fact she was supposed to be telling him about their baby also faded as her heart drummed a primitive beat perfectly at home in this deserted windswept landscape. The world of the beach shrank until there was just him and her and the sun stroking warm fingers over their skin, lulling her common sense into a stupor. His bare chest and shoulders teased her peripheral vision, his sexy stubble and wet, ruffled hair taunted her front and centre.

'I've only ever wanted you, Finn,' she murmured, her breath rough as her gaze fell to his mouth. Wanting to feel it on hers. To feel it everywhere. 'And right now all I can think about is how good we are together.'

Finn shut his eyes, images of how good they were rolling through his brain as seductively as her voice, like a siren from the sea. He opened them again and her hazel eyes were practically silver with desire. 'Evie…'

Her breasts grew heavy at the rawness of his voice. Longing snaked through her belly, hot and hard and hungry as she lifted her hand to his face, ran her fingers over his mouth. 'I've wanted to kiss you every day for five months,' she murmured.

Finn gently grabbed her wrist, intent on setting her away, but the breeze blew the scent of her shampoo, of her skin right into his face, enveloping him in a cloud of memories, and he knew he wasn't strong enough. Not after five months of denial.

'Oh, hell,' he half muttered, half groaned as he slid his hand from her wrist into her hair, pulling her head close and lowering his mouth to hers.

He'd lain awake at night thinking about her kiss. And it was as good as he remembered. Better. She opened to him on a sigh, moved into the shelter of his arms as if she belonged there and he felt the last of the cold disappear from his bones as an intense heat roared and raged through his marrow.

And then he was hot everywhere.

Their tongues tangoed as he pressed her back onto the sand, his thigh instantly pushing between hers, his hand automatically stroking down her neck, across her shoulders before claiming a breast, firmer and rounder even than he remembered, the nipple beading instantly beneath his palm.

Evie moaned as she arched her back, pushing herself into his hand more, the ache of the aroused tip mirroring the ache between her legs. She rubbed against his thigh to relieve it but he only pushed harder against her, stoking the need higher.

And then with a muffled curse against her mouth he was over her, on top of her, and she revelled in the pressure of him pushing her into the warm sand, the imprint of each grain against the backs of her calves, the feel of the naked planes of his back dry and warm from the sun beneath her hands.

Her head spun from his kiss, her breath was short and choppy and her belly dipped and tightened with every thrust and parry of his tongue. And if it hadn't been for a lone seagull landing practically on top of them and startling them both out of their stupor, Evie had no doubt they would have gone all the way, oblivious to everything but the primitive imperative of their bodies.

Evie broke off their kiss as sense invaded their bubble and she became aware they were making out on a beach and anyone with two eyes and a pair of binoculars could be watching them from the cliff top. Not to mention anyone coming down the stairs from the retreat copping an eyeful.

Finn uttered another curse and rolled off her, flopping onto his back, his chest heaving, his pulse battering his temples, his erection throbbing painfully.

'Finn.' She reached for his arm but he vaulted upright abruptly and she knew he was already regretting what had happened.

'I'm sorry, he said. 'That shouldn't have happened.'

Evie sighed as she too sat, her body still zinging from their kisses. 'Why not?' she asked. 'We're both adults, Finn.'

Finn shook his head vehemently. 'We're not going down this road again, Evie,' he said.

Evie smoothed her dress over her knees. *Tell him.* Tell him they were on the road together whether he liked it or not. 'Would it be so bad?'

'I lose my head when I'm around you and I don't like it.'

'That's a shame,' she said, trying to lighten the moment. *Tell him!* 'I like it when you lose your head.'

'Damn it, Evie,' he barked, looking at her, her lips full and soft from his ravaging. 'I don't. I don't like it. I almost had you naked on your back on this beach.'

She placed her hand on his forearm. It felt warm and solid in her palm and she never wanted to let go.

Tell him!

But she couldn't. She didn't want to use the baby to win him. 'Finn…I've known you for five years and I've never seen you so relaxed. So why don't you just…relax and see where this takes us?'

Finn shrugged her hand away. 'You want more than I'm prepared to give. And you deserve it, too.' He stood and looked down at her. 'We've got two weeks here together. Let's just stay away from each other, okay?'

He didn't give her a chance to reply as he turned on his heel. The baby thumped around inside her as she watched him stride off. No doubt it was trying to make her feel guilty for not accomplishing what she'd come to the beach to achieve.

'Sorry, baby,' she whispered. 'Not going to happen. I'll tell him when we get to Sydney—promise.'

CHAPTER THREE

AND STAY AWAY from each other they did. At least, Finn steered clear of her anyway.

Painstakingly...

His distance reminded her of how they had co-existed for years at the hospital. Aware of each other, of what might have happened that first night they'd met at the gala in Finn's honour had her father not come along and given her away as a Lockheart. Aware of something bubbling beneath the surface but neither crossing the professional divide—junior doctor and consultant.

Even her catastrophic relationship with Stuart now seemed a desperate attempt to cling to someone she could have, to distract herself from someone she couldn't.

But despite all that, their mutual attraction—subversive, unspoken—had simmered away until it had flared out of control one day and little by little she'd wedged herself into his life. He hadn't liked it, he didn't like it now, but it was simply too big to ignore.

Although she had to give it to Finn, the man did denial better than anyone she knew.

So Evie did what she had been raised to do from an early age by a father who'd prized her social skills above her brains and talent—she fitted in.

Schmoozed.

She got to know the gang. Mingled with the guys as they went about their day-to-day business—despite Finn's scowls. Took quad lessons with whoever was around to teach her. Helped Tom out at the gym and in the hydrotherapy pool. Became a sounding board for Ethan over a couple of the guys he was worried about.

And she slept in and read a book a day from the extensive library at the homestead and ate the delicious food cooked by Reginald, an ex-army chef, and soaked in the sea air and the sunshine like a giant sponge. She felt good—fit and healthy—and knew from the mirror that the tired smudges beneath her eyes had disappeared and that her skin was glowing and her hair shone.

She'd also taken to swimming after her clinic each day. She tagged along with a group of the guys and lolled in ankle-deep waters as they ran drills on the beach. Despite being a strong swimmer, she was never quite game enough to go out too far, preferring the gentler push and pull of the shallows. Such a desolate windswept section of the coastline, dominated by sheer cliffs and rocky outcrops, needed to be respected.

After a couple of hours of swimming and soaking up the sun they'd head back again. Oftentimes Finn would be on his way down. The men would greet him enthusiastically and if any of them thought Finn's reserved response was odd they never commented. They seemed to respect him and his personal space and if it made Evie sad to think that Finn came to the beach alone when he could have had company, she was obviously the only one.

Two weeks flew by so fast and Evie couldn't believe it was her last day as she dressed for her final sojourn to the beach. Thoughts of how relaxing it had been here filled her head as she rounded the side of the veranda and literally ran smack bang into Finn.

'Sorry,' she apologised as he grabbed her to steady her from their impact.

For the briefest moment their bodies were pressed together and neither of them moved as heat arced between them. Then Finn set her back and stepped away.

'Going down for your daily flirt, I see?' he said through stiff lips.

He looked her up and down as if she was wearing a skimpy bikini instead of a very sensible pair of boardies and the un-sexiest sun shirt ever made. Apart from the fact the shirt was tight around her bust due to the pregnancy, everywhere else pretty much hung and Evie was grateful for the extra layers of fabric as her bump seemed to become more and more noticeable to her by the day.

She decided to ignore the jibe. 'Have you packed up all your stuff for the trip home tomorrow?'

Her time in paradise was over—Hamish would be back tonight and she and Finn would return to Sydney tomorrow. A flutter wormed its way through her belly at the thought of going back. Part of her wanted to stay— hole up here and forget the world. With the pound of the ocean below, it was incredibly tempting. But she was a fighter, not a hider. And real life beckoned.

The thought of being in a car with Finn for five hours, of having him back in Sydney, of telling him what she knew she must, made her pulse trip.

But it had to be done.

'Nothing to pack—I still have my apartment with everything I'll need,' he said. 'And I'll be coming straight back here after Khalid's discharge.'

Evie blinked. 'You're coming back?'

Finn gave a curt nod. 'Yes. I'm done with surgery.' He hadn't been sure when she'd first arrived but two weeks back in her company had crystallised his decision.

Evie stared at him blankly for a moment then allowed the bubble of laughter rising in her throat an escape. He seriously thought he could just waltz in and do a one-off and not be sucked back into a world he'd thrived in?

Even she knew being a surgeon was like oxygen to him.

'You know as well as I do that you'll change your mind the minute you step foot in your old operating theatre.'

Finn hated how her laughter trivialised something he'd grappled with for a long time.

And that that she knew him so well.

It had been hell having her around the last two weeks. Hearing her voice and catching glimpses of her everywhere. Reminding him of them. Of his old life. Watching the guys flirt with her and then talk about her—*Evie this and Evie that*. The calm that he'd found here over the last months had well and truly evaporated and he desperately wanted it back.

The sooner he fulfilled his end of the bargain, the sooner he could find it again.

But he was scared. Scared that her prediction would come to pass. That he'd pick up a scalpel and find the salvation he'd always found there. The concentration, the focus, the intensity.

That he'd never want to leave.

Scared that he'd say yes. To surgery. To her.

And Finn didn't like feeling scared. It reminded him too much of the perpetual fear he'd lived with during his fractured childhood—for him, for Isaac. Trying to keep him safe, to keep them together.

Fear that he'd conquered a long time ago.

And frankly it pissed him off.

'Don't think you know me,' he snarled, 'because you don't. You think because we rutted like animals…' he saw her flinch at his deliberate crudity but his adrenaline was flowing and he couldn't stop '…a few times that you know me? Read my lips.' He shoved his face close to hers and watched her hazel eyes widen. 'I don't want to be a surgeon,' he hissed. 'I don't want to work at your father's precious hospital. *I don't want to be anywhere you are.*'

Evie felt like he'd taken a bloody great sword and cleaved it right through her middle, leaving her mortally wounded. A surge of white-hot bile rose in her chest as a blinding need to strike back took hold.

'You're a liar, Finn Kennedy,' she snarled. 'And a coward to boot. And to think you once called yourself a soldier!'

Finn took a step back at the disdain and contempt in her voice. No one had ever called him a coward before. No one. And he was damned if he was going to legitimise her accusation with a response.

Evie drew in a ragged breath as Finn stormed away, her insides shaking at their exchange. At her terrible insult. At the venom in his voice. Anger she'd expected—God knew, he pretty much existed in a perpetually angry state—but vitriol? That had been cutting. A block of tangled emotions rose to mingle with the acid in her chest and her legs started to shake. The urge to crumple into a heap undulated through her muscles but she refused to succumb to it.

Not here on the veranda, at least.

On autopilot she slung her hold-all over her shoulder, found the stairs, pounded down them. Hurried down the track, his angry words chasing her, nipping at her heels. And it didn't matter that she'd given as good as she'd got, that her words had been just as harsh, it was his voice that ran through her head.

Rutted like animals.

Your father's precious hospital.

I don't want to be anywhere you're at.

It was a little early for her rendezvous with the guys—it didn't matter, she had to keep moving, do something other than think, get away from his words.

Rutted like animals.

The ocean, more rolling than pounding and surprisingly calm in some areas beneath the leaden sky, lay before her and she knew it was what she needed. To cleanse herself. Let the ocean wash the ugliness of his words away.

Rutted. Rutted. Rutted.

She took the stairs two at a time, her breath choking and catching in her throat, shaking her head to jam the audio playing on continuous loop.

Her foot hit the sand, her lungs and throat burning as breath and sob fought for the lion's share of each inhalation. She ran down to the shoreline, dropped her bag and kept going, running into the water, not registering the cooler temperature or the depth she quickly reached.

She just threw herself into the waves and struck out against the ocean. Heaving in oxygen through her nose, pulling armfuls of water behind her as she freestyled like she had a rocket attached to her feet.

Getting away from Finn. Away from his words.

Away from his rejection.

She swam and swam, not looking up or around, just hitting out at the waves as her anger grew to match his.

Finn Kennedy was a jerk of the highest order.

He was a misogynist. A masochist.

Bloody-minded. Arrogant. Bastard.

And she was much too good for him.

So she swam. She swam and she swam until she couldn't swim another stroke. And then she stopped.

She had no idea how long she'd been swimming. All she knew was her arms, legs and lungs were screaming at her and the beach seemed a very long way away. And the thought of having to swim all the way back was not a welcome one.

Damn it. Now look what he'd done.

He'd chased her right out into the middle of the bloody ocean. She sighed as she prepared to swim back.

Finn stood on the cliff top, his anxiety lessening as Evie came closer to land. Stupid fool to go out swimming by herself. The water might look calm to the untrained eye but the swell often made swimming very hard going and the tide was on the turn—always a more dangerous time to be in the water. From this vantage point he could see a rip forming close to the shore before his eyes.

And Evie was swimming right into it.

'Evie!' he called out, even though he knew it was futile all the way up here, with the wind snatching everything away.

He hit the stairs at a run, his gaze trained firmly on

Evie, watching as she started to go backwards despite her forward stroke. Seeing her lift her head, her expression confused when she realised what was happening. Noting the look of panic and exhaustion as her desperate hands clawed at the water as if she was trying to gain purchase.

Thank God his raging thoughts had brought him to the cliff edge. That he'd sought the ocean to clear his head after their bitter exchange.

'Evie,' he called out again as his foot hit the sand. Still futile but coming from a place inside that kicked and burned and clawed, desperate to get the words out. 'Evie!'

It took Evie long seconds to figure out she'd been caught in a rip. And even longer seconds to stop fighting the pull at her legs and push at her body. No matter how much she kicked and bucked against the current, bands of iron seemed to pull tighter and just would not give.

Over the pounding of her heart her sluggish brain tried to remember what every Aussie kid growing up anywhere near a beach had been taught from the cradle.

Don't fight it.
Lie on your back and go with it.
Wait until it ebbs then swim parallel to the beach.
Conserve your energy.

Evie felt doomed immediately. She was already exhausted—where on earth would she find the energy to swim back again once this monstrous sucker had discharged her from its grip? She opened her eyes to glance wistfully at the rapidly receding shoreline.

And that's when she saw him.

A shirtless Finn running into the ocean, looking

right at her, his mouth open, calling to her maybe? She couldn't hear the words but just the sight of him made her heart sing. Half an hour ago she could have cheerfully murdered him but right this second he was what he'd been since that night she'd plonked herself down next to him at the gala—her everything.

She was tired and cold but suddenly she felt like everything was going to be okay and she finally relaxed and let the current sweep her along, her gaze firmly fixed on him as he threw himself into the rip and headed her way.

Her numb fingers found her bump and she whispered, 'Daddy's coming, baby.'

Finn caught up with her five minutes later as the rip swept them closer and closer to the rocky headland that divided this bay from the next.

Her lips were a pale purple and her teeth were chattering but she essentially looked in one piece and the tight fist around his heart eased a little. They weren't exactly out of the woods but she wasn't taking on water.

'You okay?' he shouted above the crash of the waves on the nearby rocks.

Evie nodded, smiling through lips that felt frozen to her face. The man didn't even have the decency to look out of breath. 'C-cold,' she whispered.

Finn knew it would be impossible to warm her up in the water. 'I think it's weakened enough now that we can swim back. That'll get the blood flowing again.'

Evie kicked into a dog paddle and managed a feeble smile. 'Yay.'

'Are you going to be able to manage the swim?' Finn asked.

Evie looked at the distant beach and thought about her baby—their baby—depending on her to manage. 'Guess I'll have to,' she said, knowing every arm movement, every leg kick would feel like swimming through porridge.

Finn could hear her exhaustion and wondered just how far she'd make it in the swell. He scanned around. They were situated between the two bays now, with the rip spitting them out directly in front of the rocky headland—the nearest piece of terra firma.

Waves thundered where the sea met rock and Finn knew they'd be smashed mercilessly, their bones as insignificant as kindling. But the bay on the other side seemed much more sheltered and he could see a couple of areas where they might be able to gain purchase on this calmer side of the headland and pull themselves out of the water.

It would certainly be quicker and less energy-sapping than the arduous swim back to shore.

'There.' He pointed. 'We should be able to get onto those rocks. Go. I'll follow you.'

Evie felt tired just looking at the waves sloshing against the rocks. He didn't consult with her or seek agreement from her. Typical Finn—used to everyone jumping when he demanded it.

Finn frowned at her lack of activity. 'C'mon, Evie,' he said briskly. 'You're cold, you need to get out of the water.'

Evie looked back at him, his unkempt jawline and freaky blue eyes giving him a slightly crazy edge. Like he conquered rough seas and rocky headlands every day.

'Evie!' he prompted again.

Evie sighed. 'Okay, okay,' she muttered, kicking off in a pathetic type of dog paddle because anything else was beyond her.

Two slow minutes later they were almost within reach and Finn kicked ahead of her, looking for the best purchase. Finding a smooth, gently sloping rock that was almost like a ramp into the water, he reached for it. A breaker came from out of nowhere and knocked him against the surface, his ribs taking the brunt of the impact. Pain jolted him like a lightning strike and cold, salty water swept into his mouth as his breath was torn from his lungs.

Evie gasped. 'Finn!'

'I'm fine,' he grunted, gripping the surface of the rock as pain momentarily paralysed his breathing. He lay for long moments like a landed fish, gasping for air.

'Finn?'

Finn rolled on his back at an awkward angle, half on the rock, half in the water. 'I'm fine,' he said again as his lungs finally allowed the passage of a little more air. 'Here,' he said, half-sitting, the pain less now. Still, he gritted his teeth as he held out his hand. 'Grab hold, I'll pull you up.'

Evie did as she was told and in seconds she was dragged up next to him and they both half wriggled, half crawled onto flatter, water-smoothed rocks back from the edge, away from the suck and pull of the ocean.

They collapsed beside each other, dragging in air and recovering their strength. Evie shut her eyes against the feeble breaking sunlight and wished it was strong enough to warm the chill that went right down into her bones. The wind didn't help, turning the flesh on her arms and legs to goose-bumps, tightening her nipples.

Finn lay looking at the sky. His ribs hurt—for sure there was going to be a bruise there tomorrow—but now they were safe he wanted to throttle her for scaring ten years off his life. He sat up. 'Let's go.'

Evie groaned. Despite how cold she was, she just wanted to lie there and shut her eyes for a moment. 'Just a sec.'

'No,' he said standing up. 'Now. You're hypothermic. Walking will help.'

And if he stayed here with her he was going to let the adrenaline that had surged through him have free rein and it was not going to be pretty. His brain was already crowded with a hundred not-so-nice things to say to her and given that he'd already dumped on her earlier, she probably didn't need another dressing down.

He crouched beside her and grabbed her arm, pulling firmly. 'Now, Evie!'

Evie opened her eyes at the distinct crack in his tone—like a whip. She knew she should be grateful, she knew she should apologise for calling him a coward when the man had jumped into a rip to help her, but she wasn't feeling rational. She wanted a hot shower and a warm bed.

Normally she'd fantasise about snuggling into him in that bed too but he was being too crabby and today was not a normal day.

'Okay, okay,' she said, letting him drag her into a sitting position and going on autopilot as she assisted him in getting her fully upright. She leaned heavily against him as her legs almost gave out.

He cursed. 'You're freezing.'

Evie frowned at his language but nodded anyway, her teeth chattering for good measure. 'Cold,' she agreed. 'Tired.'

'Right,' he said briskly. 'Let's go. Quick march. Up and over the rocks then onto the sand then up the stairs.'

Evie groaned as her legs moved, feeling stiff and un-coordinated as if they'd had robotic implants. 'Oh, God, those bloody stairs,' she complained as Finn dragged her along.

'You'll have warmed up by then,' he said confidently.

'Oh, yes,' she mocked. 'I'll be able to sprint right up them.'

It was on the tip of Finn's tongue to snap that she'd made her own trouble but he was afraid that once he started, the fear that had gripped his gut as he'd raced down those stairs would bubble out and he'd say more stuff that he regretted, like he had earlier today.

So he didn't say anything, just coaxed, bullied and cajoled her every step over the headland, gratified to see her become more co-ordinated and less irrational as her body warmed up. When they reached sand he jogged ahead of her to where her bag had been dis-carded on the beach, took out her fluffy dry towel and jogged back to her, wrapping her in it.

'You must be cold too,' Evie protested as she sank into its warm folds.

'I'm fine,' he dismissed.

Somehow they made it to the top of the stairs and into the homestead and Finn was pushing Evie into the bathroom and turning the hot shower on and ordering her in. She'd never been more grateful for Finn being his bossy, crabby self.

Thirty minutes later Evie was tucked up in her bed and drifting off to sleep on a blissfully warm cloud when Finn barged in, carrying a tray.

'Drink this,' he ordered plonking a steaming mug of something on her bedside table along with a huge slab of chocolate cake on a delicate plate with a floral border. 'Reginald insists,' he said.

Evie struggled to sit up, every muscle in her body protesting the movement. 'Well, if Reginald insists…'

She propped herself against the headrest, drawing her knees up as she reached for the mug. The aroma of chocolate seduced her, making her stomach growl and her mouth fill with saliva, and she was suddenly ravenous.

She sighed as her first sip of the hot sweet milk coated the inside of her mouth and sent her taste buds into rapture. Finn, dressed in a T-shirt and jeans, prowled around the end of her bed, slapping the tray against his legs, and she tried her best to ignore him as she reached for the cake.

Finn paced as Evie ate, reliving their moments in the ocean, still feeling edgy from the hit of adrenaline. He'd tried not to think of the hundred things that could have gone wrong when he'd been in the water and trying to get her back to the house, but the minute the bathroom door had shut and he'd known she was truly safe, reaction had well and truly set in.

They'd been lucky. *She'd* been lucky. He wondered if she had a clue how close she'd come to being a drowning statistic. The thought sent a chill up his spine.

As much as she was a pain in his butt, the thought of her not being around was unthinkable.

Did she not realise how precious life was?

Had growing up with that damn silver spoon in her mouth blinded her to the perils mere mortals faced every day?

Bloody little princess!

His ribs grabbed and moaned at him with every foot-fall, stoking his anger at her stupidity higher and higher.

Evie had eaten half of the cake before his silent skulking finally got on her last nerve. 'Why don't you just say it, Finn?'

Finn stopped mid-pace and looked at her. Her hair was still damp from her near-death experience in an unfriendly ocean and despite her obvious exhaustion she looked so damned imperious and defiant he wanted to put her over his knee and spank her. He threw the tray on the bed.

'What the devil were you doing, swimming by yourself? You could have been swept out to sea, dashed on the rocks, drowned from exhaustion, frozen to death or been eaten by a bloody shark!'

Evie blinked at the litany of things that could have befallen her. They'd lurked in her mind as the current had dragged her further and further away from the shore but she'd tried not to give them any power. Trust Finn to shove them in her face.

Did he really think she needed them spelled out?

Did he think she hadn't collapsed on her butt in the shower, shaking from head to toe at the what-ifs? That she hadn't thought about how she'd not only put her life at risk but the life of their unborn child? She'd never been more grateful to feel the energetic movements of her baby as she'd stripped off her clothes in the shower.

'I know,' she said quietly

But Finn had started pacing again and was, apparently, on a roll. 'And none of us would have known. You'd just suddenly be missing, just…gone.' He clicked his fingers in the air. 'And there'd be hundreds of people everywhere out there, looking for you. Combing the bush and the ocean, and your sisters would be frantic and your father would want to shut this place down and wouldn't rest until Ethan—' He stopped and glared at her. '*A good man doing good things* was nailed to a wall but what would you care? You'd be dead.'

Evie dragged in a rough breath at the passion of his mesmerising speech and his heated gaze that swept over her as if he could see down to her bones.

And what about you, Finn? How would it make you feel?

It hadn't been her goal to scare an admission out of him but his tirade gave her a little hope. Would he be this het up about someone he didn't have feelings for?

'I'm sorry,' she apologised.

'Well, that's not enough!' He twisted to resume his pacing but the abrupt movement jarred through his injury and he cursed under his breath, movement impossible as he grabbed automatically at his ribs with one hand and the wooden framework at the foot of the bed with the other.

Evie sat forward. 'Finn?' He didn't answer, just stood sucking in air, his eyes squeezed shut, his hand splinting his chest. 'Finn!'

'I'm fine,' he snapped.

Evie peeled back the cover and crawled to the end of the bed on her hands and knees. 'You are not,' she said as she drew level with him. 'Let me look,' she said, reaching for his shirt.

Finn stood upright, batting her hand away. 'I said I'm fine, damn it!'

She was wearing a baggy T-shirt and loose cotton shorts that came to just above her knee and she smelled fresh and soapy from the shower and she was so close he wanted to drag her into his arms and assure himself that she really was okay.

But he also wanted to kiss her hard and lose himself in her for a while, and he was more than pleased there was a wooden bed end as a barrier between them.

'Finn, I'm a doctor, remember?'

'So am I.'

She nodded. 'Which is exactly why you shouldn't be diagnosing yourself.'

'It's just a bruise,' he dismissed.

She reached for his shirt, laying her hand against his chest. 'Why don't you let me be the judge of that?' she murmured.

Her palm print seared into his chest and shot his resolve down in flames. He knew he should step back, walk away, but she was lifting his shirt and she was safe and well and so very close, looking like Evie and smelling like her and reminding him of all the times he'd seen her in the hallways at the Harbour looking at him with that aloofness that didn't fool him and making him want her even more and he couldn't make himself resist her.

Not after today.

Evie gasped at the ugly blue black bruise on his side, her fingers automatically tracing its ugly outline. 'Bloody hell, Finn,' she murmured.

But already her fingers were becoming methodical, prodding, shutting her eyes as she fell into a familiar routine. She pushed gently all around the injured area, feeling Finn's abdominal muscles tense, hearing the harsh suck of his breath.

'Sorry,' she murmured, opening her eyes, her own

breath catching at their proximity, at the intensity in his gaze. 'Can't feel or hear any crepitus,' she said, her voice unsteady.

'That's because they're not broken,' he said.

Evie nodded, her breath thick in her throat as her fingers lightly stroked the bruised tissue, exploring the dips of his ribs. 'You should get an X-ray tomorrow when we get back to the Harbour.'

Finn nodded as the light caress of her cool fingers soothed and inflamed all at once. 'Maybe.'

Evie smiled. She guessed his ribs *must* be bad for him to sort of comply so easily. She dropped her hand but he didn't move away and she didn't want him to. They were close enough for her to lay her head on his chest, have him put his arms around her.

Close enough to tell him about the baby.

The silence stretched but she just couldn't get the words out. And she needed him to come back to Sydney. Not disappear.

But she had to say something. Because if she didn't she was going to kiss him and then they'd be on the bed because a kiss was never enough with Finn and he'd find out then for sure.

'Sorry for calling you a coward,' she murmured. 'You're not. Not in the physical sense, anyway. You certainly proved that today.'

Finn grunted. Only Evie could call him an emotional coward and couch it as a compliment. 'I'm sorry for what I said too. I...'

He broke off. He what? He did want to be a surgeon? He did want to be near her? The truth was he'd spoken his mind. But he'd never wanted to hurt her with it. To throw his words at her like they were poisonous darts.

'You what?' she prompted as his unfinished sentence hung in the air.

Finn shook his head, his gaze dropping to Evie's mouth. 'You drive me crazy.'

Evie pulled her bottom lip between her teeth. 'I know.'

Finn felt the movement jolt all the way down to his groin. 'Damn it,' he muttered, reaching for her, sliding his hand under her damp hair at the back of her neck, pulling her head closer as he closed the gap from his side, claiming her mouth on a tortured groan.

'Damn it, damn it, damn it,' he muttered against her lips, as she whimpered and the urge to hurdle the barrier between them took hold and he pushed his other hand into her hair and her mouth opened as his moved against hers and he kissed her hard and deep and hungry, every ragged breath tearing through his ribcage.

A loud knock thundered against her door and he pulled away, gasping. They both were.

'Evie? Evie? Are you okay?'

Finn clutched his chest again as he took a step back, every nerve ending on fire, every cell begging him to get closer, to get looser, to get naked.

His gaze never left her face as he slowly backed even further away, her moist mouth and glazed expression slugging him straight in the groin, begging him to come nearer.

His back bumped gently against the door. 'She's fine, Ethan,' he called.

Then he turned the doorhandle and admitted his friend. And a massive slice of sanity.

CHAPTER FOUR

ON MONDAY MORNING at eight-ten precisely Finn picked up the scalpel and knew Evie was right.

He couldn't not be a surgeon.

He'd been wasting his time, his talent, his future at *Beach Haven* when his true calling was right here—surgery.

Damn it!

As he worked methodically through the steps of the quadruple bypass, as familiar to him as his own breath, the fact that the man on the table was one of the world's richest men faded to black.

Everything faded to black.

It was just him, an open chest and a beating heart. Cutting into the pericardium, harvesting the veins, putting the patient on bypass, clamping the aorta, starting the clock, stopping the heart, grafting the veins beyond the coronary artery blockages, restarting the heart, closing up.

One hundred per cent focused. One hundred per cent absorbed.

Coming out of the zone as he stood back and peeled his gloves off, a little dazed still, as if he'd been in a trance. Registering again the smell of the mask in his nose, the trill and ping of machinery, the strains of Mozart which had been Prince Khalid's music of choice. The murmur of voices around him as they prepared to transfer the patient to ICU.

'Thanks, everyone,' he acknowledged, surprised momentarily that he hadn't been alone.

Nothing had touched him as his fingers and brain had worked in tandem. Evie had been forgotten Isaac had been forgotten. The gnawing hunger of a crappy childhood forgotten.

Just him and the knife.

Taking it all away. Centring him.

And as the outside world started to percolate in through his conscious state, he knew he needed it again.

Damn it!

Finn was surprised to see Evie at the canteen half an hour later when he dropped by to get something to eat on his way to check on Khalid in ICU. Surprised who she was with, anyway. She was sitting with Marco D'Avello and they looked deep in conversation. Marco reached out and touched her hand and Finn was annoyed at the quick burn of acid in his chest. Marco was married—happily married—to Emily and they'd not long had their first child.

What the hell was he doing, touching Evie in the middle of the canteen where everyone could see them?

He hadn't pegged Marco as the straying kind.

Or Evie as a home-wrecker, for that matter.

And even though he knew that wasn't what was going on because he *knew* Evie, it irritated him nonetheless. And not everyone sitting in the canteen would be so forgiving.

He turned away as he placed his order but a sudden short burst of laughter from Evie had him looking back, and suddenly she was looking up and in his direction and her smile died, and for a moment they both just looked at each other before Evie stood up and headed his way.

The woman behind the counter handed Finn his sandwich and drink and he headed for the door.

He didn't want or need any Evie Lockheart chit-chat.

'Finn,' Evie called as he walked out the door, her legs hurrying to catch up. Drat the man—she just wanted to ask him about the surgery. 'Finn. Wait!' she called again as she stepped outside. She watched as he faltered and his shoulders seemed to fall before he slowly turned to face her.

She was in baggy work scrubs—her long, lean legs outlined with each step towards him, and he averted his eyes as he waited for her to catch him up before he resumed his trajectory.

'How'd it go?' Evie asked as she fell into step beside him.

'Fine.'

Evie waited for him to elaborate. He didn't. 'Prince Khalid came through it okay?'

He nodded. 'I'm just going to check on him now.'

They walked some more in silence and Evie could have gleefully strangled him. 'Well?' she demanded when she couldn't wait for him to be forthcoming any longer. 'How'd it feel?' she asked. 'Was it good to be back?'

Finn stopped and shoved his hands on his hips. 'Yes. Was that what you wanted to hear? That you were right? That it felt like I was coming home? Well, it did. And after I've been to the ICU I'm heading up to Eric

Frobisher's office to get myself back on the OR schedule. Eric, who is an arse and will make a huge song and dance over the *inconvenience* of it all, even though he knows I'm the best damn cardiothoracic surgeon in the country, just because he can. Are you satisfied?'

Evie wanted to be satisfied. Her heart was tapping out a jig and emotion, light and airy, bloomed in her chest. If he was here then maybe there was a chance for them. Maybe with the baby in the mix, Finn would eventually admit what she knew was in his heart.

But she didn't want him to feel trapped.

'I'm glad that you're staying. But I don't want you to be miserable.'

'Well, you can't have it both ways, Princess Evie. You can have me here doing what I do best, what I need to do, but if you want me to be whistling in the corridors and singing to bluebirds as they land on my shoulder, that isn't going to happen.'

He dropped his hands and started walking again towards the lifts.

'You don't have to work here,' she called after his back. What was the point if he just came to resent her more? 'You could do this anywhere. You could walk into any hospital in this country and name your price.'

It was a startling reality for her but Evie knew that a man like Finn had to operate. Even if it meant doing it somewhere else. Didn't they say if you loved someone you had to set them free?

Finn turned again. He knew that. He'd done nothing but turn the conundrum over and over in his brain for the last half an hour. He'd trawled through his many options but had discarded each one. Partly because Sydney Harbour Hospital had the best cardiothoracic department in the country, partly because Evie was here and he just didn't seem to be able to stay away, but mostly because it felt like home. It was the longest he'd ever stayed anywhere and deep down Finn was still an eight-year-old boy desperate for the stability of the familiar.

'I only work at the best,' he said impatiently, knowing it was only a half-truth and feeling like a coward as she looked at him with her clear hazel gaze. 'Sydney Harbour Hospital is the best.'

He marched to the lift and pushed the button. She followed. The empty lift arrived promptly. He got on.

She followed.

And because he was angry that she was still right beside him and that she was always going to be around as long as he was here, smoothing away at his edges and his resistance like bloody Chinese water torture, he lashed out at the first thing that entered his head.

'I didn't realise you and Marco D'Avello were such pals.'

Evie frowned at the slight accusation in his voice, nervous that he might connect the dots. 'I'm sorry?'

'You need to be careful. You know how easily gossip starts in a place like this.'

Evie blinked as his implication became clear. Clearly no dots to worry about! 'Don't be ridiculous,' she spluttered.

Finn held up a hand in surrender. 'I really don't care what you do, Evie, or who you do it with,' he lied, 'but maybe you might like to consider his wife and their newborn baby and how gossip might affect them.'

Evie was momentarily speechless. Which turned to outrage pretty quickly. She wasn't sure if it was because of what he was suggesting or the fact that he really didn't seem to give a fig if it was the truth or not.

That she might actually be sleeping with Marco D'Avello.

Who was married!

The lift pinged as they arrived on the third floor and the doors opened. 'Is that what you think?' she asked as he walked out. She stepped out too just as two nurses appeared, grabbing the lift as the doors started to shut. 'That Marco and I are…having some kind of affair?' she hissed as the doors shut behind them.

Finn sighed at the injury in her voice and quashed the little niggle of irritation that had pecked at his brain since he'd witnessed the canteen hand squeeze. 'Of course not, Evie. But in this place, where gossip is a second language, you can bet that others will…that's all I'm saying.'

Evie glared at him. Wanted to tell him he was being preposterous but she knew it to be true. How much gossip had she heard about herself over the years? In her first year it had been about what a stuck-up cow she was, breaking poor Stuart's heart, thinking she was too good for him even though he'd broken her heart when she'd discovered he only wanted her for her family name and connections.

And in this last year or so endless reams of gossip about her and Finn.

Evie felt herself deflate like a balloon as all the fight oozed out of her. 'Yes. People do like to talk, don't they?'

Finn shrugged. 'Well, they're going to talk anyway. Best not to feed them too much ammunition—that's my philosophy.'

Evie blinked. 'You've done nothing but feed them ammunition the entire time you've been here. Sleeping with any pretty young thing that batted her eyelashes at you.'

Even her. Not that she'd ever batted her eyelashes.

He grinned. 'It stopped them talking about my injury, though, didn't it?'

Evie grinned back at his unashamed admission—she couldn't help herself. He suddenly seemed years younger than his trademark stubbly jawline portrayed and it was rare to share such a moment with him. He was always so intense—to see him amused was breathtaking.

Suddenly Evie felt back on an even keel. Enough to begin a dialogue about the subject she'd been avoiding. 'Do you think we can find some time this week to talk?' she asked tentatively.

Finn felt the bubble of happiness that had percolated from nowhere burst with a resounding pop. *A talk* sounded as inviting as root-canal treatment.

He eyed her warily. 'I don't like to talk.'

Evie nodded. 'I've noticed.'

'Nothing's changed just because I'm back, Evie.'

She steeled herself against the ominous warning. It would do her well to take heed.

Finn Kennedy was one hard nut to crack.

'I know,' she rushed to assure him. 'It's not about that. About us.'

Not strictly speaking anyway.

She crossed her fingers behind her back. 'It's... something else.' She stopped and wondered if it sounded like the complete hash it was. 'It's to do with work...'

It was. *Sort of.* Her career was going to have to take a back seat for a while. His would be affected too if he wanted to be involved with the baby.

She watched his frown deepen. Why did she have to fall for a man who was always so suspicious? 'Look, it's complicated, okay? Can you just say yes? Then I'll promise not to bother you again.'

Finn wasn't keen on *a talk*. In his experience women's talks involved rings and dresses and happily ever afters. But it was work related…and the payoff sounded pretty damn good to him.

Never being bothered by her again was an opportunity he couldn't pass up.

It was a futile hope, of course, because he dreamed about her too bloody much to ever fully realise that blissful state of Evie-lessness and every time he saw her a very distinct, very unevolved, caveman urge seemed to overcome him.

But if she could do her bit then he could master the rest. He was used to it.

'After Khalid's discharge?' he suggested. 'A few days? At Pete's?'

Evie slowly exhaled her pent-up breath. 'Thank you.'

Finn nodded. 'I'll let you know.'

He didn't wait for her to answer. Just turned away, his mind already shifting gears.

After some rhythm complications, it was Friday afternoon before Khalid was discharged to a penthouse suite at one of the city's most luxurious hotels. It was top secret but Finn knew and Khalid had his number. Along with round-the-clock private nurses, Finn was confident the prince would have a very nice convalescence with a world-class view.

He'd seen Evie around over the intervening days—with just one VIP patient on his books, he wasn't exactly flush with things to do. In fact, glimpses of her here, there and everywhere were driving him more than a little nutty. And always, it seemed, she was deep in conversation with Marco. By the end of the week he was starting to wonder if perhaps there *was* something going on with them after all.

His idleness was driving him spare—giving him too much time to think. At *Beach Haven* it had been what he'd needed—but back in amongst the rush and hurry of *the Harbour* he needed to be busy. Eric, the CEO, had been the superior jerk he'd predicted and had refused to put Finn back on the surgical roster until after their VIP had been discharged.

But, as of Monday, he was back. Which would give him a lot less time to wonder about what Evie and Marco were up to.

To wonder about Evie full stop.

The prospect of *the talk* had kept her front and centre all week—with no surgery to do and just Khalid to see, there'd been nothing else to occupy his brain. He pulled his mobile phone out of his pocket as he made his way to his outpatient rooms. It was time to get it out of the way.

Check it off his list.

Start the new week with a clean slate.

And it was an opportunity to lay down some ground rules with Evie. They couldn't go on the way they had been prior to him leaving. He was different now—his injury was healed. He didn't need anyone's sympathy or pity or to cover for his lapses.

If they were going to co-exist peacefully in this hospital he had to start as he meant to go on.

Without Evie.

Evie breathed a sigh of relief as the electronic noise of the monitor grew fainter as the last patient from the pile-up on the motorway was whisked off to Theatre. They'd been frantic for hours and between the adrenaline buzz, the noise pollution and the baby dancing the rumba inside her she had a massive headache.

She could hear the soft plaintive beep of another alarm in the empty cubicle and it nibbled at her subconscious like fingernails down a chalk board. 'Where the hell is that coming from?' she asked irritably as her stomach growled and the baby kicked.

She looked around at the electronic gadgetry vital in a modern emergency department. The alarm wasn't one she was familiar with as she approached the bank of monitors and pumps.

'It's the new CO_2 monitor,' Mia di Angelo, her ex-flatmate and fellow emergency physician, said. 'It can't be on charge.'

Evie scanned the machines for an unfamiliar one. She hated it when they got new equipment. It was great to keep their department up to date and stocked with the latest and greatest but it was hell assimilating all the new alarms and buttons.

When she located the unfamiliar piece of equipment with its little yellow flashing light she followed the cord at the back and noticed it trailing on the floor instead of being plugged into the power supply at the back of the cubicle. She squeezed in behind, not such an easy job any more, and the baby let her know it did not like being constricted by a swift one-two jab.

She sucked in a breath, her hand automatically going to her belly in a soothing motion as she bent over, picked up the plug from the floor and pushed it into the socket.

Instead of the instant peace she was hoping for, a loud sizzle followed by some sparks and the pungent smell of burnt electrical wiring rent the air. The point where her fingers touched the plug tingled then burned, a painful jolt cramped up her arm and knocked her backwards onto her butt.

'Evie!' Mia gasped rushing to her friend's side. 'Are you okay?'

Evie blinked, too dazed for a moment to fully understand what had happened. All she was aware of was a pain in her finger and the sudden stillness of the baby.

'What's wrong?' Evie heard Luca's voice. He was Mia's husband and head of the department.

'Help me get her up,' Mia said. 'She got an electric shock from the pump.

Evie felt arms half pulling, half guiding her into a standing position. 'Evie, talk to me. Are you okay?' Mia was saying, inspecting the tiny white mark on Evie's index finger.

'Let's get her on a monitor,' Luca was saying as his fingers palpated the pulse at her wrist.

Suddenly she broke out of her daze. 'No.'

She shook her head. The baby. It was so, so still. She needed to see Marco. She had to know if the shock had affected the baby.

She had to know now.

'I'm fine,' she assured them, breaking out of their hold. 'Really I am.'

Mia frowned and folded her arms. 'You just got a zap that knocked you on your butt. You should be monitored for a while.'

Evie shook her head again and forced a smile onto her face even though it felt like it was going to crack into a thousand pieces as concern for the baby skyrocketed with every single stationary second. 'I'm fine. I'm in the middle of a hospital. If I start to feel unwell, I'll let you know.'

Luca nodded. 'Her pulse is steady.'

Mia grabbed Evie's hand. 'This could do with a burns consult in case it's worse than it looks. It'll definitely need dressing.'

Evie thought quickly. 'Yes. Good idea. It's burns clinic today, right? I'll pop in and see if they can squeeze me in.'

'I'll come with you,' Mia said.

'Status epilepticus two minutes out,' a nurse said to them as she dashed past.

And then the distant strains of a siren, a beautiful, beautiful siren, made itself known, and Evie had never been more grateful to hear the wretched noise.

'You can't,' Evie said. 'You're needed here. You both are. I'll be fine,' she assured them again, a surge of desperation to get away, to get to Marco, making her feel impotent.

'Okay,' Mia acquiesced. 'But I want to see you after you get back.'

Evie nodded. 'Absolutely.'

By the time she scurried up to the outpatient department ten minutes later Evie was frantic. The baby hadn't moved and an ominous black cloud hovered over her head. When she'd been hypothermic in the middle of the ocean her brain had been too sluggish to think of the implications for the baby. But today all her mental faculties were intact and totally freaking her out as all the horrible possibilities marched one by one through her mind.

She was on the verge of tears when she finally located Marco, who wasn't in his rooms but was chatting to a midwife in the long corridor that ran behind the outpatients department.

'Marco,' she called.

He looked up and smiled at her, his joy quickly dying as he saw the distress on her face. He strode over to her.

'Evie,' he said with that lovely lilt of his, his hands grasping her upper arms, a frown marring his classically handsome face. He could see she was about to crumple and led her away from the busy thoroughfare into the nearby cleaning closet. It wasn't very roomy and the door was chocked open but it was more private than outside. 'What is wrong?'

'I think the baby might be dead,' she whispered, choking on a sob as she buried her face in his chest.

Finn scrolled through his contacts on his phone as he stepped out of the lift and headed for the outpatients department. He wanted to spend some time looking at the case notes for his theatre list on Monday. He found Evie's number and hit the button as he entered the department.

His gaze wandered across to the corridor on the far side as he waited for her to pick up and that's when he spotted them. Evie and Marco alone in some kind of supply cupboard—embracing. He fell back a little, shocked by the image, watching them from just outside the department as they pulled apart slightly and Evie fumbled in her scrubs pocket and pulled out her phone.

'Hello?'

Finn didn't say anything for a moment, trying to decide how he should play it. 'It's me,' he said, watching her as she stayed in the shelter of Marco's body, his arm around her shoulder. 'I'm free for that talk now.'

Evie looked up at Marco as she grappled with a vortex of emotions

Now? He wanted to talk now?

'Er...I can't right now... I'm busy.'

Finn raised an eyebrow. Icy fingers crept around his heart and he leant against the nearby wall. 'Emergency a little crazy at the moment?'

Evie nodded, grabbing the excuse he had thrown her with glee. 'Certifiable.'

The fingers squeezed down hard. 'I could come down there and wait for you,' he suggested.

Alarm raced along Evie's nerve endings. 'No, no,' she said. 'I'll give you a ring when it settles and I can meet you across at Pete's.'

'Okay,' he murmured.

'Bye.'

Finn blinked at her hasty hang-up and to torture himself a little further he watched as Marco drew her against his chest and hugged her again before walking her to his rooms, his arm firmly around her waist.

He had absolutely no idea what the hell was going on with those two but he had every intention of finding out! She'd been pretty convincing in her mortification at his inference that she and Marco were *sleeping together* a few days ago but maybe she was protesting too much? Maybe there was more to Marco and Evie than she was letting on?

His heart pounded as bile burned in his chest and acid flowed through his veins. He pushed off the wall and headed in their direction.

'Finn Kennedy, well, I'll be. I heard you were back.'

Finn stopped in mid-stride to greet Sister Enid Kenny, nurse in charge of Outpatients for about a hundred years and a true Sydney Harbour Hospital icon. She was large and matronly and no one, not even the great Finn Kennedy, messed with Enid Kenny.

If she wanted to chat, you stopped and chatted.

Unfortunately for him, as he looked over her shoulder at the closed door of Marco's office, she was in a very chatty mood.

Evie was so relived she'd agreed to the ultrasound as she watched her baby—her baby boy—move around on the screen. Marco had been trying to convince her to have one all week but part of her had wanted to break the news to Finn before having an ultrasound, which she'd been hoping he would want to attend.

But after her scare just listening to the heartbeat wasn't going to cut it. She needed to see him. To watch him move. To reassure herself fully. To count his fingers and toes, to see the chambers of his heart, the hemispheres of his brain.

To know everything was perfect.

Marco was very thorough doing measurements and pointing out all the things any radiographer would have and Evie felt the gut wrenching worry and the threatening hysteria ease as her little boy did indeed seem perfect.

'Can I hear the heartbeat one more time?' Evie asked.

Marco chuckled. 'But of course.'

He flicked a switch on the ultrasound machine and the room filled with the steady *whop, whop, whop* of a robust heartbeat.

Neither of them expected the door to suddenly crash open or for Finn to be standing there, glowering at them and demanding to know what the devil was going on.

Evie was startled at the loud intrusion. 'Finn,' she whispered.

Marco turned calmly in his chair. 'Welcome, Dr Kennedy. You're just in time to meet your son,' he said.

It took Finn a moment or two to compute the scene before his eyes. The lights down low. Evie lying on the examination bed, her scrub top pulled up, a very distinctive bump protruding and covered in goo. Marco's hand holding an ultrasound probe low down on Evie's belly. A grainy image of a foetus turning somersaults on the screen.

And the steady thump of a strong heartbeat.

Finn looked at Evie and shoved his hands on his hips. 'What the hell...?' he demanded.

Marco looked at Evie as he removed the probe and reached for some wipes. 'I think I should leave you and Finn to talk, yes?' he murmured as he methodically removed every trace of the conduction gel.

Evie sat up, dragging her top down as she did so. Finn stood aside as Marco passed him, flipping on the light as he went and shutting the door after him.

'You're pregnant?' he demanded, his own heartbeat roaring through his ears at the stunning turn of events. He'd half expected to barge in and find she and

Marco doing the wild thing on the desk. He'd never expected this.

Evie nodded. 'Yes.'

Her quiet affirmative packed all the power of a sucker punch to his solar plexus. 'This is what you wanted to talk about?'

'Yes.'

He shook his head as all the control he'd fought for over the years started to disintegrate before him, unravelling like a spool of cotton.

His breath felt tight. His jaw clenched. His pulse throbbed through his veins, tapping out *no, no, no* against his temple.

'No.'

He couldn't be a father. He just couldn't. He was selfish and arrogant and egotistical. He was busy. He was dedicated to his job. He hadn't grown up in any home worth a damn and the one person who'd been entrusted to his care had died in his arms.

He was damaged goods. Seen too much that had hardened him. Made him cynical. Jaded.

Not father material.

Most days he didn't even know how to be a normal, functioning human being—he was just going through the motions.

How on earth could he be a decent father?

He looked at her watching him, wariness in her hazel eyes. But hope as well. And something else. The same thing he always saw there when she looked at him— belief.

She had no idea who he really was.

He steeled his heart against the image that seemed

to be ingrained on his retinas—his baby on an ultra-sound screen.

'You have to get an abortion.'

Evie flinched at the ice in his tone. It wasn't anything she hadn't thought about herself in those days when she'd lived in a space where denying the baby even existed had been preferable to facing the truth. But she'd felt him move now, seen him sucking his thumb on the screen just a few minutes ago, and even if she hadn't already decided against it and it had been possible at this advanced stage in her pregnancy, she knew she could never do what Finn was asking.

'I'm twenty-one weeks.'

Finn opened his mouth to dispute it but the evidence of his own eyes started to filter in. The size of her belly and the size of the baby on the screen and then some quick maths in his head all confirmed her gestation.

He groped for Marco's desk as the import of her words hit home.

There could be no abortion.

There would be a baby.

He was going to be a father.

'Why didn't you tell me?'

Evie swung her legs over the edge of the couch. 'Because you went away and I spent a long, *long* time in denial. And, honestly, I think because part of me knew you'd demand what you just demanded and even though I'd thought about it myself, a part of me wanted to put it beyond reach. For both of us. And then the longer you go...' she shrugged. '...the harder it gets.'

'You've just spent two weeks with me at *Beach Haven*. You could have told me then.'

'I almost did but...' She looked at him staring at her

like she'd just been caught with state secrets instead of a bun in the oven. 'You're not very approachable, Finn.'

He looked at her for a long moment. 'I don't know how to be a father.'

Evie sucked in a breath at the bleakness in his blue eyes. He suddenly looked middle-aged. 'You think I know how to be a mother?' she asked. 'My mother was an absent alcoholic. Not exactly a stellar role model.'

Finn snorted. She had no idea. Her poor-little-rich-girl upbringing had been a walk in the park compared to his. 'I think you'll figure it out.'

'I think you will, too,' she said, feeling suddenly desperate to connect with him. To make him understand that she knew it was daunting. But they could do it.

Finn's pager beeped and he was grateful for the distraction as he absently reached for it and checked the message on the screen. It was Khalid.

'I have to go,' he said.

He needed to think. To get away. Life events had robbed him of a lot of choices and now even the choice not to burden some poor child with his emotionally barren existence had been snatched away.

'Okay.' She nodded, pushing down the well of emotion that was threatening as she watched him turn away from her.

He needed time and she had to give him that. It had taken *her* months to adjust and accept and she wasn't Finn. A man who didn't express emotion well and never let anyone close.

She had to give him space to come to terms with it.

So she sat there like a dummy as he walked out the door, despite how very, very much she wanted to call him back.

CHAPTER FIVE

FINN WOKE UP at nine on Saturday morning, his head throbbing from one too many hits of his very expensive malt whisky the previous night.

It had been a good while since he'd overdone the top-shelf stuff. For years he'd used it to dull the physical pain from his injuries but since his recovery and his move to *Beach Haven* he'd only ever indulged in the odd beer or two.

He'd forgotten how it could feel like a mule had kicked you in the head the next day. Which might actually be worth it if it had come with some sort of clarity.

It hadn't.

Just a thumping headache and the very real feeling that he'd woken up in hell.

He stared at the ceiling as the same three words from last night repeated in his head—*Evie is pregnant*. Each word pounded like a battering ram against the fortified shell surrounding his heart with a resounding boom.

Evie. *Boom!* Is. *Boom!* Pregnant. *Boom!*

He was going to be a father. Some tiny little defenceless human being with his DNA was going to make its arrival in four short months. He was going to be *Daddy*.

Whether he liked it or not.

And it scared the hell out of him. Being a parent—*a*

good parent—required things life just hadn't equipped him with. Like compassion, empathy, love.

There'd been so little love in his life. From the moment his mother had abandoned him and Isaac to a childhood in institutions to his regimented life in the army, ruled by discipline and authority, love had been non-existent. Sure, he'd loved and protected Isaac and Isaac had loved him, but it had been a very lonely island in a vast sea of indifference.

Add to that the slow fossilising of his emotions to deal with the horror and injuries witnessed in far-flung battlefields and the death knell to any errant tendrils of love and tenderness that might still have existed when Isaac had died in his arms and the product was the man he was today.

Ten years since that horrifying day and still he felt numb. Blank. Barren.

Emotionally void.

He hadn't loved Lydia, his brother's widow, with whom he'd had a totally messed up affair and who had needed him to love her no matter how screwed up it had been at the time.

He operated with the cold, clinical precision of a robot. Always seeing the part, never seeing the whole. Totally focussed. Never allowing himself to think about the person whose heart he held in his hands or the love that heart was capable of. Just doing the job. And doing it damn well.

He hadn't felt anything for any of the women he'd slept with. They had just been pleasant distractions. Something different to take to bed instead of a bottle of Scotch. A momentary diversion.

Apart from Evie. Whom he'd pushed and pushed and pushed away and who knew what he was like but refused to give up anyway. Who could look right past his rubbish and see deep inside to the things he kept hidden.

Evie, who was having his baby.

A baby he didn't know how to love.

A sudden knock at his door stomped through his head like a herd of stampeding elephants and he groaned out loud. He wanted to yell to whoever it was to go away but was afraid he might have a stroke if he did. If he just lay here, maybe Evie would think he'd already gone out.

Because that knock had the exact cadence of a pissed-off woman.

It came again followed by, 'Finn? Finn!'

Lydia? Wrong pissed-off woman.

'Finn Kennedy, open this bloody door now. Don't make me get my key out!'

Finn rolled out of bed. It wasn't the smoothest exit from his bed he'd ever executed but considering he felt like he was about to die, the fact he could walk at all was a miracle.

'Coming,' he called as the knock came again, wincing as it drove nails into his brain.

He wrenched open the door just as he heard a metallic scratching from the other side. His brother's widow, a petite redhead, stood on the doorstep glowering at him, hands on hips.

'You look like hell,' she said.

He grunted. 'I feel like hell.'

'Right,' she said, striding past him into his apartment. 'Coffee first, I think. Then you can tell me what happened to get you into this state.'

Finn was tempted to throw her out. But he really, really needed coffee.

* * *

Fifteen minutes later he was inhaling the aroma of the same Peruvian Arabica beans Lydia had brought him the last time she'd come for a flying visit and he hadn't touched since. Grinding beans was way too much trouble, no matter how good they were. He took a sip of coffee and shut his eyes as his pulse gave a little kick.

His home phone rang from the direction of his bedroom and he ignored it as he felt the coffee slowly reviving him. Khalid only had his mobile number and everything else could just wait.

Lydia waited until he'd taken a few more sips before pinning him with that direct look of hers. She'd come a long way since the broken woman he'd comforted a decade ago. In his own grief and in the midst of their screwy relationship he had judged her harshly for that, for what he'd perceived as weakness, but she had come out the other side a much stronger person.

'Spill,' she said.

Finn thought about playing dumb but the truth was that Lydia was one of the few people who really understood how he ticked. She'd been the one who'd moved on from their half-hearted affair when she'd seen it had been perpetuating an unhealthy co-dependence. The strange mix of relief and regret at its ending had confused him but she'd never left him completely and as his one tangible link to Isaac he'd been grateful for her watchful eye and bossy persona.

'Evie's pregnant.'

Lydia blinked. 'Oh.'

Finn took another sip of his coffee. 'Indeed.'

'It's yours?'

Finn nodded. It wasn't something he'd questioned for a moment. 'A little boy.'

'Oh,' Lydia said again, hiding a smile as she sipped at her coffee.

Finn frowned. 'Are you smiling?'

Lydia shook her head, feigning a serious expression. 'Absolutely not.'

'This is not funny.'

Her shaking became more vigorous. 'Not funny at all.'

Finn plonked his mug on the coffee table and raked his hands through his hair; his chest felt tight and his heart raced. He blamed the coffee rather than what he suspected it actually was—sheer panic.

Lydia didn't understand.

Except she did.

His hands trembled as he looked at her with bleak eyes that had seen too much hate. 'I'm too damaged for a baby, Lyd.'

Lydia's smile disappeared in an instant and she reached out her hand to cover his. 'Maybe this is just what you need to help you heal?' she murmured.

He shook her hand away—how could he gamble that on the life of an innocent child? 'I never wanted a baby. This wasn't my choice.'

'Well, we don't always get what we want in life, do we, Finn? You know that better than anyone. So you didn't get a say? Too bad—it's here, it's happening. And guess what, you do get a choice about what you do now.'

Finn stared at her incredulously. 'What? *Be a father*?'

'Yes,' she nodded. 'Be a father.'

Finn shook his head as his chest grew tighter, practically constricting his chest. 'No.'

'Be the father you always wanted.'

Finn shook his head. 'I never wanted a father.'

Lydia gave him a stern look. 'Isaac told me, Finn. He told me how you wished every night for a father to come and take you both away from it all. That you'd tell him stories about him picking you up and taking you to Luna Park for the day and a ferry on the harbour and then back to his house by the sea. You can't go back and fix that, but you do get a chance to start over.'

Lydia stood, swooping his empty mug off the table. 'You want your son to not have a father either? To miss out on such a vital ingredient in his childhood? To dream every night of you coming and taking him out to Luna Park and for a ride on the ferry and to live by the sea? A boy needs a father, Finn.'

'He needs a mother more.'

She shook her head. 'No, he needs a mother *as well*.'

Finn chewed on his lip. Why did Lydia always make so much sense? But the nagging, gnawing worry that spewed stomach acid and bile like a river of hot lava inside his gut just wouldn't let up.

He looked at Lydia. A woman who had needed him to love her. A love he'd been incapable of giving. 'What if I...?' He could barely even bring himself to say the words. 'What if I don't love him?'

Lydia gave him a sad smile. 'You already do, Finn. Why else are we having this conversation? Just *be* a father. The rest will follow.'

By the time Lydia had ordered him to take a couple of headache pills and have a shower then dragged him to Pete's for brunch, Finn was feeling more human again. She'd nattered away about the weather and her job and the football scores and other inane topics, for which he was grateful, and by midday he was back at his apartment alone, with Lydia's wise words turning over and over in his head.

He wasn't utterly convinced by any of them but he had started to think that being part of his child's life was a responsibility he shouldn't shirk.

How many times as a boy had he vowed to do it different when he became a father? Back in the days before all hope for his future had been quashed. When he'd believed that his life could still be normal.

Lydia was right. A boy needed a father.

A stable, committed presence.

God knew, he and Isaac could have done with one instead of the bunch of losers that had drifted in and out of their mother's life until one had stuck and they'd been pushed out of the nest.

He could do stable and committed.

The light was flashing on the answering-machine from the call earlier and he hit the button to listen to the message.

'Finn…its Evie. I didn't really want to tell this to your machine but…what the hell…it might just be easier all round. I just wanted you to know that I know it's a lot for you to comprehend and I didn't want to tell you to…get something out of you. I'm not after money or any kind of…support. It's okay…you don't have to have anything to do with him…the baby… I just think you deserved to know, that's all. I'm happy to do it all. I'm fine with you never being a part of his life. I don't need that from you. So…that's all really. I just wanted you to know that you're off the hook…if that's what you want. Okay…bye.'

Beep...

Finn stared at the machine. *He was off the hook?* If that's what he wanted?

It should have been what he wanted. He wasn't capable of anything else—he'd just been telling Lydia the same thing. But a surge of anger welled up in his chest, washing over him with all the rage and power of a tsunami.

I'm fine with you never being a part of his life.

You don't have to have anything to do with him.

Like his own father.

Evie was going to raise *his* son by herself. Without his money. His input. His support.

Without him.

It was what he should want. It made sense. She'd love him and nurture him and provide all the things he needed.

Physically and emotionally.

Comfort and security. A real childhood. Aunties, uncles, grandparents. Birthday parties, trips to the beach, photos with Santa.

It should make him happy but it didn't. The anger dissipated quickly, replaced by something that felt very much like...craving. It slid like a serpent through his gut and whispered.

Be a father.

Damn Evie and her independence. Her grand plans. Her *happy to do it all*. Lydia was right—he did have a choice. And he'd be damned if his son would grow up without a father.

Stable and committed trumped absent any day.

An hour later Evie was examining a patient's foot in cubicle two when the curtain snapped back with a harsh screech. She blinked as Finn stood there, glaring at her with his laser gaze, looking all scruffy and shaggy and very, very determined.

'I need to talk to you Dr Lockheart,' he said. 'Now, thank you.'

His imperious tone ticked her off even as her hormones demanded she swoon at his feet in a puddle of lust. Luckily the baby gave her a hefty kick, as if to remind her she had a backbone and to use it.

'I'm busy,' she said, smiling sweetly for the benefit of the elderly lady, who looked startled at his intrusion.

But not as startled as she was!

Finn smiled at the patient as he strode into the cubicle and put his hand under Evie's elbow. 'Important cardiac consult,' he said to the grey-haired woman. 'It won't take a minute.'

'Oh, of course, dear,' the lady said. 'Off you go. Hearts are more important than my silly broken toe.'

Finn smiled at her as he firmed his grip on Evie. 'Let's go,' he said, pulling insistently against her resistance.

Once outside he dropped his hand and stalked down the corridor, naturally assuming she'd just follow him. Evie had a good mind to walk in the opposite direction and force him to come looking for her again but they did need to talk. In fact, she was a little surprised he was willing to do so this early. She'd assumed he'd be thinking about her little bombshell for a while longer.

Which meant he'd probably got her phone message.

So she followed him, glaring at his broad shoulders and the way his hair curled against his collar until both of them disappeared into the on-call room. She steeled herself, taking a moment before she entered. It had taken all her guts to make that phone call this morning when every cell in her body had been urging her to say the opposite.

But she'd meant it. She'd cope if he didn't want a bar of them. *It would hurt, but she'd cope.*

She took a deep breath and pushed through the door. He was standing waiting for her on the opposite side, his arms folded impatiently across his chest.

'You look awful,' she said.

She'd seen Finn in varying states of disarray. Angry, inebriated, in pain, high on pain pills, in denial, unkempt and hungover.

This was about as hungover as she'd ever seen him.

'Trust me, this is an improvement on a few hours ago.'

'Did it help?' she asked, trying to keep the bitterness out of her voice but not really succeeding.

Finn shook his head. 'Nope.'

Evie folded her hands across her chest. 'I left a message on your machine this morning.'

Finn gave a curt nod. 'I got it.'

'Oh.' Evie's hand dropped automatically to her belly, feeling the hard round ball of her expanding uterus. A nurse that morning had joked that she was 'looking preggers' and Evie knew that her baggy scrubs weren't going to help for much longer. 'I mean it, Finn. I don't need you to be part of this.' *I want you to, though, with every fibre of my being.* 'Plenty of kids grow up in single-parent families and they do just fine.'

Finn thought about his own dismal childhood. *Plenty of kids didn't do just fine as well.* And although he'd always thought being a father was the last thing on earth he wanted, he suddenly realised that was wrong.

His child being fatherless was the last thing he wanted.

Didn't *his* son deserve the very, very best? Everything that *he* hadn't had and more? A happy, settled, normal family life? Two people who loved him living and working together to ensure that his life was perfect?

A father. And a mother.

And a puppy!

'I think we should get married,' he said.

Every molecule inside Evie froze for long seconds as his startling sentence filtered through into suddenly sluggish brain cells. 'What?' she asked faintly when she finally found her voice.

Finn wondered if he looked as shocked as she did at the words that had come from nowhere. They hadn't been what he'd been planning to say when he'd practically dragged her into the on-call room but he knew in his bones they were the right words.

His child was growing inside her and, no matter what, he was going to be present. He was going to *be a father*. Conviction and purpose rose in him like an avenging angel.

'You can move in with me. No, wait, I'll buy a house. Somewhere by the harbour, or the northern beaches. Bondi or Coogee. He can join the Nippers or learn to surf.'

Evie's head spun, trying to keep up with Finn's rapid-fire thinking. 'A house?'

'I think kids should grow up near a beach.'

Having been dragged from one hot suburban shoe-box to the next, he wanted his son to have the freedom of space and a sea breeze and the rhythm of the ocean in his head when he went to sleep instead of rock music from the bikie neighbours or the blare of the television in the next room.

Finn's thoughts raced in time with his pulse. He was going to *be a father*.

'I'll look into celebrants when I get home.'

Evie stared at him incredulously. He had them married and living at the beach with their surfing son all without a single mention of love.

'We'll do it just after the baby's born. No need to inconvenience ourselves until necessary.'

Evie felt as if she'd entered the twilight zone and waited for eerie music to begin. He didn't even want to get married until the baby had arrived—to inconvenience himself. Could he make it any clearer that this sudden crazy scheme had no basis in human emotion? That it wasn't a love match?

Evie had grown up in a house where her parents had been strangers and she was never, *ever* going to subject herself *or her child* to a cold marriage of convenience.

'No,' she said quietly.

Finn shrugged. 'Well, maybe just before then?'

Evie blinked. Oh, when she was as big as a house and needed to get married in a tent? Was he for real? Did he *not* know how important a wedding was to a woman? Even one who wasn't into sappy ceremonies or big flouncy affairs? Didn't he know that most women wanted declarations of love and commitment when they were proposed to?

If that's what this was…

No, of course he didn't. Because, as with everything in his life, Finn just assumed that she'd jump to do his bidding when he asked.

Wrong.

'I'm not marrying you, Finn.'

Finn dragged his attention back to Evie and her softly spoken rebuttal. He snorted. 'Don't be ridiculous, Evie. This is what you wanted, isn't it?'

More than anything. *But not like this.* 'No. I told you, I can raise this baby without your help.'

Finn shoved a hand on his hip. 'Evie…come on…I know how you feel about me…'

She gave a half-laugh at his gall. 'I always forget how capable you are of breathtaking arrogance. Silly of me, really.'

'Evie,' he sighed, desperate to get on with plans now he'd made up his mind, 'let's not play games.'

Evie felt his impatience rolling off him in waves. 'Okay, fine, let's lay our cards on the table. How do *you* feel about *me*?'

Finn felt the question slug him right between the eyes, which were only just recovering from their brush with the whisky. How he felt about Evie was complicated. But he knew it wasn't what she wanted to hear.

'You want me to tell you that I'm in love with you and we're going to ride off into the sunset and it's all going to be hunky-dory? Because I don't and it isn't. Not in a white-picket-fence way anyway.'

Evie moved to the nearby table and sank into a chair. She'd known he didn't love her but it was still hard to hear.

Finn shut his eyes briefly then opened them and joined her, taking the seat opposite. 'I'm sorry, Evie. It's not you. It's me. There's a lot of…stuff in my life…that's happened. I'm just not capable of loving someone.'

Evie nodded even as the admission tore through all the soft tissue around her heart. Had Isaac's death and the other stuff that Ethan had hinted at really destroyed Finn's ability to love?

'Well, that's what I want,' she said quietly. 'What I need. Love and sunsets and white picket fences. And I won't marry for anything less.'

Finn's lips tightened. This had seemed so easy in theory when the marriage suggestion had slipped from his mouth. She'd say yes and the rest would fall into place. It hadn't occurred to him that Evie would be difficult.

In fact, if anything, he'd counted on those feelings she always wore on her sleeve to work in his favour.

'Not when there's a perfectly good alternative,' she continued. 'I'm happy…really, really happy…that you want to be involved, Finn. But we're going to have to work out a way to co-parent separately because I'm not marrying a man who doesn't love me.'

Her words were quiet but the delivery was deadly and Finn knew that she meant every single one. 'Contrary to what you might think, growing up without two parents kind of sucks, Evie. *Trust me on that.*'

Evie shivered at the bitterness in his words. 'Is that what happened to you?' she murmured. Had Ethan been right about Finn's emotional issues extending further back than Isaac's death?

She watched his face slowly shut down, his eyes become chilly. 'We're not talking about me.'

Evie snorted. 'You tell me to trust you, demand that I marry you, but you clam up when I try to get close? Well *trust me,* Finn, growing up with two parents who hate each other kind of sucks too.'

'At least you had a stable home life,' he snapped.

So he hadn't? 'It wasn't stable,' she said through gritted teeth. 'My father just had enough money to buy the illusion of stability. Ultimately my mother was a drunk who came and went in our lives while my father put nannies in the house and mistresses in his bed.'

Finn's mouth twisted. 'Poor little rich girl.' So Evie's life hadn't been perfect—it had still been a thousand per cent better than his had ever been.

Evie shook her head. He really could be an insensitive jerk when he put his mind to it. 'I won't be with a man who doesn't love me.'

She reiterated each word very carefully.

'You seemed to be with Stuart long enough,' Finn jibed, 'and Blind Freddie could have seen he didn't love you.'

Evie gasped at his cruel taunt, the humiliation from that time revisiting with a vengeance. 'At least he'd pretended to care. I doubt you're even capable of that!'

'You want me to pretend? You want me to lie to you? Okay, fine, Evie I love you. Let's get married.'

She stood, ridiculously close to tears and tired of his haranguing. If he thought this was the way to win her over, he was crazy. 'Go to hell, Finn,' she snapped, and stormed out of the room.

Finn's brain was racing as he took the fire stairs up to his penthouse apartment half an hour later. The lifts were being temperamental again and, frankly, after missing his daily ocean swims he could do with the exercise and the extended thinking time. He was breathing hard by the time he got to the fifth floor and stopped by the landing window to catch his breath and absently admire a large slice of the harbour.

Kirribilli Views apartments had certainly been blessed by the location gods.

The door opened and he turned to find Ava Carmichael entering the fire escape. She looked momentarily surprised and then grinned at him. 'We really must stop meeting like this.'

Finn grunted, remembering their last meeting in this stairwell when he'd come upon Ava crying over her broken marriage. Actually, they'd been through a lot together, with him helping her the day she'd miscarried in the lift and then she and Gladys finding him collapsed from a major infection after his first operation.

Not that they'd ever talked about those things. Ava was like that. For a therapist, she was very non-intrusive. Mostly anyway. There had been an occasion or two where she'd spoken her mind but even then she'd given it to him straight. Hadn't couched anything in vague psychological terms.

He liked that about her.

It was good to know that things had improved for both of them since. He had fully recovered from his injury and she and James had reconciled, having had their first baby just before his second operation and his desertion to *Beach Haven*.

'It's not too late,' Finn said, forcing himself to keep things light. 'We can still make out in the stairwell and no one would know.'

Ava laughed at the rumour she'd threatened to start to blackmail him into seeing her the day after he'd scared the daylights out of all of them with his infection. He'd been in an absolutely foul mood but she'd served him up some home truths anyway.

Not that he'd taken them on board.

He was a stubborn, stubborn man. But she had a soft spot for him because he'd never tried to offer any ad-

vice or interfere or make things better when things with
James had been going to hell in a hand basket. Unlike
others. And she'd appreciated that.

'I heard you were back and fully recovered. Although...' she squinted and inspected his face a little
closer '...you don't look so good at the moment.'

Finn almost groaned. Did every woman find it their
duty today to tell him he looked like hell? 'What are
you doing here? Didn't you move to your white-picket-
fence house in the burbs?'

'Just visiting the old stomping ground,' she said.

Finn turned to look back out the window and Ava
knew she had been dismissed, that it was her job to walk
on down the stairs and leave him to his obvious brooding, but there was something achingly lonely about Finn
and they'd been pretty frank with each other in the past.

Still, she hesitated. She knew that Finn was an in-
tensely private man. But then Finn turned his gaze towards her. It was so incredibly turbulent, almost too
painful to look at.

'You're a therapist, right?'

Ava laughed. 'I'm a *sex* therapist, Finn.'

He shrugged. 'But you *do* have a psychology degree?'

Ava nodded. 'Is there something you want to talk
about?'

Finn shook his head. He wanted to talk to Ava Carmichael about as much as he wanted to become a father
but...she'd always given it to him straight and he could
do with some insight into the female psyche right now.

'Evie's pregnant. I suggested we get married. She
said no. I need her to say yes.'

Ava blinked at the three startling pieces of information. She and Evie were friends, not bosom buddies and they certainly hadn't seen much of each other since her own baby had been born, but she knew more about Finn and Evie's relationship than Finn probably realised.

People told her stuff—it was an occupational hazard.

She knew Evie loved Finn. She knew Finn was a hard man to know and an impossible one to love. She knew that if Evie had turned him down it had been for a pretty good reason.

'Okay...' she wandered closer to him, propping her hip against the window sill. 'So when you say you *suggested*? What did that entail exactly?'

'I said I thought we should get married.'

Ava nodded. 'So, let me guess...you didn't get down on one knee and do the whole big proposal thing? You kind of...presented it as a fait accompli?' Finn looked away from her probing gaze. 'Am I warm?'

He looked back again, glaring. 'It was more of a... spontaneous thing. Us getting married isn't about any of the hoopla. It's about being practical. About giving our child a normal family with a mother and father living under the same roof. And Evie isn't the kind of woman that goes for all that romantic rubbish.'

Ava arched an eyebrow. 'And how do you know that, Finn? Have you ever really even tried to get to know her?'

He looked away again at the view. 'I know she loves me, Ava. Why be coy about it? Why pretend this isn't what she wants?' He looked back at her. 'This way she gets what she wants and I get what I want.'

'What? A man who doesn't love her?'

Finn wanted to smash the window at her gentle insight. 'Look, Ava...it's complicated. I grew up in a single-parent household and then...' He shook his head.

He couldn't tell Ava, no matter what degree she had. He didn't talk about his issues—he just left them behind in the past, where they belonged. Where they couldn't touch him any more. 'I don't want that for my kid.'

Ava pitied him. Finn was a man on the edge and he was the only one who didn't know it. 'Tell *her*, Finn. Not me.'

He shook his head. He was so used to burying it inside he doubted he even knew how to access the words. 'I can't.'

Ava's heart squeezed at the bleakness in his eyes. 'I do recall telling you that this would happen one day, Finn. That by pushing Evie away and not letting her in that one day something would happen and you'd find yourself locked out of Evie's life.'

Finn nodded miserably. She'd said exactly that. Yelled it at him, actually, when he was being rude and stubborn and difficult, refusing to see Evie after he'd been hospitalised with the infection.

'Seriously?' he said. 'You're going with an *I told you so* now? Where'd you get that degree?' he grouched. 'In a cornflakes packet?'

Ava smiled. 'Coco Pops, actually.'

Finn gave a half-smile before turning back to the window. 'Fine. How do I fix it?'

'Maybe it's time to stop pushing her away. To open yourself up.'

Finn pressed his forehead against the glass. She may as well have told him to stand in the middle of the hospital naked. 'What? No pill?'

Ava shook her head. 'I'm afraid not.'

'You're a lousy therapist,' he muttered.

She laughed. 'What do you expect for free?'

CHAPTER SIX

A MONTH PASSED and it was business as usual at Sydney Harbour Hospital. Finn was back on board, being his brilliant, arrogant, grouchy self. Anyone who'd thought that with him now fully recovered from his injury his mood might have improved had been sorely mistaken. Evie's recalcitrance had taken over from the pain and restrictions that had made him notoriously moody, resulting in a crankier than ever Dr Kennedy.

But given that Prince Khalid's cheque had made the hospital one million dollars richer, no one was about to call him on it. Those on his team just knew—you did your job with skill and competence and stayed the hell out of Finn's way.

Even Finn and Evie's relationship had gone back to that of polite detachment, which was causing an absolute buzz on the grapevine. At twenty-five weeks Evie could no longer hide her pregnancy and with everyone knowing Finn was the baby-daddy, speculation was rife.

Were they together?

Would they get married?

Were they already married and keeping it a secret?

Why couldn't they barely say two words to each other?

Did they even like each other?

Everything from the hows and wheres of the baby's conception to a potential wedding and the custody arrangements were red-hot topics.

Everything about Finn and Evie were red-hot topics—like they were freaking royalty.

The fact that both of them were tight-lipped with answers to any of the questions being asked didn't help.

And in the absence of truth there was gossip.

Evie soldiered on regardless of the whispers. Finn stayed away and she alternated between being mad and glad. But mostly she just wished she knew what the hell was going on inside his head and where they went from here. Sooner or later they were going to need to talk but she was damned if she was going to instigate it.

As far as she was concerned, the ball was firmly in his court!

Evie was late arriving at Pete's—the pub that had stood across the road from the hospital for twenty years—on Saturday afternoon. Bella and Lexi were already seated and deep in conversation.

Pete smiled at her from behind the bar and mouthed, 'The usual?' at her. She nodded, the usual these days being sparkling water instead of a nice cold bottle of beer.

Not that abstaining from drinking for nine months was a hardship but she did miss it occasionally after a long day on her feet—and it had been a very hectic day.

She joined her sisters, pushing into the cubicle next to Bella to give Lexi some room. Two pregnant women on one side of a booth was one pregnant woman too many, especially given Lexi's about-to-pop status.

'How's it going?' Evie asked her sister as Pete

brought her water over in a wine glass. Bless him, at least she had the illusion she was drinking something fortified.

Lexi grimaced. 'This baby is sitting so low I feel like my uterus is going to fall out every time I stand up.'

Evie and Bella laughed. They both knew that Lexi and Sam, a transplant surgeon, were ecstatic about the fast-approaching due date. Their relationship was stronger than ever now after their years apart. 'Pretty sure that's not possible,' Evie said.

Lexi laughed too. 'There's always a first time.'

They chatted for a while about baby things, both of her sisters being careful to avoid the F word even though she could tell they were dying to ask her about the latest with Finn. But what was there to say? There was no latest.

The baby kicked and Evie grimaced.

'What is it?' Bella asked. 'Did he kick?' Evie nodded, her hand smoothing over the spot where the baby was busy boogying. 'Can I feel?' Bella asked, her hands automatically gliding over Evie's belly to where her hand was, exclaiming in awe when the baby performed right on cue.

Evie noticed the wistful look on her younger sister's face as she enjoyed the show. 'I'm sorry, Bells, this must be hard for you.'

Bella had cystic fibrosis and Sam had performed a double lung transplant on her less than a year ago. She and Charlie, an orthopod the hospital, desperately wanted a baby but there were risks that neither of them was willing to take on Bella's health, not to mention the sceptre of any baby also having CF.

'It's fine. I'm just pleased neither of you carry the gene so my lovely little niece and nephew will be fine.'

She smiled at them both but Evie could tell it took a huge effort. Poor Bella had already had so much taken from her in life.

'Besides,' Bella continued, 'I get to be the cool aunty, who fills them up with lollies and ice cream and lets them watch scary movies till midnight and teaches them to drive.'

'And designs fabulous couture for their proms and weddings from your latest collection,' Lexi added.

'That right,' Bella agreed. Her new lungs had given her more freedom to make her fashion design dream a reality. 'And you can organise fabulous parties for them,' Bella said.

Lexi, an events planner, grinned. 'Starting with your baby shower,' she said to Evie.

Evie laughed. 'Steady on, there's plenty of time to be worrying about that. Just you concentrate on getting this little one…' she patted Lexi's belly '…out. We'll worry about my baby shower a few months down the track.'

Lexi shifted uncomfortably. 'Deal.'

'So, Bells,' Evie said, as Pete plonked another wine glass of sparkling water in front of her, 'tell us about your course. What are you working on?'

They nattered away for the next hour and Evie felt lighter and happier than she had in weeks. Between Finn, the gossip and the baby, she'd had a lot on her mind. It was fabulous to leave that all beyond for a while and be pulled headlong into girly, sister stuff.

Or at least it was until Finn showed up in jeans and a T-shirt, looking all rugged and stubbly and very determined. She'd seen that look before and went on instant alert despite the flutter in the region of her heart.

'Evie,' he greeted her, with a quick nod of his head to Lexi and Bella.

Evie frowned at him. 'Is there something wrong?'

He shook his head. 'I have something I'd like to show you. If your sisters can spare you…of course.'

Finn's face ached from being polite when all he really wanted to do was snatch her up and throw her over his shoulder. The refined, educated side of him was horrified by the prehistoric notion but the rampaging Neanderthal he'd become since she'd turned him down quite frankly didn't give a damn at the spectacle that would ensue should he follow through on his impulse.

'Finn…' Evie sighed. She didn't have the energy to fight today.

'Please, Evie.'

Evie blinked. Finn wasn't one for saying 'please'. Not even when he'd *suggested* they get married had he thrown in a 'please'.

'Where exactly are you taking her?' Bella asked, placing a protective hand on her sister's arm.

Bella didn't like the way he'd been treating Evie, especially his silence this last month. If she were pregnant there was no way Charlie would treat her so abysmally. He'd wrap in her cotton wool, which was no less than any woman deserved. Especially Evie, who'd been the Lockheart family rock for ever and worked such long, punishing hours.

'It's a surprise,' Finn hedged.

'Is it a good surprise?' Bella demanded. 'Will she like it, Finn Kennedy, because I don't care how much money you bring into the hospital's coffers or how brilliant everyone says you are, frankly I think you can be pretty damn obtuse.'

'Bella,' Lexi said reproachfully.

But Finn gave a grudging smile. Trust another Lockheart to tell him like it was. Bella had been pretty easy to dismiss due to being sickly most of her life but those new lungs had certainly given her a whole lot of breath! 'Yes,' he conceded, 'it's a good surprise.'

Evie's pulse fluttered at her wrist and tap-danced at her temple as Bella removed her hand. He didn't look any softer but his words were encouraging. Maybe they were going to have an adult conversation about the way forward?

'Fine,' she said, dropping a kiss on Bella's cheek before she eased herself out of the booth. Finn stepped aside for her and Evie was excruciatingly aware of the sudden rabid interest—some subtle, some not so subtle—directed towards them as she gave Lexi a quick peck.

She turned to Finn, ignoring the speculation she could practically feel coursing through Pete's like an electrical current. 'Lead on,' she said.

She breathed a little easier once they'd got out of the pub and were walking to his car, parked at the kerb outside. It was black and low with only two seats—the ultimate status symbol—and it surprised her. She'd never seen Finn's car. He walked to work as everyone who lived at Kirribilli Views did, and like everyone else at his professional level and with his abrasive personality didn't have a social life that really required one.

She supposed the women he'd dated probably thought it was hot and cool. Good-looking doctor—check! Racy car—check! But all she could think as the engine purred to life was, *Where was he going to put the baby seat?*

'So what's the big surprise?' she asked as Finn negotiated the late-afternoon traffic.

'Patience,' he said, his eyes not leaving the road. 'Patience.'

So they didn't talk for the fifteen minutes it took to get where they were going. Evie looked around bewildered as they pulled up at a house in Lavender Bay, not far from the hospital or the harbour. In fact, as she climbed out of his car—something that would probably be impossible at nine months—she could see down to the harbour where the early evening light had laid its gentle fingers and across the other side to the tall distinctive towers of the SHH and further on to the large garish clown mouth of Luna Park and the famous bridge that spanned the harbour.

A breeze that smelled of salt and sand picked up her hair, blowing a strand across her face as she tracked the path of a yellow and green ferry. She pulled it away as she turned to face Finn, who was opening the low gate of the house where they were parked.

'Okay, so…what are we doing here?'

'All will be revealed shortly,' he said as he gestured for her to follow him up the crumbling cement path.

Evie frowned. Whose place was this? Did he want her to meet someone? Someone who might help her understand him? A patient? A relative? Lydia? However she fitted into the puzzle that was Finn. His mother? His grandmother? *Did he even have either of those?* He never spoke of them.

It had to be someone he knew, though, because he had a key and as she watched him walk up the three stairs and traverse the old-fashioned balcony covered by a Seventies-style awning he didn't even bother with knocking. Just slipped the key into the lock and pushed the door open.

He turned to her. 'Come,' he said as he stepped into the house.

Evie rolled her eyes. The man was clueless. Utterly clueless. But she followed him anyway because she was dying to know who lived in this gorgeous little cottage overlooking the harbour and what they had to do with Finn.

Maybe it was a clue to his life that he always kept hidden from her. From everyone.

She stepped inside, her heels clacking against smooth polished floorboards the colour of honey. The sound echoed around the empty house. The rooms, as she moved through, following Finn, were devoid of furniture, curtains or blinds and floor coverings. Soaring ceilings graced with decorative roses added to the cavernous echo.

He opened the back door and she followed him down the three stairs to the back entertaining area and then onto a small patch of grass, the back fence discreetly covered by a thick row of established shrubbery.

'Well?' he said, turning around with his arms splayed wide like a game-show host. 'It's beautiful, don't you think?'

He was smiling at her, a rare smile that went all the way to his eyes, lighting them up like a New Year's Eve laser display, and Evie's foolish heart skipped a beat. 'Yes,' she said hesitantly, smiling back.

'It's yours,' he said. 'Ours. I bought it. As a wedding gift. The perfect place to raise our son.'

Evie stared at him for the longest time as everything around her seemed to slow right down to a snail's pace. The flow of blood in her veins, the passage of air in her lungs, the distant blare of a ferry horn on the harbour. Then the slow death of her smile as realisation dawned.

'Is this another way of *suggesting* we get married?' she asked, her quiet voice sounding loud in the silence that seemed to have descended on the back yard.

Finn shook his head vigorously. 'Absolutely not. It's a proposal. I was wrong last time just…assuming. I should have asked you. I got the call this afternoon from the real estate agent that she was mine.'

Ours, she corrected silently knowing that the gesture, while grand, was empty. It was obvious he didn't think of it as theirs. That it was just another way of getting what he wanted.

He reached out and took her hand. 'What do you say, Evie? Let's get married. Let's raise our son together, here in this house with the harbour just there and everything he could ever want.'

Evie looked into his gorgeously shaggy, earnest face. A part of her whispered, *Do it*. Say yes. Take the fake marriage. Take whatever he's offering. You can make him love you with time and patience.

And it was, oh, so tempting.

But she couldn't. She just couldn't.

She wanted more than that. She wanted it all—the whole hearts and flowers catastrophe. If she'd learned anything from her own parents' marriage and years of navigating a fraught household, it was that you couldn't make someone love you if they didn't.

No matter how hard you tried.

And you had to start as you meant to go on.

She withdrew her hand from his. 'No.'

She refused to live on Finn's crumbs as her mother had on her father's. If they were going to enter into a marriage then she wanted all of him.

'Hell, Evie,' Finn said, shaking his head incredulously. 'I bought you a house. What more do you want from me?'

'I can buy my own house,' she snapped.

'Then what *do* you want' he demanded.

'You, Finn,' she yelled. 'I want you. I want you to open up to me. To know every secret, every ugly thought, every tear you've ever shed. I want to know about every sad, sorry day of your existence. And I want you to *want* to know about *mine*. I want to know about Isaac and the day that he died in your arms and about who the hell Lydia is and how she fits into your life and about your childhood and your time in the army as a trauma surgeon.'

Evie was breathing hard as she finished and she'd just scraped the surface of the things she wanted to know about the man she loved. 'That's what I want,' she said, ramming her hands onto her hips, pulling her shirt taut across her bump. 'Anything less is asking me to debase myself. And I deserve better than that.'

Finn reeled from her list. *She wanted too much.* She wanted stuff he'd never given to anyone. Not to Lydia. Not even to Isaac.

Finn steeled himself to be the practical one. Obviously the pregnancy was making level-headed Evie a trace emotional.

'None of those things are open to negotiation,' he said, his voice steely. 'Neither are they required to make a life together. I'm sure if we're both practical we can make it work, Evie.'

Evie's temper flared at his condescension. He truly thought he could just wear her down. She'd swallowed a lot of pride where Finn was concerned because she loved him and she'd known he'd been hurting and she'd seen the injured soul under the gruff and bluff but she drew the line here. She would not become his wife—give him her all—and end up married to a stranger.

'Okay, then,' she snapped. 'Tell me how it will work, Finn. How? We get married and have a committed normal relationship where you take out the rubbish and I hang out the washing and we argue over the TV remote and snuggle in bed on the weekends with the newspapers?'

She glared at him as she drew breath. 'Or is it just a name-only thing? Do we sleep in the same bed to keep up the ruse for our son? Or apart? Do we have some kind of open marriage where we discreetly see other people? Or do we just go without sex for the next twenty-ish years and you spend a lot of time in the shower and I run up an account at the sex shop we just passed?'

Finn blinked at her vehemence, lost for words, but she seemed to have paused for a moment and was looking at him like it was his turn to add to the conversation. 'I haven't really thought about the nitty-gritty, Evie.'

'*Bum-bah*!' she snorted. 'Wrong answer. Try again. You want me to accept this proposal?' She folded her arms. 'Convince me.'

Finn picked carefully through words and phrases in his head, hoping that he found the right ones to convince her. 'I assumed we'd be sharing the same bed. In the...' he searched around for a delicate way to put it '...fullest sense of the word.'

'Well, I just bet you did, didn't you? Works well for you, doesn't it, to have sex on tap. No need for all those showers then.'

Finn wondered if Evie was maybe becoming a little hysterical but he was damned if he was going to be made out to be the bad guy here because he wanted to have sex with his wife. 'No need for you to take out shares in sex-toy companies either,' he pointed out, his jaw aching from trying to stay rational.

'Well, I wouldn't count on that.'

It was Finn's turn to snort. 'You know well enough, Evie Lockheart, that I can make you come loud enough to scare nesting birds on the other side of the harbour.'

She shrugged. 'So can a little imagination.'

He quirked an eyebrow. 'It can't hold you afterwards.'

'Maybe not. But at least it's not going to break my heart a little more each time and slowly erode my self-respect.'

'Damn it, Evie,' he fumed as his control started to slip. '*This is not what I wanted.* I didn't want to be a father but it's happening and I'm here. Do you think you could at least meet me halfway?'

Evie grappled with her escalating temper. He was right. He was here. Even if he was being a total idiot about it. She took a calm, steadying breath.

'*This*,' she said, repeating his open-armed action from earlier as she indicated the house and yard, 'isn't halfway, Finn. *This* is full throttle. Halfway is agreeing to a parenting schedule. Talking about how it's going to affect our jobs and what we can do to lessen the impact on two households. It's talking about what schools he should go to and getting our wills in order.'

Finn shook his head. She seemed much calmer now but he could feel it all slipping away. This was not how he'd planned today would go. 'What about the house?' he demanded.

'It's fabulous,' she said gently. God knew, she'd move in tomorrow if things were different between them. 'And our son is going to love being here with you. But I'm not going to marry you, Finn. Not when you don't love me.'

'I don't want some modern rubbish arrangement for my kid,' he said stubbornly. He didn't want his son to be bouncing between houses—his whole childhood had been like that and he'd hated it. 'It'll be confusing for him.'

'He won't have known anything else,' she murmured, and then she shook her head. 'It's funny, I never picked you as a traditionalist.'

'Kids should be raised by their parents. Together.'

'Sure. In an ideal world. But what we've got here isn't ideal, is it, Finn? And I'm pretty sure I'm capable of doing my bit to raise our son.'

Her calmness was getting on his nerves. He knew for sure he wasn't capable of raising a child by himself. He needed her. He needed her to provide the love and comfort stuff. The nurturing. He could teach him to build a fire and climb a tree and how to fish. He needed Evie there to make up for the stuff he wasn't capable of in all the quiet, in-between times.

'Well, you haven't exactly done such a stellar job so far,' he lashed out. 'You've got yourself electrocuted, almost drowned and followed that up by a case of hypothermia.'

Evie gasped, her hand automatically going to her belly, as if to shield the baby from the insult. If she'd been a more demonstrative woman, she might just have slapped him. 'The baby is perfectly fit and healthy and completely unharmed,' she said, her voice vibrating with hurt.

His gaze dropped to where her hand cradled her belly and he felt the irrational surge of anger from the day she'd been caught up in the rip break over him again. 'Well, that was sheer luck, wasn't it?' he snapped.

Evie wanted to scream and rant and stomp her foot but it was useless and exhausting and getting them nowhere. Finn was being his usual pig-headed self and she should know better than to try and reason with him in this mood.

She shook her head at him, swallowing down all the rage and fury and sucking up his bad temper like she always did. The only thing she had was the high ground. And now seemed like a very good time to take it.

'Goodbye, Finn,' she said, turning on her heel and marching through the house.

He followed her, calling out to her about being reasonable and driving her back, but a taxi came along just as she was opening the gate and it pulled in when she waved, and she didn't look back as Finn told her to stop being ridiculous. She just opened the door and told the driver to go, go, go.

A week later Evie was lying in bed on her day off after five day shifts, too exhausted to get up to relieve her full bladder, which the baby was taking great delight

in using as a trampoline. She hadn't heard boo from
Finn all week. In fact, she'd only glimpsed him once,
and she didn't know whether that had been his passive-
aggressive way of agreeing to do it her way or if he was
just off plotting his next grand gesture.

She suspected the latter, although right now she was
too tired to care.

Another five minutes of baby gymnastics and she
could ignore the need to go no longer. She rolled out of
bed and did her business. She was heading back again
when there was a knock on her door. She wistfully eyed
the corner of her bed, which she could see through the
open door.

It was probably just Bella, who had taken to dropping
in all the time to check on her. She could probably just
ignore it but the knock came again and she didn't have
the heart to leave her sister on the doorstep.

Except it wasn't Bella when she opened the door. It
was Lydia.

Evie blinked, feeling like an Amazon next to the tiny
redhead. She tried to suck in her belly but that was no
longer possible. 'Oh… Hi…Lydia?'

Lydia smiled at her as she checked out Evie's belly.
'Well, he's right,' she said. 'You're definitely pregnant.'

'Er…yes,' Evie said, struck by how truly bizarre
this moment was. Not knowing Lydia's exact relationship with Finn made this meeting kind of awkward.
For her anyway. Lydia didn't seem ready to scratch her
eyes out—in fact, she seemed friendly—so maybe they
didn't have that kind of history?

'Do you think I could come in?' Lydia asked. 'I've
come on behalf of Finn.'

Evie groaned—Finn had sent an emissary? She was

too tired for this. 'Look, Lydia, if Finn's sent you to offer me some crazy incentive—money or diamonds or the goose that lays the golden eggs—I really need to let you know right off the bat that you're wasting your breath.'

Lydia pursed her lips. 'Oh, dear...the house,' she tutted. 'It's worse than I thought.'

Evie frowned. 'Huh?'

'Can I, please, just come in and explain?' Evie hesitated and Lydia dived in to reassure her. 'I've come on behalf of Finn but he doesn't know I'm here. *He'd be furious if he did.* But I haven't seen him this...bleak in a very long time and I can't bear it any longer.'

Evie could hear the woman's genuine concern and worry as she had that day Lydia had told her Finn's whereabouts. She got the sense that Lydia loved Finn and the spike of jealousy that drove into her chest almost knocked Evie flat. She reached for the door to steady herself, the overwhelming urge to slam it in Lydia's face warring with her curiosity.

Curiosity won out.

Part of Evie needed to know where Lydia fitted into Finn's life.

Evie fell back and ushered her inside. She played the perfect hostess, fixing Lydia a cup of coffee and some green tea for herself. They sat on opposite sides of the coffee table, sipping at their drinks for a moment or two, and then Evie voiced what she'd sensed from the beginning.

'You love him?'

Lydia nodded. 'Yes.'

Evie gripped the cup at the other woman's calm response, her pulse pounding in her ears. What must

Lydia think of her? Carrying Finn's baby. Did Finn love her back? Was that why he couldn't love her?

'I'm sorry, I didn't know…' She put a hand on her belly. 'I would never have…if I had known he was with you.'

Lydia frowned. 'What?' She made an annoyed little noise at the back of her throat. 'He hasn't told you about me, has he?' She reached across the coffee table and patted Evie's hand. 'Finn's my brother-in-law. I'm Isaac's wife. Widow, to be precise.'

Evie felt a rush of relief like a slug of Finn's whisky to her system. She let out a pent-up breath in a loud rush. 'His sister-in-law?'

Lydia grinned again. 'Yes.'

'Oh,' Evie said, lost for words as the high robbed her of her ability to form a complex sentence. 'That's good.' She smiled. 'That's good.'

Lydia nodded. 'Although in the interests of full disclosure we did have a…relationship. A very messed-up one for a few years after Isaac's death. I was a complete wreck…it was a very dark time… I think we both held on for much longer than we should have because we were each other's link to Isaac.'

'Oh,' Evie said again, still having trouble with sentences but this time because of Lydia's frankness. Finn and Isaac's widow had been lovers? 'Did he…did he love you?'

Lydia shook her head. 'Not in that way, no. I wanted him to…needed him to at the time…but he's been through a lot…seen a lot…he's a complex man. He doesn't love easily.'

Evie nodded slowly. 'Tell me about it.'

'You love him?'

'Yes.'

'And yet you won't marry him.' Lydia smiled. 'You have him quite riled up.'

Evie shrugged, looking into the bottom of her cup. 'He doesn't love me. And I'm not settling for anything less.'

'Good for you.' Lydia laughed. 'If it's any consolation, though, I think he does love you.'

She looked up at Lydia sharply, expecting to find her looking as flippant as the remark, but she seemed deadly serious. 'Well, I think he does too,' she said. 'But he has to say it. He has to admit it. To himself more than anything.'

Lydia nodded. 'Yes. For a man so bloody intelligent he can be exceedingly dim-witted.'

Evie laughed and Lydia joined her. When their laughter died Lydia suddenly sat forward and grabbed Evie's hand. 'Don't give up on him, Evie, please. He needs you.'

Evie was reminded of Ethan's words. It spoke volumes that Finn had people who loved and cared about him.

'I need him too,' she said. 'But I need all of him.'

Lydia let her hand go. 'Of course you do.' She sipped at her coffee. 'He showed me the house,' she said after a while.

'Ah,' Evie murmured. 'The house.'

'You don't like the house?' Lydia asked, her brow crinkling.

'I freaking love the house,' Evie muttered. 'But I don't want grand gestures from him.'

Lydia gave her a sad smile. 'You have to understand what that house means to Finn.'

'Oh, yes?' Evie asked, trying to keep the jealousy out of her voice. 'And what's that? Believe me, I'd love to know. But he doesn't tell me anything. He just wants to install me there like bloody Miss Haversham.'

Lydia pursed her lips again as if deciding what to say next. Evie hoped and prayed she'd say something, anything, that would give her some insight into the man she loved.

'Finn and Isaac grew up in the system,' Lydia said. 'Their mother abandoned them when Finn was eight. Isaac was six. It was…tough. They got passed around a lot. Finn fought to keep them together, which was hard when most families only wanted one troubled child and that was usually the much sunnier Isaac. There was a lot of rejection. A lot of…bouncing around. Finn would tell Isaac stories about their dad coming to take them away to Luna Park for the day and a ride on a ferry then bringing them back to his home by the sea.'

Evie sat for long moments, letting the import of Lydia's words sink in. Finn had bought his childhood fantasy home for his own son, the house he'd never known, with the hope of providing his child with an upbringing he'd never had.

She sat very still, moved almost to tears. And yet she was blindingly jealous too. Why had she had to hear this story from Lydia? Why couldn't he have told her himself? If he'd told her this the day he'd taken her to the house she might not have been so bloody angry all week.

'He told you all this?' she asked, looking up at Lydia.

Lydia shook her head with a wry smile. 'Good grief, no. Isaac did. Finn never speaks of it. I doubt he's ever told anyone.'

It shouldn't have made her feel better. The story was tragic and awful. But somehow it did. Somehow knowing that he hadn't told any woman about his younger years gave her hope. Hope that he would open up to her about it eventually.

Over time.

Which was what they had now. Time. Before the baby was born.

Maybe she could use it wisely to get them what they both wanted?

CHAPTER SEVEN

Ava had been in her office for one minute on Monday morning when the door opened and Finn stormed in.

'What do women want?' he demanded.

Ava looked up from the mail she'd been opening. He was in his usual work attire of a carelessly worn suit, his tie pulled askew. 'And good morning to you too, Finn.'

Finn waved his hand dismissively. 'I bought her a house—*a goddamn house*—and she still turned me down.'

'You bought her a house because…you love her?'

He shoved his hand on his hip. 'This has nothing to do with love. I bought her a house so our son has a roof over his head.'

'Right…so you bought her a house but you don't love her? Goodness.' Ava tsked. 'That's a tad ungrateful.'

Finn glared at her. 'There's no need for sarcasm.'

Ava sighed as Finn prowled back and forth in front of her desk. 'Okay. Did she say why she turned you down?'

Finn stopped pacing. 'She said she could buy her own house.' He shot her an incredulous look. 'Like I'd offended her feminist principles.'

Ava nodded patiently. Of course Evie Lockheart could buy her own house. With or without the Lockheart fortune behind her. But years of being a psychologist told her there was a lot more to Evie's refusal than an affront to feminism.

'What else?'

'What?'

'Did she say anything else?'

Finn took up prowling again and Ava leaned back in her chair to wait him out.

'She wants me to *open up to her*,' he said eventually.

Ava suppressed a smile. Opening up was not something that Finn was known for. He made it sound as if Evie had asked for a sparkly unicorn or some other such nonsense.

'And you don't want to do that?'

'How does talking about my past have anything to do with raising our son together?' he demanded.

Ava swung slightly in her chair, watching Finn pace. 'Because it's what couples do?' she suggested.

'We're not a couple,' he snapped, coming to an abrupt halt.

She quirked an eyebrow. 'And yet you want her to marry you…?'

'None of that stuff is important to a successful future together.'

Ava knew he was dead wrong and she suspected that somewhere beneath all the injury and barriers he knew it too. But it wasn't her job to tell him he was wrong. 'Is it important what *you* think or what *she* needs?'

He glared at her. 'Goddamn it. Can't you just give me one piece of useful advice instead of answering every question with another question? You're a sex therapist, aren't you supposed to be full of practical ideas about making relationships work?'

Ava sighed. He was far from ready for practical exercises and she should be annoyed that he wanted her to give him a magic wand without doing any of the hard yards he obviously needed. But this was Finn, who wasn't a client, and for Evie's sake maybe she could help.

'Fine.' She folded her arms across her chest. 'Woo her, Finn.'

He frowned. 'Woo her? Are we living in Shakespearian England all of a sudden?' he scoffed.

Ava knew that good wooing took time and if Evie was smart she'd use it to her advantage. 'You wanted my advice.' She shrugged. 'You got it.'

'I've already got her pregnant—don't you think it's a little late for the wooing?'

Ava shook her head. 'It's never too late for wooing.'

Finn shut his eyes. *Bloody hell.* He'd bought her a house and now he was going to have to *woo* her as well?

He opened his eyes. 'Gee, thanks.'

Ava grinned at Finn's look of distaste. 'Don't mention it.'

Finn knocked on Evie's door that night in his suit, juggling some flowers and a bag of Indian takeaway. He knew she was on days off because he'd checked the emergency department's medical roster at lunchtime.

He'd been brooding about Ava's advice all day and by the time he'd finished his afternoon theatre list he'd decided it might be a worth a try. He had time, after all, and instead of rushing like a bull at a gate, which was what he had been doing, maybe a little subtlety *was* called for.

But it had better show dividends pretty quickly because, come hell or high water, they would be married by the time the baby was born.

The door opened and he suddenly felt awkward and unsure of himself standing there with flowers. Women usually came to him—flowers and that kind of thing weren't his style.

Evie blinked. 'Finn?'

'I have flowers,' he said, pushing them into her arms. He lifted up the plastic bag in his other hand. 'And Indian takeaway. Have you eaten?'

Evie shook her head, the aroma of yellow roses and oriental lilies enveloping her. 'I was just doing some... yoga.'

Finn noted her workout gear. Skin-tight Lycra knee-length leggings. An equally form-fitting top with a round neckline and spaghetti straps that bared her shoulders and stretched over her full breasts and rounded belly. Her hair had been scraped back into a messy ponytail.

'I see,' he said, exceedingly self-conscious as he tried not to stare. She seemed to get bigger every time he saw her.

'Come in,' she said, falling back to allow him entry.

Finn stepped inside and then followed her through to the lounge room. There was some low Gregorian chant playing from a sound system somewhere and he noted the yoga mat on the floor. He sat where she indicated on the three-seater lounge and started to pull the containers out while she took the flowers out of sight.

He heard water running, a fridge door opening then shuffling of crockery and tinkling of glasses as he pulled the lids off. He almost called out to just bring some cutlery but he supposed part of the wooing process was to eat off good plates rather than straight from the containers.

Evie, her brain busy trying to fathom what Finn was up to now, was back in the lounge room in a couple of minutes, balancing a tray and the vase of flowers. Finn, who'd taken off his jacket and tie, stood and relieved her of the tray as she placed the vase on top of the television cabinet and used a remote to turn the music off. When she turned back he'd unloaded the tray and her plate was waiting for her, the napkin a bright slash of red against the snowy white pattern.

He was pouring them both sparkling water and he smiled at her as he handed her the glass. A smile that went straight to her insides. She sat towards the end of the lounge, tucking a foot up underneath her, being careful to leave a cushion's distance between them as he asked her what she wanted then proceeded to plate it up for her, passing it and the napkin over when he was done.

She took it and sat unmoving for a few moments as he turned his attention to his own meal. When that was done he smiled at her again and then tucked in.

'Okay,' she said, placing her plate on the coffee table. 'What's going on?'

Finn, in mid-swallow, thought about feigning obtuseness as Bella had already accused him of being obtuse anyway. But he was a cards-on-the-table kind of guy.

He finished his mouthful and took a drink of water as the spicy lamb korma heated his mouth. 'Ava thinks I should woo you.'

Evie frowned. 'Ava? *Ava Carmichael?*'

Finn nodded. 'The one and only.'

'You're seeing Ava?'

'Yes. No. Not like that. We just…chat sometimes…'

Evie was lost for words. 'I…see…' What on earth could she say to such a startling revelation?

It was Finn's turn to frown. 'You don't like it.' He shook his head. 'I knew it was a dumb idea,' he muttered.

Evie shook her head. 'No, I just…' Just what? Was shocked, amazed, flabbergasted? That Finn Kennedy had not only asked a sex therapist for advice about their relationship but had also obviously taken it on board. 'It's sweet…really sweet,' she ended lamely.

'Great,' Finn grumbled, as he also put his plate down. 'Why don't you just pat me on the head and tell me to run along?'

Evie watched as he ran a hand through his hair. This was her chance to start making inroads into his reserve. If he'd finally dropped his bullying tactics and was willing to take others' advice he might just be open to doing things her way.

She leaned forward, resting her bent elbows on her knees. 'I don't want you to woo me, Finn.'

Finn gave a self-deprecating smile. 'Probably just as well. I obviously suck at it.'

Evie laughed. 'You were doing fine. I'm sure with a little practice you'll be perfect.'

He glanced at her. 'But it's not what you want?'

She shook her head slowly. 'How about I do you a deal? I *will* marry you *after* the baby is born if we spend these next few months getting to know each other first.'

Finn's heart started to pound in his chest. It was the same thing she'd told him she wanted at the house. Except she'd made a major concession—she was promising to marry him. 'You've changed your tune,' he said warily.

Evie nodded. 'I spoke to Lydia. She thinks you're worth a little perseverance.'

Finn felt every muscle in his body tense. 'Lydia?'

Evie almost shivered at the sudden drop in his tone. 'She told me a little about you and Isaac growing up in the care system and what the house at Lavender Bay symbolises for you. She asked me not to give up on you. So, by the way, did Ethan.'

Finn wanted to roar at the interference. How dared they talk about him behind his back? This stuff was deeply, deeply personal! 'Lydia *and Ethan,*' he ground out, 'should really learn to keep their big mouths shut.'

'They care about you, Finn,' she murmured. 'As I do. And I'm willing to meet you at this halfway you wanted, to marry you, but only if you're willing to meet me halfway. I want us to get to know each other, Finn. No holds barred. No topic off limits.'

Finn felt the slow burn of anger being doused by hope as the push and pull of emotions seesawed inside him.

He could have what he wanted.

But at what cost?

Was she hoping her amateur attempts at psychology would result in some breakthrough? 'Do you think me spilling my guts to you will make me love you somehow? Is that what you're hoping for, Evie? Because it's probably just going to make me resent you.'

Goose-bumps broke out on Evie's arms at the conviction in his voice. She shrugged. 'Well, I guess that's a risk I'm prepared to take. This isn't about making you love me, Finn.'

'Isn't it? Isn't it?' he demanded, his emotions swinging again. 'So when we get to the end of it all and you know all the sordid details of my life, especially the bit where I don't know how to love anybody because I grew up without any and I still can't give you the love you want, you're still going to marry me? Is that right?'

Evie swallowed at the stark facts he hadn't bothered to sugar-coat. 'Yes. That's right. I just want to know you better. Is it so wrong to want to know the man you're married to? The father of your child?'

Finn hated that she was so bloody rational. They were talking about his life and there was nothing rational about that. He stood and glared down at her. 'So you want to know how it felt to have Isaac die in my arms?' he demanded. 'And my awful childhood with a mother who abandoned us? You want to know all my dirty little secrets?'

Evie nodded, knowing it was vital to stay calm in the face of his consternation. She understood she was asking a *very big thing* of him. It was only fair for him to rail against it for a while.

'Yes,' she said quietly. 'I don't want you to tell me everything in one night. We can build up to the hard stuff but…yes, I want to know it all.'

Finn felt lost as the storm raged inside him. He'd thought she'd back down in the face of his outrage but she wasn't even blinking. He felt angry and scared and panicked as he contemplated what she wanted.

Cornered.

And then Evie slipped her hand into his and it was like the storm suddenly calmed and he had an overwhelming urge to tell her everything. Completely unburden himself. 'Sit down,' she said. 'Eat your curry. It's getting cold.'

Finn sat, his heart beating like a bongo drum as he raked his hands through his hair. She picked up his plate and handed it to him and he took it, eating automatically as his thoughts whizzed around and collided with each other like atoms on speed.

'What do you want to know?' he asked eventually after half his meal had been demolished and he couldn't stand the silence any longer.

'It's okay,' Evie said. 'We don't have to talk tonight. Just…tell me about your day.'

He frowned. 'My day?'

Evie gave a half-laugh at his bewildered expression. 'Yes. Your day. You know, the stuff married people talk about all the time.'

It was awkward at first but they were soon chatting about safe hospital topics—his theatre list tomorrow, how Prince Khalid was going, some new whizz-bang monitor he wanted for the cath lab and the new salads on the canteen menu. And before Evie knew it, two hours had passed and Finn was on his second cup of coffee.

Even he looked surprised when he checked his watch as he drained the dregs from his mug. 'I guess I'd better get going,' he said, looking at her, curiously not wanting to leave.

Evie nodded. It would be the easiest thing in the world to ask him to stay. He'd actually been acting like a human being for once and he looked tired and stubbly and masculine and it had been so long that she wanted to reach across the gap and sink into his arms. But she didn't want to mess with what she was trying to establish now.

Sex would just distract them.

Suddenly the baby gave a swift kick that stole her breath and she gasped involuntarily and soothed her hand over the action.

Finn followed the intimate action, struck by the notion that he'd put the baby inside her. That it was his son, his flesh and blood that blossomed in her belly. 'Baby awake?' he said, feeling awkward again.

Evie looked up, a grimace on her face, which died quickly. Finn was staring at her belly, or rather at the circular motion of her palm, and he seemed so alone and isolated, so untouchable, *so Finn*, way over the other side of the cushion, that it almost tore her breath from her lungs.

'Do you...?' She hesitated, unsure of how to broach the subject. 'Would you like to feel him moving?' she asked.

Finn mentally recoiled from her quiet suggestion even as his fingers tingled at the possibility. His pulse kicked up a notch. His breath thickened in his throat.

Lay his hands on her? Feel his son moving inside her?

He was used to touching women. Used to touching this woman. But as a prelude to something else. Not like this. Not in a way that bound them beyond just a physical need for release.

He would know his son soon enough. He didn't need to feel his presence to understand his responsibilities.

'Ah, no,' he said, standing, gathering his jacket and his tie and taking a pace back for good measure. 'I'm good.'

Evie tried not to take his rejection personally. They'd taken a big step tonight—she didn't want to scare him away by going all militant mummy on him. 'That's fine,' she said, plastering a smile on her face as she also stood.

They looked at each other, Finn avoiding her belly, Evie fixing on his collar. Finn cursed the sudden uncomfortable silence. The night had gone well—considering.

He cast around for something to say. It seemed only fair, given that he'd been the one to ruin the atmosphere. 'Do you want to have dinner with me tomorrow night?'

Evie blinked. She suddenly felt like a teenager being asked on her first date. 'Ah…yes.'

He nodded. 'I'll pick you up at seven.'

And that set the pattern for the next couple of weeks. Going out or staying in, keeping things light, getting used to just being together without arguing or tearing each other's clothes off. One night Evie pushed a little and asked Finn about his life as a trauma surgeon in the army, and for the longest moment as he hesitated she thought he was going to shut her down, but he didn't and she found herself asking a bit more about it each night. About the places he'd been and the people he'd met.

He was more close-lipped about the specifics, about the horrors he must have seen, but each time he gave away a little more and a little more, even mentioning Isaac's name a couple of times before he realised and then stopped awkwardly and changed the subject.

But for every backward step Evie felt as if they were inching forward and they had plenty of time. She was determined not to push him too far too fast.

Evie was almost twenty-eight weeks when Finn called one night to say he'd been delayed at the hospital and would miss their restaurant booking. 'How does a spot of telly and a takeaway sound?'

Like an old married couple, she almost said, but, already exhausted from her own full-on shift, she readily agreed.

'I could be a while yet,' he warned.

'Whenever you get here will be fine,' she assured him. She took great delight in kicking off her pregnancy jeans, which she hated, and her bra, which felt like a straitjacket around breasts that seemed to get bigger by the day, and getting into her sloppy pyjamas. The shirt had a tendency to fall off her shoulder and the legs were loose and light. One day soon it wasn't going to meet in the middle but for the moment the ensemble was holding its own.

That was one of the advantages of their unconventional relationship. There was no need to dress to impress. The man had already seen everything she had. She could sloth around in her daggy pyjamas with no bra and no real shape and he was prepared to marry her anyway.

Besides, she didn't think he found her pregnant body much of a turn-on. He'd studiously avoided looking, touching or getting too near her belly. He didn't refer to it, he never remarked about how big she was getting or comment when she rubbed it.

She knew that was partly to do with his issues but she had to face facts—she'd put on some weight, her breasts had doubled in size and her belly had well and truly popped out.

Hardly a sex kitten.

So there seemed very little point making an effort and there was something very comforting about a man

who was a sure thing so she threw herself down in front
of the telly, her feet up on the coffee table, and waited.

It was nine o'clock when Finn finally knocked and Evie
was almost asleep on the couch, but her belly rumbled
as she admitted him and she realised she was ravenous. For food and for him. There was something very
sexy about the total disregard with which Finn wore a
suit. The way he never bothered to do up the jacket so
it flapped open all the time or how he couldn't care less
about doing up the collar buttons on his shirt and how
his tie was always just a little skew. The whole look
said, I'd much rather be in scrubs.

Which pretty much summed him up.

He'd brought beer and pizza and they ate it out of
the box while he told her about the emergency thoracot-
omy he'd had to perform on an MVA that had come in
after her shift had ended and they watched TV re-runs.

Finn shook his head as Evie laughed at some ridiculous antic. 'I can't believe we're watching this.'

'Hey, I love this show,' Evie protested. 'The nanny
used to let us watch it if Lexi and I had done our home-
work.'

'What about Bella? Didn't she watch it?'

'Of course, but none of them made Bella do anything
because of her CF.'

'Poor Bella,' he mused. 'How did she feel about
that?'

Evie opened her mouth to give him a flippant reply
but it suddenly struck her that Finn was asking *her*
about *her* life, seemed interested in *her* life. After two
weeks of gently pushing his boundaries back with a
feather, he was actually taking an interest in her past.

It was beyond thrilling. She smiled at him. 'She played on it for all she was worth.'

An hour later, with Evie having fallen asleep on his shoulder and snuggled into his side, Finn decided it was time to leave. His arm was numb, which was the stuff his nightmares were made of, and frankly with a large expanse of her cleavage exposed to his view she was just too tempting.

He'd tried not to notice how her body had burgeoned over the last weeks. Tried to concentrate on her, on sticking to his side of the bargain, but her athletic body was developing some fascinating curves, which he'd need to be blind not to notice, given how much time they were spending together.

It was taking all his self-control not to reach for her. To remember she was pregnant. As her bump was getting bigger, it shouldn't have been that difficult but here, now, with her all warm and cosy and smelling fresh and soapy with her hair all loose and her shirt half falling off, exposing the creamy rise of most of one breast and the light from the TV flickering over her skin, it was very difficult.

Finn liked sex. And he was good at it. Even when he'd been practically crippled with pain and numbness in his arm, he'd been good at it.

He and Evie were especially good at it. He reached a plane with her that he'd never reached with anyone else. There'd always been something more than physical. Kind of like what they'd been sharing these last few weeks.

But she was pregnant and they were trying to build a relationship beyond what they already had so making a move on her right now, when things were going so well, was just plain stupid.

He tried to slowly ease away from her but she shifted and murmured and seemed to cling to him even more firmly, pushing her soft breasts into his side.

He prayed for patience, or deliverance.

Whichever came first.

'Evie,' he whispered, and shook her gently, trying really hard not to watch everything jiggling nicely. 'Evie.'

She stirred a little and murmured sleepily. 'Hmm?'

'I'm going to go,' he whispered, trying to ease away again.

Evie dragged herself back from the dark abyss of sleep towards the lure of Finn's whisper. Her eyes fluttered open and her gaze slowly fixed on his face as awareness filtered in. She'd crashed on his shoulder and was smooshed up against him like some crazy stalker.

She removed her hand from his biceps and sat back a little, snuggling her head against the couch instead of his shoulder. She gave him a sleepy, apologetic smile. 'Sorry,' she murmured. 'I'm perpetually tired these days.'

Finn felt the low note of her voice hum along his veins like a tuning fork. 'It's fine,' he said, also keeping his voice low and his gaze firmly trained on her face and not the view straight down her loose top.

'Thanks for the pizza.' She rubbed her belly. 'It was delicious.' The action pulled her shirt down a little more and Evie was surprised to see Finn's eyes widen slightly.

Finn looked. He couldn't help himself. Her breasts were so lush and so…right there. He grimaced as he looked back at her. 'I should…definitely go,' he murmured.

Evie felt her insides dissolve to mush at the look of naked lust she saw heating his gaze to a blue flame. Her hormones, suddenly not sleepy, roared to life. 'You don't have to go,' she said.

Finn sucked in a breath at the shimmer in her soft hazel eyes. 'Evie…'

Evie leaned forward, her breasts tight, her internal muscles quivering in anticipation. 'Stay,' she murmured, and pressed her mouth lightly to his. The beer on his breath was sweet and heady.

Finn, everything north of his groin burning up, groaned the second her lips touched his, ploughing his hands into her hair and deepening the kiss. He pulled back, pressing his forehead against hers as he sucked in air. He felt his control unravelling, as the urge to push her back against the lounge and ravage her pounded through his system. 'I want this too much,' he said on a husky whisper.

'Good,' she breathed, picking up his hand, placing it on her breast and muttering, 'So do I,' as she sought his mouth again.

Finn held her back. 'Wait,' he muttered. 'Not here.' Too many times they'd had rushed sex, hastily parted clothes and a dash to the finish line. Not tonight. Not in her state. He stood and held out his hand. 'Your bedroom.'

Evie would have been perfectly happy with the lounge or the wall or the floor but she was touched by his consideration. But once they hit the bedroom he swept her up and she felt his control shatter on a guttural groan as he kissed her deep and hard.

And then they were pulling at each other's clothes. Shirts and buttons and pants and zippers seemed to melt away as their hands sought bare flesh. And then they were standing before each other naked, his erection jutting between them. His hands brushed against her belly and he pulled away from her, looking down at it, looking down at where his baby was growing. He reached for it again, slid his hands over its rounded contours then slowly up over her breasts, fuller than he remembered, the nipples bigger.

He looked back at her face. 'You're beautiful,' he whispered.

Evie felt beautiful when he looked at her like that. When he touched her so reverently. 'So are you,' she murmured, pressing a kiss to both flat broad pecs.

She trailed her fingers where her mouth had been, trekking up to his shoulders, tracing the scars on his right shoulder before moving down to his biceps. Then slowly shifting, moving around his body until she was standing behind him, her fingers trailing over his back, finding the shrapnel scars she'd only ever felt before, each one breaking her heart a little more.

'Did you get these the day Isaac died?' she asked, dropping a kiss on each one, rubbing her cheek against the puckered skin of his back.

Finn shut his eyes as her kisses soothed and healed. It reminded him of the time she'd tried to offer him solace after he'd lost a patient on the table and for a moment in the operating theatre's change room they'd stood like this, fully dressed, her cheek to his back, him drawing comfort from her simple gesture.

'Evie…'

'I hate it that you were hurt,' she whispered, her lips brushing his skin. 'That you had to go through all that. That your brother was taken from you.'

He opened his mouth to tell her it was a long time ago but it felt as raw right now as it had back then. 'There wasn't anything I could do,' he murmured.

Evie squeezed the tears from her eyes. She'd expected him to say nothing, to clam up. The anguish in his voice was unbearable. She kissed his back. 'I know,' she murmured. 'I know.'

And then she circled back to his front and kissed him with every ounce of passion and compassion she'd ever owned. And then they were on the bed, stroking each other, caressing, kissing and teasing as if they were getting acquainted all over again.

And when they could take it no more Finn looked down at Evie, stroked her belly and said, 'I don't want to hurt you...'

And she hushed him, rolling up on top of him and Finn had never seen anything more beautiful than Evie pregnant with his child, her hair loose, her full breasts bouncing, her belly proud as they moved in a rhythm that was slow and languorous and built to a crescendo that was so sweet Finn knew the sight of Evie flying on the crest of her orgasm would be forever burned into his retinas.

She collapsed on top of him, spent, and he didn't know how long they lay there but at some stage she shifted and he pulled her close, fitting her back against his chest, curling around her, his hand on her belly, kissing her neck, all to the hum of a phenomenal post-coital buzz.

And then he felt the baby move.

And the buzz evaporated.

He waited for something. A bolt of lightning or a beam of light, a trill of excitement—but he got nothing. Life, his own DNA, moved and shifted and grew right under his hand and he felt…nothing.

Panic rose in him. Shouldn't he feel something?

Other than protective? And an overwhelming urge to provide?

Shouldn't he feel love?

Evie, oftentimes oblivious to the baby's movements due to their frequency and this time due to a heavy sexual fog, only became aware of them as she felt Finn tensing around her. She felt him about to withdraw and clamped his hand against her.

'It's okay,' she whispered. 'It's just the baby moving.'

But it wasn't okay and Finn pulled his hand away, eased back from her, rolled up, sat on the side of the bed, cradling his head in his hands.

Evie turned to look at his back, the scars affecting her as deeply as they had just moments ago. She scooted over to where he sat. Her fingers automatically soothed the raised marks and he flinched but didn't pull away, and she kissed each one again as she had earlier. 'What is it Finn? What are you worried about?'

Finn shut his eyes. He wanted to push her away but her gentleness was his undoing. 'Something died in me the day I got these scars, Evie. The day Isaac died. I don't think I'm capable of love.'

He heard her start to protest and forced himself to open his eyes, forced his legs to work as he broke away to stand and look down at her, gloriously naked, her belly full of his baby.

'I'm worried I'm not going to love him.'

Evie smiled at him gently. 'Of course you will. That's what parents do.'

Finn shook his head and the sadness in his eyes cut her even deeper than his scars had.

'Not all of them, Evie.'

CHAPTER EIGHT

EVIE DRAGGED HERSELF through the next few days. She hadn't seen Finn since he'd picked up his clothes and left the other night and there was a small part of her that was beginning to despair that she might never be able to reach him.

But after three punishing day shifts in a row she was too exhausted to care when she crawled into bed at eight-thirty and turned off the bedside lamp. Her feet ached, her back ached and she wanted to shut her eyes and sleep for a week.

She'd worry about Finn tomorrow.

Except that wasn't to be.

Evie woke from a deep, dark sleep with a start several hours later, a feeling of dread pushing against her chest. Her heart was racing. Something was wrong but for a moment she couldn't figure out what.

As she lay in the dark, the luminous figures on the clock telling her it was two-thirteen a.m., she slowly became aware of a feeling of wetness. She reached down, her hand meeting a warm, wet puddle. Had she wet herself?

Before she could apply any logical thought process, a spasm that caused her to cry out and clutch at her belly, pulsed through her deep and low.

Was she bleeding?

The pain eased and panic drove her into a sitting position as she kicked off the sheet and reached for the light, snapping it on. The bed was saturated, clear liquid soaking into the sheets and mattress, her wet pyjama pants clinging to her legs.

Her pulse hammered madly at her temples as she tried to think.

Clear. Not blood. And a lot of it.

Not urine. Too much. She hadn't the bladder capacity for more than a thimbleful for what seemed for ever.

Another pain ripped through her and she gasped as it tore her breath away and she suddenly realised it was amniotic fluid in the bed.

Her membranes had ruptured.

And she was in labour.

The spasm held her in its grip for what seemed an age and Evie failed miserably at doing all the things she knew you were supposed to do during a contraction—stay calm, breathe deeply—by intermittently crying and then holding her breath to try and stop herself from crying.

She collapsed on her side, reaching for the phone on the bedside table as soon as she was able, quickly stabbing Finn's number into the touchpad. It rang in her ear and she hoped like crazy that he had the same special powers that every other doctor who spent half of their lives on call possessed—the ability to wake to a ringing phone in a nanosecond.

He picked up on the third ring but she didn't give him a chance to utter a greeting. 'Finn!' she sobbed. 'It's Evie. My membranes have ruptured. I'm contracting.' As if to prove her point the next contraction came and she almost choked as she doubled up, trying to talk and gasp and groan all at the same time. 'The baby... is coming...now!'

'I'll be there in one minute.'

But she didn't hear him as the phone slipped from her fingers and she curled in a ball, rocking and crying as the uterine spasm grabbed hold and squeezed so tight Evie felt like she was going to split open.

It was too early. The baby would be too small. She couldn't do this. She wasn't ready. The baby wasn't ready.

She heard Finn belting on her door a minute later and she cried out to him but the contractions were coming one on top of the other, paralysing her. She just couldn't get up and open it. She was conscious of a loud crash and Finn calling out her name, his voice getting closer and closer, and she cried out to him again and suddenly he was stalking into her bedroom.

Finn was shocked at the sight that confronted him. Evie—strong, competent, assured Evie—curled up in a ball on the bed, her pyjama pants soaking, her face and eyes red from crying, a look of sheer panic on her face.

He threw himself down beside her. 'Evie!'

'Finn,' Evie sobbed clutching at his shirtsleeve, her hand shaking. 'Help me,' she begged. 'It's too early. Don't let our baby die.'

The words chilled him, so similar to the words Isaac had used as he'd reached out a bloodied hand to Finn.

Finn! Finn! Help me. Don't let me die.

Words that had haunted him for a decade. The promise that he'd given haunting him for just as long. One he hadn't been able to keep in the middle of hell, injured as he'd been and with precious medical help too far away.

But he could make a promise right here and now that he could keep. Last time he'd been powerless to help.

But not this time.

'I won't,' he promised. 'I won't.' He was damned if he was going to let down another person he cared about.

He stood and dragged the light summer blanket that had fallen off the end of Evie's bed away from the mattress and wrapped it around her then scooped her up as she moaned in pain and sobbed her heart out.

There was no point in ringing an ambulance—he could be there in three minutes at this hour of night.

He strode out the door he'd damaged trying to get in and pulled it shut behind him—he'd get the lock fixed later. The lift arrived within seconds and a minute later she was ensconced in his car and he was driving out of the garage. He dialled the emergency department and got the triage nurse.

'This is Finn Kennedy. I'm three minutes out with Evie Lockheart, who has gone into premature labour at twenty-eight weeks. I need the neonatal resus team there stat.'

He hung up and dialled another number, zoning Evie's anguish out, doing what he had to do, drumming his fingers on the steering-wheel as he sped through a deserted red light.

The phone was picked up. 'Marco? It's Finn Kennedy. Evie's gone into labour. I'm two minutes out from the hospital. The baby is coming now.'

Whether it was that particular note of urgency one doctor recognised in another or the background noise of Evie's distress, Finn wasn't sure, but Marco's 'I'll be there in ten' was all he needed to hear before he hung up.

He glanced at Evie and reached for her hand. 'Everything's ready. The neonatal team will be there and Marco's on his way. We're a minute out.' He squeezed her hand. 'Hold on, okay?'

Evie squeezed back as contractions battered her body. She knew she was a snivelling mess, she knew she shouldn't be, that she should be calm and rational and confident in modern medicine and the stats on premmie births, but fear pounded through every cell, rendering her incapable of reason.

Right now she was a mother. And she was terrified.

Finn screeched into the ambulance bay fifty-five seconds later. Mia and Luca were there with two nurses and a gurney, and they had a hysterical Evie inside in a cubicle within a minute. The neonatal team was already there, a high-tech cot with its warming lamps on ready to accept the baby, and Finn suddenly felt superfluous as the team went into action around him.

He felt lost. Outside his body, looking down. Usually in an emergency situation in a hospital setting *he* was the one in control. But not now. Right now he could do nothing but just stand around helplessly and watch.

Just like with Isaac.

'Finn!'

Evie's wretched wail as she looked around for him brought him back to the present, to the trilling of alarms, to the hive of activity.

'I'm here,' he said, stepping closer, claiming a position near her head, reaching for her searching hand. They weren't in the dirt in the middle of a battle zone and she wasn't dying. They were at Sydney Harbour

Hospital with as good a medical team around them as anywhere in the world and she wasn't dying. 'I'm right here.'

The curtain snapped back and Marco entered, and Finn knew everything was going to be fine. 'Well, Evie,' Marco said in that accented way of his, 'this is unexpected but don't worry, you are in very good hands.'

Evie was grateful Marco was there but the feeling was swept away by a sudden overwhelming urge to push. She half sat forward, dislodging two monitoring electrodes and causing a cacophony of alarms to go off. 'I need to push,' she said, the noise escalating her panic to full-scale terror.

Marco nodded. 'Don't push, Evie,' he said calmly as he snapped on a pair of gloves. 'Pant. Let me just check you.'

Evie gritted her teeth. 'I…can't…' she groaned as her abdomen contracted of its own accord.

Finn leaned in close to her ear, kissed her temple and said, 'Yes, you can, Evie. Yes you can. Here, do it with me,' he said, as he panted.

Evie squeezed his hand harder, fighting against the dictates of her body, trying hard to pant and be productive and not let the panic win.

'Okay, the baby is crowning,' Marco said.

'No,' Evie pleaded. 'No, no, no.' She turned to Finn, clutching their joined hands to her chest. 'It's too soon, he's too small.'

'And he's in the best place,' Finn said, hoping it was the right thing to say, the thing she needed to hear. He wished he could take the fear and anguish from her eyes. That he could take her physical pain and bear it for her. 'And we're all going to fight for him.'

'Okay Evie, let's meet your son,' Marco said.

Evie cried and shook her head, still trying to stop it, to hold inside her the precious baby who needed more time, but the urge coming over her again couldn't be denied and although she didn't assist, she couldn't fight it either, and because the baby was so small he slipped out into Marco's waiting hands in one smooth movement.

'Got him!' Marco exclaimed, as he quickly clamped and cut the cord and passed the still newborn into the warmed sterile dressing towel held by the neonatologist.

'He's a good size,' Marco said, looking up at Evie.

Finn and Evie only vaguely heard him as they both held their breath, straining to hear a little cry through the rush and hurry around them.

'He's not crying,' Evie murmured.

Finn kissed her forehead as the suction was turned on. 'Give it a sec.'

But there was still no gurgling first baby cry. No annoyed, indignant wail at having a plastic tube shoved up its nose. They could hear terms like *bradycardic* and *low sats* and *starting compressions* and *get an IV* and *need to tube him* and Evie turned her face into Finn's shoulder and cried, quietly this time, as a scenario she'd been part of on many occasions played out.

Only this time it wasn't some anonymous person off the street—it was happening to her.

'He's going to be fine,' Finn said, his head close to hers. 'He's going to be fine.'

If he said it enough times, it might just be true.

Then he heard *I'm in* and he looked up as the tone of the sats monitor changed. *Sats improving. Heart rate picking up.*

He kissed Evie on the head. 'They've tubed him,' he whispered. 'He's improving.'

Evie looked up, the normal sound of the sats monitor like music to her ears. She turned her head towards the flurry of activity around the cot. 'How's he doing?' he asked.

The neonatologist turned around. 'He was a little flat. He needed some help with his breathing—not unusual at twenty-eight weeks. Hopefully we can get him straight on to CPAP. We'll put in an umbi line and given him some steroids down the ETT. We'll take him up to the unit now, it's the best place for him.'

Evie nodded vigorously. 'Of course, go, take him,' she urged. She wanted him in the best place, with the best people looking after him, but she couldn't deny how bereft she felt. She'd given birth to him but she hadn't even touched her little boy yet or seen his face.

Her arms ached to hold him. To be near him right now.

She turned to Finn. 'Go with them,' she said.

Finn frowned. 'What? No Evie, he's in good hands, I'll stay with you until you're settled upstairs and then I'll go and check on him.'

Evie, feeling strong now, dashed at the moisture clinging to her cheeks. 'I don't want him up there by himself, Finn.'

'He's going to be surrounded by people,' Finn said gently.

'No.' She shook her head vehemently. 'Not people who love him. That is our son up there and I want him to know that every second of every day we're right beside him. Go, please, please go. If you don't, Finn, I swear to God I will, placenta delivered or not.'

Finn caught the eye of Marco, who indicated with a quick flick of his head to hop to it. But he was torn. He wanted to be with his son, but he didn't want to abandon Evie either.

Evie grabbed his sleeve. 'I'm going to be fine,' she said. 'I'm sorry, I know I've been a mess tonight but I'm fine now. And I need you to do this. Promise me you'll stay with him until I can get there.'

Finn blinked at the zealous glow in Evie's eyes that turned them from soft hazel to a supernatural hue. He nodded, knowing it was another promise he could keep. 'I promise,' he murmured. 'But don't be long.'

Evie gave a half-laugh. 'I'll try. Now go!' she urged as the cot and the team headed out of the cubicle.

Finn stopped by Marco, who was pulling gently on the umbilical cord to deliver the placenta. 'I have my mobile. Call me as soon as you're done here.'

Marco nodded. *'Assolutamente.'*

Five hours later Ava strode into the isolation room they'd put little baby Lockheart in because there were some perks to being on staff and because they were quiet enough at the moment to allow it. Not that it was exactly isolated—large windows on three sides kept it fully visible to the entire unit.

She smiled at the nurse making notes on a computer console before spying Finn sitting in a chair beside the open cot, valiantly trying to keep his eyes open, his head bobbing up and down as he intermittently lost the battle before regaining control.

'Finn,' she said bending down to push her face closer to him when he didn't seem to register her presence.

He looked as if he'd been pulled through a hedge

backwards. His jeans had a stain down the front and his shirt looked like it had been crumpled in a ball in the corner for a week. His stubbly look was bordering on haggard. His feet were bare.

Finn shook his head as his name was called again and the figure in front of him came into focus. 'Ava.'

She pushed a takeaway coffee towards him. 'You specialise in looking like hell, don't you?'

He gave a half-smile, accepting her offering gratefully. 'Only for you.'

Ava looked at the cot, seeing more tubes than baby. 'Big night, I hear.'

Finn nodded. He stood and looked down at his son, who had rapidly improved in just a few hours and was now only on CPAP via the ventilator to lightly support his own breathing rather than the machine doing the breathing for him.

'This is just the half of it. Evie needed a manual removal of her placenta then part of it was left behind so she had to have a D and C as well. She only got back to her room at six.' He still felt sick thinking about the fist that had squeezed a handful of his gut when Marco had come to tell him the news personally.

Ava nodded. 'I know. I've just come from there.'

Finn looked up, eager for firsthand news of her. 'You have? How's she going?'

'She's sleeping. Bella's with her.'

Finn nodded. He had called Bella a couple of hours ago because he didn't want Evie to be alone. Lexi had been his first instinct but she was also dealing with a newborn and he figured she needed the sleep more. Bella had popped in briefly to see the baby, taken a picture, then gone to her sister.

'Evie made me promise not to leave him until she got here.'

Ava smiled. 'Of course she did. She's a mum now. And what about you? How are you feeling now he's here and it's all a little more real?'

Finn shook his head. 'More like surreal.' He looked down at his tiny son, just over one kilo, everything in miniature but all still in perfect working order. His chest rose and fell robustly despite his little bird-like ribcage and his pulse oximeter bleeped away steadily in the background, picking up the strong, sure beating of his heart.

'I'm scared. Worried. Petrified.'

'But he's doing well, yes?'

Finn nodded. 'But I keep thinking about all the possibilities. Immature lungs. Intracranial haemorrhages. Infection. Jaundice. Cardiac complications. I can't breathe when I think of all the things that can go wrong.'

'Well, that's one of the hazards of knowing just a little too much, I guess. But this little tyke is probably stronger than you think. He's a tough guy, just like his daddy.'

Finn felt his heart contract and then expand so much it felt like it was filling his chest, the cold bands that had clamped around it the day Isaac had died shattering into a thousand pieces. He gazed at his son. 'I love him more than I thought it possible to love anything.'

Ava smiled. 'Of course, you're a dad now.'

Three hours later Finn was watching his son take his first breaths off the ventilator. He'd done so well the team had extubated him and popped on some high-flow humidified nasal prongs. He'd fussed at first, his little hoarse squawk pinging Finn's protective strings, but with a couple of sleepy blinks he'd settled and was, once again, getting on with the business of breathing unassisted.

Finn was watching his son through the open cot's glass side panel when he heard some squeaking behind him and turned around to find Bella pushing her sister into the room in a wheelchair.

'Evie?' Finn stood, shocked by her pallor, covering the two steps separating them quickly, sinking to his knees in front of the wheelchair. She had dark rings under her eyes and her lips were dry. 'Are you okay? I don't think you should be out of bed.'

'She shouldn't be,' Bella agreed. 'But she threatened to pull her drip out and make a run for it if I didn't bring her.'

'I'm fine,' Evie dismissed. Nothing else mattered to her right now more than seeing her baby. The little boy who'd been impatient to make his entry into the world.

He'd been the first thing on her mind when she'd woken from her anaesthetic and after letting weariness, exhaustion and well-intentioned people fob her off for the last few hours, she'd made her stand.

'Push me closer, Bells,' Evie demanded, bouncing in her seat a little, trying to get a better view. If she'd thought she could walk and not faint, she'd have been by his side already.

Finn stood. 'Here. Let me.'

Bella stepped back. 'I'll give you two some privacy,' she said. 'Ring me, Finn, when Evie's ready to go back and I can take her, or I can sit with the baby for a while if you like so you can stretch your legs.'

Finn nodded his thanks and pushed Evie over to the cot side. 'Here he is,' he murmured. 'Master Impatient.'

Evie felt tears well in her eyes, overwhelmed by the fragile little human being they'd created dwarfed by the medical technology around him. He was wearing the tiniest disposable nappy Evie had ever seen and a little blue beanie. He looked like a doll and the mother in her wanted to scoop him up, clutch him to her breast, slay anyone who dared come near him, but the doctor knew he was better off right where he was for now.

She flattened her palm against the glass, too low in the chair to be able to reach in and too sore and weak to be able to stand but feeling the strength of their connection anyway. Their unbreakable bond.

'Hello, baby, I'm your mummy,' she whispered.

And she listened as Finn pulled up a chair beside her and recounted what had happened since they'd left her in the department. About how their son had improved in leaps and bounds and how incredibly stable his blood gases and body temp and sugar levels had been.

'He's done everything right, Evie.' Finn placed a hand on her knee. 'He's a real little fighter.'

Evie nodded, tears blurring her vision. 'Of course,' she said, placing a hand over his and giving him a squeeze. She looked at him. 'He's just like his daddy.'

Finn's heart almost broke at the shimmer of tears in her eyes. He never wanted her to hurt again. He'd watch her go through hell last night and then she'd gone through even more without him, and he didn't want to ever be away from her again. He wanted to wrap them both up and love them for ever.

Finn turned his hand over and intertwined their

fingers. 'According to your father, he has the Lock-heart brow.'

Evie laughed. 'My father's been?'

Finn nodded. 'He and your mother called in briefly earlier. She agreed.'

'My mother?' They'd been making some inroads to their relationship in the last months since Bella had received her new lungs but Evie knew there was still a long way to go.

'Well, they're both wrong,' she said, gazing at her son's tiny face. Even all wizened, she could see the mark of Kennedy genes everywhere. 'He has *your* brow. *And* your chin. *And* your nose. I don't know about those fabulous cheekbones, though…'

Finn stared at them as he'd been doing for the last eight hours, trying not to remember why they were so familiar. 'They're Isaac's,' he whispered, finally admitting it. 'According to Lydia, Isaac had cheekbones that belonged in Hollywood.'

Evie glanced at him. His voice was tinged with sadness and humour and regret. 'I'm sorry he never got to see his nephew,' she whispered, holding tight to his hand.

Finn nodded. 'So am I. He'd have been a great uncle.'

And for the first time in a long time he remembered the happy times he and Isaac had shared instead of how it had all ended, and he could smile. How Isaac had always managed to find a baby to cuddle or a toddler to give a piggy-back ride to, wherever they'd ended up.

The baby squirmed, making a mewling noise like a tiny kitten and waving his little fists, no bigger than gumballs, in the air, dislodging a chest electrode and tripping an alarm. Evie's gaze flew to the cot, her pulse spiking as a moment of fear gripped her, suddenly understanding how nerve-racking it must be for her patients to be in an unfamiliar environment with strange machines that made alarming noises.

'It's okay,' the nurse said, unconcerned, as she pushed the alarm silence button. 'Just lost a dot.'

She located the AWOL chest lead and replaced it back just below a collarbone that looked to Evie as spindly as a pipe cleaner. 'There we go, little darling,' the nurse crooned. 'All fixed.' She smiled at Finn and Evie. 'Is there a name yet? Because we can call him little darling for ever but he might get teased when he goes to school,' she joked.

Evie looked at Finn and then back at the nurse. 'We hadn't got that far,' she said helplessly, already feeling like she'd failed her tiny little son twice. Once for not being able to keep him inside where he'd desperately needed to stay for a good while longer and now not having a name to give to him.

'Well, there's no rush,' she murmured. 'But a wee little guy like this needs a warrior's name, I reckon.'

Evie couldn't agree more and as the nurse fussed over the lines in the cot she knew with sudden clarity what to call him. 'Isaac,' she said to the nurse. 'His name's Isaac.'

The nurse smiled. 'Isaac,' she repeated. 'Ooh, that's good. Strong. Noble.' She looked down at the tiny baby in her care and said, 'Welcome to the world, Isaac.'

Evie smiled through another spurt of tears as the nurse bustled away. She turned to face Finn. 'Is that okay with you?'

Finn's chest was so tight he thought it might just implode from the pressure. He was shocked to feel moisture stinging his eyes and a lump in his throat that barely allowed for the passage of air. He forced himself to look at her instead of turning away or blinking the tears back, like he'd done for so many years. He couldn't even remember the last time he'd allowed himself to cry. Not even as the life had ebbed from his brother's eyes had he broken down.

He'd just shut down. Gone numb.

And it had taken this woman and this tiny scrap of humanity to bring him back.

'I think that would be quite wonderful,' he whispered, his voice thick with emotion.

'But could you hear it every day, Finn?' she probed, her voice gentle. 'Would it make you sad every day?'

Finn shook his head. 'No. I've spent a decade of my life trying to forget what happened and all I've managed to do is erase all the good things as well. I think it's time I remembered them also.'

Evie nodded, squeezing her hand. It sounded like a damn fine plan to her. 'Do you think Lydia will mind?'

Finn smiled. 'I think she'd be delighted.'

'Good,' Evie murmured. 'Good. Isaac it is.'

They smiled at each other for a long moment then turned to gaze lovingly at their son. Finn slid a hand onto Evie's shoulder. 'I've been such an idiot,' he said as he watched Isaac's little puffy breaths kick his rib cage up and down.

'You were grieving,' Evie dismissed, also watching her son, trying to absorb every tiny detail about him.

'I don't mean that. I mean about what I said the other night. After we'd...'

'Oh,' Evie said, glancing at his profile. 'That.'

'All I have to do is look at him and I feel this incredible surge of love rise in me.' Finn didn't take his eyes off Isaac's face. 'And I don't even know where it comes from or that I even had it in me but I do know that it's deep and wide and unfathomable and if I live to be a hundred I'd never get to the bottom of it.'

He looked at Evie then and she was watching him so intently, and he needed her to know, to understand so she could never, ever doubt that he loved Isaac. 'I was so, so worried that I wouldn't, Evie. I was terrified. But it's like…it's just there. It's suddenly just there.'

Evie felt his relief and wonder and even though she'd never really doubted that he would feel this way about his own flesh in blood he'd been so bleak, so convinced the other night when he'd left that she'd felt her first prickle of unease.

She smiled at him. 'I know.'

'It's like a…miracle.' He laughed. 'This love is like a bloody miracle. It's so different from anything I've ever felt before.'

Evie smiled but it felt forced in comparison to his obvious high. She was ecstatic that he knew what she'd always known—that he'd take to fatherhood, revel in it even. But part of her wished a little of that miracle was coming her way.

That he'd look at her and talk about the miracle of the love he felt for her. A very different love from what he was talking about now.

Because while Isaac needed Finn's love, so did she. The kind of love that would fill her soul and warm her days.

A man's love for a woman.

'And you,' Finn said, shaking his head, in awe of what she'd been through. 'You are amazing. Incredible. What your body has done is truly awesome.' He looked at his son, so small but so perfect. 'Isaac and I are so lucky to have you and I'm going to spend the rest of my life taking care of you. Nothing…nothing will be too good for the mother of my child. I love you, Evie,' he said, watching Isaac. 'I couldn't have picked a more perfect mother if I'd tried.'

Evie's breath caught at the words she'd been waiting to hear ever since they'd met at that hospital function five years ago. And they felt so empty.

He was on his daddy high and she was the mother of his child swept up in the raw newness of him coming inside after a long cold winter.

Suddenly she felt overwhelmingly tired.

CHAPTER NINE

AN HOUR LATER, after Evie had expressed for the first time and they'd watch one mil of milk disappear down the gastric tube Finn had insisted that Evie go back to bed. She looked exhausted, the black rings around her eyes had increased, her shoulders had drooped and she was sleep staring at everything with long slow sleepy blinks.

He made a mental note to check her haemoglobin with Marco when he saw him later.

'What about you?' she protested. 'You've been up since two with no sleep.'

'Yes, but I haven't given birth or had an emergency operation. I'll catch some sleep tonight in my office if everything stays stable.' He'd spent many a night on the surprisingly comfortable couch.

It felt wrong to leave Isaac but Bella and Lexi had eagerly volunteered to keep vigil while he pushed Evie back to her room and he had to admit it felt good to be out, stretching his legs.

She was quiet on the trip and his concern for her condition ramped up to another level. 'Are you okay?' he asked as he pulled the wheelchair up beside her bed, crouching down in front of her. 'Have you got pain? Do you feel unwell?' He placed his palm on her forehead, checking for a temperature.

Evie shut her eyes, allowing herself to lean into his hand for a few seconds. 'I'm fine,' she said, avoiding his gaze as she opened her eyes again. 'Just tired.'

He frowned as she seemed to evade eye contact. It seemed more than that. 'You need to be rested and well for your milk production.'

Evie blinked. As a doctor, she understood what he was saying was correct. She'd told many a patient exactly that and she had the pamphlet in her hand to back it up. But it wasn't what she wanted to hear him say. She wanted him to hug her, rub her back and tell her she was beautiful.

Which, of course, he wouldn't, first because he was Finn and, second, she really wasn't beautiful, more classically interesting, and last she doubted she'd ever looked worse. Although she guessed it didn't really matter what you looked like when you'd stopped being a woman and become the milk supply line for a premmie baby.

'I see you're going to be the milk police,' she said, her voice brittle.

Finn chose his words carefully to her irritable response. There *was* something bugging her. 'Colostrum is vital for Isaac's immune system.'

Evie took a steadying breath as despair and animosity battled it out inside her. This was typical Finn in tunnel-vision medical mode. All about the facts.

'Yes, I know,' she said, scooting him aside so she could crawl onto her freshly made bed. She almost groaned out loud as the crisp white sheets melted against her skin like snowflakes and all her cells sighed in unison.

Finn stood up and watched as Evie's eyes fluttered shut. He had the distinct feeling she was trying to block him out. 'Evie…?'

He hesitated, not really knowing how to voice his concerns to a woman who was probably experiencing a hormone surge not unlike Chernobyl's meltdown. Even if he did love her.

'You seem…down…and you know PND can start very early post-partum and it's particularly high in mothers with premmies.'

Evie sighed. *There he went with the facts again.* 'Finn,' she said sharply, opening her eyes and piercing him with her cranky hazel gaze. 'I've just given birth to a twenty-eight-weeker who's in the NICU and I'm two floors away. I feel like an utter failure and my arms *literally* ache to hold him. Yes, I'm *down*. No, I *do not* have postnatal depression.'

Finn sat on the side of the bed. 'Oh, Evie…' He reached for her hand.

Evie really did not want to be pitied so she evaded his reach. 'Look, just go, will you, Finn? Go back to Isaac. I'm tired and not thinking straight. I'm sure I'll feel a lot better after a sleep.'

Finn opened his mouth to say something but Marco entered the room, greeting them in his usual jovial way. 'How are you feeling, Evie?'

'Tired,' Finn murmured.

Evie glared at him. 'A little tired, otherwise fine.'

'What's her haemoglobin, Marco?' Finn asked.

'Ten point nine,' Marco said, not having to consult the chart in his hands. 'She lost very little blood,' he assured Finn, before turning to Evie and asking a couple more questions. 'I think we take down that drip now and discharge you tomorrow morning if everything goes well overnight.'

Evie nodded, feeling ridiculously teary again at the thought of going home without Isaac. 'I won't be going far,' she said.

'Which makes me even more comfortable with discharging you.' Marco smiled.

They chatted for a while longer, talking about Isaac, and Marco smiling over his own little one's antics before he noticed Evie yawn. 'I better get on,' he said. 'I'll see you in the morning.'

Finn stood and shook his hand. 'Thanks, Marco. You were brilliant last night.'

'Yes,' Evie agreed. 'You were fabulous. I'll never forget how you came in when you weren't on call.'

Marco winked at her. 'Anything for Evie Lockheart.'

Finn rolled his eyes. 'I bet you say that to all your mothers.'

Evie shut her eyes as Marco chuckled and Finn once again relegated her to a role instead of a person. Would he ever see her as a woman again? Love her as a woman? Or would he always just love her because she was the mother of his child?

'But thanks,' Finn continued. 'Evie's right. I owe you.'

Marco chuckled. 'I hope that is something I never have to collect on. My cholesterol is good and there is no cardiac history in my family.'

'Well, how about I buy you a beer at Pete's as soon as Isaac is home instead?'

Marco nodded. 'It's a deal. Although let's make it a red wine instead—just to be sure.'

Marco left and Evie faked a yawn. She had the sudden urge to bury her head under the covers and not come out. Maybe Finn was right. Maybe she was going through those baby blues a little early.

'I'll go too,' he said, satisfied to see her already look a little less exhausted around her eyes, even if she did seem to still be avoiding eye contact. He sat on the side of the bed again. 'Ring me after you've had a sleep and I can come back and get you.'

Evie nodded, a lump in her throat at the tenderness in his voice. Then he leaned forward and pressed a chaste kiss on her forehead. He stood and said, 'I love you, Evie,' before walking out the door.

Evie let the tears come then. She wasn't sure what had been more heartbreaking, his throwaway line about loving her or the kiss currently air-drying on her forehead. His declaration of love—his second—was about as heartfelt as that kiss. Something he might bestow on an aged great-aunt with whiskers growing out of her chin.

Asexual. Perfunctionary. Expected.

Was that what she had to look forward to now she was a *mother*? Some idealised figure who was a nurturer. And nothing else?

Finn was going to put her on some bloody pedestal and turn her into something holy and untouchable.

After a full night's sleep Evie was almost feeling human again at barely five a.m. as she crept down to the NICU by herself to visit with her little man and do some more expressing. Finn was there, still maintaining his vigil beside Isaac's incubator, and for a moment she just stood in the doorway, watching him watch their son.

Her heart squeezed painfully in her chest at the sight. She could feel Finn's love for Isaac rolling off him in waves, encompassing the cot and the tiny little scrap of humanity inside it as if he was the most precious child that had ever lived. The area around the cot practically glowed with the force field of Finn's love.

It was exactly what she'd wanted. And yet she was suddenly incredibly jealous.

Which was selfish, hateful and greedy.

And she had to let it go because their son needed her to concentrate on him and his needs and the long haul ahead. Not on any insecurities over Finn. And this morning at least she was feeling more in charge of herself to do just that.

She shuffled forward in her slippers and slid her hand onto Finn's shoulder. He turned and looked up at her and he looked so weary and sexy she plastered a smile on her face.

'Morning,' she murmured. 'How's our little warrior?'

Finn smiled back, hopping out of his chair for her to sit in. 'He's doing well. They've reduced his oxygen. He's coping.'

'Did you sleep?' she asked.

'No,' the nurse piped up.

'I dozed on and off,' Finn corrected her.

Evie looked up at him standing beside her. He looked like he hadn't slept in a hundred years—his lines had lines. 'You look exhausted,' she said.

'I'm fine.' Finn brushed his tiredness aside. '*You*, on the other hand, look much, much better.'

'I feel a hundred per cent better,' she admitted.

Finn squeezed her shoulder. He'd been worried about her yesterday but she looked like the old Evie and he felt one of his worries lift. 'Good.'

'In fact...' Evie stood, gently reaching out and stroking Isaac's closest arm, the warm fuzz covering it tickling her finger '...I'm going to go and express then I'm going to come back here and stay until Marco's round at eleven for my discharge and then I'm coming straight back. So I want you to go and catch up on some sleep.'

Finn looked at the determined set to Evie's chin and felt that protective part of him that had refused to let him leave Isaac's side relax as it recognised the strength of Evie's protective instinct. 'Okay. I'll go to my office and have a couple of hours.'

Evie shook her head. 'Finn, you need a shower, a decent meal and a proper bed. Go home. Rest properly.'

He shook his head. 'I can't leave you sitting here all day. Not so soon after your discharge. You need the rest more than I do.'

Yeah, yeah. The milk. But she let it go, refusing to dwell on something that was fact anyway.

'It's okay. Bella and Lexi will be in and out fussing around all day, making me go for walks and feeding me well. And seeing as your theatre cases have been reassigned this week, I'll let you take the night shift again.'

Finn laughed. 'Why, thank you.'

He hesitated. The offer was tempting. He'd been in the same clothes for almost thirty-six hours. And they hadn't been clean to begin with. If it hadn't been for Ava persuading Gladys to let her into his apartment, he probably still wouldn't have shoes. He'd used the toothpaste and toothbrush from the care pack he'd been given by one of the NICU nurses.

A shower and his own bed did sound mighty tempting.

He looked down at Isaac and felt torn. What if something went wrong while he was away? He'd been rock-steady stable but Isaac was in NICU for a reason.

'I promise I'll call immediately if anything happens,' Evie murmured, sensing his conflict and knowing it intimately. How much had she fretted during the hours she'd spent away from him?

'Okay,' he said, giving in to the dictates of his utterly drained body. 'Thanks.'

Finn was back at three o'clock. He'd eaten, showered, slept like a log for two hours longer than he'd planned and zipped quickly into town to do something he should have done weeks ago. Then he'd left his car back at Kirribilli Views and walked to the hospital. It was a nice day and it gave him a chance to think things through, to plan. He stopped in at the canteen on his way to the unit and bought two coffees and some snack supplies for later tonight.

'Hi, there,' he said, striding into Evie's room.

She looked up from changing Isaac's nappy. It was the first time she'd touched him properly and even though it was a thick, black, meconium bowel motion, she was vibrating with excitement. Perfectly functioning bowels were another cause for celebration.

'Poo!' she announced to Finn. 'Who'd have ever thought you could be so happy about a dirty nappy!'

Finn caught his breath. Her eyes were sparkling and she looked deliriously happy. He didn't understand why it had taken him so long to figure out he loved her when just thinking about her now made his heart grow bigger in his chest.

He laughed, understanding an excitement that might seem bizarre to others. 'That's our boy,' he said.

Lexi, who was also in the room, shook her head and pronounced them nuts.

Evie finished up and Finn hovered nearby, talking to his son, whose eyes fluttered open from time to time indignantly as his sleep was disturbed. When she was done he passed her the coffee, gave his to Lexi and they filled him in on the day, including the news that the oxygen had been reduced even further.

'He's a little marvel!' Lexi exclaimed.

Finn couldn't have agreed more and to see Evie with her eyes glittering and her skin glowing was a sight for sore eyes.

'You're just in time,' Evie said. 'I was about to go and express. You can entertain Lexi.'

Finn glanced up. 'Actually, would you mind going solo for a bit, Lex? I wouldn't mind having a chat with your sister.' He looked at Evie. 'If that's okay with you?'

Evie felt her breath catch a little at the intensity in his blue, blue gaze. She'd forgotten with all the madness of the last couple of days and a side whammy of maternal hormones how it could reach right inside her and stroke her.

Was she okay with him watching her express? It should have been an easy answer—it wasn't like he hadn't seen her naked before. They'd made Isaac together, for crying out loud. But she hesitated anyway. It was pretty damn obvious he'd already relegated her to mother status—surely that would only enhance his opinion more?

Lexi noticed her hesitation. 'Why don't you let the poor woman and her leaking breasts be, Finn Kennedy? I won't bite and after she's done I'll stick around so you can take Evie outside and talk without the slurp and suck of a breast pump serenading you.'

Finn looked at Evie. He could tell she was relived at her sister's intervention and he didn't know what that meant exactly. He'd felt on the same page with her during their getting to know each other weeks but due to the rather dramatic interruption of Isaac's early arrival he wasn't sure about anything any more.

He was, however, grateful for a little bit of sanity from Lexi. What had he been thinking? Breast-pump music was not the ambience he was after.

'Of course.' He smiled. 'Good plan.'

Forty-five minutes later Finn and Evie were ensconced in a booth at Pete's. He'd chosen it over the canteen for its relative quietness at this time of the day. Weekday hospital staff didn't tend to arrive until after six o'clock so they had plenty of time to be uninterrupted. Unlike the canteen, where they'd have been swamped with well-wishers, their conversation stifled.

And he could do without their private life being aired on the grapevine—for once.

'So I was thinking,' Finn said as he placed a sparkling water in a wine glass in front of her and a Coke in front of him, 'that you should move into the penthouse with me while we're getting the Lavender Bay house set up.'

Evie, who had chosen that moment to take a sip of

her drink, almost choked as she half-inhaled it in shock. She coughed and spluttered for a while, trying to rid the irritation of sparkling water from her trachea.

'Is it that shocking?' Finn joked as he waited for her to settle.

'Yes,' she rasped, clearing her throat and taking another sip of water.

Finn reached across the table and covered Evie's hands with his. 'It makes sense to me. We'll be getting married as soon as Isaac is home and as we both live in the same building anyway, it seems silly to keep two places going.'

Evie looked down at their joined hands as the very practical reasons for her moving in with him sank in. 'Right,' she murmured. She had to admit he made good sense even if it had been thought about in that logical way of Finn's.

But…where was the emotion?

The *I can't live without you one more day*. The *I love you, never leave my side*.

She drew her hands out from under his. 'Finn…I don't think this is something we should be worrying about at the moment. I just want to focus on Isaac. On what he needs.'

Finn felt her withdrawal reach deep inside him. He knew she was right, that Isaac had to come first, but they also had to look after themselves. There was no point being run down from stress and lack of sleep when Isaac finally came home.

Home.

The word resonated inside him and settled easily, warming him from the inside out instead of echoing around all the lonely places as it always had.

He had a home. And a family to share it with.

'You still need a base, Evie. A place to have a quick shower and change your clothes, lay your head for a few hours maybe, collect your mail…that kind of thing.'

She nodded. 'Fleeting visits, yes. But I plan to spend as much time on the unit with Isaac as I can without totally exhausting myself. I can't bear to think of him there all by himself, Finn.' She took a sip of water as she felt a thickening in her throat. 'There certainly won't be any time to be shifting apartments.'

Finn nodded. There was no point reminding her that Isaac wasn't alone because he knew exactly how she felt. It felt wrong being away from him, leaving him in the care of strangers—no matter how excellent or vital it was.

He nodded. 'Okay, fine, but…' He put his hand into his pocket and pulled out a burgundy velvet box. 'I want you to have this.'

He opened it to reveal the one-carat princess-cut diamond—a princess for a princess. It sparkled in Pete's downlights as he pushed it across the table to her. 'I realised that I hadn't given you one yet and that was remiss of me. I want you to have it, to wear, so everyone knows we're going to be a family.'

Evie was rather pleased she wasn't drinking anything when he put the box on the table or she might well have choked to death this time. Her pulse thundered through her ears as she picked it up. The ring was exquisite in a platinum antique setting.

'It's beautiful,' she whispered. It was the kind of ring she would have picked out herself and just for a moment she wanted to hold it and look at it and marvel. 'It must have cost you a fortune.'

Finn shook his head. 'No price is too high for the mother of my child.'

Evie felt a hysterical sob rising in her throat and swallowed it down hard. Everything she had inside her wanted to take the exquisite piece of jewellery and put it on her finger and never take it off.

To be Finn's wife.

But she knew if she did, if she compromised what she needed from him, she'd lose herself for ever. With more self-control than she'd known she possessed, she snapped the lid shut and passed it back to him, keeping her gaze firmly fixed on the bead of moisture running down her glass. 'I'm not going to marry you, Finn.'

Finn frowned as a prickle of unease scratched at his hopes and dreams and he was reminded of how she hadn't been able to look at him yesterday. 'What?'

Evie fiddled with the straw in her glass. 'I know I told you I would but…that was before all of this.'

Finn put his hand over top of hers, stilling its swishing of the straw. 'Look at me, Evie,' he said.

Evie fleetingly thought of telling him to go to hell but this was a conversation that they might be better having now so Finn knew she couldn't be waited out, persuaded or bullied. So she looked at him and tried to keep the hurt from her gaze.

'What's really going on here?' he asked.

Evie sighed at the brilliant, clueless man in front of her. What would Lexi or Bella say to him? 'You suck at proposing, Finn.'

Finn snorted. She was having some kind of female hissy fit because he hadn't gone down on bended knee? 'I'm sorry I've been a little busy to organise a flash mob and a blimp.'

Evie felt tears well in her eyes and for an awful second she thought she was going to cry. Right here in the middle of Pete's. Wouldn't that be great for the gossips? 'I don't need grand gestures, Finn,' she said quietly. 'Not a flash mob or a blimp or even a bloody house. But I *do* need to hear three little words.' She paused and cleared her throat of its wobble. 'I'm not marrying you because you don't love me.'

Finn frowned. That was the most preposterous thing he'd ever heard. 'Yes, I do. Of course I do. I've told you that.' He had, hadn't he? More than once.

'Sure,' Evie said bitterly. 'Suddenly the love is flooding in for Isaac so much it radiates out of you and you're dragging everything nearby with you like some bloody comet, and I've been swept up in it too.'

He shook his head. 'No, Evie, that's not right.'

'Isn't it?' she demanded in a loud, angry whisper, sitting forward in her chair. 'I'm the mother of your child—of course you love me, you have to. You've got me all set me up as this esteemed mother figure. As this revered nurturer. The provider of milk and changer of nappies.'

If Finn could have kicked his own butt he would have. 'Of course you mean more to me than that. I love *you*, Evie.'

Evie felt as if he'd struck her with the words, so obviously an afterthought. 'Then why in hell do I get a ring pushed across the table accompanied by a *This was remiss of me*. If you loved me, really loved me, as a woman, not just as the mother of your child, then you would have told me that. That's what men who love the women they propose to do. But you didn't. And do you know why?' she snarled, uncaring who might be

overhearing their conversation, 'Because it never occurred to you. Because it's not the way you feel. Well,
I'm sorry, Finn,' she said, standing up, not able to bear
the look of total bewilderment on his face. 'I need more
than that. I know that you had a terrible upbringing and
you need a home and a family and you've got this whole
fantasy going on around that, and I thought I could live
with just that. But I can't. I won't.'

She sidestepped until she was out of the booth. 'Do
me a favour, give me an hour with Isaac before you
come back.'

And she whirled out of the pub before the first tear
fell.

Lexi was alarmed when Evie arrived back with puffy
eyes and insisted she'd ring her babysitter to stay longer, but Evie sent her on her way, assuring her she was
fine, just Finn being Finn on top of the worry and stress
over Isaac.

By the time Finn arrived back she had herself under
control and was determined to stay that way. He looked
at her tentatively and despite how he kept breaking her
heart, she felt sorry for him. Finn was a man who'd shut
himself down emotionally to deal with a crappy life.
Opening up like this couldn't be easy for him.

'Evie, can we please talk—?'

Her quick, sharp headshake cut him off. 'Listen to
me,' she said, her voice low so the nurse wasn't privy
to their conversation. 'I do not want to talk about what
happened today until after Isaac is home and we know
he's safe and well. For the moment, for the foreseeable
future, he is the *only* thing that's important. *The only*

thing that we talk about. The only thing we concentrate on. *Just Isaac.*'

In the time she'd had to herself, looking down at the precious little bundle that connected her to Finn, Evie had decided she wasn't going to snivel about what had just happened. She'd drawn a line in the sand and that was her decision, and until Isaac was well enough to come home she wasn't going to think, cry or argue about it again.

'Can I have a commitment from you that you'll do the same?'

Finn opened his mouth to protest but Evie was looking so fierce and sure, and after the bungled way he'd managed the whole ring thing he wasn't keen to alienate her further. By his calculations, if everything went well Isaac would probably be discharged in a month or so once he hit a gestational age of around thirty-two weeks or a certain weight.

He could wait a month.

Live by her edict for another four weeks.

But after that she'd better prepare herself. Because he intended to propose properly and leave her in absolutely no doubt of how much he loved her.

He nodded. 'Fine. But once Isaac is home, *we will be revisiting this, Evie.*'

Evie shivered at the steel in his tone and the flicker of blue flame in his eyes. 'Fine.'

Four days passed. Four days of tag-teaming, polite condition updates and stilted conversation. Evie taking the days, Finn the nights. Four days where Isaac continued to grow stronger and put on weight and have most of his lines removed and Evie was finally allowed to have her first kangaroo cuddle with him.

As she sat in the low comfy chair beside the cot, a squirmy, squeaky Isaac held upright against her naked chest, both of them wrapped up tight in a warm blanket, Evie wished Finn was there. The nurse took a picture but it wasn't quite the same thing. This was the kind of moment that parents should share, watching their tiny premmie baby snuffling and miraculously rooting around for a nipple, even finding it and trying to suckle, no matter how weakly.

She felt teary but determinedly pushed them away. She'd been strong and true to her promise not to dwell on it—stress and exhaustion helping—and she wouldn't do it now, not during this simply amazing moment when she and her baby bonded, skin on skin.

On the fifth morning Evie woke early and couldn't go back to sleep, trying to decide if Finn would mind having his time cut short. Or at least sharing a bit of it with her. It made sense to go in—all she was doing was lying there thinking about Isaac anyway and she could feel her breasts were full.

May as well head to the hospital and pump.

Evie was being buzzed in through the main entry doors half an hour later. She noticed a group of nurses standing off to one side of the station and frowned. She smiled at them as she went past and they smiled back, indicating for her to hush and stay with them for a moment. Bemused, Evie turned to see what had them so agog. Her smile slipped as she realised they were watching Finn kangaroo-cuddling with Isaac through the isolation room's windows.

It was a touching, tender moment, stealing her breath and rendering her temporarily paralysed.

Her two darling boys.

'The great Finn Kennedy,' one nurse whispered.

'Who'd have thunk?' said another.

Evie left them to their amazement. Not that she could blame them. She doubted anyone, Finn included, would have ever thought he could be brought to his knees by a tiny baby.

She stood in the doorway for a moment, just admiring them from the back. Finn sitting in the low chair next to the cot, obviously shirtless if the bare shoulder blade just visible through the folds of the blanket was any indication, skin on skin with his son.

She swallowed hard against the lump in her throat, preparing to enter. But then she realised that Finn was talking quietly to Isaac and she hung back, not wanting to intrude on a father-son moment.

'There we are,' Finn said, 'I think we've got you comfortable now you've realised no matter how much you look for it, I'm just not your mummy. She'll be along later. She won't really talk to me because she's mad at me and she'll only have eyes for you anyway.'

Evie's ears pricked up at the conversation and she leaned in a little.

'My fault, I'm afraid, little mate. Totally stuffed everything up there. Take it from me, women may be complicated but in the end all they really want is for you to love them. I've never been good at that stuff, couldn't even tell your uncle Isaac I loved him until he was dying in my arms. You're a lot like him and I promise I'm going to tell you every day. And hopefully I'll get a chance to tell your mum as well. Trust me on this, matey, never make *I love you* sound like an afterthought. Stupid, stupid, stupid.'

Evie held her breath.

'And now she thinks I only love her because she's part of some package deal with you. That I only see her as *your* mother. And I can't tell her she's wrong, that's she's the sexiest, smartest woman I've ever met and I'm crazy about her because I promised her I wouldn't talk about it until you were home. So you need to hurry up and get home, you hear?'

Evie blinked back a threatening tear as she listened unashamedly now.

'Because the truth is I don't want to live a day of my life without her in it. I love you, little guy, and the same applies to you, but it's different with your mother. I want to hold her and touch her and kiss her and make love with her and do all those things that people in love do. You probably won't ever realise this because she's your mum, but she's one sexy lady.'

Evie blushed at the rumble in Finn's voice.

'And of course I love her because she's your mother and there are things she can give you that I can't, but I love her also because she can give *me* things that you can't—a different kind of love. And I never thought I'd hear myself say this but I need that. And I want to give her the love that you can't. I want to love her like a woman deserves to be loved. And I never want to stop.'

Evie let the tears come this time. She didn't try to stop them. She pushed off the doorframe and was at his side in five seconds. Bending her head and kissing him two seconds after that.

'Why,' she demanded face wet, eyes glistening, 'didn't you say those things in Pete's?'

Finn looked into her beautiful, interesting face made even more so by two wet tear tracks, his heart thudding in his chest. 'Because I'm emotionally stunted and incredibly stupid.'

She laughed and kissed him again. 'Do you really mean all those things? About loving me as a woman, not just as Isaac's mother?'

Finn smiled. 'Of course. You wouldn't let me tell you so I figured I'd tell him.'

Evie crouched beside him, peeking inside the blanket at Isaac snuggled up in a little ball against Finn's chest. 'I'm glad you did.'

'So am I,' Finn murmured, looking down into her face. 'I'm just sorry I got it so wrong for so long, Evie. I *do* love you. Just as you are. Evie Lockheart. No one's mother or sister or doctor. Just you. You helped me love again, feel again, and I need you in my life. All of you.'

Evie nodded, two more tears joining the others. 'And I love you.'

Finn dropped a kiss on her mouth and it was the sweetest thing Evie had ever known.

'Don't think you're off the hook for the flash mob and the blimp, though,' she warned as they broke apart.

Finn grinned. 'I'll consider myself on notice.'

And then a tiny little snuffly sneeze came from under the covers and they smiled at each other, brimming with love.

EPILOGUE

EVIE LOOKED UP from watching Isaac happily crawling around the back yard to see her husband approaching with a massive wrapped box.

Finn grimaced as he set the heavy box on the ground. 'Delivery for the birthday boy.'

Isaac turned at the interesting new arrival and crawled their way, gurgling happily. It was hard to believe a year had passed since the frantic night of his birth and while the doctors still corrected his age to nine months, it was still his *birth* day.

His milestones were behind, he was only just crawling and he was smaller than most kids his age, but he was bright and engaging and his parents were besotted with him.

Finn bent and picked his son up off the grass, kissing him on the head. 'What do you think about that?' he asked him.

Isaac kicked his legs excitedly and Finn and Evie laughed as they helped him pull the paper off the box and get it open. Inside sat the most exquisitely carved and decorated rocking horse Evie had ever seen.

'Finn,' she breathed reverently as he pulled it out and placed it on the grass. 'It's beautiful... Where did you get it?'

Isaac squirmed to get down and Finn obliged. 'It's not from me,' he murmured, upending the box and searching for a card. A piece of thick embossed card slipped out.

Finn read it. 'It's from Khalid,' he murmured.

Evie stared at it. A Saudi oil prince had sent Isaac a first birthday present. The sun shone down on the exquisite workmanship and they both admired it for a moment.

'Is that…gold leaf?' she asked.

Finn nodded. 'I think so.'

They looked at each other and laughed. Then they heard Isaac giggling too and looked down to find him peeking out of the box at them.

'But who needs gold leaf when you've got a box?' Finn smiled.

And Evie watched with joy and love in her heart as Finn pushed a giggling Isaac round and round the yard in his cardboard car.

* * * * *

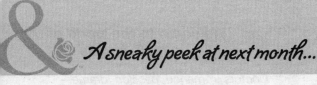

A sneaky peek at next month...

Medical Romance™

CAPTIVATING MEDICAL DRAMA—WITH HEART

My wish list for next month's titles...

In stores from 5th April 2013:

☐ NYC Angels: Unmasking Dr. Serious — Laura Iding

& NYC Angels: The Wallflower's Secret — Susan Carlisle

☐ Cinderella of Harley Street — Anne Fraser

& You, Me and a Family — Sue MacKay

☐ Their Most Forbidden Fling — Melanie Milburne

& The Last Doctor She Should Ever Date

   — Louisa George

Available at WHSmith, Tesco, Asda, Eason, Amazon and Apple

Just can't wait?

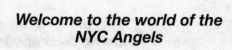

Welcome to the world of the NYC Angels

Doctors, romance, passion, drama—
in the city that never sleeps!

Redeeming The Playboy
by Carol Marinelli
Heiress's Baby Scandal
by Janice Lynn
On sale 1st March

Unmasking Dr. Serious
by Laura Iding
The Wallflower's Secret
by Susan Carlisle
On sale 5th April

Flirting with Danger
by Tina Beckett
Tempting Nurse Scarlet
by Wendy S. Marcus
On sale 3rd May

Making the Surgeon Smile
by Lynne Marshall
An Explosive Reunion
by Alison Roberts
On sale 7th June

Collect all four books in this brand-new Medical 2-in-1 continuity

Find out more at **www.millsandboon.co.uk/medical**

0413/MB409a

Join the NYC Angels
online community...

Get all the gossip straight from the hospital on our
NYC Angels Facebook app...

- Read exclusive bonus material from each story
- Enter our NYC Angels competition
- Introduce yourself to our Medical authors

You can find the app at our Facebook page

Facebook.com/romancehq

(Once on Facebook, simply click on the NYC Angels logo
to visit the app!)

 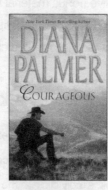 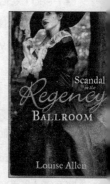